His Blood Like Tears

Gwen Hunter

BellaRosaBooks

BellaRosaBooks

His Blood Like Tears
ISBN 978-1-933523-42-2

Copyright © 2012 Gwen Hunter

First Edition: January 2012

Library of Congress Control Number: 2011961445

Printed in the United States of America on acid-free paper.

Also available in ebook form: eISBN 978-1-933523-86-6

Cover illustration by Joyce Wright – www.artbyjoyce.net

BellaRosaBooks and logo are trademarks of Bella Rosa Books.

10   9   8   7   6   5   4   3   2   1

His Blood Like Tears is dedicated to
Bobbie Joyce Hennigan Wright, my mom,
who never gave up hope that this book would be published.

Acknowledgments

Many people influenced this book over the years. I am especially grateful to the following:

Joyce Wright for her unfailing support and for painting the cover from my dream.

Kathryn Hege, who has loved and encouraged me through all the many revisions.

Christine Cogburn and Pat Gentry, members of the Four Leaf Clover Prayer Group.

Lee Williams (deceased) of the York County Public Library.

Carla Damron for a wonderful developmental edit.

Rod Hunter for standing by me in every way that counts.

Author's Note

This book is a work of fiction. In no way have I tried to remove anything from, or add anything to, the scriptures or church history to make a better story. While it is meticulously researched, it is a product of my imagination, not doctrine, not scripture, not fact. It's just a story that asks my favorite question, "What if?"

His Blood Like Tears was my first novel, started just after high school, and back then, no publisher wanted it. I could have given up on the novel, but I loved it too much to simply put it under the bed and leave it there forever. I went on to have a good career in the fiction market in several genres, under the names of Gwen Hunter, Gary Hunter, and Faith Hunter, but this book was the child of my heart. I came back to it every few years, reading over the manuscript, making changes, knowing that there was something special about the story, and hoping that someone, someday, would agree.

As I worked on the manuscript, I would have dreams about the story or the book cover. The title and cover art are directly from those dreams.

And now it is finally in print. I am so thrilled! I hope you like the story. I hope you like the characters.
—Gwen Hunter

www.gwenhunter.com

Prologue

Magdala: Possession's Last Moments

The Pharisee pulled aside from the wailing woman, careful not to touch her. She chattered and keened through rough, cracked lips, her tone dropping down into a moan, a dirge-like refrain as she rocked slowly back and forth. She was filthy and coarse, caked with grime, hair matted, her gums swollen, frothy pink spittle spewed as she sang. But it was her eyes that caught and held his gaze. They were alive with the opaque light of demons and dark places, sorcery and death. They laughed as she reached for him, ragged nails slashing.

The Pharisee leapt away, gathering his robe to avoid the slightest contact. She cackled louder at the near miss and settled a steely eye on him. He made the mistake of meeting her stare. The spirits in her gaze swirled, coalesced, and gripped him with frozen claws. They pulled and he fell forward, dizzyingly, into her mind, into the long shadows that marked her possession. The wails silenced. The day fell away. Darkness surrounded the Pharisee and he floated, suspended in the uncommon night.

"Romans did it," a grieving voice deep inside her said. The words resonated within her, almost calm, in defiance of the wild crooning that had come from her mouth. The voice dropped lower and he turned in the dark place, floundering to catch the source of her next words. "Yes, and Romans will do it to you, Pharisee. To you."

Abruptly he was back in the heat and noise of the market, and he stumbled, arms flailing, away from the mad woman. The demons in her eyes danced. She laughed and spat into the dust at his feet, a few tiny pink globs settling on his sandals. Instantly he thought of the cost of the temple baths and the purification necessary to cleanse himself of the woman's filth. The damp of her spit slid to his toes and, suddenly nauseated, he turned away from the mad thing and her demons and her Romans. He fixed, un-expectantly, on the startling eyes of the Nazarene. The Pharisee reversed his course and lowered his gaze to the man's chest as sweat prickled down his spine. In his own way this Jesus was as alive as the strange mad woman cackling between them. The Pharisee stepped back trying to keep away from them both.

And then a bizarre thing happened. Jesus, the man the Pharisee leaders had sent him to watch, reached down to the filthy, spindly fingers of the devil-possessed woman and took her hands in his own.

The Pharisee turned away, a grim and exuberant satisfaction replacing the unease in his chest. After less than a day in Magdala, he had his answer. Jesus of Nazareth was ritually unclean. Pharisees need have no fear of a man who would touch filth. He could go home to the temple baths of Jerusalem, purify himself in the grottoes, and bask in the knowledge of a job well done and quickly. Relieved, The Pharisee did not look back to where Jesus stood.

From the corner, a gangly boy watched, his gaze on the woman. He picked at a scab on his knee, scuffing his bare feet in the dust. She was still possessed, and no threat to them. Satisfied, he too turned away and joined the small trading caravan heading to Capernaum.

Chapter One

Magdalene

She was quiet for a moment. Her inner being so still that she saw her whole soul as God must see her, a tapestry woven of history and possibility and pain. She was broken, torn, there were holes in her soul, threads fluttering in the breeze of God's breath. The tattered cloth was stained and faded. But strangely there was no shame—only an objective awareness of her own incompleteness.

From the holes in the cloth of her spirit, strange forms emerged, bent and misshapen things, eyes full of hate and anger. As each departed, they stared at her, as if memorizing the openings in her soul for a future return. There were seven of them. Seven beings like nothing she had ever seen. Darkness that made her shiver. As they left, the threads of her soul lifted in the wind of God's breath, seeking their rightful place in the tapestry, waving and whirling as if alive. *How very odd.*

Slowly, she opened her eyes, and when the mist cleared from her vision, she found herself gazing into soft, gentle brown eyes, fringed all around with thick, black lashes. There was compassion there, in those eyes, as if he too had seen the inner vision of her and the things that had departed. The tender warmth in his eyes sent a surge of strength into her shredded soul. It was almost as though some of the broken strands of the torn soul-cloth rewove themselves under his stare, which all knew was impossible even for the best weaver. As if still watching outside herself, she watched as the image of her incompleteness took form in the tapestry, shaping into a woman. She stirred, stretched, and stood amid the frayed threads, wobbly as if after a long sleep.

Hands, still grasping hers, lifted her to her feet. Her legs wouldn't carry her, and she nearly fell, but the brown eyes continued to share their strength, and the hands steadied her. The silence of his gaze was bottomless.

She never took her eyes from his, but allowed herself to absorb his features. He was dark all over, with tangled black hair pulled back from his face, which was half hidden beneath a dusty beard. He was smiling, and his smile was both gentle and strong, his teeth even and smooth. He was robed in white over dark brown and black, *desert clothes*, her mind flashed. His hands moved on hers and calluses scraped on her flesh. She smiled. Calluses meant he was real. Her dreams never had calluses.

The man turned away; his eyes disappeared. His hands released her. The sounds around her clashed together, roaring over her still, calm being. Her vision of herself—for a moment seeming to be of whole cloth, healing, reweaving on a loom—ripped. Ends flaying and flying, her soul disappeared into the roar.

Human and animal sounds rushed together like waves meeting, crashing over her, sucking her down. Screaming, laughing, braying washed over her, suffocating her, drowning her in the clamor. The stench of dead and putrefying fish filled her nostrils. Someone fell against her and she stumbled, caught herself. Colors danced and swirled—clothing and rugs and fresh fruit and the stuttering images of running children and a trotting donkey. Panic rose in her like bile; she opened her mouth to scream but there was no breath for words. *I am alone.* She closed her eyes against the bright light, shutting out the myriad colors.

Brown eyes flooded her memory; calm wrapped around her like a new cloak. Suddenly she knew that if she could find those eyes she would never again be alone. Bare feet apart in the dust, she caught her balance. Opened her eyes again and looked around, recognizing a marketplace.

The colors steadied and firmed. There was something familiar about the walls and the tents. But the one with the eyes was striding off in the crowd. His white scarf disappearing in the crush. He was lost in it. But she could find him again. She must find him again.

Slowing often to rest, to catch her breath, she followed where the eyes had led, but the crowd thickened and she was pushed away from its center, to the outer edges where the children played.

She turned to go around the crowd, too weak to push through, for surely he was just beyond. But she was so tired. Her breath was wheezing like a sick child's, or like an old woman's lungs, filled with the fluids of death.

She paused in an alleyway, resting against a clay wall. How long since she had eaten? She rubbed her stomach to ease its cramps and felt ribs, stark and boney.

"Hey! Demon woman! What visions do you see?"

Turning, holding to the wall for support, she saw a small boy, perhaps ten years old, and behind him in a ring were others, younger than he. They were laughing.

"Do you see Romans and dead Jews?"

"Where is your keeper, demon woman?"

"My father says she's possessed and if he had the say she would be stoned."

From somewhere a pebble was thrown and bounced off her temple. Pain spiraled out and she made a small sound, touching the bleeding place. They were joined by other children, running at her, boys, all of them, laughing and throwing stones. She held up her arms to ward them off. A large rock cracked against her elbow; others beat into her clothes. Bruising.

Frightened, confused, she spun and ran down the twisting alley, blundering into another, pushing between people to escape the pelting. The boys and the reek and noise of the market fell away, but still she ran, her hunger forgotten, her eyes blinded by tears and strands of oily hair. Cold sweat trickled down her sides beneath her arms. Sour perspiration matted her clothes to her frame. A cramp started in her side and pulled at her with hot pinchers. Breathing became a torment and at last she was forced to stop. Gasping, she lay against a wall, the stone rough on her shoulder through her clothes, her fists pressed against her sides. The world whirled around her. And again soft brown eyes touched the edge of her memory. They beckoned.

After long minutes the pain lessened and she started forward again. The street was packed mud, littered with animal refuse, and as she lifted the hem of her robe to avoid a fresh pile of dung, her eye caught on the fabric in her hand. It was caked with the greasy grime of long accumulation. She pushed the edge of the robe aside and pulled out the dress beneath it. It was so filthy as to be un-recognizable and there were old, dried stains along the hem, like blood. A glance around assured her that the boys had fallen behind. She was safe for the moment.

She dropped the folds of crusty cloth and looked at her hands. They were black with soot and grease, the skin rough and worn, cracked and split—swollen, as if with little pressure they might bleed and water. Her nails were chipped and cracked, lined all around with filth. She lifted a lock of hair; it was tangled, twisted through with sticks and straw. She shuddered as something ran out of it and into her clothes. Darker things moved more slowly—lice. Their nits clung to each strand.

Her feet were scratched and blistered as though she had run through briars and stepped into hot ashes. There was a sup-purating boil on one ankle. Her boots were gone. So dirty. She must look like the old women by the gates, beggars, dirty diseased vagrants, widows, and bastards who littered the city streets on feast days like the droppings she had just passed. And she had lost her mantle.

I need a bath. It was a simple thought, but she was vastly pleased to have made it. A bath. The stream near the house was fresh and . . . Her mind veered away. No. Not the stream. Something bad had happened there. There would be another place.

Her pace increased as she worked her way toward the city walls. She passed fewer people now and was glad, for they looked at her so strangely, increasing her confusion. Was tonight the start of the Sabbath? Or a feast day? She hadn't bathed. Her husband would be ashamed of her. If only she hadn't lost her mantle. A woman's hair and head should be covered. It was almost sun-down. She had to hurry. She had to get home.

Keeping to the shadows, she passed back around the marketplace and out the city gates. The path out of town was well traveled and the smooth dusty earth felt good on her bare feet. She hoped Jason wouldn't be angry that she had lost her shoes. She must have left them at Rebecca's house, but why would she have come out without putting on her shoes? And how had she gotten so dirty? Jason had good cause to be angry. Perhaps she had fallen. Her husband would understand that. And when she told him her secret he would be so excited that all his shouting would be happy. He might buy her another pair of boots, perhaps of red leather.

She touched her stomach. She would have to eat more. He had wanted another child for so long and he would expect a fat, healthy child again. And this time it would be a girl. *A girl.* Rebecca had said she would be beautiful and dark like her own mother. Rebecca knew these things. It was a gift. A baby. There were so many things to prepare. If only she weren't so tired.

Increasing her lagging pace, she rounded the curve in the path. The turnoff was just ahead. Almost running now, she laughed as the path came into view, but the laughter died in her throat. The path was overgrown and choked with weeds, as if it had not been traveled in years. Something was wrong. Maybe she had missed the path. Or was it just ahead? Where was the mark Jason had put on the cedar? Uncertainly, she turned and started to retrace her steps, but stopped, turned again and stepped into the brush. There was the mark, scaled and overgrown with new bark, hidden by the high foliage.

She gasped, her breath hot in her throat. Prickles of fear started at her scalp and ran down her spine like spiders. The tiny hairs on the back of her neck raised. Something bad. Something . . . *Run,* her mind whispered, the remembered gibbering of darkness, far more familiar than the path she now trod. *Get out of here.*

She swallowed. Ignoring the voice, she stepped along the obscure path that led to her home. And with each slow step her fear increased. The air was warm, yet she shivered. It was too silent. No chickens or fowl clucked, no donkey brayed. The smell of fear and death filled her nostrils. The fear was her own, the death . . . Her mind twisted away from the memory, like a broken thread wisping free from a loom.

The cedars were tall; she stepped between them lightly. Jason had planted these trees not long ago, intending them to be a shield against the wind when they were grown. Surely they had grown far too fast. Bewildered, she stopped and stared at the clearing. Her house should be here. Right here.

Her heart beat like the wings of a bird held loosely in a hand. The shadows from the cedars cast long strips of darkness across the clearing. Weeds grew waist high in the center of them, but her house was gone. A stone foundation pushed up through the weeds. Within were the remains of roof and walls. They had caved in. Only a few tall beams were left standing, lonely and stark in the lengthening shadows. But her house was gone.

Scarcely breathing, she stepped into the brush, slowly, dazed and confused, her feet dragging. She stumbled, bruising her toes against something protruding from the weeds. Carefully, as if any sudden motion would shatter her, she bent to pick it up, her hair sliding forward and hanging to the ground, snarled as old roots. The thing in the ground was cold and rusty, old metal. Her fingers slid along it. Without knowing why, she grabbed it with both hands and pulled. Half buried in earth and tangled weeds, it held at first, then broke away, sending her sprawling. She hit the ground, bruising her hip, and rolled. Dirt showered over her. She lay in the lowering gloom. Overhead, the first stars had appeared in the darkening sky. Head whirling, it was a long moment before it occurred to her to look at what she held.

It was a sword. Turning the sword, she traced its shape in the murky light. About sixteen inches of blade and six of hilt. Leather covered the grip, the leather cracked and broken. The blade was a bit less than the width of her hand where it joined to the hilt. Rusty, the blade had been nicked, a small irregular place about the size of her little fingernail. But even damaged, a sword was valuable, its loss not to be taken lightly. Its name came to her. A Maintz Gladius. Roman short-sword . . .

Memories tore through her. Sharp and ripping as if tearing through old cloth. That day. She remembered *that day*. She had rushed into the clearing, exhausted, heart pounding, following the smell of smoke and burned meat. She had tripped over the . . . over the sword. That day and this day melded. Became one.

The breath she had drawn burned as she breathed heavy smoke, choking. Her throat worked against the spasm. Suffocating, her fingers clenched around the leather of the hilt, twisting. The leather was cracked. Broken. Her swollen skin split, tore. A tiny drop of watery blood trailed across the back of her filthy hand. Slowly, it fell. As it dripped, it caught the last light of day and seemed to draw with it precious air from her laboring lungs. The blood splattered on the ground at her feet.

"No. Her lips moved, soundlessly. "No . . . No . . ." *Holding the sword, she turned to the last standing beam of her home. "Jason. Oh, Yahweh, have mercy! Jason." Tied to the center beam of the ruined house, was her husband. His beloved, precious face, a twisted death-mask, his mouth slack and cheeks sunken in, drying clots of blood everywhere. Oh my God. Yahweh! What have they done?* Her mind skittered away from the memory. She looked back at the sword in her hand. Romans. Romans had done that to Jason.

Where was her son? Where, where, where? She looked frantically, tearing her hands in the brush, striking at it with the short-sword, rushing through the clearing, calling for him. She saw a flash of red cloth and knelt in the trees. But . . . No! He was gone. Gone.

The smoke and the reek of burned flesh filled her nostrils. The outer walls of her home, Jason's special labor, smoldered in ruin about her. She turned again to Jason, hanging on the beam. Tears coursed down her face as the memories plunged into her, twisting, staining, a crimson and violent agony that left her gasping.

She saw again her own tapestry, frayed and twisted upon the loom of her mind, the cloth writ with her own inner darkness, the savage violence of her own past. The violence of memories that rumbled, thundered, crushed and buried her, leaving her broken and torn. Thousands of memories, superimposed each on the next so that in an instant she saw and relived them all.

Somewhere, a shrill scream began, growing louder until it beat in her chest and deep in her soul. A high-pitched rhythm that matched her breath, matched her heartbeat. Pain greater than dying whipped through her, ripping like claws. She plunged the sword into the ground again and again, each time screaming . . . screaming.

It was dark when she woke. Her fingers were clamped tightly around the sword. Her mouth was dry and her throat raw; she tasted blood when she cleared it. Her muscles were stiff and cold, creaking as she pushed herself to her feet and slowly stood. It must have been hours since she had eaten; she was weak.

A stream gurgled nearby and she started toward it, but progress was slow for there was no moon and the countless stars shed only thin light. Weeds held her, grabbing at her dress and hair. Small cedars had sprung up; she stumbled into one and fell. Now too weak to stand, she crawled like a child on hands and knees, her dress ripping, dragging the ground.

Pushing through the last thick brush, she reached the stream. Water ran past her. It would be cold and fresh, washing away the thirst that gripped her. And yet, here by the stream, the memories still battered her. The baby. She had lost the baby. She had buried the small clot of blood at the base of the tree, there. Her eyes welled and she wept, huge silent sobs. Her breath shuddered in the night.

Tears felt strange on her face, in her dry eyes. How long since her last tears? It must have been years since the day she had walked into the clearing and saw her life dead and hanging from a tree. That day the pain had come, and now, suddenly, there was no defense against the agony. No anger, no dullness from the passage of time, no death cries or tender words from friends. Not even the empty wail of madness and demons that had once separated her from the memory of her family's death; it was all burned away.

How long had she kept the pain, the horror, at bay? Years? And why had the gentle eyes in the marketplace forced it all back into her?

Alone. She was alone. And she had been alone for a long, long time. Her tears dried into cold crusty streaks, the night's cool breeze brushed her. Alone. There was no one.

Much later she raised herself to crawl the remaining inches to the stream. The water was frigid, numbing her hands as she drank. She could have released her hold on the bank and fallen into the water. It would have been an easy death as the winter-cold snowmelt rushing from the hills carried her body heat away. After a few moments, she wouldn't even have felt the cold. Instead, she crawled from the water's bank, curled into a tight ball and stared into the night sky. Multitudes of stars hung there, uncountable, unknowable. They blurred and danced in her tears. Eventually, the sleep of exhaustion claimed her.

• • •

Stones pressed beneath her back. Stones? Muzzy clouds eddied through her, confused and frozen. Slowly, she became aware of light just outside her eyelids, bright as noonday sun. A stream gurgled nearby. She put out a hand to find sand beneath her fingers. She was lying on the ground. She opened her eyes, felt the crack of sleep in the corners. Blue—brighter, more beautiful than any color she had ever seen before, stung her eyes. It was the sky, with soft clouds floating in it, and the sun straight above her.

Jason . . . And my son, gone. The sky began a slow whirl, speeding and spinning crazily above her. Jason. Dead for so long. My pretty little boy. Gone. *Oh my God, my Yahweh.*

Brown eyes floated at the edge of her memory. The brown eyes that had caught her and held her steady. They settled themselves firmly in her memory. There was nothing else, but his calloused hands, strong as they lifted her from the bank of the stream. She was standing. Though she was alone, they carried her. She was too weak to walk alone.

Her mind seemed detached and floating somewhere above and behind her as she cautiously walked back to the clearing where her house once stood. A distant awareness told her that her body ached, that she was hungry, but the pain was muted. There was nothing she could do about either. Her reality was the immediate—brown eyes and the clearing ahead. Fleetingly, she wondered where Jason was buried. Then that thought too slipped away.

A peaceful breeze touched her cheek, brushed through her clothes. The wind moved the tree tops so slowly, like dancers. A bird floated by on the breeze. She waited for it to fall. Surely it would fall. Its pace was too sluggish to sustain flight. She turned her head, following it into the brush. It didn't fall.

The clearing came into view. It was hard to see as the trees wavered and melted. She lifted a hand and touched her face. A tear sparkled on her finger. She wasn't moving well. She had to be careful or she might fall, and the beam was still so far away. Weeds tore at her ankles, hiding them from view. It would be much easier to walk if her feet touched the ground. She stumbled and watched as her arms reached out to break her fall. Slowly she fell forward, closer to the beam. Her hands touched the smooth cedar of the tall timber. She felt the jolt as her body's momentum stopped, but distant. She held the beam hard to her chest, resting against it, so close it was difficult to focus.

There were blood stains on it still. She closed her eyes. Time and space were soughing sounds in her mind, like wind and rain. The past had form and shape within her, its own reality. Time wavered, past and present melding together. She opened her eyes.

A noise was coming closer, like singing, but no one would sing at a funeral. No one would sing where the dead had hung from a bloody tree. Perhaps it was wailing instead. *It is wailing of the mourners. It is time for the mourners. For Jason. For the family she lost. Her whole world was gone.*

The mourners will prepare his body. They will wash Jason and wrap him in spices and fresh cloth. She turned her head and looked around. There was tall grass and new cedars, piles of rubble. Where was Jason? She had laid him just *there*, only moments ago.

He was gone.

The Romans must have taken him, as they took her son. Romans; had they been here when she came? No, they had left. The Romans were gone. They had destroyed her family and left her no one to mourn. Who would be so cruel as to leave no one to lament?

Mourners filled the clearing, but without bodies to mourn, they would leave her and she would be alone. She had to speak, to explain. Her mouth hung open, but her throat closed upon the words, aching. Fresh tears coursed down her face.

One of the group stepped forward, her tears blurring his face. "Someone." Her voice was a dry croak. "Someone took his body. But I can't mourn alone. They took him, but you'll stay, won't you? Someone must mourn."

There was a long pause. "All people mourn."

She blinked again, dragging a hand across her face, blinking to focus. It was he! The one with the brown eyes. He had carried her here across the clearing from the stream so she would be ready when he came, though that was foolishness beyond bearing. He said again, "All people mourn." She put out a hand, shaking and filthy, toward him. She could rest now, there would be

women in the group who could find Jason's body and prepare it.
There would be mourners.

She swayed and he caught her. Carefully, he settled her to the
ground. He was speaking. It was a wonderful voice, rich, resonant,
with an intensity that made her want to listen. She strained for the
words, but she was too tired and caught only the deep tones and
something about wounds. Good. He knew about them, about the
wound upon her family. Watching his mouth work as he gave
orders, it occurred to her how strange to have a man direct a
mourning, a ceremony usually left to elder women. But it was
right that he should be here; he belonged in this moment.

"Rest . . ." He said something about rest. She would like to
rest, but there was Jason to mourn, and her son who was lost to
her, and the baby she had buried. She must not forget the baby
she had buried. Tears trickled down her cheeks. She closed her
eyes.

There was movement near her. Looking down she saw that
someone was washing a hand. There were cuts on it, long
scratches and a deep gouge that was filled with yellow pus. Jason's
hand, they were letting her help wash Jason's hand. She loved him.
Even with him dead she could feel the pain of the washing; it was
both cold and hot where the water entered the cuts. She watched
as the hand was dried and a salve spread over the skin. She could
feel the soothing release in Jason's hand. Soft strips of cloth were
wrapped around the fingers. Where were the herbs? They had left
out the herbs.

"He will stink if you don't wrap him in herbs," she
whispered. "There is all that you will need in the cedar trunk."

A woman who was wrapping the hand looked at her
strangely. It was a gray woman. A tender, gentle woman with
silvered hair and gray-black eyes. A kinswoman of the man,
perhaps. She wore a gray robe. But her head was uncovered,
which was unseemly in a mourner. Perhaps they were from a far
place. She would be gentle when she told her. But all mourners
must be covered. "You have no mantle. It is not seemly that you
should go about so."

"But I used the mantle to bandage your hands. We had no
other cloth soft enough for them." Her voice was mild, musical

almost. But she had said bandages. Bandages.

Looking again at her hands wrapped and folded in her lap, she remembered. Jason's body had been taken away. These were her own hands. That is why she felt the water on them so keenly. A single tear rolled down her stained cheek. No body to mourn. Yet the mourners had not left, but stayed to help, and one used her own clothing. She watched as the woman lifted the hem of her soiled robe and prepared to dress her feet as well.

Kindness was not common. Most mourners cared nothing for the living, only for the bodies and the death, and the excitement of the wailing. Here, there were no bodies, and death had been long ago and gone. The bodies had been taken.

Time did a small swoop, like the bird floating into the brush without falling. And she understood. The past and the present fell into place with an almost audible click in her mind.

The gray woman worked for some time, and she caused no pain in her ministrations. She dressed all the sores and inflamed places with a mixture of olive oil, crushed lamb's ear, and the ruined mantle. The woman tore through her soiled dress and washed her filthy body. The woman didn't turn away from even the smallest kindness, leaving her clothed in a clean, soft dress. There were no rough mourning clothes, but soft ones of dark dyed wool. She remembered when Jason had given her the cloth to make them. He had been laughing and singing, praising her; she had given him a son. The son who was now gone. And Jason was dead. His gift felt good on her skin. "I have a mantle of new gray wool. It is yours for your kindness." Thinking for a moment she added, "It is in the chest."

The gray woman's mouth lifted into a small smile, but her eyes never rose from her work. "You should sleep. Sleep is healing," she said.

Her eyes closed, opened, and slowly closed again. Sleep was close. It was hard to stay awake. *Jason. Jason, my love.* Bodies mutilated and bleeding, drifted by on the edge of consciousness, bloated and distorted. One, its arms detached but drifting near it, came closer. It rotated to face her, and through slack toothless gums, called her name.

"Jason!" Jason!" Screaming, she jerked fully awake. "Jason," she whispered.

"A dream, child. It's only a dream. Sleep. Rest. It was only a dream."

The gray woman's voice lead her back to dreams. She curled up and allowed sleep to take her. This time there was no blood, no floating bodies. The drifting darkness was a slow tide, pulling her deeper.

Chapter Two

Aemoa

"That will have to do." Mary surveyed the bandages on the sleeping young woman—or old woman—her age was impossible to judge. The bandages were adequate, but just barely. She didn't carry a large supply of clean rags on a short journey and had quickly run out, trying to treat the woman's injuries. Her wounds had gone for some time without proper care, and some were inflamed and festering.

The sleeping woman was so dirty. There were years of grime ground into the cracks of her skin, beneath her nails. It would take many more baths to get her really clean, and with her wounds, she could not be *ritually* clean for a long time. She had to wonder why her son didn't make the woman well, but she didn't ask. There were too many things about him that she didn't understand, and his healing gift was one of those.

And the clothes the woman had worn. Mary hated to burn clothes, it went against the heart. But even the meanest peasant would shy from them.

Mary sighed, looking at the tangled mass of black in her hand. She had cut off the woman's hair. The lice alone would have been reason enough to cut it, but the knots could never have been combed out. She threw the thatch into the fire and the reek of burning hair rose on the still day. Perhaps by the time the woman was well enough to go about in public it would have grown out. Until then, she could keep herself heavily mantled. Once it was known that she was not a woman of low reputation, but had been ill, few would speak badly of her.

Mary stretched and watched the others digging about in the ruins. Already there was a pile of salvaged goods, among them the clothes she had dressed the woman in, and the pile continued to grow as she watched. Someone pulled out a box of some sort which her son took and examined.

Well, the poor woman would probably sleep for hours, if not days. She might as well join in the fun as there would be no getting the traveling companions to set up camp until they had picked the ruins clean. She pulled the back hem of her dress through her legs, tucked it into her waist, out of the way, and waded into the center of the foundations.

Several hours and many treasures later she surveyed the chaos and laughed. They would need a train of donkeys just to carry the bounty home. It was amazing that no one had plundered the wrecked house before. The Law allowed excavation of abandoned places, but there were many local superstitions and perhaps one guarded this spot. Or perhaps this had been the woman's home and she watched over it.

Thinking of the woman, Mary looked for her son. It was dusk and her eyes were failing. Old age she supposed. Not unusual for a woman who had survived forty-six years. Finally, she spotted him among the cedars sitting on a stump, still holding the box she had seen him take earlier. It looked like a writing box, inlaid and finely made. He would appreciate so delicate a work. She watched as his fingers traced a seam where wood joined stone. Her eyes filled with unexpected tears. Joseph had once touched wood in that respectful, almost reverent way. It was amazing that her heart still ached so. It had been years since he died, but the pain still pierced whenever she thought of him.

Her son glanced up, caught her sadness and smiled. It was a wonderful smile, pushing away her pain, and she smiled in return as she moved the last steps to his side. The thing she had come to say was hard, for she knew that if he agreed, they would be separated for a whole season. At a loss, she held out her hand, no longer meeting his eyes.

"May I see? It's beautiful." Gingerly she took the box. "Tell me about it," she said, not liking the way her voice sounded. Conniving. Or innocent. She didn't know which was worse.

He looked at her speculatively, the faint smile hovering at the edges of his lips. "It's a very fine piece," he said at last. "From Egypt, I'd say. The mother-of-pearl and green malachite are of excellent quality, unblemished by whatever happened here and the years since. It's so delicate that I'm surprised it survived the destruction of this place." His eyes on the ruins, he said, "Open it."

Carefully she folded open the box, exposing inkwells, mortar and pestle for crushing dried pigment, a cake of red from blood-stone, another of ocher, and the black from vegetable soot. She handled the pens carefully, setting them down when one, a dried and cracked reed, crumbled in her fingers.

"It has probably been buried here for years, but it's not warped or water damaged," she said, glancing back at the ruins. "In fact, quite a number of things survived the destruction."

Her son pushed himself away from the stump and stood where he could get a better view of the remains of the house. "The roof was well made. Beams of cedar and cypress," he made a circle of his hands to show her the size, "with overlapping, baked clay tiles. It looks as if the walls were pulled out and the roof simply fell in. It landed mostly in one piece, keeping the rain out. And the box," he said, turning to her again, "is of cypress and olive wood. The finish is dull and in need of polishing, but I can make it beautiful."

Not having wasted the late night discussions between car-penter husband and son, she understood his analysis. "Beauty, tarnished but restorable, and underlying strength. "She cocked her head and met his eyes. "Just like the woman, yes, my son?"

"Just like the woman. Yes, Aemoa," he said gently, using the Aramaic word for mother.

There was no question now what she was coming to; even to herself she was predictable, but he added to throw her off track, "Her name is Mary, like yours." He opened the box and handed her a rolled parchment. Mary unrolled the dry, crinkled paper to reveal a smudged page.

"It's a letter from her," he said. "She wrote it herself."

"You seek to dissuade me from my intent," she said, her tone lofty. This was an old game, played out in many variations over the years. He would change the subject by making some outlandish, unrelated statement. The tactic had saved him from many a scolding in the *tap* and *elemi* stages, but she wasn't so easily fooled now. "Women," she said primly, "are not taught to read and write."

"This Mary was."

She chuckled in the quickly darkening gloom, but the sound faded. He was serious. The implications of a woman who could write filled the space between them. The only women in modern society who were taught to write were the heterai, the servants of a false goddess, the mistresses of wealthy, Gentile men. She looked back at the sleeping woman. Had she fouled herself further by tending to the wounds of a *fallen Gentile* woman? "Perhaps a scribe—?"

"If she is the woman who lived here," her son said, "then she was a godly woman, and she wrote this. It was ready to be dispatched by courier and it is signed Mary of Magdala. It is not the work of a well educated woman," he said, to put her mind at ease, "but the hand of a beginner." He rolled the letter, set it into the writing box, and closed the lid, leaving it in her hands and walking away. He went to help the other men gather firewood for the evening fire, as she stood in the falling dark, caught up in her own surprise.

Later, when the evening meal was cooking and all were engaged in their usual tasks, Mary sought out Jesus again, still determined. She found him back at the stump, staring off into the distance, and immediately launched into an intricate description of her plan. It was a few moments before she realized he wasn't listening, and she ended on an exasperated sigh. He was rocking slightly, to and fro, and she should have recognized the motion. He wouldn't hear a thing for a while, he never did when he was thinking or praying. He turned all conscious thought inward and shut out the world.

She settled herself to a fallen tree to wait, wrapped her robe tightly around her and watched the camp members in the darkness, their movements illuminated by the fire or hidden in shadows. The first round of men were eating, there was a thread of song from three others who were setting up tents and placing bedrolls. It was always the same; in the past few months the evening chores had become almost ritual, the cooking of the food, the feeding of the men in small groups, the singing and story-telling, the after-meal discussions lasting long into the night, the women gathered to the side, eating, gossiping, chatting, and listening to the men talk. She relaxed against the tree at her back and prepared to wait.

Although it was now completely dark, and his face was trapped in shadow, she knew the moment his eyes rested on her. She could feel the power of his gaze. "Mary." She started. He never called her anything but *Aemoa*. "Mary," he said again, his voice so soft she almost lost it in the darkness. "There was a dream once, long ago, about a woman. I could see only the top of her head, but I knew that she was crying, and that her tears were for me. I wanted to comfort her and I called her Mary." Abruptly he broke off, reached down in the darkness and picked up an object in the shadow of the stump. Handing it to her, he said almost wonderingly, "I can't understand why they didn't kill her too. It isn't like them to let anyone live." He dropped something cold and heavy into her hands, turned, and stepped into camp, his body limned by the firelight, throwing her deeply into shadow. He was gone.

The thing he had dropped into her grip was cool, metal, and she turned it in the dark to search out the sense of it. In the shadows, her fingers saw what her eyes couldn't. A short-sword. Heavy. Rusty. Roman. Suddenly she understood, and looked at the clearing, the foundations of the house, the place where the woman slept. There were many things she should have seen and understood, things she should have pieced together.

The house had been destroyed as an act of will, not by storm, not by fire—though there had been that too—but by deliberate action. Systematically. Unexpectedly, for there had been the remains of a meal on a brazier inside, neatly folded clothes, the everyday things of life, both insignificant and of great value. The implication of that had eluded her all day, but now she knew. Romans had been here, and they didn't tear down a house and leave the family to rebuild. They killed them all. Always. Except for this time. This time there was the woman, left alive.

Her mind shied away from too many imaginings, too many memories. She had seen the work of Romans—drunk and rampaging, or precise and controlled—either way the deadly result was the same. She shuddered at the memory of the corpse of a young boy, the result of a humiliating and obscene punishment of a criminal of the Roman state. The boy had been an orphan, hungry, and had stolen bread, but his need hadn't mattered to Roman law. Then there were the reports of slaughter when an uprising was put down, the whispers of shame about women beaten and raped by soldiers, and there were the tales of the Bethlehem massacre—hideous, lurid stories, visions of which had invaded her dreams for years.

Still, sometimes late at night, when she would be waked by the sound of a baby crying nearby, or by the sound of wailing at a newly discovered death, she would again feel the nauseous, choking fear that had accompanied her own family's escape from Bethlehem only days before the Roman slaughter. An escape that had begun with the grim recounting of a dream by Joseph. His face had been taut and lined with horror, his hands trembling as he reached for her in the night. His voice had been urgent and shaking as he told her to gather their things, that they must leave Bethlehem. *Now!*

She gripped the short-sword, remembering Joseph's frenzied movements as he packed their things on the donkey, taking everything they owned, leaving not a trace that anyone had ever lived in the house. Then they had simply run. A frightened, tireless master, Joseph had driven them mercilessly for two days and nights, pausing only long enough to eat and change the child, until she had fallen in exhaustion at his feet and begged for rest.

She had heard the bloody details of the massacre later, in the Jewish community in Egypt. The stories of babies tossed high in the air and spiked on Roman swords, of tiny heads dashed against stone, of raucous laughter and screaming women, and town leaders begging to be told why. *Why?*

And she remembered holding her son to her breast during the stories as if to protect him even then from the awful death. Jesus had been the only child younger than the *gamul* age to survive; Jesus had been called charmed from that moment on.

They had been celebrities for a short time in Egypt, among her Jewish compatriots. She had never again doubted the wisdom of her husband. They had become truly a family at that time, Joseph at last accepting Jesus as his son. Her mouth stretched into a smile, her skin tight in the cool night, her hands cold from the rusty metal of the sword.

Shaking herself, she stood, her eyes alighting dimly on the sword, all but obscured in the darkness. No wonder the Magdalene was so ill. She had lost everything to a massacre. Perhaps had been forced to watch. And the frail woman was still living the terror, still seeing the horror. But why was she still alive?

Mary walked back to camp and found herself at the foot of the pallet where the sleeping woman lay. Simon the Fisherman took the sword from her nerveless hands as she studied the features of this other Mary. A dark Jew, the Magdalene's age could be anywhere from twenty-five to forty-five. It would be a long time before her ravaged looks would again be the measure of her years. She needed constant care and rest, time to heal. Sleep was the best remedy. Already the patient was hard to wake for feedings as her body struggled to repair itself.

Aware that her thoughts were straying, Mary forced them back to practicalities, and spread her bedroll next to the sleeping form. There were so many things to decide, to plan. The first being that she still had to talk to her son. Then there were packs to be reconstructed for the new valuables, and perhaps they should send someone into Magdala to look for the woman's family. One of the men had broken his sandal in the ruins yesterday and it needed repair. Jesus should make a list of priorities. Her head touched her sleeping mat and instantly she slept.

Just before dawn, early in the gray-dark hour before sunrise, the camp was awakened by loud braying, shouting, shrill screams, and laughter. Disoriented, groggy, it was a moment before Mary could decide where to look. Figures, clad only in tunics and loincloths were running, converging on the path, becoming a mass of arms and legs. After a few moments of frenzied struggle, three old donkeys were led into camp—apparently docile, but clearly masterless.

Mary looked at her son. He grinned impishly and lifted both shoulders as if to say, "I didn't do it, Aemoa. I promise." She shook her head and stretched. Sometimes she thought he went too far in his *coincidences.*

Later that morning, however, the oldest donkey stood, head down, nuzzling at the feet of the sleeping woman, the other Mary, and she wondered again. Perhaps this time, her son had been innocent—perhaps the three beasts had belonged to the Magdalene once, though it was strange that they had appeared when they did. She sighed, finished tying a bundle of clothing as perspiration trickled down her sides, and went in search of her son. "Jesus?"

At the sound of her voice, he turned from strapping a pack with rope thongs. Eyes twinkling at her approach, he got in the first sally. "You did well with her, Aemoa. She sleeps like a babe. But then you have always been good with the sick. How long will you nurse this one?"

Her mouth hung poised over her carefully planed speech. She closed it and sighed, irritated. She mopped dampness from her brow. "If you continue to respond to unspoken statements, I'll forget how to talk."

"I should be so blessed." His laughter echoed across the camp. When she put her hands on her hips and narrowed her eyes at him, he held up his hands for peace. "Truly, Aemoa, you may do what is best; she needs care and I won't leave her behind. I only laughed because no one ever stopped you from doing any-thing once you set your mind to it, so why ask my permission?"

Laughing still, he started to turn, but caught the gleam in her eye and stopped. "There's something else?" he asked, appre-hension in his tone.

"Nothing alarming, son," she said wryly. "The Magdalene can't walk or ride one of the half-wild donkeys that just *happened* by this morning. She needs a litter."

"I should have thought of that." He looked at the cedars, his mind clearly devising a litter out of the saplings. "I'll send Simon back into Magdala for a few things I'll need. Oh," he said, interrupting before she could form the thought, "while he's there he can check on any family she might have and ask the truth of what happened here."

He turned back to his pack and stifled a laugh when she muttered, "Why bother to think?"

"And, Aemoa?" he said over his shoulder, amusement in his voice. "Dragging a litter, our pace will surely be hampered. We'll be at least two days late getting back to Nazareth and we'll miss the wedding of the Jehosheba girl. Your good deed will cost you the wedding feast."

Mary's face fell as he turned his back but not before she saw his grin. She stamped away. "No need to rub salt into my wounds," she mumbled, ignoring his chuckles.

Several hours later they set out, the men strapped with sleeping mats, cookpots and other essentials. It was late in the morning, within two hours of the noon meal and rest time, but, being so far behind schedule, they needed to make it as far as possible today. The going was slow in the glaring sun, as their pace was set by the slowest among them, the pack animal encumbered with the Magdalene's litter. The old male donkey moved like cold leben, even with Mary walking beside him, pulling on his lead, encouraging him to move faster. He treated the device he half-pulled, half-carried as an anchor, and each time she let go the lead's tension, he stopped, and Mary had to find a way to get him moving again. Finally a young boy took over, leaving Mary free to watch over the Magdalene. She was fairly certain there was no fever, but the woman was having dreams, some violent, where she clawed the air with bandaged hands, screaming the name Jason.

The slow pace allowed her to think over what Simon had learned in the town. Five years ago, a household, on the spot where they had camped the night before, had been slaughtered, presumably by Romans from every land in the Empire, from Thracia and Narbonensis, from far away Lusitania and Belgica. The oft whispered charge had been sedition and encouraging an uprising. Among the dead had been a man named Jason Ben Shahar, found killed on a tree, a servant, and a slave. The servant, who had acted as a scribe and tutor, and the slave had been found days later hanging by the neck from trees on the road leading out of town.

A Roman citizen in the town had claimed that the soldiers had used torture, but the charge had been dropped after a visit by a leading Roman official of the area. Any evidence had vanished when the chief complainant, Mary, Jason's wife, disappeared. Later, the woman had reappeared, quite mad, possessed by demons, prophesying truths that made others fearful. She had been cared for by an old woman named Rebecca until her death last year. Since Rebecca's death, Mary had drifted, living off scraps and what little charity there was in Magdala. She was referred to simply as Mary the Possessed, or Mary of Seven Devils, most certainly the Mary of Magdala in the letter. And yes, some claimed she had been able to write.

Mary felt rather than saw her son step near for the first time since they started the day's walk. He adjusted the screen he had erected to protect the woman's skin from the burning sun. Rising up, he noticed her own uncovered head and face and frowned. "Why are . . ." Glancing down, he saw the familiar cloth of the bandages on the woman's hands and sighed. "Why?"

"I used all of our bandages."

"The sun will burn you brown as an Ethiopian in two days time. Sometimes you're too good, Aemoa, especially as I have an old tunic you may have used just as well. What will you do for a mantle now?"

"Perhaps I'll use your tunic," she teased.

"That would make the gossiping old crones in Nazareth happy," he said, his tone droll.

"The Magdalene said that I might have a gray one in the oak trunk and—"

"She spoke to you?" he interrupted. "When?"

"As I bandaged her hands. I examined the mantle and it has no moth holes. Do you think I might have it? It's lovely, embroidered in dark blue on the hem. I haven't had anything new since Joseph died. Do you think she meant that one, and would it be proper?"

He lifted his hand, smoothing back a strand of silvered hair along her cheek, his touch rare and treasured. "The things we dug from the ruins of the house are hers to give as she wishes. If she has given it, take it." He looked up at the sound of his name, and cast her a quick smile before moving to the front of the procession.

His smiles didn't stop the sun's burning. Perhaps she had best search out the promised mantle and cover herself. Or maybe she would just use the extra tunic. Grinning with mischief, she went in search of a covering.

A long slow sigh escaped Aemoa as she sank gratefully against the wall of the booth. It was wonderful to feel clean and smell of scented oil rather than donkey and sweat. She relaxed even deeper into the rushes beneath her. They were fresh but dry, left in a pile, extras from the quick construction of the bathing booth against the back wall of the house. It had been a full day, arriving back in Nazareth, putting the house in order again, making places for the Magdalene woman's things, followed by the surprising command to bathe. Her son seldom demanded anything, but perhaps the stink of the Magdalene had affected even him. She had been filthy, and most of the afternoon had been devoted to her.

While Jesus and his friends had constructed the bathing booth, the other women had carried great quantities of water from the nearby well and placed the casks in the sun to warm. Their efforts had freed Mary to begin the arduous task of stripping the Magdalene and combing out what was left of her matted hair. Bathing the woman and binding her sores had taken the last hours of daylight, forcing the rest of the women to bathe by lamplight. They would all sleep with wet hair tonight.

Salome had left her a comb, and absently, she pulled it through her long hair, rubbing it with a strip of drying cloth. She could hear Susanna around the brazier preparing the evening meal, and the savory smell of rich stew saturated the night air.

She was wasting time lounging while the others worked, but she couldn't bring herself to put back on the dirty, dusty shift and robe which were her only clothes. Though they had been beaten and shaken, what they really needed was the attention of the town's fuller for cleaning. That process would leave her naked, however, and Jesus might frown. She grinned. *Oh well. Dirty clothes are better than no clothes at all, especially with a room full of men inside.*

The other women had taken the lamp with them when they went to prepare the meal, leaving her in darkness. She pushed herself from her resting place almost regretfully and reached for her shift on its makeshift hook. It wasn't there. Moving carefully in the dark booth, she felt along the reed walls and then over the ground beneath the place she had hung her tunic. Suddenly echoing in her head were the words, *Dirty clothes are better than no clothes at all.* She curled her hands into fists. Practical jokes? Well, tonight she was too tired to be amused.

"Susanna! Susanna, come here! Susanna? Joanna? Salome?"

At the sound of her voice a light appeared in the doorway of the house. Moving slowly toward her was a lamp, carried high, leaving the bearer obscured in shadows. Quickly she stepped back into the booth, wrapping the drying cloth about her as protection.

"Susanna?"

The lamp was lowered to the ground just inside the opening to the booth. A package was placed near it and footsteps plodded heavily back to the house.

Baffled, hoping no one would see her, she snatched the package away from the lamplight and retreated. In her hands was a soft cloth wrapped in twine. Quickly, with clumsy, water-wrinkled fingers, she loosened the knots and shook out the linen cloth. It was a shift. In the dim lamplight, it looked gray, dyed dark at the hem, with a tiny geometric pattern embroidered along the neckline and sleeves in scarlet silken thread. "Oh. How lovely," she whispered.

Reverently, she slipped the shift on over her shoulders and smoothed it out along its length. It was beautiful. There was no question that Jesus, gave her this. She stroked the soft cloth, smoothing out the wrinkles, and twisted her hair into a neat bun. Reaching for the lamp to carry it back to the house, she stopped. In its far glow, were two more bundles of cloth.

Slowly, she bent past the flickering flame and lifted one into the light. It wasn't bound and fell away, revealing a dress, this one of warmest wool. Though dyed like the shift, the dress was embroidered with geometric designs in all the colors of the rainbow. The silken threads shimmered in the lamplight, blending as her tears swirled. Holding the dress close, she bent and picked up the third gift, a larger one still, similarly dyed, but of heavier, woven wool. It was a robe. A full set of clothing—a year's pay for her carpenter son. And in the far shadows, was a small handloom, just like the one she'd had in her father's house so long ago. Clutching the soft cloth, she stared into the darkness. A form appeared near her, wavering in her tears.

"Are you pleased, Aemoa?"

"They are most beautiful . . . most . . . most beautiful . . ." Her voice trailed away as her gathered tears overflowed, spilling down clean cheeks.

She heard his quiet chuckle in the shadows. "I never thought to see the day when you were speechless. I should have found a way to do this sooner."

"Don't laugh," she whispered. "I have done nothing to deserve this. This should have been for your wife. For your children. This is too fine. I had nothing so fine for my own dowry." Silence met her statement, until she finally asked "Jesus?"

"I will have no wife, Aemoa. No children."

"You speak of now, of the next few years. But, what of the future? Of when you're older? Then you'll want children to warm you. To carry on your work."

He didn't reply for a long moment. Then, with a strange timbre in his voice, he answered. "There will be those who will carry on my work, Aemoa. But they will not be of my seed. I will have no children."

"Shhh," she placed her fingers over his mouth, looking into his eyes. "Don't speak such things. Of course you'll have a wife, and children to give you grandchildren. Your vows are not forever."

Jesus took her hand from his mouth, holding it as if he would say something more. Instead, his eyes took on a teasing glint. "You had no mantle. Should my beautiful mother flaunt her beauty about Nazareth? It might cause rioting among the younger men."

She forced a chuckle at his nonsense, on safer ground than

the topic of his holy vows, but his tone gentled.

"I've been planning this for over a year, Aemoa, a Seder gift, but then you tore up your mantle for the Magdalene woman, and forced my hand— What's so very amusing?"

"You gave me everything *except* a mantle, my son. Though I have no complaints at all."

Like a magician at one of the town festivals, he produced a long triangular piece of cloth and wrapped it around her shoulders and head with a flourish.

She sighed in delight, stroking the delicate weave of the mantle. "Oh, Jesus. I don't deserve this. But it's too beautiful to refuse. Too wonderful. And the loom . . ." She reached up again to stroke his face above his beard. "Joseph would be so proud of you. So very proud."

She heard him murmur softly. "I will always see you cared for, Aemoa. Though I will have no children, you will always have a son."

Chapter Three

Magdalene

The strong, pungent smell of onions, herbs, and lamb roused her to the rowdy sounds of laughter and men's voices. Fear scraped along her like claws. She struck out, fighting off the sounds, but her hands swiped through air. No one was there.

Heavy-lidded, she sat up and knuckled open her swollen eyes. For a moment, she couldn't understand what she was seeing. Then the scene resolved itself, though it still made no sense. Perhaps thirty men were sprawled across rugs on a packed clay floor in a room built to hold half that many. They were being served by several women who stepped carefully among them carrying earthenware bowls of steaming stew. Her stomach cramped, groaning at the smell.

She watched, hoping to catch the eye of a woman, but no one glanced her way. The room was unbearably hot from the mass of sweating bodies and smoking lamps.

Fighting to stay upright in the suddenly whirling room, she pushed herself into a higher sitting position against the wall at her back. The room made a lurch, and she caught her breath, squeezing shut her eyes. When she opened them she was staring into the kindest eyes she had ever seen. Gray eyes, clear as the most perfect glass, gazed back into her own. They were familiar, but no single memory would separate from the confused jumble tangled in her mind. And then the woman smiled, and all the pieces fell into place. Crisp and clear was the memory of the woman who had given up her clothes to bandage dirty hands.

She considered how best to address this strange woman. There were several titles of respect she could have used, and she finally settled on the formalized Aemoa—mother. It indicated both middle age, successful child-bearing, mostly sons, and, often, financial success in the marketplace.

"You have a new mantle, Aemoa. It's very beautiful."

Surprise registered on the older face, followed quickly by delight. "You remembered! Jesus will be delighted! Yes, it is lovely, isn't it, child? It was a gift from my son. So is this shift and so many other things. He promised a new pair of sandals will be delivered soon. His generosity meant I did not need to accept the kind offer of *your* mantle.

"Oh listen to me rattle on. You must be hungry. Good," she said at Magdalene's nod. "I'll get you some broth."

A bowl of clear broth and a large piece of warm bread appeared quickly and there was more prattle, but most of the chatter bounced away, leaving the impression of coddled safety and gentle concern. It was hard to get the soup to her mouth. Her hands, though no longer bandaged, were weak, shaking. She didn't try to drink the thin broth, but dipped in the bread as a sop. Her stomach needed little to fill it, having been empty so long, and soon she nodded into a contented sleep.

She groaned softly, hearing herself through the muzziness of dreams. There was sun on her face. Turning away from the brilliant light, she sought to find the escaping dream. She put out her hand and touched gravel. The touch brought her suddenly awake. She was outside, on the ground. Again.

With eyes still tightly shut, she slowly raised up, pausing as the world beneath her heaved dangerously. When the earth steadied, her fingers relaxed their hold on a small stone and the blades of grass that had anchored her. She cracked open her eyes and tried to focus on the scene before her, blinking into the brightness until her vision cleared.

Immediately before her was an L-shaped house. It was made of wood, mud, and stone, with a carved wooden door propped open and hung on wooden hinges. There was one large window with an ingenious wooden casement and solid shutter, thrown open to admit the sun. Hugging the side wall of the house was a narrow mud and stone stair, showing signs of recent work. Piles of reeds and poles lay nearby, perhaps the remnants of a bathing booth. But it was the courtyard that drew her. Enclosed by the house on two sides and walled on the other two, the entire yard was tilled and planted with herbs, their muted shades blending into one another. It was a picture of serene beauty, enhanced and bordered on the two open sides by a flowering grape vine creeping over the low, dry-stack, rock wall. Raked and patterned sand swirled around a small bench and the cistern that collected rain water. To the side there was a stump of twisted cedar heart wood, shaped like a windswept tree on a mountainside. Everything here was stark and set apart, yet there was complete harmony.

She took a deep breath of the hot, herb-scented air and released it. Almost accustomed by now to waking in strange places, she wasn't frightened to have been lying in the middle of an unfamiliar courtyard in the hot sun. Taking another deep breath, her mouth watered, for over the scents of dill, thyme, rosemary, and mint, there was also the smell of fresh hot bread. And she was hungry—ravenously so.

The distance to the house grew as she considered how to make it to the doorway, but before she could move, a woman stepped through the opening and into the bright courtyard. It was the gray woman, the one she had called mother.

She felt a sudden shyness in Aemoa's presence. The woman had bathed her, bound her sores, fed her broth. How does one greet someone who has done so much? The gray woman bent close and read her confusion. "Child?"

The voice was soft and kind, and no single word could have been more perfect. In that word Mary found her first answers. She was welcomed and would not be made to leave. Almost unwillingly, she smiled.

"You have a beautiful smile," Aemoa said. "How are you? Besides weak, that is." The words were slow, measured yet lilting.

Saying the first thing that came to mind, she croaked out, "I'm hungry."

The other woman laughed. "I'm not surprised, though you ate broth only moments ago. You don't remember do you? I thought not. Your eyes looked odd, like sleepwalking. I have fresh-baked bread and buttermilk cooling in a crock. Would those satisfy?"

Mouth still watering, Mary scrambled to stand. She promptly sat back down. Hard. Onto a bucking and rolling earth that refused to be still. Over the roaring in her ears she heard, "I said you were weak, child. You will have to move slowly for quite some time. Give me your hand."

"Yes, Aemoa. But please make the world stop moving," she whispered. Soft laughter answered her complaint and she joined in, for as the earth settled to a gentle roll she saw herself sitting, bony legs splayed out on the pallet and her tunic twisted tightly around her hips.

Looking up, their eyes met and if Magdalene felt any shame, it was swept away by the compassion she saw in the mother's eyes. Silently she placed her skeletal hand into the outstretched palm.

On their sixth day back in Nazareth, Mary woke, fully alert and lucid. That still surprised her. She knew exactly where she was, how long she had been here and what she wanted. *Food.*

Her appetite was enormous and already she had put on weight. According to Aemoa, the hollows beneath her eyes weren't so bruised and Mary thought she could feel a little meat on her ribs when she brushed her healed fingertips across them.

Outside, the day was young, the sky a dull gray. Somewhere a cock crowed. Carefully so as not to disturb Aemoa, she reached for the ceiling joists, then bent to touch the floor, pulling at muscles and joints that were just beginning to move without pain. Still stiff, she judged, but there was improvement.

She touched her hair and grimaced. After two shampoos and the judicial application of a blade to even up her ragged locks, she looked more presentable, however, it would be many months before she could be seen without a heavy mantle. Her emaciated body, her shorn head and the constant fight with chills made that seem almost pleasant.

There had been a round of visits from the Nazarene women, all of them curious about the strange guest. Aemoa, who was also named Mary, had made it clear to the townspeople that "the

Magdalene" was too weak for visitors and so entertained on the roof, sparing her their prying eyes and probing questions. But soon she would have to face the visitors and visit in return. It was expected. Soon—after the Sabbath.

For now, her days were spent sleeping, eating, and healing, and the two widows talked, catching her up on the world that had gone on without her for so many years. Her stomach rumbled in impatience and she pressed in on the hollowness there. It was too early break the fast.

A rustle sounded from the other pallet. "You renew each day, and constantly throughout the day, the work of creation," Aemoa said. Then, "Good morning, Magdalene. The Lord be with you today."

"Thank you, Aemoa." Her stomach rumbled again, sounding like a thunderstorm had been trapped inside her.

Soft laughter filled the room. "You're hungry. Even after you eat, you're hungry." Magdalene's stomach gave another loud complaint, and Aemoa threw off the robe she slept beneath and stood quickly, adjusting her tunic and finger-combing her hair, hands moving with fluid ease.

Magdalene was awed at the strength of the older woman—from sleep to instant motion—in contrast to her own body. Slowly, like a withered and crooked grandmother, she rolled to her knees, and, with a hand propped against the wall for balance, she stood. Her breath came at a gasp that left her lightheaded, but the older woman helped her through her morning ablutions and back to a three legged stool.

She watched the bird-like movements as the older woman stirred the embers in a small brazier. The stove was a heavy but portable clay bowl with arms reaching up to hold a cooking container, also of clay. Aemoa added bits of charcoal and cloth fibers to the smoking embers and soon water was boiling.

Using her hands as scoops, Aemoa measured out handfuls of ground oats and added a pinch of salt as seasoning. While the oatmeal cooked, she set out smooth wooden cups and bowls, and two large crocks, one containing figs and the other nuts. There was cool buttermilk in a third crock, and honey and bread from the night before.

Voraciously, Mary attacked the food. By the end of the meal, she had consumed three servings of oatmeal, two cups of buttermilk, half the figs in the crock, and most of the bread. Her teeth were too loose from malnutrition to eat the nuts or they would be gone as well. Satisfied, she sat back and propped herself on both arms. Her stomach stuck out under her shift. She looked pregnant.

She averted her head until the sudden tears passed. *That was a long time ago*, she told herself. They had calculated and it had been at least five years. She had mourned long enough and been a burden on others far too long. It was time to be well and care for herself, though she was making only slow progress. Tomorrow she would make breakfast and sweep out the house. All that activity would make her hungry.

For the first time since coming here, eating didn't make her sleepy, and she watched as Aemoa carried the dishes outside to rinse them at the water jar. She then dried and stacked them on a low shelf just inside the door. The shelf was made of smooth plastered clay, a part of the wall, and it went all around the room. It was filled with Aemoa's treasures, as were the pegs, higher on the wall.

The house was small, only two rooms, but sturdily built of stone walls overlaid with clay that was plastered white. The huge beams that held up the ceiling and roof were ancient, smooth, and browned by time. The front room was large and simply furnished, with beautifully carved wooden stools and a low table around which seating mats could be placed for eating. A small handloom stood in the corner, covered with a length of half-finished cloth. The floor was of hard packed clay, but a few woven reed mats and rugs were scattered about, and one elegant rug lay in a conspicuous place near the door. The house, with its sleeping room to the side and the lovely courtyard, was that of a craftsman, yet, so far, she had heard mention of only one son. Memory was hazy concerning him, but Magdalene was certain she had met him.

There was no long table and covered couches for lounging, no tiled floor, and no bath. It was a far different type of house from the one to which she was accustomed—the lovely house Jason built. But Aemoa's home was comfortable and secure from the summer wind and the latter rains.

In the shadows of the winter sleeping room, a windowless cell that could be warmed easily, Magdalene saw a jumble of things, less neatly piled. Curious, she rolled her body off the stool and then to her feet. It was tortuous standing; her weakened muscles had stiffened in the crouched position and she was cautious walking. The object that gripped her attention was a lyre of polished sandalwood inlaid with mother-of-pearl, newly strung, and smooth beneath her hands. Familiar. Absently, her fingers plucked the strings. This had been a gift from Jason on her wedding day. Chills crawled up her spine like spider legs. She jumped at the voice behind her.

"I see you found the gift. It's the surprise I promised you today. One of my cousins strung it yesterday. Do you like it, Magdalene? Child?" When she didn't reply, Aemoa repeated gently, "Child?"

"It was wrapped in a lace veil," Magdalene whispered. "Such beautiful lace, stiff and intricately woven." She blinked and a tear coursed down one cheek. "Jason gave it to me on our wedding day." She closed her eyes to the pain of the memories that followed. Darkness, a velvet shroud, slipped over her.

Vaguely, she heard the words, "Come. Lie down. You tire so easily. Rest now, child. Rest." Clay, cool, and smooth, pressed against her feet as she was led; her knees buckled as she sank onto her pallet. Eyes still closed against the past, she sighed. Gentle hands smoothed her brow and a lullaby hung on the edge of her consciousness, sung in a soft, vibrant voice. She slept.

When she awoke, it was near noon. The first thing she saw was the lyre, propped against a stool near her hand. Reverently, she stroked the shining wood and plucked a single string. The note hung on the warm, dry air. Sitting up, she took the fragile instrument on her knee and tested the sound of each string in turn. She adjusted the tuning of several and strummed once. An old melody came to mind unbidden, a lullaby she had sung to calm her son. Hesitantly, she plucked at the strings until she had the right sound, and then swept through the song almost flawlessly.

"That was lovely. Play it again?" Aemoa sat on the rug inside the doorway, holding a small loom, her hands poised as if she had just stopped the shuttle. There was a smile on her face and Mary realized that the melody was the song she had heard as she fell asleep. More slowly, she played the melody, and this time the rich voice she remembered from her dreams sang the words.

When the last syllable fell away, Aemoa said, "I sang that to Jesus when he was a babe. Not that it ever put him to sleep." The smile lines to either side of her mouth pulled deep.

"I sang it to my son as well." She strummed a chord, slightly dissonant. "This lyre. It was destroyed." Tears brimmed her eyes. "Everything was destroyed."

Aemoa rose, leaving her loom in the light at the door. After a few rustling moments, she returned, holding a flat box. Dazed, Magdalene took it. "My writing desk," she whispered.

"There's more. Magdalene, we found many things in the ruins of your home. You are a wealthy woman. Do you understand? We can . . . we can sort through the things if you like."

The mist that had enveloped her began to clear. "I have something left. All those years and I didn't know. They didn't take everything . . . All those years." A laugh pulled at her face. "I have something left!" She gripped the lyre, the sharp edge cutting into her palm. "What else is there?"

A soft light in her eyes, the older woman gestured into the sleeping room along the back wall. "All of that is yours."

Magdalene clasped her hands together, feeling the sting in her tender palms. "All that?"

The older woman chuckled. "Yes, and there is an old, bedraggled donkey outside that must have been yours as well. My son borrowed two others from you to carry supplies. I didn't think you would need them, and he will return them much more docile than we found them."

Aemoa told of the fray that had resulted when the donkeys had first been loaded with packs. It had been years since they had been strapped for travel and there had been jammed fingers and bruised shins before it was all over. It would have been a much easier chore if they had been in Nazareth, with the animals in a pen, but with them loose in the clearing where they were captured, it was laughably difficult.

"Go ahead. See what you have." Aemoa returned to her handloom and resumed work on a man's tunic. A bit bemused, Magdalene set aside the lyre and took up the desk. Malachite and mother-of-pearl caught the light in the olive wood surface as she opened the top on its new hemp hinges. The exploration of the writing box took only a few minutes, yet touching the stylus, small brushes, and the pottery vial of dried ink, caused a vague feeling of apprehension. She set it down, the green-veined stone shining with a dull gleam, and took up the lyre again. The pile of other things in the shadows beckoned but she hesitated, half afraid and not knowing why.

The lyre sang a melancholy tune beneath her fingertips, yet, below the sorrow of the notes, there was a tight bud of solace, a seed of remembered pleasure, of laughter. Someday, it might germinate and push to the surface. Someday she might even feel peaceful, the way she had felt as a child living in the protected confines of her parents' home. There had been no mourning when she was a child, and perhaps there should be no more mourning now. It had been years since her tragedy, years of horror and mourning. It was time to put her pain away, to go on. She played for some minutes the song of Deborah, trying to recapture in the notes the proper sound of triumph. Over the last notes of the song came a loud groan, her stomach rumbling again. Embarrassed, she glanced at the mother.

Aemoa held the shuttle still and said. "Don't say a word. You're hungry. Well, before you see what was recovered from your home, why don't *you* prepare us lunch. Something light. Today will be too warm for full stomachs."

Awkwardly, Magdalene rolled to her feet. On wobbly legs, she surveyed the room. There were large jars and crocks on the farthest wall from the door, standing or hung on pegs, closed with heavy lids to keep out pests. She spotted the one that held the figs remaining from breakfast and tried to lift it from its pegs. Though she pushed until she was dizzy, it refused to budge. Breathless, she leaned against the wall, her heart an irregular pain against her ribs.

"Try the serving bowls, child."

The voice was cool, almost nonchalant, but when Magdalene turned, she saw the intense concentration of the older woman, watching, evaluating. She washed her hands, chose a wooden bowl, and lifted the clay tops from the crocks. It was easier than she expected, and quickly she filled the bowl with fresh figs and grapes, and cut up a small melon. In a separate dish she mixed sliced leaks, cucumbers, wild artichokes, and tore a few strips of bull's tongue—a bitter, leafy green. She poured a ladle of olive oil over the vegetables and wiped the utensil clean before replacing it, smoothing the oil into her rough skin.

To the communal bowl, she added a handful of nuts. Pleased with her efforts, she turned to call Aemoa to eat. The room behind her was empty, the loom back in its place against the wall.

She walked to the open doorway and blinked into the sunlight. Near the outer wall of the courtyard, Aemoa knelt over a low mound of earth. Magdalene watched as her hostess moved aside a stone from the mound and, using thick cloths to protect her hands, Aemoa pulled out a convex metal sheet. There were six small loaves of steaming bread on it and Magdalene felt her mouth water. At some time in the morning, Aemoa had built a fire in the earth oven. When the flame burned out in the enclosed space, it left the oven and rocks inside heated, and the mother had formed the dough in to balls and set them on the tray inside the oven, sealing the opening with a stone.

Magdalene moved back to the crocks on the wall and ladled out a helping of honey into a small bowl. From a goatskin bag she dipped the last of the leben—cold butter curds—into a clay bowl. The two women washed, spoke thanks for the meal, and ate with their fingers, drinking water from wooden cups.

During her last helping of figs and melon, Magdalene heard Aemoa's mumbled comment about how much easier it had been to feed a growing boy. She liked this candid and gentle woman. Aware that the mother could have left her in the Magdala ruins, or worse, pitied her into total helplessness, she was grateful for the warm bullying and concern. Somehow, while living in this small house in Nazareth, she might remember how to live. Alone.

The word thudded dully through her. *Alone.*

The afternoon was warm, but the women chose to forego the

customary mid-day nap in favor of exploring the plunder from Magdala. Alternately chattering and silent with grief, they opened the heavy storage crocks. Most of their contents were unrecognizable: the remains of dried fruit had fermented into a gummy, sticky mass coating the sides and bottoms of several crocks; nuts had dried into wrinkled powder filling two small ones; grain, green and fuzzy with mildew filled two larger ones; a small block of salt, gray with lost savor, was in a special mortar, attached with rotted cord to a pestle for grinding. The women pulled the crocks out into the courtyard and dumped them, rinsing them with water from the cistern to loosen the clingy muck.

Of the kitchen and cooking supplies, there were a few things still usable. A small pottery crock held crystallized honey and a large sealed cask, higher than her knee, contained wine more potent than any Magdalene had ever tasted. A cache of spices, some precious, were tightly capped in small individual stone jars and vials; the box holding them was of fine, charcoal-toned soapstone, its lid carved in intricate geometric designs. The box had been a gift from her mother-in-law, who had died soon after her marriage to Jason. In a box with similar carving, though larger and less valuable, were herbs, musty and stale, which she tossed out. A wooden box had held each day's bread, and on the Passover the leaven was placed in it and carried out of the house.

A special crock, made of white stone which glistened when the light struck it, contained a heavy cloth bag. Magdalene had no memories of the crock and felt certain that she had not seen it before.

"You found this at my house?"

Aemoa's face was mischievous. "One of my son's friends found it buried beneath the foundation. How he found it there I'll never know. Go on. Open it."

Magdalene pulled at the half-rotted string and when the bag fell away, she was holding coins. The air seemed to stutter and pause before swirling around her again. Magdalene dipped into the coins and lifted a handful. They clinked dully and several slid down her dress to roll noiselessly across the floor. The importance of the soft shining metal escaped her for a moment, and then, stunned, she gasped. It was gold. A fortune in gold.

There was a deep silence in the house as Magdalene stared at the money in her hand. Resting on her dress. Scattered on the floor. Slowly she closed the rotting cloth bag and placed it in the crock. Crawling on her knees, she gathered all the coins that had rolled into the corners and dropped them in with the bag, replacing the stone lid with a faint clunk.

Aemoa had called her wealthy, but this money wasn't hers. She and Jason were prosperous, but not to this extent. Never this affluent. *Where did Jason get this money? Where had he ever gotten his gold? He never discussed his business with her. Where did Jason go on his long trips, for so many years? What had he sold that earned him such riches?*

Shadows of suspicion danced through her mind, but no insight came. Silent, aware of Aemoa's gaze, she set the stone canister to the side. Aemoa, not understanding her disquiet, and clearly interpreting it as grief, gestured to the next pile of household items. Magdalene shoved her thoughts aside for more private consideration and found a smile for her hostess.

Resting upside down was an oversized bronze caldron in need of polishing, its ladle nearby. Beneath the caldron was a black basalt grinding mill, the large size requiring two women to turn. Proper etiquette would not allow her hostess to refuse an outright gift and Magdalene immediately presented the caldron, ladle, and mill to her new friend. Though still shadowed by a worry she had never known before, she was touched by the older woman's childlike excitement and honored when two of the gifts were placed with the special riches of the house, items reserved for Seder and Purim feast days. She knew their value, and clearly the caldron and ladle would be lovingly polished and treasured, handed down as a cherished heirloom to the wife of the son.

The mill would receive more mundane usage. It took the combined efforts of the two women to drag the mill to a place near the small loom. As they worked to position it, Magdalene's heels digging into the clay floor and her heart pounding with effort, she gasped, "How did the mill come to be transported . . . all the distance from . . . Magdala?"

Aemoa gave it one last shove and they both plopped to the ground, the mother running her hands over the black basalt topstone. "My son's friend, Simon the Fisherman, has giant shoulders," Aemoa held her hands out to show the size. "He carried the mill."

"I must find a suitable gift for his effort," Magdalene said as her heart steadied and the pain in her chest subsided.

The last thing left to be explored was a large cedar chest, water-stained and warped, its beauty permanently marred. The long heart-of-cedar handles had been replaced with hastily cut saplings. The latch had been broken, the scratches of recent tampering fresh on the face of the chest. She ran her hands over the scratches, the metal rough beneath her fingers.

"My son wasn't quick enough to stop one of the men in our caravan from breaking the latch," said the older woman in a soft voice. "He offers his apologies and promised to repair the latch when he returns. The contents were thoroughly rifled also. I'm sorry."

Magdalene was silent before the chest, her knees clasped tightly in her arms. Perhaps recognizing her pain, the older woman chose to leave her to her grief. After placing a chisel by her side to help with the water-swollen wood, she slipped into the courtyard.

Tears welling in her eyes, Magdalene traced the wooden inlays with a fingertip. The once-smooth edges were rough with weather and some of the inlaid pieces, weakened from exposure, had popped loose, leaving depressions of wood, pale and faintly scented. She knew what was inside without even thinking. Inside were her family's clothes. Her bridal gifts. Her lace veils for weddings and feast days. How many times had she knelt before this chest to withdraw a length of fabric or to replace a washed tunic? Inside were the memories and mementoes of a lifetime, for in truth, the old Mary was dead and buried. She didn't even know this new woman, the one called Magdalene.

Grief prickled at her eyelids and, before a single tear could trickle down her cheek, she wiped her eyes, took a steadying breath, and picked up the wood chisel left by the mother—a carpenter's valuable tool. She inserted it into the tight crack, prying up and down.

The wood, so long left unoiled, groaned and cracked. A splinter fell to the clay floor. Afraid that she would damage the chest even more, she moved the chisel to the other side of the lid and tried again. Working slowly around the tight seam, she eventually widened the crack, prying and working until the force of the wood itself sprang the lid loose. Feeling a sense of accomplishment far too great for the simple task, she fell beside the chest breathing heavily. She had done it alone! How many years since she had done anything useful alone?

The sun had shifted around, no longer sending a ray of light through the window and open door. The room had grown gloomy, long gray shadows obscuring the disordered state of her plunder. She fumbled about in the darkness of the room and found a lamp, lit it from a coal in the brazier.

Placing the lamp on the low table, she pushed the heavy cedar lid far back on its wooden hinges. The swollen wood caught before the lid was fully open, leaving the contents in shadow. Impatiently, she readjusted the position of the lamp, and its feeble light fell on a chaotic pile of wrinkled cloth, leather, and stone. On the top was a small dress, highly embroidered with silken thread. Her hands trembled as she touched the fabric. Tears slipped silently down her cheeks. She saw his little face clearly, all covered with mud and scraped from a fall. His leg was shaking with the impatience of youth interrupted at play, a game he was winning, just to try on this silly dress for next feast day. Had he ever worn it? She couldn't remember. He and Jason were gone. Only she was left to suffer.

A gentle hand stroked back her hair, cradled her bony body, rocking her as though she were a child. Her pain-wracked sobs had carried on the evening air and brought Aemoa. "He did this to me. The one with the eyes." Her words roared inside her skull, drowning in her sobs. There was a break in the rhythm of the older woman's body as if she were surprised or about to speak. Then Magdalene continued, the rhythm slower. "He made me remember," she whispered.

Brown eyes slipped into Magdalene's memory. Calm and gentle, they smiled. Slowly her anguish subsided. A strange lethargy, almost like peace, filled her. And still the eyes smiled. "He had brown eyes. He seemed kind." There was a long silence and no answer from her new friend. "Why would he make me remember? And why did the Romans kill Jason?"

The older woman patted her shoulder and rose, to begin gathering food for the evening meal. "I don't know why Romans do anything."

Later, after another meal, this one with a bit of meat, they cleaned out the trunk. She now had three changes of clothing, one an elegantly embroidered dress that had never been worn. Jason's father's cloak, heavy wool and three generations old, the Magdalene set aside. It would have been for her son at his coming of age. Now it would pass out of the family unless she could find Jason's brother. The men had been estranged for many years; it wasn't likely she could locate him now. Her husband's leather winter boots were tangled in the clothing and she set them aside, uncertain what to do with the valuable shoes. Leather boots were worth a year's wages.

About midway down in the trunk hidden in the deepening shadows were several hard objects. A heavy black stone, flat and grooved on the surface, was wrapped in a length of fabric. It was the playing board for a game Jason had taught her. The pieces were scattered among the heaped clothing. Jason's best tunic held in its folds a jewel box. Within were her gold and silver-worked bracelets, the gold gleaming dully, the silver tarnished. There were two pairs of earrings set in the Greek manner, one silver and one gold, and on the bottom were her rings. All this was a part of her dowry.

She found one pair of sandals with soft leather laces, brightly dyed, and her favorite pair of boots. These were the boots her father had made with his own hands when she had finally come of marriageable age. She slipped them on, and the boots still fit though the leather was hard. Every village had its cobbler, and she knew they could be oiled to usefulness again. She set both pairs of shoes aside for repair. There were a pair of baby shoes, really nothing more than once-soft pieces of leather slashed at the corners and laced to the feet. These she set near the baby dress. It was all she had left, except for a small ragged toy made of cloth. It had been found in the ruins of her home, not in the chest. Rats had used it and there was little left. She placed it with the dress, though the toy would never be of value to anyone but herself.

Before she had even touched the last bound object,

Magdalene recognized what it was—her glass dishes! Gingerly, she lifted out the package and placed it on the floor. She untied the corners of the cloth, one knot holding tight against her fingers. She jerked and it fell away, revealing the green glass goblets that had been her greatest prize.

Aemoa gasped at the carnage. One goblet, though somehow intact, was shattered, like so many spiders had tried to trap it in a web. Two of the others had been damaged as well, one nicked on the rim, the other with a minute hairline crack at the handle. One glass, the last, was untouched and beautiful. Magdalene lifted it out.

Using the edge of her tunic, she polished the glass inside and out. The lamp, catching on the goblet, cast a green glow into the room, winking in and out as she turned it. Smiling, she wrapped it back in the cloth that had bound it and pushed the three broken ones away. They would have to be taken to a glass merchant and sold at a fraction of their cost. Then perhaps she would commission a trader to find her three new ones to replace the old. After all, she was now rich enough to afford an extravagance. And this one was important. To her, if to no one else.

The last things in the chest she lifted out and set on top of the others: a bolt of bright blue silk, her lace veils, and a pair of Jason's sandals. At the very bottom of the chest, a dull gleam caught her eye. Her girdle of coins! The last piece of her dowry.

The priceless gold and silver girdle abandoned at the bottom of the chest was almost ruined—it was twisted, tangled, bent, and several of the coins had come loose from their settings. The weight of the other contents, thrown haphazardly on top of it, had crushed the fine mesh at a thousand different angles. It looked as though the girdle had purposely been thrown into the bottom of the trunk to be mangled. Feeling the first burble of anger, Magdalene lifted the twisted girdle from the trunk and spread it out on the nearby table.

It was the only girdle of its kind in this country. Her mother's mother's mother had brought it from a distant land, and for all these generations it had been passed on to the eldest daughter as dowry. Angrily, she smoothed the delicate wires, trying to restore the coil to its lost beauty. "I will know who did this," she hissed, her voice sounding strange in her own ears. "This was not some accident. This is not from before, for the wires are freshly bent, not yet crushed flat. Who? Who did this?"

Aemoa's voice was subdued. "I think it must have been one of my son's friends. The Law says what is taken from ruins is the property of the finders, and several wanted to sell the girdle for the group's coffers—the girdle and all else we recovered. Jesus told them to return the girdle to its embroidered bag and place it with the other things. I don't understand why it was put on the bottom. It's very delicate and couldn't bear such weight. Perhaps it was an accident?" The words hung lamely in the air, countered by the condition of the girdle and the way the contents had been tossed into the trunk. "Jesus was adamant that nothing be taken. He said all these things were yours. I'm sorry, Magdalene."

She stood over the trunk, the priceless girdle in her hands, aware she was being studied as the words slowly sank in. *He was adamant that nothing be taken . . . all these things were yours.* She realized what Aemoa's son had done for her. Anyone else would have taken everything of value and fled, leaving her to fend for herself. But these people had not only bound her wounds and taken her into their home, but had seen to it she retained her possessions. They had left her a very wealthy and protected woman. Aemoa was right. This was far more than they legally had to do. More than they morally had to do. Her shoulders relaxed and Magdalene breathed deeply, her anger evaporating. She owed this Jesus a great deal.

No one had ever given her so much. Not Jason. Not her father. Women didn't own property. They *were* property. Jason had even said as much to her one day. She shook the memory away. It was replaced with a vision of eyes, the strange, powerful eyes that had come to her in Magdala and in the ruins. Both times they had brought her peace. She was certain that they belonged to Jesus. Eyes like that did the unexpected.

Slowly she smiled, feeling her face light up from within, as it had as a child. She placed the girdle between the folds of blue silk and hugged it close to her shrunken chest.

Softly she said, "Thank you."

Chapter Four

The Zealot

A hot, desert breeze filtered dustily through his tunic. Around him, the night was black and moonless, the dark the best camouflage. The Roman soldiers, encamped in the bottom of a dry riverbed, couldn't see him where he sat, out of range of their firelight, and just beyond the perimeter of the guards' paths. Simon was close enough to hear the words they spoke, echoes bouncing off the low canyon wall to the west and to the east.

One complained about missing supplies. Another swore about the hot wilderness wind. Others grumbled about the guerrilla attacks in the region and about a woman they had captured and used in the last town.

All of it made his lips stretch across strong teeth, a fierce and violent smile, where he hid in the darkness. They were making it so very easy. It brought him brutal delight, for Nirit, for his little flower, Nirit. Because someday he would find the ones who took her.

For now, though, these filthy men who talked about the rape of a woman with such pride and boasting would earn the worst of his punishments. When he was through with these Romans, even their own mothers would not be able to tell one from the other. He closed his mouth on his smile, hiding his teeth in the night's inky blackness. He waited, patient, unmoving, until the fire burned low, the embers faint glowing spots in the ashes, until the moon began to set, darkening the night. The guard nearest sat with nodding head.

Slipping from his crouch, Simon stood and stretched slowly, restoring circulation. He checked his weapons. Three knives, each honed to razor sharpness. One in each hand, and another, his last resort, sewn into the lining of his loincloth. Shoes, soft chamois for silence.

Advancing with the pace of a stalking cat, Simon was right in front of the guard before the man woke from his half-doze. Incredulity died on the face of his enemy before he could scream. The best warrior the Others had, he caught the man and his weapons before they hit the ground and alerted the sleeping soldiers. Carefully, he slid the man down and wiped splattered Roman blood from his face. Roman blood. It was good.

Stealthy, he crept from man to man, his knife slicing through the arteries and windpipe of each throat, then wiped the blade clean on the beard or hair or tunic of his victim. Twelve in all. Simon smiled again, that terrible grimace that was more pain than joy, and returned to the first man. He took the sword, personal knife and money pouch, slipping them into the large travel pouch he carried. He bent again. Quickly he severed the man's right ear, and, moving aside the man's clothes, his testicles. He moved to the next man. And the next.

The animals would do the rest. He had a certain instinct for horror. When these men were found, days from now, their faces and genitals gnawed away, there would be reaction. Strong reaction. Horror. Right in every Roman soldier's deepest heart.

Minutes later, bowed beneath his plunder, he walked into the undisturbed night air and vanished into the darkness. In hard, muscular shape, not a hint of fat on him, he quickly found the pace that was his night-travel run, and headed for the mountains to the north. Roman blood dried on his body, cracking and flaking. Though it was fifty miles to the cave, he could cover half of that before dawn and be so far from the campsite that even if it was discovered at dawn, he could never be tracked.

Simon ran through the dark, stopping only twice, once at a stream to wash the bits of flesh he carried and the blood from his body, and the second time to hide the heavy weapons. At daylight, he holed up in the branches of an old olive tree and slept lightly, so alert he heard the buzzing of bees collecting for honey. At dusk, he ate some of the hard bread he had brought and sipped his water. Good Jewish water in a stolen Roman flask. Then he started out again for the mountains and the cave where the Others waited. They had sent him to kill one man and steal weapons if he could, but his instinct for death was strong. He had smelled it on the wind, felt it brush against his skin. A Roman patrol. Instead of one man, one example, he had killed twelve and stolen all the weapons, all the food, all the money, and a little reminder from each man to hang on the cave walls where he slept. They would again ask him to become a leader, and once again he would refuse. He liked the killing too much; leaders were too valuable to risk in forays and raids.

He arrived at dusk the following day, pausing twice to give a cryptic sign, and once to pass the secret word before moving into the bowels of the mountain, and the arms of his compatriots. They were astounded at his success, and immediately sent couriers to retrieve the weapons he had hidden on the journey. Over a celebration of wine and more food than the starving band had seen in months, he told and retold the story of the attack. For Nirit, all for Nirit. And even in his drunken state, just before he lay down, or fell down, Simon remembered to tack the ears and small bits of flesh that had been testicles to the walls of the cave above the place where he slept. Now there were fifteen sets. All for pretty little Nirit, with the flies that buzzed over her body and dipped their tongues into her blood.

He woke slowly, his head splitting wide, as if it were a melon halved cleanly by the single stroke of a sword. He knew where he was. The dim cave light never changed, day or night, summer or winter. He knew it even with his eyes closed against the pain. He squinted his eyes open. Above him, directly in his line of sight, pinned neatly to the natural arch that was the sloping cave ceiling, were small wrinkled trophies. The memory of the camp, the soldiers, and the butcher work returned. He rolled to his side with a violent motion and vomited on the sandy floor. It was sour, and the stench blended in with the smells of unwashed bodies, old wine, urine, and the peculiar, almost sweet, sickly smell of rotting flesh.

Feeling better, he drew up the memory of Nirit, forced her into his conscious mind, past the sickness from the drunken night and the memory of the soldiers. He remembered her sitting in a field of flowers, sitting before a fire, spinning thread, drawing water from the city well. Laughing. But the good memories faded, leaving only his last sight of her, swarming with flies. The dark memories were good. They kept his hate alive.

Simon rose and went to the back of the cave where a stream rose for a few feet before disappearing again into the blackness. A torch flickered in a hole someone had dug in the cave wall, the oily flame throwing more smoke than light. Besides the anonymous location, the small stream of water was the only thing the cave had to offer.

Stepping carefully, he squatted in the frigid water and flexed his toes into the slick, black bottom. Using a coarse sponge, he scrubbed his skin and splashed water over himself, the stream taking away his filth. The shock of the water eased his headache and he drank a small mouthful where it rushed out fresh. Standing, he flung off icy drops with his hands instead of reaching for the communal towel. The sound of hard palms slapping sinewy thighs echoed through the cave. Hungry, he went into the sunlight.

The three leaders were staring at a map. A real map on fine Roman parchment penned with delicate ink lines. Near it was a familiar leather pouch, and he knew the map must have been in the pouch he had taken from the commanding officer of the soldiers. He hadn't bothered to look in it. Hadn't cared. The leaders looked up at him, standing in the mouth of the sleeping cave, and paused, a tiny hesitation before they resumed their conversation.

Though his face reflected nothing, he was surprised. He had been with the band for over three years, but this was the first time the leaders had talked within his hearing. It was another indication that they hoped he would join them as a leader. He would make a terrible leader. He would rather kill.

The two other leaders continued speaking as Reuven, the oldest of them studied him with his one good eye. In his gravely voice, Reuven said, "Simon. We offer the next mission to your leadership if you want it. It will be a major incursion against the Romans." The grizzled old man lifted his chin to the map and raised a finger, indicating he should draw nearer and sit beside them at the low Roman table they had stolen in some raid, somewhere.

Leader of a raid. Now, that he could do. He sat on the bare ground, lower than they, uncaring of his position or the dust beneath his body.

"By bringing this, you have put an opportunity before us." Reuven cleared his rough voice, spat in the dirt, and pointed to the map. "It's the travel route of a well-guarded Roman merchant. There will be immense wealth on this caravan. It will be a great coup."

"Tell me," Simon said. He heard their words, the guile in their voices, saw the false smiles in their eyes as they told him of the route and discussed possible ambush sites. They wanted the riches. He wanted to kill. He would take the mission. He always took them, though this would be his first as commander. Yet, when they finished, he grunted, "I'll think about it."

Standing, he moved for the darkness of the cave. His head hurt. He needed wine and hot gruel, and fresh hot bread with soured milk and butter and honey. His stomach rolled drunkenly as he strode from them out of the blinding light and heat, in search of darkness and food.

Later, near the close of day, his stomach calmer and his head again lightened on warm wine, Simon sought out the leaders and found Reuven sitting with his face toward the evening sun. Silently, he knelt near the bent old man and waited to be recognized.

"So. You have kept us waiting long enough, do you think?"

Simon smiled, almost a real smile. "You knew I would take it."

"Yes. I knew. But the others," he shrugged a bony shoulder, "they were not so sure. Some men would not wish to go back out this soon. But I know you. I trained you myself before the pain in my hands got bad." Reuven looked at his gnarled knuckles, swollen and red. "I know how the lust sits upon you. The killing lust. I have seen it before. I thought it would burn out of you," the old man paused, tilting his scared face to the dying sun, "but I was wrong. You breed hate like a Samaritan breeds heresy." He turned his head and the sunlight cast sharp shadows across his ruined cheek. "You will die with a sword in your belly and a growl on your lips, spitting at the man who downs you. "The old man shook his head slowly.

Ignoring the man's prediction, Simon scooped up a small handful of sand and let it drain through his fingers. "Save your pity. Tell me of the mission."

In a raspy, unemotional tone, the old man outlined the plan. Timing, supplies, distance, the number of Romans guarding the caravan, the number of men he would take, the weapons each would carry. Simon memorized each word as it was spoken. The old man used the same measured cadence that a village Rebbe used to teach a group of schoolboys their first scriptures. Later, Simon would memorize the map and the locations of the landmarks. He had little time. The men he would lead had already been chosen.

"This caravan will have hired mercenaries, desert fighters." Reuven tilted his head up, his one good eye piercing. Reuven had once been a desert fighter and had given all his knowledge to Simon. He had pounded in lesson after grueling lesson until battle was more instinct than knowledge. Reuven had taught him *everything*. "You leave at the second dawn."

Simon shrugged. One day was as good as the next when it came to killing Romans.

Chapter Five

Magdalene

The morning before the Sabbath, the two women cleaned the house, straightening and sweeping, smoothing the clay floor with water and their bare hands, polishing and scrubbing until the house was organized and spotless. Magdalene was exhausted at day's end though she rested often and napped at midday. By sundown, the start of the Holy Day, the table was graced with flowers and the symbols of the Sabbath. There were candlesticks, twisted Hallah loaves, stuffed fish, wine and a bit of lamb. Just before the sun set, Aemoa lit the candles. She shielded her eyes from the light in order not to see it and spoke the Berakhah, the blessing of light to begin the new day. "Barukh attah . . . vetzivanu lehadlik ner shel Shabbat." *Blessed are You . . . He . . . commanding us to kindle the Sabbath light.*

While Magdalene watched through lowered lashes, the mother silently prayed.

Because Magdalene had been too tired, they had not gone to the synagogue, and thus had not heard the Sabbath proclamation. The Mitzvah of the two widows was short because there were no children present for them to bless, no Praise of the Valiant Woman by a husband in honor of his wife, and there was no adult male to pass the Kiddush wine and speak of the import of the seventh day.

During the ritual of the Sabbath, the Magdalene was aware that Aemoa wasn't giving lip service to the traditional words. The older woman was *worshipping*; her hostess believed, *really believed*, that God heard her words. When Aemoa opened her eyes after the Mitzvah, her home had received the Sabbath, and a soft smile lit her features. That smile tore into Magdalene. That smile was so full of safety and contentment and . . . and *satisfaction.*

Aemoa, though a widow, had a home, a purpose, a place in Jewish life and tradition, a tradition that revolved around children, around sons. A widow, with no living children, Magdalene had no place in the society of her people. Even with the bag of gold, she had nothing. Like a boat with no tiller and no sail, she was adrift, helpless in her aloneness. *Alone.* Utterly and totally *alone.*

A vision of torn cloth, frayed and flapping in the wind came to her. Grief and rage tore through her, slashing like ravens' claws. How could God let her family die? How could he let her be *alone?* She had done no sin. She had not profaned her God. And yet he had punished her. Maybe he didn't even exist, as some Greeks, and even some great Jewish thinkers, postulated.

Anger and disbelief warred in her as shame dripped down her soul like tears. She pressed her mouth tightly shut and took in a deep, whistling breath, trying to find the calm in her center, a calm that had once been sourced by Yehowah-rā-ah—the Lord, my Shepherd—but her soul was shredded and torn, the fabric that had been her life nothing more than rotted threads waving in the breeze, releasing calm, to dissipate like morning mist. She was empty of Yehowah Elohim, the creator of heaven and earth. A dark hole was ripped through the place he had once filled, leaving an emptiness so vast that it seemed able to draw down the entire world, an emptiness that took the place of her own most recent years.

Tears built behind her lids as she studied the emptiness, the darkness within her. She remembered only bits and pieces, fear and running and that overwhelming darkness leaping onto her, within her, a crushing, devouring loneliness.

Magdalene dropped her head so that Aemoa couldn't see her rage. And what followed—covetousness toward her hostess who still had so much. *It isn't fair!* She had even lost her own name. She was no longer called Mary, but the Magdalene, a woman no longer named after a father or a husband or a son, or even an honored woman in the family. But named after a *town.* Aemoa had everything, a home, a son who was revered and called teacher. She remembered that much. Rabboni. Beloved teacher. While her own son was gone, stolen.

A rational part of her knew it wasn't Aemoa's fault. But worship wasn't possible for her. She had lost too much.

The morning of the Sabbath dawned clear and red with a strong southerly breeze, and Magdalene lay on her sleeping pallet in the main room of Aemoa's house, staring into the rafters overhead. Her bones didn't hurt quite so much as when she rose yesterday. Her breath came easier. She was healing. But for what? Why had Yehowah-rapha, the Lord who heals, let her live?

A song of thanksgiving, the traditional greeting of the day, rang out from an early riser next door. Out over the village, the greeting song came from many houses, from roof tops and unsecured windows, echoing into the morning air. It was hot early this year and summer sleep patterns had already begun, making the village one family, rising and going to sleep as one, rather than dozens of families each closed into its home, keeping its own hours, as in wintertime.

From her room at the back of the house, Aemoa sang, her voice low and pleasing. Magdalene didn't join in the familiar refrain. Instead, she rose with the singing and splashed water on her face and body, her voice silent, her heart empty and dark.

The special Sabbath clothes she had placed out the night before were her finest, given back to her by her hostess, salvaged from the ruins of her home. Quickly she put on her embroidered dress and jewelry. All the best things were for the Sabbath, in clothes and dishes and food and thought. She could carry nothing, so all that she needed for the day she wore.

Having no Gentile servant to do the Sabbath day's chores, the two women had done all they could before dusk, the beginning of the Holy Day; all else would have to wait until after sundown. The day's food simmered in its own juices in thick, sealed earthenware. The lamps were full of oil, ready to be lit. The utensils for eating and drinking were laid on the table. According to Law, of the thirty-nine work prohibitions for the Holy Day, eleven of them concerned the growing and the preparation of food. Neither woman would have thought of breaking even the smallest of the Laws.

At the appointed time, they stepped into the street and began the long slow walk to the synagogue. Her mantle pulled low across her face to hide her cropped hair, Magdalene peered out at the town as they walked. Especially compared to Magdala, it was not a particularly attractive town. Most of the houses were mud and wattle—dried mud and sticks—with a few dried mud brick houses interspersed. Only a few were stone overlaid with clay and whitewashed plaster, and limestone was nowhere in evidence. Few of the houses would have been visible from a distance; the whole town seemed to have pushed up from the earth around them, rounded or squared off globs of mud.

The path on which they walked was rough and pitted from last year's rains, climbing sharply uphill. Her weak ankles twisted on its uneven surface and, forced to ignore the unprepossessing little town, she picked her way carefully. Until they neared the synagogue, she kept her gaze low, though as they climbed, she felt the buildings lean away from the path and a cool breeze pressed into her clothes. When she looked up, the view—so unexpected— took her breath away.

Nazareth was perched on top of a circle of hills dotted with olive groves and majestic cypress. Regally, the dirty little town spread its arms and looked down into the greatest valley in her nation, the Jezreel. The Armageddon. The valley of every major battle in her people's history. From here she could see it all.

Her breath, frozen in her chest, tightened painfully. Tears, so ready to her eyes these days, gathered and spilled down her cheeks. Below her, in the Armageddon, were broad fields of new wheat, carefully tended grape arbors, the rounded masses of fig trees, and even a few young grape vines tied to wood frames. A battlefield in time of peace.

Around her, the homes which had looked so mean before, she now saw in a different light. Each had a small garden with herbs, lilies, verbena, a rare olive tree or bougainvillea. The browns and tans of brick and dried mud, and the gray of stone formed a pleasing, almost soothing palette. Though nothing was whitewashed, it was a pleasant little town, and strangely peaceful.

It took a moment for her to determine why she saw it as serene. Nowhere were there Romans, no single sign of them. The road leading from Nazareth to the valley was ancient, a fully Jewish track, untouched by Roman engineers. There was no Roman dress, no clink of sword. No Roman bathhouse or Roman banner above a small outpost.

Until then she had not realized she held her breath and, slowly, a long sigh passed between her lips easing the pain in her chest. No Romans. Not one.

She hurried to catch up with her hostess, relieved in ways that she didn't completely understand. In a doorway as they passed stood three women, their heads close together. They were dressed in the coarse cloth of simple peasants and their words which reached her ears were rough and uncouth in the dialect of the region. It was obvious they intended her to hear.

"Jesus' mother and her *guest*."

"The one with shorn hair?"

"Why ever did she take *her* in?"

"Mary and her stray cats. She takes in anything with a *limp* or a *sniffle*. It's a surprise she hasn't taken in beggars."

"Why did they cut her hair? Was she cast out? Did her husband catch her in *adultery*?"

Magdalene's skin blazed with shame that wasn't hers to feel. She had not sinned, no matter how her God had punished her.

"*I* heard she did it in mourning."

"That's what Mary is saying, but *I've* heard otherwise."

Aemoa's head went up high and her lips pressed closed, her nostrils flaring in anger. She came to a stop and Magdalene shuffled to a stop behind her, though she wanted to run fast and far. Magdalene pulled her mantle higher over her face. Nazareth wasn't so pleasant after all, but at least there were no Romans. She watched from the safety of her mantle as Aemoa let her eyes travel slowly over the women. Her gaze was steely and the three quieted, turning away. Head high, Aemoa turned back to the path and the climb to the synagogue.

Silent, she followed her hostess into the place of worship, to the women's side, separate from the men. The two Marys sat on the back wall of the synagogue, and Magdalene breathed deeply after the climb, trying to find comfort on the hard bench.

The reading of the Torah was a dull rumble. The discussion

afterward was desultory, all between the men. The women were traditionally silent, and Magdalene had to struggle to stay awake. She was exhausted long before the meeting concluded and made the trek downhill to Aemoa's house only by force of will. She took to her pallet as soon as they were inside.

She had slept this last week with only vague dreams, but today they were darker, malevolent, steeped in dread. The figures which always haunted her nightmares were clearer—swords and blood and terror. And though she knew them to be dreams, she couldn't turn away. A dismembered hand reached for her, touching her face. A faceless corpse whispered obscenities. A river of blood carried bloating, festering dead closer. Clotted blood lapped at her feet. Her clothes were steeped in the crimson tide. The wind roared and she covered her ears, but it tore her hands away, ripping her hair, slashing her clothes. A body paused in the frothy blood at her feet, rotated and raised its arm in accusation. It was Jason, his voice a stunning clarity. "You did this. You. The guilty one. *You!* Shame. Shame, shame, shame."

Her thrashing and her scream woke her as Aemoa fell to her knees on the edge of the sleeping pallet, her face rigid with concern. Magdalene sobbed out the dream, her voice hoarse and anguished, her hands griping the folds of Aemoa's gown. She buried her face in the cloth, the new dye stringent in her nostrils. When she calmed, Aemoa rose and brought back a damp cloth, the excess wrung out. "You shouldn't," Magdalene said. "The Sabbath prohibits—"

"Shhh. The Law allows us to care for the sick. You are un-well."

Magdalene took the cloth and wiped her own tears, the cool water soothing on her flushed skin. Aemoa stroked her hair as if she were a child, murmured soft words, holding her until her breath eased and her fear quieted. After long moments, Aemoa finally spoke.

"Can you tell me about that day, Magdalene? Mary? The day your family died."

"Jason didn't *die*," she whispered, sitting up, pulling away from the comfort of her new friend's arms. "He was tortured to death."

"By Romans?"

"They came though town. They passed me. A few said . . . things, as they always do. I was on my way to Rebecca's house, to learn if I was with child. Rebecca had a woman's gift, to discern if a woman was blessed with a babe. She said it was a girl."

Magdalene pressed her hand to her stomach, hollow with malnourishment. "She said my child would look like me." A bitter smile twisted her face. "I spent the whole day with her. It was late when I left. Almost dusk when I passed from the city walls. I saw smoke when I was a long way off. I *knew*. And I started running. I came through the trees, smoke trailing through them heavy with the rank smell of burned flesh. Our house, everything, was gone. It must have happened right after I left. Jason was cold and stiff."

Aemoa's breath caught. Magdalene pulled away from her hostess and stared down at her hands in her lap. The skin was red and rough, scars redder still. "Jason was tied to the center beam of the house. He had been burned and beaten. His teeth knocked out. His face bruised and swollen. And he had been . . ." She took a slow breath, "He had been skinned like an animal."

Aemoa's body trembled in horror, but she said nothing. There was no sound in the small house, no sound in the silent village, as everyone turned their Sabbath thoughts to God, or napped in the afternoon heat. Magdalene didn't look up, just folded her fingers together like a basket and held them, studying them as if they might capture and hold all the pain that occupied the empty place in her torn and ruined soul. *Ahhh. That is why there is no God within my heart. There's no room for him* and *the pain.*

Her throat ached, but she forced the words out. "Our son. They took him." Aemoa's hands twitched, but she said nothing. The darkness swelled within, pressing on her heart, on her lungs; her chest ached.

"I don't know how I got him down off the tree. I don't remember much of anything. Except that later, by the stream, I lost the baby. But I don't . . . think it was that same day. I don't remember when that was." Magdalene looked up from her hands and found Aemoa's eyes on her. There was no pity or condemnation there, only a great sadness. A sharing. Tears gathered again in Magdalene's eyes. "I should have been with them. I was drinking tea and toasting the child that would never be, celebrating with wine and eating sweets and they were dying. If I had been there I could have—"

"Died with them. Been tortured in turn. Raped."

Magdalene shrugged and wiped at her face with her sleeve. Tears smeared and burned her partially healed skin. When she spoke, her voice ripped along her throat like talons, the words strangled and hoarse. "It was *my place*. I should have died. *I wish I had died with them.*"

"Look at me." Aemoa's voice was soft and gentle, and when Magdalene looked up, she found eyes full of compassion. "You are not at fault for living. You survived by a quirk of God's providence. That doesn't mean that it was the will of God for your family to suffer, only for you to survive."

"That isn't what the scriptures say."

"It is what they mean. My son is learned and he says God does not punish us by punishing the ones we love. God is merciful."

"God is a merciless killer." The words, blasphemy that came from her mouth, shocked them both.

"Listen to me," Aemoa said, when she could speak. "No, don't shake your head. I do know whereof I speak. And I do know how it feels to have avoided death and disaster when your friends and family could not escape. I do know. *I do.*" Her eyes were intense, focused bright as candles in the dim light of the house. "You cannot give up and die because you didn't go with them. You can't. You're alive. God wanted you alive."

Silent. Attuned to Aemoa's words and the pain beneath, she listened, though her heart whispered, *But if there is no God? If it was only the whim of living and not action with purpose? Can there be both God and the accident of fate? Can there be anything other than his judgment? And if he doesn't judge fairly? If he punishes the innocent?*

She felt and heard Aemoa take a great breath, heard the tears in her throat as it threatened to close with the pain of remembering. And then her new friend talked. About her husband and her pregnancy when she had no husband and knew only vaguely about the physical relationship between man and woman that produced children. About the village's reaction to her large, swollen belly. And she talked about Bethlehem. The massacre of the children, all those precious children of her friends, who had not been saved by Joseph's dream.

And for a moment, a single soft, gentle moment, Magdalene felt less alone. That moment stretched out. And out. The feeling didn't fade as she expected it to.

For all of the hours of the Sabbath, as Aemoa talked with her, she listened and was calm. It was a cleansing Sabbath and at sunset, Mary, who was called Magdalene now, found a faint, tattered sense of peace and a return of strength.

Near sunset, the two Marys went to the village Rebbe's table, invited to share a meal, and they listened as he spoke of divine mysteries and revealed instruction. The peace that wanted to weave about her became more real as he spoke. Perhaps God wasn't vengeful or capricious. Perhaps. Though the darkness was still a ragged emptiness within her.

The Rebbe spoke of the Messiah, the promised one, and of the miracles that would happen when he came. It was nonsense, tales for children, but she felt the peace, the peace of new friendship and the shared paths of women.

The first three stars appeared in the evening sky and the Rebbe, who was also the village's cantor, spoke the evening prayer. "Vehu rahum . . ." *He is compassionate . . .*

The traditional words continued, and at Motzaei Shabbat, the Exit of the Sabbath, they called upon Elijah to stand by them during the week, to protect them, to help them to succeed. It was beautiful, but it wasn't worship. It was possible that she would never worship again.

But Magdalene recognized that it *was* a beginning of something, something new. Her new life, whatever it might be.

In the dark of the moon, the young man watched the two women walk back along the rough, dried mud streets to their humble house. It had taken him weeks to find the woman, and his employer would not be pleased to know that she had been healed by the meddling Rebbe. Not pleased at all.

● ● ●

Simon slept hard and ate well; the time passed swiftly with preparations. The mission set for him by the leaders of the Others would be difficult only in location and groundwork. The killing would be simple—the death of Romans, even merchants, always was. So he kept his mind empty, like a well is empty, except for water, conserving his strength.

The second dawn came, and they were on the road, out of the hills, heading south, keeping to the shadows, leaving no trail, moving fast. No campfires at night meant dried meat and crusty bread for three days. The men grumbled about the rations and the speed of travel. He ignored them, pushed them. The bloodlust burned through him—a killing heat.

On the fifth day, the scouts he had sent ahead jogged back. The caravan was sighted west of the expected trade route, off just enough to make it hard to spot by common bandits. But they were not common bandits. He ran on ahead, along the track of his scouts, choosing the site of attack, determining where each man would be placed, before rejoining his team. His heart raced with the pounding of his feet and the burning breath in his lungs, and he ran back to his team, his limbs fired with death lust.

They worked like madmen that night, sleepless, muttering, preparing the trap. He pushed them until they were ready to drop. Some griped loudly, the complainers among the new men, the new recruits. When one untried braggart complained too strongly, Simon struck out with his fist, knocking out the man's front teeth. After that, the men were afraid of him. They stopped complaining. Finally satisfied, he allowed them to rest as the dawn drew near. Lack of sleep could make men nervous, edgy. They were more likely to attack too soon or too late when they were tired. He *had* to let them sleep. They lay in position, hidden in brush and behind rocks, waiting for the appearance of the caravan outriders. Simon, unable to rest, was cold now, days of travel and the hard night's work having worn the rough edge off his high energy. He watched the brush, shifting his eyes to check each man, running through the plan for any mistakes, any needed revisions. But it was perfect.

Just after noon, his thoughts were interrupted by a sign from the lookout perched on the highest point. The caravan had been sighted. Not trusting that they would wake themselves, he sent his scout to alert all the men.

The caravan moved slowly into range. The sun beat down onto his overheated body. Simon breathed deeply, sweat tricking down his sides. It seemed hours before the camels and donkeys moved into place, in the low area of the poorly marked trail below them. There were five outriders, one wearing a Roman military breastplate, a retired soldier perhaps. This would be a good day.

His men kept their places, no foolhardy soul giving them away, or running toward the caravan waving a spear. He had seen a young man slashed to bits by outriders once. The boy had wagered that he would be the first to bring down a Roman. He had failed; his failure had cost them the mission.

Simon gave the signal. At first nothing happened, then a great cry erupted from the throats of the men, a Zealot battle cry, echoing across the dry ground. The bloodlust fell on him and he screamed out his hate. Rushed in with the first wave of men, slashing the throat of the old Roman. Took the head of an outrider. He didn't look back.

Suddenly it fell quiet, the eerie silence of death. He blinked and looked around, his lungs sucking in air for his starved limbs. He was standing in a swarm of bodies and blood, the stench of death rising on the day's heat. It was over.

When he caught his breath, Simon walked among the dead, counting. There were thirteen enemy fighters dead, three Roman, the rest desert mercenaries. He thought he had killed all but one of the desert fighters himself, most bearing his signature sword stroke to the throat.

There had been more soldiers than expected. Simon stood, and counted again. Thirteen dead. Fierce exultation shot through his veins, like the echo of the wounded men's screams as they were dispatched.

He remembered to look to his own men. There were six of his original twenty men left. He was the seventh, and they all looked exhausted, stunned to be alive. One man swayed and fell, blood spurting from beneath his right arm. Then gushing out, and last trickling, as the man coughed and died. Now there were six of them. Six. And all these riches. All the others dead. Dead for the gold the leaders wanted, and there weren't enough men left to carry it back with them. He laughed. Silently at first, and then with great guffaws. It was a victory. A great coup. And no way to take it all back with them.

"You laugh, imbecile. Barbarian!"

The voice was young, high and shrill. Female. He turned, and the sight of a young woman armed with a Roman short-sword made him laugh even harder. Even as she advanced on him, he laughed. As the sword came down on his neck, he laughed, twisting only slightly to avoid the sharpest edge of the sword. As his blood spurted, he laughed. And fell.

From where he lay, in a fast-spreading crimson pool, he watched and choked on blood and insane laughter and sudden, frenzied tears. Tears for what the remaining men did to the woman. Over and over again. Long after she died from it all.

His tears were for Nirit. All for Nirit.

He didn't remember seeing the men arrive from the cave. Nor did he remember being bandaged or carried to a nearby village. It was days before he remembered anything, and then Reuven came and carried him back to the cave where he was welcomed as a hero. No one mentioned the girl the men had raped and killed. No one.

He spent his days trying to blot it from his mind, the sound of her screams and cursing and begging, her whimpers. The harsh sound when her breathing stopped. He had been unconscious when the men finished with her, but he still saw her, laying in a pool of blood . . . She looked like Nirit. The same flies buzzed around her. He was sure of it.

Perhaps it was shock or loss of blood, but he couldn't get warm now. He was cold all the time with a bone-chilled cold like that of death. He had called the Romans bastards, savages, swine, animals for what they did to his Nirit. And now Hebrews had done the same thing. The same thing, though to a Roman girl.

He volunteered for no more missions, no more killing, sitting instead in the sun before the cave. Recuperating, the leaders said.

What they meant was dying. His soul was dying, shriveling like the pieces of Roman flesh hung in the cave. He could smell the stink of his own rotting soul.

Nirit . . . Nirit . . . He had not protected her either. He had been fishing all day on a ship with a large cask of wine and four other men and much drunken laughter. He had been laughing when his own men took the woman on the caravan too.

He had to get away before he killed them in their sleep. Away from the killing, the missions, the death, and the smell of his own rotting soul. He had to get away from the men who raped the girl. He couldn't bear to see their faces. He couldn't bear to wake again and see the bits of rotting flesh tacked to the cave roof. Worse, he couldn't bear to kill again.

Weeks later, an opportunity came for a man to go to Galilee as a spy. Simon volunteered, packed his sack, and left, Reuven's parting words reverberating inside his head.

"I fear that all the bloodlust has been burned out of you."

Chapter Six

Magdalene

Undulating waves of heat rose from the earth around her; the sun beat down on her neck, an unmerciful demon. She blinked and her lids felt gritty. The glare was so bright she shielded her light-sensitive eyes each time she looked up. Pulling her mantle higher, Magdalene tried to settle herself more comfortably on the ground as she made leben. The heat and the rhythmic sloshing of milk in its goatskin bag dulled her mind and slowed her breath, her heartbeat, down to the slow push-pull.

It was past noon, the hottest part of the day, in the midst of a smothering heat wave, her fourth week in Nazareth. The south winds had blown in three days before, bringing desert-dry air, making daytime activities miserable, and sleep nearly impossible. She felt limp and weak, but leben wouldn't wait. It was one foodstuff that was tastier for the heat, though warmth could also cause the mixture to spoil if she stopped rocking the bag, so she sat in the sun before a short tripod slung with a goatskin bag of goat milk, swinging it, churning milk to butter and butter-like curds.

The endless swaying made her arms ache and she rolled her shoulders to relieve the strain, drinking sparingly from a cup of water. If the heat continued, water might become scarce sooner than usual this year, and the prospect of long months drinking last season's old wine was unpleasant. The vinegary taste always left her more thirsty. Carefully, she replaced the cup in the hollow she had dug to keep it cool. The wind blew in, gritty and filled with the scent of desert and the hardy herbs of the garden.

The sloshing in the bag was growing heavier. Soon she would be able to stop and get out of the sun for a nap. She yawned and scratched her foot. The last wound was almost healed, but it itched intensely. Listlessly, she patted her greasy face. The palm oil she used to moisturize had mixed with sweat, and short strands of hair stuck wherever they touched her skin. Her shift, newly washed, was already sour. There was a fine dust in the air and she wished desperately for a bath she wouldn't get until after the next rain. Sweat trickled steadily down her back. She hated south winds.

A soft rasp sounded nearby, the almost-silent sound of cloth grinding against stone. She was suddenly, uneasily aware that she was not alone. Blinking painfully into the blinding light, she saw a hooded figure seated near her, resting with his back against the courtyard wall. He sat without moving, legs extended before him, blocking her escape to the house. His feet were dusty and the smell of feet and man-sweat was heavy on the air. His face was shadowed by a white head covering pulled low over his forehead, the tassels gathered in his lap. Though she couldn't see his face, she sensed he had been watching her for some time. She could feel power in his hooded gaze, and prickles rose on her sweaty neck as if she were suddenly cold. How had he gotten so close to her without attracting her attention?

Moments passed. Her hands still swung the goat bag, her lungs continued to pull in air as though nothing had changed. But her heart pounded and her eyes darted toward the house beyond the seated figure, mentally begging Aemoa to appear. The doorway remained empty.

The man was still, not attacking, not moving at all, and she fought off the desire to scream for help. He was dressed in light traveling clothes, his sandaled feet dirty beneath desert robes. Her apprehension faded slowly as she watched him. He made no move toward her. In fact, he made no move at all. Perhaps he was just resting. The pain building in her chest eased somewhat with his stillness.

The folds of cloth at his sides moved and a huge calloused hand appeared. It gestured to the forgotten cup in the hollow at her side. The water was very warm by now, but she nodded at his unspoken request. The hand that took the cup was rough, the dirt of travel ground into the skin and beneath the nails. Lifting the cup to his mouth, he drank. He looked vaguely familiar with his dusty beard and dark-tanned skin. A thin curl of wood fell from the tonsures near one ear to tangle in his beard, proclaiming him to be a master craftsman, a carpenter. She tilted her head to see better, the bag of leben still rocking but almost forgotten. He drained the cup and held it. Turning it slowly, he viewed the cup from every angle, the carved, orange acacia wood smooth beneath his fingers. The wooden cup was quite ordinary, but he seemed almost fascinated, and, she thought, saddened by it. He replaced the cup in the hollow by her side and pulled back his head cloth.

She jerked, the bag coming to a halt as she recognized his eyes. These were the eyes of the marketplace in Magdala, the eyes of the clearing, the eyes of the journey to Nazareth. These were the eyes that had calmed her nightmares, given her strength to deal with the memories, and brought her a measure of peace. Her mouth opened to speak, but words failed to come. Shaken, she simply stared. After a moment, she resumed rocking the bag, the goat milk sloshing.

"Mary?" He smiled, a gentle smile, his voice soft and deep. "Mary. You remember." Slowly, as though he feared she would shy away like a fledgling bird, he reached out and closed her gaping mouth with a click of her teeth. She had not been aware that it hung open. His fingers were rough, just as in that crystalline memory in the marketplace.

His hand pulled away. "I'm glad you came," she said, into the silence. "You are Jesus, yes?" When he smiled, she asked, "Will you stay for a time?"

"Yes, Mary. For a day. Perhaps two. Will you please go and tell my mother I am here?"

She smiled back and, grabbing up the goatskin bag, she rose and ran for the house.

There was no midday nap that day, not for Magdalene. She lay in the sweltering heat listening to the irregular beating of her heart, itchy prickles along her skin, down her fingers.

She had washed his feet and hands earlier in the day, carrying water and clean cloths. It was the proper gift of hospitality and the duty of the women of the household to a returned elder male. As she worked, she had studied him from the corners of her eyes, listening as he told his mother about his travels. But he was still an unknown, and his eyes still made her hands ache and her breath come fast. She wanted to wake him where he slept so silently in the other room, touch his hand to prove he was real, and look again into his eyes. Mostly that, for there was something in his gaze that pierced beneath her skin, beyond her confusion and into her deepest heart, and did it with compassion.

She rolled on her pallet, listening for the slightest sound he might make, and wiped at the sweat that beaded on her body. He was quiet, seeming to lay perfectly still, not turning miserably the way she did. Even his breathing was silent, while her own rasped noisily in her ears.

Later, much later, there was a rustle in the doorway that separated the two rooms, and she turned in the semi-darkness to face him. His features were obscured, but she knew he was watching her, and quickly she stood, waiting, scarcely daring to breathe.

"Is there water?" he whispered, to keep from waking Aemoa who still slept in a darkened corner. Without speaking, she moved to the water jar by the doorway to the courtyard and located a cup on the low table. She filled the cup with water and drew one for herself as well, handing him his. She drank, matching his swallows, matching his breathing. Chill bumps raised on her skin and tightened. Sensing her discomfort, he whispered, his voice was so soft she barely heard his words, "It's cooler now. Would you speak with me in the courtyard?"

Magdalene followed him outside. He perched on the low courtyard wall, sitting with his back against the house. She sat silently a little distance away, careful not to intrude, careful not to sit too close as though she had a right to familiarity. And she waited.

A breeze, cooler than the day's worst, but still hot, swirled dustily through the courtyard, raising again the scent of herbs, the rosemary and dill strong and astringent. He drained the cup and held it, empty. "Who are you, Magdalene?"

The question surprised her and she paused, her own cup

halfway to her mouth.

"Does your mouth always hang open when you are startled, Magdalene?" he chuckled. When she didn't speak, his face grew thoughtful. "Is my question too difficult for you?"

Slowly she put her cup aside, leaving her with empty hands and eyes that didn't quite focus. "Yes," she answered, her voice low. She turned her head away from him. "Yes, it is hard for me. I don't know who I am now. I am no one. Nothing." *It's your fault. It's because of you that I remembered. Because of you I am alone.*

"Be at peace, Magdalene," he soothed, as if he could hear the words in her mind.

Despite her anger with him, her breath eased, finding a calm she didn't feel, and she blew her anger into the dust settling around her. She forced her hands to relax and then stubbornly curled them tightly around the cup. She refused to look at him.

"I won't ask then, about your present. But what about your past? May I ask about your past?" At her stiff nod, he continued, his voice slow, as if he spoke to a young child or a wild animal. "Who were you? Before. In Magdala."

"Before." She relaxed slightly, in thought. "Before, I was the wife of Jason Ben Joseph, a trader of Magdala, and the mother of Amos Ben Jason. And I was carrying the Lord's blessing of a second child who was to be a daughter. I was happy. I sang and played the lyre. I embroidered well enough to always sell my tunics in the marketplace. I was a dutiful wife, the child of my mother, though she was dead."

"When you were Mary, when you were all those things, did you worship in the solitude of your heart?"

She smiled. "I was born Jew. Of course I worshipped, every day, in each activity, each motion I made, in each Mitzvah, I worshipped."

"Do you worship now, Magdalene?"

She didn't answer, and the silence between them grew cloying. She knew it was useless to dissimulate. Somehow, he would know the truth anyway. "No."

He did not move from his place nor did he speak. He seemed to be waiting, and anger fell on her again. "Why should I worship? I have nothing left to praise Him for. I was good. Pious. I left nothing undone. Yet . . ." Her chest heaved with the effort of speaking in hushed tones when she wanted to scream. "Yet I was punished. And I don't know why. Punished with death, with destruction, with loneliness." Tears welled in her eyes, making his image waver in the setting sun. His very stillness made her fierce. "Why should I worship now?" she demanded. "Why? I am nothing now. I am no one." She hissed, "I am nothing to Yehowah. Less than the birds of the field. Just as the death of a sparrow in the talons of a hawk goes unnoticed by the Most High, so did the death of my family. I am nothing to Him. And He is nothing to me." Her voice wrenched at the blasphemy.

"You are still Jew. And El Roi still sees you." With those words he rose from his seat at the wall and walked silently across the courtyard, leaving her to collect herself.

El Roi was the *"almighty who sees me"*. Jesus was saying that the Most High who watched over them all was *still* watching over her, despite her loses. She heaved and fought tears, swallowing painfully, forced her nails into the palms of her hands until she thought the new, tender skin would break.

"Magdalene who does not worship," he called softly from across the courtyard, "come here. I want to show you something."

She looked at him, feeling the fire in her eyes. He was smiling almost gently at her, as though he didn't know she wanted to shout at him, even slap him for his insolent cruelty. Movements jerky, she slid from the wall to the courtyard. But she stood too quickly, and the world swirled blackly around her. She put out a hand to steady herself and he caught her fingertips, just the tips, and held her. Her vision returned slowly, like a mist that clears before a wind, and she found herself staring into his eyes. Without speaking, he led her to the cedar-heart carving of a windswept tree in the far corner of the courtyard. And with each step, her hand secured by his, she felt her anger slipping away.

"You see, Magdalene? How chisel and knife worked a piece of wood into a thing of beauty? I found a twisted branch in the desert heat, desiccated and withered. The bark had been removed by wind and sand, followed by layers of the living wood, until there was only the block of rose heart-wood left. I brought it home, yet its torture was not over, for it had to dry again, evenly all over, inside and out. I dried three branches of tree to get this *one*, Magdalene. The first two cracked and split when they dried and were useless to me. They were . . ." he seemed to search for the word "faulted . . . within. But this one was strong. I carved the tree with chisel and file, and polished each limb, each twig with sand and stone. Now it's beautiful, yes?"

"Yes, Rabboni . . . It is beautiful. Surpassing."

"You are like this tree, Magdalene."

She laughed a quick note, like the yelp of a small dog, a hand flying to her face.

"You had your protection—your bark—ripped away. Your roots. And the living wood also. Then you dried in the hot sun and fierce winds for years while the sap, the life that was, dried out of you. Yet you did not crack. You are strong, and you will make a tree of great beauty, Magdalene, woman who is carved by the hand of Yehowah-rā-ah—the Lord, my Shepard." He was smiling into her eyes, and she stared back. The gold flecks in his irises seemed to have a light all their own. Dropping her fingers, he rubbed his stomach. "I'm hungry for that leben you made today, and fresh bread." Calling for his mother, he turned and strode across the yard and into the house.

Gently she lifted the hand he had held and touched her face. *A tree of great beauty.* She stroked the skin of her cheeks. It *was* softer. And she *was* healing. But somehow she felt he had meant something else.

After a small meal of leben and fresh bread, the Rebbe left the house and stayed gone into the night, visiting with relatives and friends in the village. She worked outside, cleaning the rest of her casks, scrubbing out the remains of dried food, with very little of the precious water. She could see him, Jesus, from the slight elevation of the house, as he stopped and entered various homes. Once, the breeze caught his laughter and carried it to her from the well where he spoke to two women who drew water there.

Such a strange man to speak to women so easily. Even Jason, who had loved her, had not spoken to her as though he felt she might actually comprehend the meaning of his words. And never had he told her she was strong. Or a tree of great beauty. Not once.

This man, this Rebbe Jesus, was different, radically so, from any man she had ever known. He was a rebel, in a soft and gentle way, to the customs of his people. He handled dirty children, scratched a stray kitten behind its ears, helped a neighbor hold a sickly calf while it was medicated, all with his hands, and he seemed not to feel contaminated by contact with that which was physically unclean. He even stood near the doorway of a suko and spoke to the woman within, though she was menstruating and unclean, kept apart by Law. He was . . . *different*. Revolutionary. She felt a quiver of excitement deep inside as she watched him.

The three of them ate together that night in companionable silence and retired early. Magdalene slept deeply until the early hours before dawn, when the dreams came again. This time there were no bodies floating in the air around her, but blood, swirling, sucking at her feet like waves at the shore. And hands reaching for her.

She tried to run, but her feet slipped and she fell into the cold, clotting blood. She tried to crawl away, thrashing and fighting in the slippery ooze. The heavens opened and blood fell steadily onto her, a bloody rain. She couldn't breathe, and woke choking.

The house was completely dark, the lamp having spluttered out during the night. She fought to sit up, staring at the sleep tunic that had wrapped around her hips in the thrashing nightmare. The salty taste of blood was strong in her mouth, and her lips ached. She had bitten into them in the horror of the nightmare, and she swallowed the blood.

The small house was silent, stifling. She rose from her pallet and found a cup for water, washing down the blood. Without awaking Aemoa, who still slept near her in the corner, Magdalene slipped from the house, into the courtyard. The night breeze was cooler, though arid.

Her eyes adjusted slowly to the moonlight, and it was some moments before she saw him sitting in the yard, his hands uplifted in prayer. Embarrassed, she paused, wanting the relative cool of the night air, but not wanting to disturb him, afraid he would think her spying if he looked up and saw her. She turned and reentered the house. Her pallet had cooled somewhat in her absence, and she lay down, closing her eyes to uneasy dreams.

She worked hard the next day, watching for him, but it was evening before they happened to meet. Jesus had built a booth of palm fronds on the roof of the house, and carried up their pallets and the low table. In the cooling air, high enough to feel the breeze from the valley as it rushed up along the hills, they reclined on their pallets in the rapidly falling night and dipped chunks of warm fresh bread into a single pot, mother and son laughing as they licked the greasy vegetable and mutton stew from their fingers.

Even after all these weeks Magdalene still ate more than any two healthy people combined, causing her some embarrassment at their playful jibbing. But she had gained weight, and her hair, while still shamefully short, was acquiring some of its original luster, now curling, black and rich around her cheekbones and her black eyes. Crunching into a handful of walnuts, her favorite, she grinned at them and said saucily, "Don't look at me like that. I'm not a glutton, no matter how many walnuts I eat."

"Yes," Aemoa responded pertly. "Walnuts, honey, fresh bread, every vegetable the village can grow. You would gnaw the mutton bones if your teeth were strong enough."

"Don't suggest it, Aemoa. She might try," Jesus said, laughing.

"No. No bones. But I'll have that last piece of bread if you don't mind." She pointed to the crust.

The older woman passed it to her and shook her head as Magdalene wiped the bowl clean of the last film of stew.

"Jesus, be sure to position Mary's pallet across the joists of the roof to give her more support. Otherwise, she is likely to fall though the roof tonight."

They all laughed, and with the easy feeling that enclosed the small group, Magdalene decided that it was a good time to broach a subject that had been on her mind.

"I . . ." Her voice gave out and she started again. "I am grateful for all you have done for me. But I have far outlived and out-eaten your duty as host. I wish to recompense you for your kindness," she said pointing to the empty bowl. "I've been keeping track of what I eat and—"

"What?" her hostess gasped, her brows shooting high. "*Pay me?*" Her back straightened and her chin rose, casting indignant shadows against the booth walls. "You gave me your beautiful caldron and mill. You will not insult me by offering payment for your stay. *Never.* You are a guest in my house and I am not so measly as to—"

"No," Magdalene said quickly. "I didn't mean to imply—"

"Well then, you will not mention it again," Aemoa interrupted hotly. "You are my *friend.* And friends don't pay one another when they come for a visit."

Magdalene looked at her hands. They were smooth now, the skin healed of the nicks and cuts, the nails rounded and even. And clean. Turning them over, she studied her palms, and when she spoke again, it was softly, her eyes never leaving her hands. "Thank you, Aemoa. But what am I to do with all that money? It's useless to me. I have no one to support, no family left anywhere, except a brother-in-law who hated my husband. I have no place to go. And only you, whom I have come to love, with whom to share it."

Around the low table was silence, the rustling of palm fronds in the faint breeze the only distraction. Ordinarily, the wealth in the ruins would have belonged to the finder, or to Jason's brother. But since her brother-in-law had not claimed it in the more than five years since the destruction, and since he had not done his duty by Law to care for her, she owed him nothing. She knew that, and took a breath that shuddered faintly along her throat. "I am," she said, "quite alone." She looked to Jesus, who, as head of the house, would have the final say in her request. "I would become part of your family, a sister to Aemoa, if you will have me. And if you will welcome a widow into this household.

"I have funds. I could build a room onto this house. Put tile onto the floors. Bricks along the walls . . ." She stopped. It was starting to sound like pleading, and she did not want to burden them with her need. She could sense without looking up, that mother and son were conferring with their eyes as only people who have lived closely for many years can. She waited, feeling the tension along her shoulders, down the back of her neck. But she was determined not to cry, and not to look up lest the fear and pleading in her eyes sway them. She clenched her hands. The waiting was unbearable. She wanted so very much to stay.

"Why don't you travel with us, Magdalene?" Jesus said.

It was not the answer she expected. Looking up, she met his eyes.

"My mother travels with me most of the year. She only stayed in Nazareth these last weeks because you were too weak to care for yourself. But now, or at least soon, you will be well and you both can rejoin us. We would be happy to have you travel with us. And return with us here when we rest from my mission. And you have funds to buy or rent a house anywhere. A house of your own."

Her eyes sparkling with unshed tears, she blinked hard, and clasped her hands together, gripping them tightly before her. "Travel? I have never— Oh, yes. That would be— I would love— Oh, please. Yes."

"It isn't easy, Magdalene," Aemoa said. "We walk wherever we go. Some towns do not welcome my son's teaching. We are sometimes greeted with threats."

"Threats?"

"My son has a reputation, child," Aemoa said wryly. "He has a gift for healing and . . . other things. And he . . ." She glanced swiftly at Jesus and then away, her expression enigmatic, "he forgives sin."

Into the silence, Magdalene said carefully, "Only God can forgive sin," She had blasphemed God, but this was worse. It was tainted, foul.

Aemoa pressed her lips tightly, her face strained, as if hiding a secret disapproval or a furtive fear. Jesus was expressionless, watching his mother's face. Was there a hint of pain there, hidden in the night?

Uncomfortable, Magdalene shrugged. "I've never traveled,

except the move to Magdala when I married." When neither replied, she tried to steer the pair into waters less troubled than the forgiveness of sin. "Will we go to Jerusalem? And Tyre?" She paused. "I grew up there. It's a beautiful city. The market is miles wide with so many things to buy, and . . ." her words went silent. Neither had responded. This wasn't working. "What about the money?" she asked firmly. "We were talking about the money."

Jesus said, "Invest it."

"Invest it?" Magdalene's relief that he responded was colored by confusion. "I know nothing about money. Jason handled our funds, as is right and proper."

"Aemoa, why don't you send her to one of your friends near Capernaum? Someone will be happy to help her."

Aemoa seemed to shake herself and pursed her mouth in disapproval. "Yes, well, that would be true if she were a man, but no one will help a *woman* with money."

Jesus ignored the comment, rose and rolled his pallet. "Be well and grow strong, Magdalene," he advised as he backed out of the booth. "We travel in all weather, fast some days, and often we travel hungry. You will have your donkey to ride, but he will be unable to carry you all the way. Exercise. Walk." And he was gone, his sandals pattering down the steps on the side of the house.

Magdalene looked at her hostess, Aemoa's face pensive. Magdalene wanted to ask about Jesus forgiving sins, but now was not the time. She curled on her side in her bedroll and closed her eyes. Aemoa blew out the lamp and the night closed in around them, cooled by night breezes. Magdalene feigned sleep as the moon rose, staring at the night sky through the leaves and branches of the booth, until near dawn when sleep finally took her. Her dreams were of Tyre—its clamorous marketplace, the harbor filled with swaying boats, its shores loud with seamen's jargon. Not once did she dream of blood.

When she woke the next day, the sun was high in the sky, filtering through the drying palm fronds and leaves. She stretched and groaned with pleasure, for muscles and tendons that no longer ached with the dullness of hunger. She rolled the sleeping mats

into tight bundles and carried them down the steep, narrow stairs
to the courtyard and into the house. Aemoa, sitting in the
doorway, nodded to her without lifting her eyes, hands flashing on
the handloom. She was silent, her face brooding. Magdalene
stepped into the relative darkness of the house and saw that Jesus'
bedroll and travel pack were gone, which explained part of
Aemoa's unhappiness. How much of the brooding was also
related to Jesus' near-blasphemy, she didn't know, but it was clear
that she was not going to have company or conversation today.

Magdalene placed the mats in their proper places against the
wall and studied the room. It was still disordered—her property
piled on the floor, on the shelves that circled the room, and
hanging from the pegs on the walls. Though she hadn't broken
her fast, she threw herself into the disarray, and by the time for
the noon meal, her belongings were neatly stacked in the sleeping
room against the wall. The shelves and pegs were organized and
the floor was swept.

"You've worked hard this morning," Aemoa said, her voice
distracted and vaguely sad.

Magdalene frowned. "Where have you been, so lost in your
thoughts?"

Aemoa sighed, stood, and flexed her fingers. "We can talk
while we prepare the meal." She pulled crocks and a basket to the
table and began laying out wooden dishes. As she worked, she
talked and her mood seemed to lighten. "I spent the hours from
just before dawn until just before you woke, at a birthing. I made
soothing teas for the new mother and her attendants and
comforted the father. It was his first child, and her water broke all
over him in the marriage bed." She grinned suddenly, eyes
sparkling. "His scream woke half the village. He thought she was
dying." She laughed and Magdalene smiled with her. "New fathers
are so terrified." She flapped a hand as she laid out fresh figs. "But
it was an easy birth, and Shaul and Adi have a son," she said.

"I'll get the bread, you slice and peel the melon." Aemoa
went out to the oven in the noonday heat. Magdalene did as she
was bid and soon they had a meal of hot barley bread, melon, figs,
and yesterday's leben.

Though she hadn't taken part in the delivery, and therefore

didn't have to be ritually cleaned, Aemoa washed her hands and arms with special care and diligence, before eating. After her prayer of thanksgiving, she said, "Today we will walk, Magdalene. We will go to market. We will stop to visit friends. It will do us both good." She tilted her head, her eyes compassionate. "What's the matter, child? Are you unwell?"

Magdalene twirled a short strand of hair around a finger, examining it as though she had never seen it before. "Is it not too soon to be seen in public? My hair is still short."

"What do you think traveling with my son will be, hibernation?" Aemoa asked with some asperity. "You'll have to become accustomed to being seen in public, and here is a good place to begin. These women are my friends and will accept my explanation about your illness and shorn hair. You didn't protest when we went to synagogue on the past Sabbaths, so why do you fret?"

"I've heard them talk, the women here. They think I was a . . . was put away by my husband for adultery."

"I'm sorry you heard that. Only a few of them would say such things. They are sad, sorry creatures, and not my friends. Rest easy, child. You are accepted here."

Magdalene applied herself to the food, but she knew that she would be the object of speculation wherever she went even if she kept herself heavily veiled. She ran her fingers through the curling mass of hair as she chewed, and wished for a mirrored surface to see herself, but her mirror hadn't been among the items brought from her home. And that was vanity, after all, a sin. She pushed the desire away and ate.

In the coolness of early evening, she washed sparingly with water in a bathing bowl and put on a clean tunic before carrying the water to the herbs in the garden, careful to use every drop. Her everyday dress went on over the tunic, and she smoothed it in place before wrapping her lace veil around her head, beneath her heavier wool one. She put on her best Sabbath jewelry, the glass beads and bracelets, the gold and silver—her dowry—all but the gold mesh girdle. She tried not to think about the ruin in the trunk. Just before they left, Aemoa poured licorice tea into a cooling crock and carried it in under one arm.

The walk through the village was pleasant but the visit was far worse than she had imagined. When they arrived at the house of Aemoa's distant cousin, three women were in a booth on the roof, giggling and whispering, seated on carved stools with rounded bottoms. The conversation stopped abruptly when they entered. It was clear they had been gossiping about her.

Magdalene's face burned and she kept her shoulders hunched, her face down, as Aemoa took the last chair, and Magdalene seated herself on a rug. It was the finest house in Nazareth, the village below them only partly obscured by palm frond walls. Three rugs covered the mosaic tile floor. The plates were turned stoneware, glazed green. It was a rich man's house, though not so rich as her parent's home in Tyre had been, or her own in Magdala.

The Gentile servant girl wore linen and carried a blown glass plate as she served them tiny pastries flavored with mint and saffron. When she offered Aemoa's licorice tea, it came in handleless glass cups; Magdalene took her own with nerveless fingers. The servant was quiet and unobtrusive, the only one of the women who didn't steal furtive glances at the silent guest. As Magdalene had feared, she was scarcely seated when the probing began, but it wasn't a polished, polite curiosity. It was far worse.

Eglah, wife of Caleb, said rashly, "You are a guest in our city and we must needs protect our good names. Why did your husband set you aside in Magdala?"

There was a stunned silence as the other women suddenly found their drinks and pastries fascinating, knowing Elgah had gone too far. Aemoa spluttered, clinking her cup to the floor. "How dare you, Eglah! That was uncalled for. Shame be on you and your house! You owe Magdalene your apologies. And me as well."

"No!" Magdalene hadn't meant to sound gruff, nor to speak so loudly. But she did at least have their attention. She drew herself up on the rug, as she had not been offered the courtesy of a stool, and looked each woman in turn in the eye, at last fixing her eyes steadily on Eglah. Slowly, she pushed the mantle and lace veil off her head exposing the short hair. "I can defend myself," she said, "but thank you, Aemoa. And Eglah does, after all, deserve an answer to her question, however discourteous it was." She ignored the outraged gasp of the small, dried-out woman and continued. "There has been talk, most of it stupid, said by fools who have no consideration for the victims of . . ." She faltered and swallowed, ". . . of Roman soldiers. So to keep others from making Eglah's foolish mistake and speaking recklessly, I'll tell you my story. I'm sure you *ladies* will see to it that my story is spread over this sorry little village by sunrise."

Except for Eglah, who sat in insulted silence, she had their attention. She smoothed her bracelets out where the gleam of gold and silver could not be missed, and continued. "My husband was a trader in Magdala. We had a house much like this one, though larger, located just beyond the town walls, by a stream. I was away from the house, visiting friends in the city. I had passed Romans on the way into town but I thought nothing of it. Who would? But when I came home, I found my husband tortured and crucified to the tallest beam in the center of what had once been my home. My son was gone, my home destroyed, my servants dead or run off or carried away. *Romans*," her voice shook, "are *blasphemers* before God, *licentious*, and *cruel* beyond human under-standing. They took *everyone* and *everything* from me." She took a steadying breath, wanting to add, "And God allowed this evil," but she didn't, for Aemoa's sake.

The silence on the roof was broken by the serving girl's sniff. She was hiding a smile. The other women seemed to find great interest in their hands, their laps, the crumbs of food.

"The shock of that day was too much for me, and I lost the child I was carrying. For five years I had nothing to live for, until Aemoa came, and found me at the site of my home, and became my friend. She made me well again." Large, gentle, brown eyes nudged her memory and she felt a slight uneasiness at the partial lie, but she went on. "Her son restored my wealth to me. His traveling party brought me here to heal. I have been ill. My hair," she said, turning a short strand around one finger, "which seems to have caused this slander, Aemoa had to cut. I know little about healing, but Aemoa does, and when she cut my hair, it was necessary. I owe her my life and you owe *her* your respect, if not common etiquette to her guest."

She hadn't told them the whole story, for she couldn't bear to remember the details of that day. It was enough though, the uneasy silence around the booth being proof. One of the women moved from her stool, uncurling her legs as she stood. She walked to the serving girl and prepared a plate from the best delicacies on the serving tray. Choosing the best cup, she poured more licorice tea and knelt.

"Mary of Magdala, forgive me. You are right. Many foolish things were said when you were too weak to defend yourself. I'm sorry. I am Ofira, wife of the fuller, and your hostess. You are welcome in *my* house as a much treasured guest."

The other women nodded in agreement—all but Eglah, who rose and swished out of the booth and down to the street, footsteps padding on the clay steps. Her leaving was like a signal and the women gathered around, the conversation suddenly relaxed. The last of the visit was pleasant, though Magdalene tired and soon begged to go home. The recounting of the loss of her family, however watered down, had left her exhausted. Yet, when she left, it was with the promise to return and tell of Magdala and Tyre, known far and wide as some of the most beautiful cities of Galilee. The women were eager to hear about the markets and the rich, opulent houses, which were finer than anything Nazareth could offer. She supposed she had friends now, but she also had an enemy in Eglah. Her last memory, before she closed her eyes to sleep that night, was the face of the woman, glaring in hatred.

Chapter Seven

Aemoa

Mary watched her guest as she slept uneasily in the unrelenting heat of the night. Unable to sleep herself, she sat in the light of a spluttering lamp and worked at her loom, her eyes going often to the sweating, slender figure, trembling and twisting in unhappy dreams. She had been amazed at Magdalene's poise and composure that evening when her own friends and family had baited her. And her heart had wrenched at the emotion on Magdalene's face when she told of the Romans. Her lips had curled into a snarl, her voice had held such horror, such terror and hate.

She was frightened by the intensity of Magdalene's feelings, and needed Jesus' counsel, but he was far away, and she was alone to deal with the passions in the soul of the angry woman. Her heart was like a wound that grows inflamed and consumes its victim. Mary was faced with something that seemed too great to simply take to God and leave there. It wasn't that she felt Yehowah couldn't handle whatever problem she handed Him, for, in her faith, He was stronger than her fear. Rather, she felt that He wanted her to do something, and she didn't know what.

She half smiled, remembering that evening. Magdalene was of good lineage and had been brought up to act with dignity and self-assurance. She was no child to be coddled or protected. She had handled the confrontation well, had defended her husband and herself admirably, and if Eglah was insulted, it was no great loss. The haughty, gossipy woman needed to be brought down a peg or two. Her tales had long been a village problem; in that respect, the Magdalene had been right. It was difficult to talk in front of Eglah because one knew that the entire conversation, or rather, Eglah's interpretation of it, would be all over Nazareth and the surrounding countryside by dusk. By morning at the very latest, the story of the sick, wealthy visitor who had been the victim of Roman pillage would have been carried to every household for miles.

She wished she could sleep, because daybreak would see the arrival of visitors, each exclaiming how happy they were to meet the Magdalene and eating her out of house and home. Not that the Magdalene had left very much in the house to be eaten. She would have to bake early in the morning and go to market as well. Hopefully, any potential guests would see her leave and wait until she returned before they descended. Even more hopefully, they would bring a guest-gift of food.

The shuttle caught and she worked loose a knotted thread. Jesus' tunic was nearly done and the Magdalene had volunteered to purchase some good silk thread and embroider the hem. It would be a fine garment and she would be proud to see him in the synagogue of any city when he stood up to read or pray, wearing this tunic. Men sometimes did not realize how a dirty or torn garment could make them look less refined and less deserving of being listened to. If only he would cut his hair and shave his face. He was a good carpenter, like Joseph, and with a shaved face, he would look so grand, not like the strange, devout teacher from Galilee with his holy vows. In her secret heart, she wanted grandchildren. It would be nice to have him quietly married and the father of three or four children.

Her eyes misted over and she stopped the shuttle, closing her lids on the present. Joseph had been a great man, tall and pious, learned in the Torah as well as in his craft. She never failed to feel pride when he spoke in the synagogue, and other women often looked at him with pleasure and at her with envy. His dark looks had been much like the Magdalene's, with rich wavy hair the color of the sky at a new moon, and eyes so deep that she could fall into them. It had been good to be so loved.

Dawn was a pale gray glow when she put down the shuttle for the last time and stretched to her feet. She needed little sleep, and though the cost of burning midnight oil was high, she could now sell tunics, children's clothes, or swaddling clothes and make a profit.

She offered praise to God for the day and for His blessings, including the new loom, washed herself from the water jar and dressed. Tomorrow was the Sabbath, and so much needed to be done. Almost, she regretted taking Magdalene to visit, for the extra work it would mean. And then, remembering the expression on Eglah's face, changed her mind. It was worth it.

She washed her hands again and mixed fresh dough for the day's and the Sabbath's bread, and while the oven was heating, she checked her purse for a coin to buy fish for the holy day meal. As usual, Jesus had left her several. She mixed up a concoction of dates, raisins, and dried mandrake root, sweetened the mixture with a pinch of granulated honey and coated it all with a little cinnamon. Closing it up in a crock as a surprise for Magdalene, she donned her heavy robe and left the house for early market while the bread cooked.

There was plenty of time to browse as the farmers set up their booths for early market, and she always lingered over the freshest selections. She bought melons and more mandrake, not because she needed the effect of its fertility properties, but because she liked its taste. Spotting some tart bull's tongue and mallow, she purchased the greens and also a little flavored vinegar to season it. They would be wonderful with the Sabbath meal, mixed with sorrel, dandelions, and chicory from her own garden. It was nice to have someone refined to cook for, instead of twenty or more men interested more in talk than in the seasonings of the food.

Purchases in hand, she hurried to the fish section of the market and selected a large fresh fish. Once she had haggled the vendor down, the change she had left from the vegetables was just enough to buy it, and she raced off to remove the bread from the oven, the sound of his mutterings in her ears. "It is people like you who keep me in rags. The Lord knows I am a charitable man." Her back to him, she smiled. It *had* been a good buy. His other customers would not fare so well today. The way his wife ate, he could only afford to be charitable once.

The day was as she expected, filled with visitors, many of whom hadn't seen the inside of her home in years. It seemed that the entire village turned out to welcome the Magdalene, everyone but Caleb and Eglah. She was saddened by the loss of a friendship she had managed by force of will to keep for years. But not too saddened.

Later that afternoon, when she was finishing up the Sabbath chores, making certain that she would leave nothing undone, she caught sight of Eglah peering around the side of a nearby house at the spectacle of the last gaggle of women leaving. Eglah had tougher skin than she had thought. It would not be very many days before the woman had enough of hearing the latest gossip about the Magdalene and her clothes and her jewelry and her dowry trunk, and come for firsthand information. Mary made a mental note to save a special tidbit for her, so that Eglah would have something to tell to make her important again in the eyes of the townswomen. Her isolation would end quicker if the injured parties were seen to speak.

After the Sabbath meal, at sunset, which they took in private, she studied the Magdalene. There were dark circles beneath her eyes, and the mixture of greens had scarcely been touched. "Are you unwell?"

Magdalene twitched like a reed in the wind. "No. I'm not hungry. Just tired." Sipping at her wine, the guest-gift of the fuller's wife, she turned a strand of her short hair around a finger, an action that had quickly become habitual. "Why did they all come here today?"

Aemoa said, "They all wanted to see the only woman in town who ever had the courage to stand up to Eglah."

Magdalene spluttered and almost choked on her wine. "Not really. Oh, no. What an awful thing to be remembered for."

"Not so awful. I was remembered for having an illegitimate child for years. But now hardly anyone even thinks of it. Besides, Eglah will come around soon enough. Don't be surprised if she becomes one of your staunchest supporters."

"I don't think she will ever get over it. You didn't see the way she looked at me. I know hatred when I see it and that woman hates me. She'll never forgive."

Remembering the sad face that peered at the house earlier in the day, Mary just smiled and said, "Don't be too sure, Magdalene. Don't be too sure. Now. I have a surprise for you."

"I don't think I could handle another surprise today."

"Oh, you will like this one." She moved to the corner where she had placed the crock, on the floor so as not to break the Sabbath by lifting it down. The stone top came free. The smell of honey and dates from the treat she had prepared earlier filled the room.

The young woman leaned back on the rug and sniffed appreciatively. "Dates," she sighed happily. "And cinnamon? It's seasoned with cinnamon, isn't it? I *love* cinnamon. Did you use mine? Good. If you won't accept payment for my keep, at least use some of my spices before they go completely bad. I'll get clean bowls."

"Well, you can have as much as you want as long as you finish your greens first."

"You sound like my own mother," Magdalene said, grumpy. "But I'll eat the greens. Appetites restored, they finished the meal and ended up eating the whole bowlful of sweets.

The desert air blew away in the night, leaving a fresh westerly wind, scented with salt from the great blue sea. The smell, so much a part of her guest's childhood, prompted the Magdalene's sluggish memory, and they talked for the next several days of Tyre and her family. Magdalene had been a loved but spoiled child, full of the artless innocence of all children that grow up in small, wealthy households where there is never want or hunger. The scent of the sea was like a window into her past, and the memories that blew through seemed to make her glow. She appeared younger, stronger, and able to travel soon.

She looked so well, that Mary began laying plans to leave Nazareth. She missed Jesus. They shared an extraordinary bond, a special closeness, perhaps even more intense in his case, because of the circumstances of his birth. He knew her thoughts, her needs, and when they were separated for too long, she felt his absence with a keenness that was like the slow cut of a cold knife.

She saw Jesus' face in the well when she went to draw water, heard his voice in the wind as it raced from the sea, felt his touch on her hands as she pushed the shuttle on her new loom. The children of her large, extended family, couldn't replace the comfort of being with her son. Nor could the Magdalene.

She began to speak of him with her guest, of his childhood and the way he charmed the village's people. He always went with her when she carried her basket of herbs to tend the sick. As a youth, Jesus would sit with the children outside while she brewed a special tea or made a poultice for the sick ones within. And he had always loved to laugh. She could hear his laughter even now, though he was far away.

There *was* laughter on the wind. She shivered. It was not the soft gentle chuckle of her son, but the raucous guffaw of strangers, coming down the road. She looked around the house, feeling disoriented and uncertain. Magdalene was on the roof, sleeping in the cool of the booth, taking a midday nap. The laughter grew stronger, and she was able to pick out voices, the clop of horse hooves . . . and the clink of steel against steel. The sound of Romans.

She swallowed convulsively. The last time Romans had come through the small village, they had commandeered the use of a house and the use of several townswomen. The horse stopped just outside her courtyard, and footsteps came toward the house.

"You in the house. Jew. Come out."

She stepped to the doorway. There were three men in Roman uniforms lounging against the courtyard wall and another man seated on the horse. Not an officer, that one, though only Roman officers rode. This one was dressed in Roman traveling clothes, a civilian important enough to merit three foot soldiers as guards. The air in the village had gone still and silent as her neighbors heard the voices and identified a threat. The soldier nearest gestured to her. Squaring her shoulders, she stepped into the yard. "Sirs," she said softly. "What do you require?"

One of the men laughed, the one who had spoken merely smiled. "Water. For my men. The horse can use the cistern."

Turning back into the house, she chose four wooden cups, placed them on a tray, and filled them with water. Then, as an afterthought, she picked up a bowl and broke some of yesterday's bread into it, added a small amount of leben, and walked back into the yard. The men and the horse had all come into the courtyard, disturbing the careful arrangement of rocks she had placed there, trampling on her herbs and the horse was slurping noisily from the cistern. She kept her frown hidden behind a neutral face. The cistern would have to be drained and cleaned and seen by the village Rebbe before it could be used again; the loss of water in this season was a hardship, and she could only hope they stopped there in their Roman desecration.

The men took the tray from her without a word of thanks and drank the water, their slurping almost as loud as the horse's. When they finished, the soldiers ate the bread and leben with dirty fingers, then licked them clean. Though she didn't react, even the youngest Jewish child knew better than to eat without first washing his hands.

"We require the use of a house for two days," the man on horseback said. She fought a glance up, and pulled her mantle closer. "Do you live here alone?" She had no doubt why he asked. He had a certain look in his eyes, and he grinned at her obvious fear. At his gesture, one of soldiers walked slowly around the yard and peeked into the house.

"Woman. I spoke to you."

She swallowed painfully, her hands twisted into tight balls. "I am not entirely alone."

Her speech was interrupted by the sound of a hoarse wretch from the rooftop, then other sounds, like thrashing, followed by the unmistakable sound of vomiting. And more vomiting.

"There's sickness in this house? You would feed us food from a sick-house, woman?" One soldier threw the plate to the ground, and the four cups followed as they each divested themselves of anything that she had touched. Hope and fear warred inside her and she crushed her dress in icy fingers. "You would feed us and not speak a word?" he spurred his horse around and out of the yard and motioned the other men out. "How many are sick, woman? One?" When she didn't answer, he asked, "Two? We'll find another house."

He was almost out of the yard before she could think, and

she ran to the civilian man, caught the hem of his robe and pulled. He raised his arm and struck her a strong blow across her head, but she held on to his robe.

"What do you want, woman," he spat, "to give me your disease? Let go of me."

"But sir," she called loudly, loudly enough that all her neighbors might hear. "The sickness. It is all over the village. There is hardly a house free from the fever and vomit. You must help us. We need the healing only the learned Romans can give us." From the next house, she heard the sound of groaning, from another the sound of retching. "Please help. Ride through the village if you don't believe me. It is almost deserted from the death!" she shouted. "Help us!"

The Roman jerked his foot free and kneed his horse. The foot-soldiers almost ran, taking the shortest path to the trade route to the north. They vanished at a steady trot, the men outpacing the tired horse.

She shuddered at her narrow escape and whispered a prayer of thanks for the sounds that came from the roof. The one thing that frightened Romans was the thought of dying far from their homes of a disease that could not be cured. She gulped a breath and laughter caught her. She pressed a hand over her mouth to arrest its sound and wiped her hand across her face. Turning, she climbed wearily to the roof. The cleaning of the cistern and the yard could wait until later. The Magdalene was sick and retching painfully.

She found the young woman curled into a fetal position in a pool of her own vomit, clutching at her stomach and shaking as with a fever. Growl-like mutters escaped from between her clenched and grinding teeth, and her face was a fierce mask of misery. Although clearly sick, it was not like any disease she had seen before. Standing over the writhing woman, Mary tried to recall what it reminded her of. And then the Magdalene spoke.

"Romans . . . Romans . . . Soldiers. Run . . . run." Her voice was rough, her breath gasping, as if . . . As if she might once again be possessed of demons. But Jesus had healed the Magdalene. Surely there was no chance one of the evil things had returned. Surely this was only fear and grief. "Romans! *Romans!*"

"Ahhh," Mary breathed. Magdalene was caught in the death scene at Magdala, her illness caused by the presence of Romans. But how could she protect the woman from *Romans*? The conquering army was everywhere.

She studied her guest, curled into a tight ball. "They're gone," she said. Magdalene's eyelashes fluttered and she went quiet. Tears pooled at the corners of her eyes. Earlier, Mary had brought a small crock of water up to the Magdalene, ready for washing after her nap. Now, she took up the crock and washed her guest's face with the cool water and a cloth. "They're gone," she said. "*You* chased them away, Magdalene. The soldiers are gone." Finally, the words penetrated and Magdalene went utterly still, as if the blood in her veins had ceased to flow.

She opened her eyes. "Gone, Aemoa?"

"Yes. Thanks to you and the hand of the Almighty."

By evening, the Magdalene was almost her normal self, the roof was clean, the bedding aired, her shift dry after washing and hanging on a line, the cistern cleaned and seen to by the Rebbe, and the sand, rocks, and herbs in the garden tended to. It was as if the event had never happened. And they had done none of the work at all. It seemed that the whole village knew of the episode with the Romans, and had turned out to help. Every family had sent at least one member to get the story firsthand and to convey thanks in the form of services. They all thought a village-wide illness was a wonderful ploy and she and the Magdalene were heroes.

Aemoa never found out who had spread the story, but she had a sneaking suspicion it was Eglah, for soon after, the woman took Magdalene under her wing and became a constant companion, the story becoming highly embellished in true Eglah style. But no one ever admitted a thing. Only that the Magdalene was special. The Magdalene was a hero.

Magdalene

"We leave for Bethsaida Julius, near Capernaum the morning after the Sabbath."

The excitement loosed by those words still sang through her body, damping the ache of muscles abused from the first day's travel, muscles that now stiffened cruelly on her pallet beneath the stars. They had camped off the road. Their bedrolls placed close together made a small perimeter for the armed guards hired to protect the trade goods in the caravan. A Nazarene vendor, going to Capernaum for trade, had included them in his company for a fee.

Though their companions made a large group, thieves were known to attack a traveling party no matter the size, especially if there were women to be had. Women could easily be carted to the shore and put on a slave ship to vanish forever. Their jewels, which no decent woman would travel without, would be stripped from them and sold at the markets of the ritually unclean, to the Gentile women. And the men, if they lived, would be injured, beaten, possessions lost. It was dangerous to travel. But the carefree group was still close to Nazareth. No bandits had been seen for months and they had a sense of security and safety.

A guard crunched gravel as he passed by, the stout metal-tipped pole he carried as a weapon swished softly. Two pallets over, a snorer burbled and rearranged himself. Further off, the bell she had attached to her donkey's halter tinkled softly as the pack animals, also guarded, grazed. From out of a dream Aemoa laughed softly and snuggled beneath the blankets, shoving the bundles and baskets that rested between them for safekeeping into Magdalene's side. The familiar laughter brought back a conversation from several days earlier.

"What are we to do with your things while we are gone?" Aemoa mused. "Almost all I own goes with me, and my family usually watches over the house. But this time there are your things to consider." She looked around the crowded room. "You have so much to store, it would take the whole village to keep it all. Eventually you will have your own house and all your belongings will be safe, but until then, we have to think of some place to keep them." She tapped her slender finger against her pursed lips, taking silent inventory of the riches. Eyes twinkling, she tilted her head to one side and said, "How about Eglah? She has a large house and would be delighted to store your valuables."

"Humph. Store, no. Use, sell, break, destroy, discard, maybe. But store?"

The older woman laughed. "Be charitable, child. She has tried to be kind to you. And she has made it a point to bring you special treats from her own hands. You enjoyed that saffron cake she brought you," she reminded.

"Yes, and the whole village enjoyed the tale of my spilling the honey down my shift. Except that, by the time I heard it, I had spilt the entire crock, not just a single drop."

"Why, child, I do believe you're sullen. Shame on you."

"Shame on me? Why . . . What about her?" Magdalene spluttered.

Aemoa laughed. "You will never be able to stand the men's humor while we travel if you can't take a little teasing from me."

Sheepishly, Magdalene grinned.

"Well. You will get over it soon enough if I know his followers. Now back to Eglah. She has her ways, but she is a good soul. You would never know it but she is always giving to the poor. Her home is full of the smell of cooking for the sick and for anyone who can't afford food. And she has a warm heart."

"A heart warmed by the trouble she causes. And heated on gossip," Magdalene muttered.

"What?"

"Oh, nothing. If you think Eglah would be the best one to keep my things, then Eglah would be the best one to keep my things." Even to her own ears she sounded petulant.

The older woman smiled wider. "I think you will learn to love her. Or you would if you stayed in Nazareth. She's always been a good friend."

Good friend or no, Magdalene didn't like Eglah having access to her cedar trunk. She had a wager with herself that her bolt of blue silk would be on Eglah's stout frame within days of their departure. Wisely Magdalene had kept her fears quiet. She had wanted no animosity between Aemoa and herself.

The snorer paused, burped loudly, and fell silent. Scavenging for wild greens, herbs, and roots was the women's job as they traveled, and the results tonight had been a strange variety of tastes and textures. The merchant had packed a small supply of dried meat for the journey and there had been a soup, salad, and fresh bread. In the evening, while the men set up camp, the women dug an earthen oven and started a fire to heat rocks on which to cook small flat loaves of coarse bread and the day's food findings. As they traveled, nearing the Great Sea, the assortment of foods would begin to include dates, fresh melons, tree-ripened olives and horse beans to augment the wild onions and garlic-flavored greens. The food was highly seasoned, and in the cool of the evenings, men tended to overeat, their burning stomachs eased with watered wine.

An oiled pitch basket stabbed through her shift as Aemoa moved the baskets again. Gently she shoved against it, heard her friend mumble and turn in her sleep. The extra inches were welcome on the narrow pallet, but she missed the blanket the Aemoa took with her. The nearby snorer again worked up to a deafening soliloquy, the din echoing on the still air until someone punched him. Hard. He grunted as the air whooshed from his lungs. A hissed conversation ensued before the camp finally quieted.

Jesus didn't snore. Jesus. The man of the deep gentle eyes and large calloused hands. A teacher of hard lessons and unflinching words as she had already learned. An orator in great demand. Excitement blossomed fresh in her tired limbs.

Jason had never allowed her to hear any of the fine orators who chanced to come through Magdala, assuming her to be incapable of understanding what was said. Yet, she had always yearned to listen and learn. She had been taking secret lessons from their son's tutor, learning to write— The thought broke off. Jesus had said something about her writing a letter. Strange that she had not recalled such lessons. Jason had come in on her one day working with her tutor and flown into a rage. Shaking her head, she rolled over.

Jason in a rage . . . *Forget,* her mind told her. *Don't think about Jason. Men are just that way. They can't accept some things. And when they get angry, they do . . . they sometimes do things . . . But that doesn't mean that one is unloved. Jason had done a great deal to make up for the way he had treated her. For the bruises.*

Gentle brown eyes wavered in her memory, seeming to speak her thoughts a lie. His eyes smiled in her mind, leading her gently to sleep.

Chapter Eight

Magdalene

Following their arrival in Bethsaida, the exhausted Magdalene slept through twenty-four hours; it was late afternoon when she woke. She stretched and scratched her head, yawned and pulled at sore muscles. Her shoulders and legs were swollen and stiff, her feet bruised, and all she wanted to do was go back to sleep. Instead, propping herself on her elbows, she brushed the tangled, short hair out of her eyes, and studied the empty house.

The home of Simon the Fisherman was large and airy, floors and walls of limestone tiles pressed into clay and rolled smooth. This room had three windows facing east with heavy wooden shutters latched open. Around the floor were bedrolls and satchels and cloaks, as if an army lived here. The room she was in led off to two other rooms, one on each side. Through one doorway, she could see the main room, where a wooden door was propped wide and shielded with a gaily woven cloth. There were couches there and at least twenty stools pushed under two long tables. Against the far wall, was a pile of woven rugs and reed mats, bright pottery and crocks. As usual, at the sight of crocks, her stomach complained with hunger.

The clutter brought a strange desire to run. She clutched at the bedcover, pulling it higher. Her life was so different from the life she had anticipated so long ago when she went to live with Jason. Now it was filled with uncertainty and disorder, with people who weren't hers and weren't Jason's. She had no place here. She was alone in a house of strangers.

The ceiling above her groaned, and soft giggles floated in through the windows. The patter of feet descended along an outside stair that she could see through a window. One pair, the last, were strapped into new sandals which she recognized as Aemoa's, and some of her feelings of abandonment vanished. In a moment, three women entered, laughing and speaking all at once.

"Magdalene, you're awake. Good. We could use some help with the greens in the yard."

"They are early and bitter. What we will serve with them is beyond me unless those sons of mine can manage to find at least a few fish."

"Did you finally get enough sleep?"

"Can you get up by yourself?"

"Do you wish to wash?"

She looked from one woman to another. She knew only Aemoa, yet the other two spoke as though she knew them also. Her confusion was evident, and Aemoa gestured to the other women. "The skinny one is Joanna and the short one with the heavy load is Simon's wife's mother and my dearest friend. She thinks she's younger than the rest of us, but you should call her Mother just the same."

"Don't lay there all day, Magdalene. There's work to do," the short woman said.

"Don't pay her any attention, child. She's always working and expects us to work just as hard," Aemoa said, laughing.

"If you did, this place wouldn't be so messy."

"It's perfectly clean. There simply isn't enough room for all the things the men bring."

While the voices battled pleasantly around her, Magdalene slowly worked herself to her feet and rolled up her bedroll. Stacking it against the wall, she combed out her tangles and washed at an ewer in the corner before wrapping up in her mantle. She was cold, and walking was uncomfortable on her sore feet. Her calves were swollen and hard as rocks. But she had a feeling that if she were to be accepted in this house, she would have to get over her aches in a hurry and get to work. She waddled out into the yard and over to the pile of new greens. It was impossible to bend over to work. Her first attempt to stretch the injured muscles brought tears to her eyes and she gasped with pain.

The older woman, a short squat ball of energy, noticed her tears and ran to her. "Don't try to use your muscles, Magdalene. I forgot you had been sick. Here, sit on this stool and I'll bring you some greens. You can be our washer woman. Be sure to wash all the bug eggs off. Wait. Let me look at those legs."

Without asking, she pulled aside the wrinkled shift. "Child, these legs look awful. They're feverish. You clearly were not accustomed to walking so many miles. You should have said something. Let me get some liniment. It stings like the fires of Gahanna and smells almost as bad, but it'll ease the swelling."

She bustled off, leaving Magdalene with her head spinning. The short woman talked so fast, it was hard to follow. The mother of Simon's wife. So who was Simon's wife? And who was Simon? She sighed. It wasn't going to be easy, traveling with the Rebbe and his mother.

The short woman was back, carrying a small crock. Quickly she bent and pushed up the wrinkled shift again. With deft movements, she opened the crock and poured a generous amount of dark liquid into her hand. It stank. The smell was so strong, it cleared Magdalene's head and stung her eyes as she watched. The liquid was oily, but it rubbed into her skin easily. At first, there was only the barest tingle of burning, followed by a warmth that radiated into the sore muscles and up her leg. But as the woman continued to rub, the burn became more intense until she thought her skin would smoke. It did burn like the fires of Gahanna, the constantly burning waste pile outside the walls of Jerusalem. And probably smelled worse. However, no smoke appeared and her skin didn't curl up, but only turned a bright shade of red.

"Now," the woman said, slapping the crock into her lap. "You use this before you go to sleep tonight and again when you rise. If you rub it in every day, the soreness and swelling will go down soon. You get busy washing these greens. We've got at least twenty men to feed tonight, plus three or four women who think that food appears on the table by magic." Grumbling, the woman was gone.

It wasn't as difficult as she had feared, to fit in and find a place in the band of people. As long as she did more work than she believed she could, the short woman was satisfied, and as long as she walked every day to loosen her muscles and garner strength, Aemoa was satisfied, and as long as she listened to the Rebbe speak at night and on the Sabbath, *he* seemed satisfied. But Magdalene wasn't sure that *she* was satisfied.

The work exhausted her, and the walking seemed pointless as the crowds followed the Rebbe wherever he went. His teachings were different from any rabbi she had ever heard, insisting on compassion and love and forgiveness. She didn't hate anyone, nor was she planning any revenge, and so she allowed his teachings to pass through her unheard. And after the first time her feet were trampled and she was elbowed to the side, she stayed away from the crowds. Until she overheard the disciples talking about things that had happened in the days or months past—miraculous things. Healings. Fascinated, in her second month with the group, she began again to follow the Rebbe when he went into the countryside to talk and to preach. She only went when there was little work to do, and she always followed at a distance. Discreetly.

The things she saw there left her breathless. If it was some kind of sorcery, she couldn't see how it was done. No magician would allow anyone to watch closely at his feats of magic, nor would a magician or charlatan stay for long in one place, least his duplicities be discovered and the townsfolk turn against him. But the Rebbe did both. He was surrounded by vast crowds every day and if he was using spells to accomplish his miracles, then they were very strong, because they didn't wear off in a few days' time, leaving the victims as ill as before.

Her interest in the healings led her to listen more closely when the Rebbe taught at night around the brazier, and in the hills around Bethsaida Julius or Capernaum by day. She didn't understand all of what he said, but as the other followers seemed to have the same problem, it didn't worry her.

As she healed, her mind grew sharper, and memories of the past came clearer. She began to remember the last days of Jason's life, bits and pieces, fragments of happy memories. But she also began to remember the years after he died, and these memories she fought. They crept up on her as she worked with the other women, or when she was falling asleep, or as she walked alone. Angry memories haunted her, intent on her hurt, painful slivers of the life she had lived for five years. There were snatches of conversations, scenes of dream places she had never been. She couldn't push them away, but found that as long as her mind was occupied, it was easier.

To fill her time and engage her mind, she followed the Rebbe, and practiced with her lute, and she found herself a teacher. Not a teacher in the usual way, for she was uninterested in holy scripture or in prophecy like that taught by John the Baptist. This was a business teacher—an old man she met at the city gates. He had turned out to be Bethsaida Julius' richest man, and its loneliest. She would meet him at the entrance to the market twice a week, bringing him a treat from the kitchen and would stay to hear him talk. Often he let drop a comment about money, and she would encourage him to continue, though she professed to be incapable of following his words. How much she fooled him she wasn't sure, but she saw a twinkle in his eye several times when she would press him to explain some salient point or describe a certain person who was looking for investors.

After a time, she began to follow his advice. Slowly, she began to invest her money in projects and land. Within a season, she owned part of a vineyard and a share of two fishing boats. The old man mentioned a skilled woman, a widow with young children, and Magdalene set her up in business as a dyer of scarlet and a weaver of fine cloth. She found a man to distribute the products in the town markets of Galilee, and helped the woman to hire skilled workers in the growing business. She spent her money in the same way she followed the Rebbe. Discreetly.

She was careful to attract no one's attention with her spending and she enjoyed the intrigue of pretending to represent a young son when she talked to some man of business looking for investors. This seemed to work in her favor as she ended up with a goodly share of profits, and even acquired a business manager in the person of a young scribe. It was exciting to be a woman in business but she didn't want to be tied to Bethsaida or the region near Capernaum. The scribe would allow her the freedom to travel.

The Rebbe's group was growing every day as more people heard about the teacher in the north of the Galilean region who spoke with the authority of the great prophets and who did great things in the name of the Lord. The inn—a covered place to camp near the large market square in the center of town—was filled to overflowing with new followers and with families of the sick and infirm who flocked to hear the preacher and to be healed. The vendors of nearby towns, hearing about the crowds gathered near Capernaum, packed their wares and traveled, selling what they had, to return in only a few days, to gather a new selection and race back to the north of the Sea of Galilee and its quick profits. One day there were a thousand people gathered on the hill by the sea to listen. Other days steady crowds of five hundred sat quietly in the heat and listened to the words the Rebbe roared into the wind.

Living with the Rebbe was a thing of laughter and excitement, a varying landscape of new faces, new ideas, and work. She was learning how to cook with new herbs, new fruits, and in great quantity for they now served at least thirty men, crowded at night into the central room of Simon's house. The men would devour whatever was set before them in silence, and then the talking would start. The men spoke about their day, the things they had seen as they worked beside the Rebbe or wandered through the crowds of people. The men wanted to hear an explanation of the day's teaching from the Rebbe, but he often sat silent with closed eyes and let them talk their way into and out of theological corners. A lot of what they said must have been amusing, for, from where Magdalene sat in the shadows near the door, she could sometimes see the Rebbe's mouth twitch with laughter. And still he would only listen, waiting for a serious discussion, one that would involve almost all the men or loud groups of three or four. At these times the pitch of excitement would rise so high that arguments broke out which raged for hours into the night before the Rebbe would step in and quiet the men with a few words of explanation, or scripture, or just common sense.

It was these evening talks that Magdalene began to love most, for here she could relax, invisible and silent in the shadows, her head propped against a water jar while she watched and listened. It was soothing at the end of a day. And it was wonderful to be a part of it all, to be needed, for occasionally the Rebbe would seek her eyes and smile in the darkness, sharing with her and her alone some amusing point one of the men had made. She wondered for a while why he turned to her for this and not to the man himself. It was later that she realized he would not embarrass the speaker by exposing his ignorance or appear to laugh at him. There were other ways to teach. And so she waited in the darkness for when he needed her to smile, and to recognize the laughter in his eyes.

To many of the others who could not see laughter in the eyes of the Rebbe, he was a quiet man. Subtle. Full of great words and serious of spirit. Perhaps even brooding. To her, these men were obtuse and she avoided their company when she came upon them talking for fear she would commit the crime the Rebbe himself avoided and laugh at them.

The summer wore on, growing hotter once the first harvest was over, and the ground became dusty on her walks. It seldom rained in summer, but a steady breeze blew east from the Great Sea, assisting in the harvest, blowing away chaff from the heavier wheat kernels during the winnowing process. Magdalene bought a newly planted field in summer, her money going to pay the harvesters, and she watched the process of threshing and winnowing from an isolated booth of fronds at the edge of the field. At the end of the day, she would be covered with chaff and dust as she walked home, carrying a large bundle of wheat from the winnowing fields as apology for her lateness. When the crops were sold, she reinvested the principle and most of the profit in another venture, taking a small portion to support herself, to buy food for the men, and to purchase new sandals for the Rebbe.

The women managed to feed the group by scavenging the countryside for edible wild plants, gleaning from harvested wheat fields and fruit trees, and bargaining the poor vendors with determined desperation. Her profits, though not large, went toward feeding and clothing the motley group of men, and to the poor.

At first, she had turned the profits over to Judas the Judean, called the Iscariot. He acted as treasurer for the men, taking in donations and allotting it back out to the poor and destitute for food. But later, though she could not have said why, she stopped giving the Iscariot money, preferring to carry it in her own money belt and using it as she thought best. After that, the Iscariot never liked her much, and she avoided his accusing eyes.

A New Disciple

He stood, watching the women draw water at the well in the cool of the morning. With his practiced eye he had eliminated the ones too young and too old, the pregnant, the infirm, the ugly and the recently widowed. His eye had settled on the shorn-haired woman. She piqued his curiosity.

She was a pretty little thing, but far too skinny for his taste. Lonely widows, or those set aside for adultery, or wealthy women with husbands who traveled too often and too far were his favorite kind of females—though he liked all women. *All women!* And this one with the fine clothes and gentle movements was an oddity to him. Almost too refined to be a woman of pleasure— almost—her shorn hair gave her away as either a harlot or an adultress. Watching her, his finely chiseled lips lifted slightly. He was lonely. He had been on the road too long without female company.

He was a handsome man, with short curling black hair and fair skin and Greek blood flowing in his veins. It was the Greek blood that gave his nose the definite curve, his jaws the strong angle, his lips their sensuality, and his family their money. He had found life an easy game, with few challenges except for learning scripture and commentary, and conquering reluctant women. His understanding of each was prodigious.

That she would draw water with the other women, opening herself up to the possibility of ridicule and slapping or even stoning, showed strength and a fighting spirit. And when her mantle slipped, falling to her shoulders, the other women looked at her with . . . Was it pity? She was willow thin, as she pulled at the rope tied around her jug, but more graceful than any woman he had seen, except of course for his mother. Keeping a distance from her, he followed her through the winding streets of the town, surprised that she walked them so easily. Her step never faltered, and she spoke often to those she passed. Had he been able to see her face he felt she would have been smiling. Strange conduct even for a happily widowed woman.

Always delighting in anomalies, whether they were scriptural or female, he was enchanted with this one, and determined to ferret out the reasons for her behavior, and for her acceptance by the townspeople. If she was a harlot, then the townspeople did not know. If she had cut her hair for some type of mourning, then she wouldn't smile or speak to passersby until her hair grew back out. Indeed, a strange woman.

She entered a house larger than most, well built, in a horseshoe shape with a central patio and an extensive medicinal and flavor herb garden, colorful with flowering plants. The house was whitewashed, its shutters open to the sun. It was a charming house, but lacking in the usual indications of a house of pleasure, no phallus carved into the door or molded into the garden walls. In fact, a fish was carved above the door here—indicative that, at some point, a fisherman had lived here.

He watched the house for a time from across the street, lounging against a tree. Several men went in and later left. Two women followed them. It was a busy place, if it was a house of pleasure. The puzzle was delightful. Three men left the house together, calling back inside to, "Use the money for wine and pickled fish. We will be thirsty and hungry when we return." *Use the money . . . It* was *a house of prostitution!*

He stepped to the house and banged importantly on the door with his fist, said the proper words over the lintel, and stepped inside. The woman whirled, framed in a halo of sunlight streaming through an open window.

"Who are you? What do you want?" It wasn't exactly what he had expected to hear. Best to move slowly.

He lifted a brow, calculating its effect on her. She seemed unmoved. *Interesting.* "I have business with your husband, woman. Call him."

"I have no husband."

He smiled. "No husband?"

"No. I am a widow for some years. Perhaps you mean one of

the men who stay here."

Stay here? Did she run an immoral boarding house? he wondered.

"Perhaps Simon the Fisherman or his brother? Or one of the women?"

He continued to stand, staring at her, trying to decide what to say next. She was clearly puzzled, but he couldn't think how to answer her.

"Are you here for the Rebbe?"

A rabbi was one of her customers? Thoroughly confused, he repeated, "The Rebbe?"

She smiled. It was a beautiful smile, lighting her features from within. "He isn't here today, though I expect him back by nightfall. If you wish to wait, please sit." She indicated a stool and added, "Let me pour you some wine."

When she turned, he dug into his purse and withdrew three small silver coins. It was more than he usually left with a woman, but he didn't quite know how to pay this one. She turned, again, now carrying a cup of wine. He took it and pushed the coins into her palm. "Will this be sufficient?"

She looked at him strangely. "There is no charge for the wine." When he didn't respond, she asked, "Is this an offering?"

He opened his mouth and closed it with a snap. He had had no trouble winning his way with a woman in years. He was always sure what to say and what to do. But with this one, he was standing on sinking sands. The sensation was not unlike the way he felt the first time he approached a woman. He had been a boy at the time, and shame had washed over him, a feeling like drowning, which had stayed with him for years. He thought he had overcome it.

He should be holding her by now, leading her to her carpet, telling her what he wanted. Instead he sat like a foolish boy, gawking. His discomfort rose, suffocating. He stood, set the wine to a low table, untasted, and grabbed the woman. Ignoring her struggles, which had no place in the carefully planned scenario which had already gone so sour, he kissed her soundly. And found himself sitting on the floor gasping for breath and cupping his searing genitals in his hands. The pain was like lightning, bringing tears to his eyes. He gagged and rolled to his side, knocking the cup of wine to the floor beside his head.

"What are you doing?" she hissed.

He looked up, blinking the tears away. She stood like an angry goddess the Greeks might have worshipped, brandishing a heavy, short-handled broom. Her mantle and veil had fallen away, and her eyes flashed dark flame. He rolled toward the door. "I gave you the money. Was it not enough?"

"Enough for what? It was a generous donation, and will keep some poor child from going hungry tonight."

He grunted with pain, "Is . . . Is this not a house of pleasure?"

Suddenly the woman standing in front of him changed. Her face, which had been so wild the moment before, now smiled, and from her smile grew laughter. Peals of amusement echoed around the room and, as his pain faded, he felt the memory of that first time with a woman growing. The humiliation.

He stood, leaning to one side with residual pain. He turned and limped toward the door. But he had forgotten the cup of wine. Still puddled on the limestone, his momentum was just enough to cause him to slip, and he tumbled again. He hit the floor, his breath whooshing out in a grunt. The woman laughed harder.

"Are you not a prostitute?"

"No. I'm Magdalene."

"That's good, I think. I'm Jude Thaddeus, a distant kinsman to James, and I no longer need one."

The Zealot

He sat facing the sun, its sharp rays piercing even behind his lids. It was a calm day, peaceful, like the day before and the day before that. He had never known such peace. Worn by the sight of death, its blood, its stench, he thought he had become so cold to all else that nothing could touch him ever again. But since coming here he had found that life might be different, new, alive. Here, it was death that couldn't penetrate beyond the peace.

He had come to watch this new man, this new leader. He was sent to listen, to gauge the mood of those who followed him, to determine how the revolutionary new rabbi could be used by the Others in their war. Instead, he was being used by the teacher to feed the poor, to carry children. Ah, the weight of a child in his arms again. It had been so long. He was listening, yes, but instead of listening for the Others, he had begun to listen with the intent to learn. He was caught up in the words and the meaning and the excitement, especially the excitement, in a way he had not thought possible since the Others first came to him and gave him a reason not to die.

War. The Others had given him war, death, intrigue, hatred, the cries of the injured, the reek of blood and emptied bowels. He had been part of their dreams, their vengeance. The lives he had taken had helped to ease the pain in his heart each time he thought of little Nirit and the things the Roman soldiers did to her. Each time he had plunged his knife into a black Roman heart, he had pictured her in his mind, the way he last remembered her, lying in a congealed pool of blood, her body mangled, covered with flies.

It was only lately that the killing was no longer enough. He wanted to live again, to bury the hate and feel the sun on his face. To hold a child. To love. And that was what the Rebbe Jesus was giving him, in doses too large to swallow. He was drowning in the understanding he saw in the man's eyes. Simon the Zealot, fiercest of the guerilla warriors, seeking peace and the look of brother-hood in the eyes of a man who denounced violence. It was *not* what he had come for.

The Others had wanted a speaker who could weld the people into fighters, willing and fearless, and had sent him to convince this man, this Jesus of Nazareth, to join them, to recruit him for the day when his words would make the people rise up and fight the Romans, wresting their homeland from the grip of foreign devils. But he had not tried to recruit the man. Instead, he sat at the feet of the teacher and listened. It was changing him. Part of him fought the change, wanting the hatred that had sustained him for so long, yet, it continued to slip away, slowly, and he had no will to stop it. It was the children that changed him. The Rebbe sent him to them every chance he could, almost as if he knew the changes that were taking place in the cold heart that sat at his feet.

Simon turned, following the sun, its rays having moved to the side, and remembered the first time he had heard the Rebbe speak. He had surveyed the town twice; Bethsaida was wealthy, boasting a thatched-roof inn and walled bathing area, when most towns had only a fenced compound and a shallow cistern. He had learned its twisting streets and empty buildings, places to hide in the event he needed to run. It wasn't necessary, he wasn't planning a midnight raid, but the practice of long years of running, hiding, held firm. This careful reconnoiter had saved his life many times and he couldn't abandon it had he wanted. Satisfied, he had sauntered into town on his third day, just before dusk and the start of the Sabbath, dropped his few things in a corner of the inn, and washed himself.

By the time the cantor climbed to the roof of the synagogue to blow the shofar, signaling the end of the day and the beginning of the Lord's day of rest, he was fully entrenched in the temporary community of the town. He offered a coin to join the travelers' Sabbath meal and ate silently, keeping to himself, and listened to the talk around the fire about the great rabbi who sat at meat in the house rented by Simon the Fisherman. Two of the men held the attention of the rest of the group by recounting the healing they had witnessed the day before. A young woman, once beautiful, had been restored to fresh loveliness by the slightest touch of the Rebbe's hand. Before the eyes of those assembled in her house, her body had been wiped clean of thousands of black moles and lesions that had covered her. Even the birthmark that she had carried as a child on the inside of one arm was gone.

Intrigued, Simon, always a loner, moved closer to the group, hoping they would say more. He wasn't disappointed. Through the rest of the meal, they talked of nothing else. How the Rebbe's voice was so powerful it could be heard over the roaring of the desert wind, his presence so authoritative that he seemed to stand a head taller than any other man. They recounted a teaching the Rebbe had given: "Blessed are ye that hunger now: for ye shall be filled. Blessed are ye that weep now: for ye shall laugh." Those words had pierced him deeply. For he hungered. And he wept.

He had known, even in that first moment, this could not be the one for which the Others had looked for so long, the speaker who would bring about the revolution. This man was peaceful. Kind. Not a revolutionary to lead the people into war.

When the townspeople gathered that evening at a small synagogue for scripture reading and interpretation of the Law, Simon followed and sat in the shadows on the men's side in the back of the austere room, his eyes watching those already seated along three walls on wooden benches and stools. The center of the room filled with latecomers, sitting on rugs they brought or the bare tile floor, to hear the scriptures read and the Law expounded. Last to enter was the resident rabbi and another man, only slightly taller than the first, both in belted white tunics and fringed prayer shawls. They stood before the curtained chest containing the sacred scrolls, their faces lit and shadowed by flickering lamps. The resident rabbi read the scripture and spoke first, and his knowledge of the Law was great. He called up from memory alone, the comments of six great teachers on the interpretation of the fine point of Law from which he had read. He used their names with conviction, and the crowd listened quietly, a few men adding or questioning a small point.

Then. The other man took the place of the first at the head of the crowd, and an excited whisper fanned back through the group like a desert wind. Simon felt the hairs on the back of his neck lift. A feeling like the shivering of the air before a storm raced down his fingers. He leaned in, toward the man, Jesus, at the front of the room, and slid closer to the edge of his narrow bench, filled with an unaccountable excitement. The Rebbe read a short passage from the first book of Chronicles. "Behold, a son shall be born to thee, who shall be a man of rest; and I will give him rest from all his enemies round about: for his name shall be Solomon, and I will give peace and quietness unto Israel in his days." And then Jesus returned the scripture to the box and he spoke. "Blessed be the kingdom of our father David, that cometh in the name of the Lord. Blessed be the Lord God of Israel; for he hath visited and *redeemed* his people. *His* people! For God loves his people."

His words filled the room with intensity as he taught with authority on the scripture, using no other man's reasoning or name for his words. He spoke of redemption and peace, and the love of God to all men. His words permeated the room with power and with promise. This Jesus made them a people again. A people of pride, of destiny, a people of sinners redeemed. And when he finished, the assembled let out a breath with one great collective sigh, some clapping, others running up to touch the man, to kiss his face. Though it was late, many stayed on and questioned the Rebbe while others formed smaller groups and talked about what he had said. Even the women's side of the synagogue remained full, the women staying to hear.

Simon sat unmoving in his place, his eyes closed, feeling the strength move slowly back into his body. He was afraid even then. If he stayed in this town, he knew he would change in ways he couldn't fathom, and he felt the fear natural to any creature threatened by a greater outside force—the unknown. He slipped from the synagogue, meaning to gather his pack and leave, no matter the Sabbath prohibitions on carrying and on travel. But somehow, on his way back to the inn, his fear lessened and by the time he had found his pack, he was ready to laugh at himself for a fool. So he had stayed. But indeed, his first impulse had been correct. He was changed. He had lost the one thing that had defined himself. His hate had vanished.

It was the Sabbath again, though weeks after his first with Jesus, and he sat in the sun, waiting for the evening worship at the close of the day. It was peaceful here and warm. What he felt might be the calm joy of a child in the arms of its mother. He was happy, and he already knew that he would never go back to the Others. But they would come after him. He knew too much, too many secrets for them to let him disappear. He had some time yet, but soon they would come to carry him back, or kill him if he refused. And he *would* refuse.

There was a footstep beside him, and he looked up into the eyes of the Rabboni. When had he become Master in his mind, and not simply Rebbe? It wasn't important. Many others had begun to call him Rabboni. Jesus lowered himself, and sat back on his heels, his knees up high. Simon smiled, the feeling still strange on his mouth. For years, he had never smiled. Now, he did it without thought.

"You're smiling, Simon. When you first came I thought you would never smile."

"You made me. You *re*made me."

"I remade you?"

"Yes. By the words of peace you speak. By the expression in your eyes. There is peace there, such joy."

"Not everyone sees peace, Simon. Perhaps only one who has known war sees true peace."

Simon stiffened. The Master watched his eyes and Simon shuddered with the certainty of his banishment. He had never told Jesus about his past, yet, somehow, the Rebbe knew, and now he would be sent away. A man of peace would reject a Zealot, a man of death and murder, ambush and terror. Tears threatened and the impulse to cry was so new to him he couldn't control it. Salty tears ran down his face as, silently, he begged the Rabboni to let him stay. His only home was by his side.

"I wish you to speak the grace and thanksgiving after the evening meal tonight, Simon. Do you know what you will say?"

Simon blinked, his ears having deceived him, until he saw in the eyes of the Rabboni the confirmation of the words. In a swish of robes, he rose and was gone. Simon wiped his face, knowing exactly what he would say and for what he would give thanks.

The first time he saw the Magdalene, he was surprised. The things he had heard had not prepared him for the woman, for her frailty, her ravaged but almost ethereal beauty. He had come into Simon's house looking for Mary, Jesus' mother, to give her a small message. He had thought the house was empty, until he moved from the doorway and light entered behind him. He saw her then, perched on a stool, a lyre in her hands and a look of fear on her face. Immediately, he saw the resemblance to his Nirit. Oh, her face was thinner than the memory he carried of Nirit, and her eyes were perhaps a darker shade of brown, and, of course, her hair was shorter. They had prepared him for that so he didn't stare. But the line of jaw, the rich luster of coal black hair, the fearful way she stared past him when he entered the house, as though she searched for protection in the empty doorway, these were all the same. And the look in her eyes when he dipped his head in a sign of respect and held out his hands to show her he was unarmed, that was the same. The very same relief he had seen on the face of little Nirit the first year he knew her.

Uncertain, he stood in the doorway, shuffled his feet in the thin layer of dust that coated the floor no matter how often the women swept, and finally, not finding anyone else in the shadowy corners of the rooms, he spoke. "Ah . . . ah, message from the Rebbe. Is ah . . . is she here?"

Smiling at his stuttered unease, she said, "No. She and Salome have gone into the market to purchase for the evening meal, for Simon will be on the boat all night and will bring no fish today."

He glanced up at the woman before dropping his eyes to his feet. He felt the Magdalene's smile, and he writhed inwardly. Wanting to speak, he wracked his brain, but no words would come. His face flushed. Perspiration poured hotly beneath his clothes. His feet sweated into his sandals, and the stench of his unwashed body rose.

"You could leave the message with me, if you like," she said, her tone gentle.

Explosively, the short message burst from him. He whirled and fled the house, flinging drops of sweat. It was only later that he realized his words had come out in the wrong order.

After that first meeting, he sought out every opportunity to speak to her, but only when he had memorized the words he would say, and the exact inflection his voice would take. He was careful not to stay in her presence too long, fearing she would ask him a question and his brain would freeze. He never looked at her while he spoke his cautious words, and her response was answered back softly, as careful as his own. She never couched a response that would force him to speak again, seeming to respect his difficulty with speech when she was present.

He could almost predict the exact words they would say to each other each time. Every conversation was similar to the ones before it, and to the ones which would come after. It gave him a continuity to his life that he needed. And that he knew would not last.

The Others had not yet come though it had been two months and three weeks. Each day the confrontation drew inevitably closer. Each day that he saw through to dusk was a joy, for he knew he had another night to listen to the Rabboni, to sit and talk with the disciples, his friends.

It was a mystery to him, but these learned men had become friends, real friends, who looked to him to speak as though he had something important or special to say. Of course, he was often wrong, the things he said would be foolish or simply unlearned, but that didn't matter to them. They would clap him on the back, guffaw and continue the conversation. It was wonderful. But it didn't stop or postpone the day that the Others would come after him.

Each night was glowing, each day filled with promise, and he told himself that he was ready to die when they came. But the thought made him infinitely sad. It seemed that only his conversations with the Magdalene helped him deal with the dread. He had begun to think that if he went to her with his story, with his fear, she would understand. She would not withdraw from him in horror. He had planned several times to speak, to tell of his past, but each time, when the silence sat like a chaperon between them, words failed. The speech he planned seemed foolish. She was a lady, and one didn't burst out gory details of one's past in the presence of a lady.

What if he was wrong about her acceptance of his past and she ran screaming from the house, or—God forbid—fainted. Either prospect filled him with such dread that he swallowed his words and the silence continued. He sighed, and grinned wryly. He sounded like a lovesick schoolboy, not the greatest guerilla fighter that the Zealots boasted. He sighed again, and stretched to his feet. There was work to do. But his thoughts stayed with the Magdalene.

He sought her out again. She was sitting on the roof of the house spinning through a yarn bowl, humming. He came closer and sat at her feet, liking the sound of her voice and the simple childhood tune she hummed. Before he knew it, he was singing along with her, surprised at his bravado. At the end of the song, he risked a look at her face. She was smiling. "Simon the Zealot, you have a wonderful voice. You should sing often."

He started. *She knew.* She knew and still she smiled at him and sang with him, and even dared to be alone on the roof with him. The confusion and wonder must have been apparent on his face, because she laughed, the sound tinkling.

"Yes, I know about your past. Everyone thinks it is very romantic, your being a Zealot."

"Everyone . . ." Swiftly, he said, "I am not a Zealot now. Not since I met Jesus."

She held her smile, her eyes on the thread. "I know. No killer ever had such peace on his face. I knew you were a gentle man from the first time I saw you. I never was afraid."

"Never? Even a little?" He almost felt disappointed.

"Well, perhaps just a little when you first came through the door of Simon's house. You walked so silently, you were in the doorway before I knew you were there at all. You more startled me than frightened me though."

"That was part of my training, to walk silently." The usual silence fell between them, and he realized that they had had a real conversation and not a planned speech. She *knew.* And it didn't matter.

"Did you have friends in the mountain cave the soldiers found and raided?"

He felt himself grow cold and stood swiftly at a crouch. *The mountain cave.* The Romans had it now? He looked at her, a stunned expression in his eyes. "Romans . . ."

She turned her soft, deep, black eyes to his, puzzled. "Yes. Didn't the men tell you? It was days ago, before the last Sabbath."

"No one said a thing. Nothing." Facing her, he touched her for the first time, grasping her shoulders, pulling her to her feet, making her to look into his eyes. There was a dull thud as the spinning bowl fell to her feet. "Tell me. Tell me everything you know." His voice was stern and her lips quivered at his tone. He eased his grip, and forced his voice to remain calm. "It's important, Magdalene. It could bring Romans after me if they had the forethought to torture the Others before they killed them.

And Romans would be dangerous. Do you understand?"

Her eyes clouded over, she seemed to shrink in on herself, as if the light went out of her. He had seen it before in the faces of small children, the effect of too much fear, too much pain. They withdrew into themselves and blocked out the rest of the world. One had to be gentle with them then, not press them too hard, but give them time to heal, to grow. But he might not have time to be gentle. The Romans could be laying a trap even now. It was conceivable that they would attack a whole town to get one man. They had done it before.

"Magdalene." He shook her slightly. Some of the clouds in her eyes slid away as she focused on him. "I was a member of that group before I came here. If the Romans forced them to talk before they killed them, then the Romans might be after me. I need to be away before they come here. Do you understand? I have to protect my friends, the Rebbe, and this town, from the Romans. But I can't do that if I don't know what to expect. Do you understand? Tell me what you heard." He wanted to shake her in his fear.

She wiped a hand across her eyes, seemed about to fall and he tightened his grip on her shoulders. "They said that Pontius Pilate's soldiers had trapped a large group of Zealots in a cave. A mountain cave." Her voice was so soft he could barely hear it, and he strained with impatience. "They killed them all and brought their heads back to Herod's city and hung them on the wall. That's all I know. You will have to ask Simon the Fisherman for the details. He was the one who first heard the story. Ask Simon. Please." Her eyes pled, and he dropped her in his haste to find the Fisherman, leaping down the steps to the ground, worrying, *Why was I not told?*

It was mid-afternoon before he located the Fisherman and Thaddeus at the seashore cleaning fish for pickling—to sell in the market—and for the evening meal. They were carrying on a lively conversation, an argument about some trivial matter the master had brought up that morning. His emotions under control, having run the fear out of his lungs on his race to the sea, he sat near the beached small boat, catching his breath, feeling the fire of danger warm him. It was the first time he had felt like a man, the vital, elemental creature he had always seen himself. Was it the threat? Was he one of those strange ones who faced death and dismemberment with glee, flinging themselves into battle like whirling madmen? He didn't think so. Nor was there that intense excitement he had seen on the faces of professional killers.

He drew swirls in the sand, thinking, surprised at his inward thoughts. The run had made him feel alive. It was *good* to run with need again. To feel the wind whip through his loincloth and hair. To know his actions had meaning and importance.

He half smiled at his fingers in the sand, knowing it wasn't the same killing-grimace he wore during the years he killed Romans, yet it wasn't the insipid, gentle smile he wore each time some trusting maiden thrust a child into his arms. Perhaps it was the smile that would have been his had he led a normal life, with children and a wife to protect. His thoughts flashed back to the timid Magdalene. This must be how a husband might feel toward his wife. Protective.

He didn't know what he would do if the Romans were after him. A man could only run so far. But he would protect these people with his absence if he could. He could go to Jerusalem and join the Zealot group there. But the killing . . . He didn't think he could kill now. And he didn't think he could be a leader, instructing new recruits in the art of death and subterfuge. So if he ran, it would be to nowhere. And alone.

A rowdy voice interrupted. "Do you always sit in the shade while others work in the sun for your supper?"

Hoisting his slender frame, he sauntered over to the smooth, sandy place where the fishermen worked, surrounded by fish entrails and flies, and picked up a sharp knife. Deftly, he sliced a large fish from gill to tail, made another incision and skinned it. He then filleted it, discarded the bones and head and started on another one. The men worked in amiable silence, the piles of waste growing, and the fish stretched out in a long line in the sun. Finally, Thaddeus stopped, flexed his fingers and opened a barrel. The stench of vinegar filled the air, and they layered fish and spices into it. Other fish, they salted whole in a separate barrel, non-kosher foods for non-Jews.

Glancing at the piles of waste, the Zealot smiled. Although it had been years since he had cleaned fish, his own pile was almost as large as the Fisherman's. "Did being a Zealot teach you such skill with a knife?" the big Fisherman asked.

It wasn't meant to be an opening, or to be unkind, it was simply the thoughtless kind of question one associated with Simon. Thaddeus, however, looked up with alarm. So. They did know. Unaware of their reactions, Simon rattled on. "Now, Thaddeus here had to be taught how to hold a knife. He's a slow learner. See that scar on his thumb? Ha! He thought he was going to bleed to death."

Thaddeus, embarrassed at the story and at the Fisherman's oblivious comments, bent his head to his work. The Zealot grinned, hiding his amusement by wiping his face with the back of his arm. "Well, I have had a bit of practice with a knife. We Zealots are quite proficient with them, you know." He almost laughed when Thaddeus' eyes bulged.

The Fisherman, however, never even looked up. "Is it true you practice morning and evening with weapons, even when you are injured?" the big man asked blithely.

The Zealot realized he was enjoying the conversation. Nodding seriously, he said, "Yes. And if one of us becomes too badly injured to fight, we kill him and eat the poor bastard."

"True?" the Fisherman said incredulously.

Straight faced, the Zealot answered, "Oh, yes. We ate seven last year alone. Raw." Simon the Fisherman laughed, throwing back his head before filleting another fish with a single slice.

"Tell me what you heard about the raid on the Zealots in the mountain cave," The Zealot said.

Without pausing in his deft slicing, the Fisherman told the story. "The Prefect's soldiers followed an injured man back to the cave, waited until dark, and attacked. The Romans lost as many men as the Zealots, even though they surprised them. But, you know what else I heard?" he continued. "They found pieces of Roman soldiers tacked all over the walls, ears and other parts, dried to the walls of the cave. They tried to get them down, but some stuck." He laughed gleefully. "When the Romans found the dried ears, and other *things*," he enunciated again with a wink, "they grew so angry that they killed all the prisoners. Didn't save any for the Roman tortures. I heard it was a massacre. Not one of them was left alive."

He laughed again and cast a sidelong glance at Simon. "All the warriors died at the scene. Lucky anyone who wasn't there at the time, eh? The Romans think they killed the entire group. Every last one of the northern Zealots wiped from the face of the earth." He lay his blade on the cleaning board to watch the effect of his words. "Anyone not there is safe. As safe as if he lay against his mother's breast."

The Zealot looked at the big, blood-splattered Fisherman. The silence between them was thin and sharp as the blade in his hand. He said, "Thank you." He lay down his knife and walked away. The Fisherman wasn't as dumb as he sounded most of the time. He knew exactly what he was talking about, and how to tell another man he was free to live without fear. Simon walked along the bank of the small sea, watching the way his feet landed in the dust and lifted back up again. He was free. Perhaps for the first time in his life.

He squared his shoulders, staring at the city in the distance, thinking of Nirit, his little kinswoman. Not as he had last seen her, but as she had been the day before her death, laughing and gay, free from the memories that had pursued her for so long. He remembered her delicate face, her soft expression as she sat in a fallow field, surrounded by wildflowers and laughed up at him. Though still young, only a child really, she had just become a woman with the start of her womanly flows. She had told him she was all grown up now and wanted to marry. He had been heartbroken, wondering who the lucky man was to be, and she had laughed again at his dismay. Had he really been so transparent? "I want to be *your* wife, dear Simon. *I want to be your wife.*"

Chapter Nine

Magdalene

She was humming a quiet song as she worked, her hands deftly turning a saffron and honey cake, alternately smoothing and rolling it until it reached the proper consistency. There would be a wedding in town in two days, and she had been asked to prepare some of the delicacies for the weeklong festivities. It had been a long time since she had been part of a wedding, and never one so grand as this.

Hanani, the daughter of a merchant family, and Shmeil, the son of the bronze-smith had been betrothed since the girl's second birthday when a seer had determined that the girl would be virtuous, as well as wise in market ways. As an afterthought, the seer had added that the girl would also be beautiful, a prediction that had earned her another silver coin. However, a seer cannot be right all the time, and in this instance, the girl was only passably pleasant to look upon, her beauty marred by a large flat nose and a slight odor perfumes couldn't hide.

Since she had defeated the promises of the seer in regards to beauty, her family had taken great precautions to insure that she kept to the letter in all the other predictions, sending her to be educated in the warehouse of her uncle. There she had learned the secrets of making perfume and scarlet dye, how to store food and wine for travel in all kinds of weather, as well as the ways that sacred anointing oil could be stored for export. Not that her uncle ever did such things, but it was good to know how other, less scrupulous businessmen worked. She also learned how to choose the best wools and silks, linens, and flax for resale.

She had been found to have an astute mind. Privately, her mother, Azania had worried that she would become a nag, a domineering woman, bullying her unlucky husband into misery. Wisely, she kept such thoughts to herself, hoping that the large dowry prepared for her would entice both the groom and his father into thinking that they had made a good bargain.

As the occasion neared and her fears of disaster became clearer, Azania had needed to confide in someone. For reasons known only to herself, she had picked the Magdalene. For three weeks Magdalene had been subjected to constant tears and fears, listening to the obese woman moan about her sleepless nights and awful days, her husband who ignored her, and her daughter who was so educated that she no longer needed her mother's advice. It was sad. It was heartrending. It was boring.

Magdalene had taken to hiding from Azania, going on long walks early in the morning, and returning late at night by another route. When she couldn't leave the house due to the amount of work pending, she hid in a booth on the roof, silent when the woman called for her. Thankfully, the rotund caller had bad knees, and didn't climb the steep stairs to seek her out. The other women who stayed at the house sharing the work, helped Magdalene in her deception, because they too, were tired of the constant complaining.

The thought of the wedding made it worth it all. Invitations were begged for, and then jealously bragged about, food was being prepared in almost every home in the city, wine was being brought in from the east, and a fatted calf waited in the girl's family compound for slaughter and blessing by the prescribed ritual. Except for the coming of the Rebbe, it was the most exciting thing Bethsaida had seen for years.

The Huppah, the tabernacle tent that the happy couple was to stand beneath for the wedding ceremony, had been woven of silver cloth, and stood in the yard of the groom's family by day, so all could see it and know that two wealthy families were to be joined by marriage contract. There were wagers of the lowest sort in the back streets, and bets were placed, not on whether the bride was virgin, for no one had ever considered relieving Hanani of her precious burden, but on whether the groom was capable of breaking her fierce maidenhead. Privately, it was considered too strong to break, and that the virtuous woman the seer had foreseen would remain so. Magdalene had tried not to listen to the bawdy jokes on her walks, but some of the men, aware that she was dealing with money—an unladylike occupation—seemed to find great pleasure in speaking aloud in her presence things no decent man would. She ignored the words and phrases as best she could and ignored the men, but occasionally one of them spoke too loudly and she had to tighten her lips against quivering with amusement.

She patted the saffron cake a little harder. She had learned some interesting things while on her walks, and the insight into the typical male mind about weddings and women in general fascinated her. She would enjoy this wedding from the shadows if she could, listening and watching to increase her education a bit more. The Zealot could be her escort, or Thaddeus. She felt Thaddeus could be trusted now, and her lips tweaked at the memory of their first meeting. Yes. After an introduction like that, any man would be trustworthy.

The nights of the wedding week had been lovely. The weather was mild with an eastern breeze, the sky was clear and sparkling with stars, and the town was loud with drunken laughter, singing, and dancing in the streets. Magdalene had avoided the bride's mother, Azania, all week, determined to remain a spectator and not one of the unlucky souls caught in the streets and herded into the bride's house as temporary slaves, serving, cooking, washing dishes. This was a night to remember. A night of dancing, of secret rendezvous, a night of courting, of drinking, toasting, excitement, and eating more food than one could comfortably hold.

The bride and every unwed girl of marriageable age in the town had gathered at the bride's house in their best clothes, hair washed and combed, smelling of scent if their families could afford it and rubbed with fresh flowers if they could not, draped with bangles and necklaces, bracelets and rings, faces often painted, though only after they arrived and their mother's departed for their own part in the festivities. The girls sat draped across lounges and stools, their lamps nearby, their clothing spread carefully around them to avoid wrinkling, and they talked, gossiping and whispering about the secrets of the marriage chamber.

Never pretty, and tending to be squat, Hanani sat spread-legged on the sturdy lounge, eating fresh grapes coated in honey, saffron cakes and bread spread with leben and butter, sweat staining her bridal clothes. Terrified and excited.

Magdalene peeked through the window into the room along with the other women all recalling their own weddings with soft smiles or sad eyes. The festivities went on long into the night, until the groom was suitably drunk, and the bride had imbibed enough wine to calm herself. In fact, her mother had to take precautions to keep her from becoming too calm, as the groom seemed to be in no hurry to claim his bride.

Magdalene had drunk far too much wine, knowing she would pay for it before morning and all the next day as well. But it was so wonderful, so exciting to be part of it all, that she overate, if that was possible, and over-drank on both wine and fruit drink. Thaddeus was nowhere in sight, having vanished hours before, and the Zealot had followed soon after, almost as if it had been prearranged. In fact, she noticed as she stroked her numb face, none of the most faithful followers were to be seen.

It was good to be a woman, to be free and not chasing after a man. Even the followers, though they were men, had become tied down, studying so hard with the Rebbe that they missed a wonderful party only to sit at his feet. Disciples . . . students . . . *men*. She hiccupped and went in search of more food.

Close to midnight, an hour later than was tactfully proper, the groom's men ran through the streets carrying torches and shouting. Most of the men remembered to say the ritual words, "The bridegroom cometh," but a few, drunk on expensive wine, shouted other, improper things, as they led the way to the bride's house. Magdalene, slumped against a wall in the shadows, giggled to herself as she listened and promised to remember some of the more choice phrases. Staggering, she followed the crush of young people to the bride's house, seeing in the distance the flickering light made by virgins' lamps as they walked to meet the torches of the groomsmen.

"Magdalene?"

She turned and squinted in the darkness. "Thas'seus, she slurred, "you finally got back, did you? Well, you missed the—the bes' food I ever ate. All my saffron cakes are gone already." She grinned into his face. "But theresss some real good wine left. Come on, lets go fin' us some. It's a party."

Delicately, Thaddeus turned his face from her and gulped clean air. "My dear girl, I assure you it is not necessary for me to go anywhere to find a source of inebriation. Standing next to you is wine enough. You smell worse than a Samaritan."

She tilted a smile to him. "You have suddenly become terribly proper, haven't you, Thasseus?" she said smoothing her dress. "But I remember when you weren't so proper with me." She slipped an arm across his shoulders. "Do you remember that, Thasseus?" She breathed into his ear. "I remember. An' I haven't said a word to the Rebbe about it either. I been a good girl, haven't I, Thasseus? So," she said more briskly, standing straight and removing her arm, "I deserve a good time. Good girls deserve a good time. I'm not as stuffy as the rest of you have become, and I'm going back to the party. You comin' or not?"

Thaddeus sighed. "I suppose someone should be around to care for you and carry you home when you pass out. And," he said looking around and finding them alone, "it looks as if that someone is me, though I had other things planned for tonight."

"Ohhh . . ." she said archly. "Other *things*. Did you finally find a willing widow or some lonely wife in need of your *special brand of comfort?* My, my, my. You are making the supreme sacrifice tonight, aren't you, Thasseus, dear?" She waggled her fingers at him. "I wonder who is really keeping whom out of trouble tonight."

"Don't push, Magdalene," he growled. "I really had other things to do tonight."

"Mummm. You sound irritable, Thasseus. Perhaps I should go to the party alone. You mus' need another kind of entertainment after all."

Still growling, he grabbed her arm and yanked her down the street after the fading torchlight. Magdalene, smiling to herself in the darkness, hummed a little song and pranced a wedding dance at his side. Her giggle and a hiccup followed them into the night.

• • •

Slowly, so as not to rock the boat she was obviously lying in, Magdalene cracked open her eyes. A lamp-lit ceiling swirled over her head, and she clenched her eyes shut against the motion. Not in a boat. But still moving. Ugh. *The party.* What time had she gotten in last night. No, not night. The sky was light. There had been gray streaks in the sky as she was carried home over someone's shoulder. What time had she gotten in this morning? And who carried her home?

She remembered becoming sick and being dropped to the ground, left there for what seemed like hours. And had someone stripped her and thrown her into the sea? She vaguely recalled drowning in cold, cold water, and then floating on the surface. She had been with Thaddeus. The ground moved dangerously beneath her. Had he been the one who stripped her and threw her into the water? Had anything else . . . She strained to remember and felt sickness rise again. She fought off the nausea and forced herself to think of calmer things. No. She remembered a woman's voice at the water. There had been at least one woman present when she was stripped and bathed.

"Oh. My head." she moaned. "I need water." She looked around. The room was empty. "I'm talking to the furniture." She sat up and propped herself on her arms, locking her elbows to steady her wavering. She inspected the room. This was definitely *not* the house rented by the Fisherman's mother. And it was not the house rented by the Rebbe's mother. So whose house was she in? And whose clothes was she wearing? They were far too large. The soft linen tunic reached all the way to her toes and hung off one shoulder. Two of her could have fit into it. She would like to have seen the dress that went with it.

A head peeked around the corner. "Oh. You're up." The voice boomed in the large room and echoed inside her head. She grabbed it one-handed and moaned.

"I'm not surprised you have a headache. I've never seen anyone so drunk in my life. When my Thaddeus brought you here, I was of a mind to turn him down, but I never turn Thaddeus away when he's in trouble. And you looked like a heap of trouble.

Where did he get you anyway? He wouldn't say. Can I be expecting an irate husband to come looking for you and Thaddeus?"

Magdalene realized that the large apparition before her, arms akimbo, had asked a question. "Wh . . . What?" she rasped.

"I said, are you married."

"N . . . No. A widow. Please don't talk so loud. My head is ringing like a thousand bells."

"And so it should. You have been unconscious in my front room for ten hours, drunk on wine. Why Thaddeus thinks he can bring me his doxies I'll never know."

"I'm not a doxy. I'm his friend."

"Humph. No such thing as friends where Thaddeus is concerned. You're either his sister or his doxy. He never had a friend in his life, at least not one as pretty as you."

"I'm not pretty. Besides. The first time I saw Thaddeus, I kneed him in the groin and threatened to hit him with my broom. May I please have some water?"

"Hit him *where*?" said the woman as she brought a drinking cup.

"I kneed him where he needed it most at the time and he hasn't touched me since. At least not that I know of," she said, remembering the cold water. "Did you perhaps throw me in the sea last night?"

A hearty laugh shook the rafters and echoed inside Magdalene's skull. "You got him where it hurt the most, did you? Yes, I threw you in the water and stripped and dressed you myself. I was wondering this morning why Thaddeus was so unco-operative last night. He acted like he wasn't supposed to be looking at you. Not that he didn't steal a few peeks when he thought I wasn't looking." The too-loud laughter boomed again. The woman seemed to want to cause the most pain possible.

At least he hadn't stripped her himself. And possibly she could forget the part about him stealing looks at her. No . . . She couldn't. "I need a bath. And I need to scrub my teeth and I need to get back to the house. Can you point me in the right direction," she said as she tried to find her feet and her balance.

"Thaddeus said you would want all that, but said I wasn't to let you out of my sight. So, come with me, we can get to the baths if we hurry, and you can have your own clothes back. They're clean now, but you can't leave my house alone. The walk back to Bethsaida Julius is dangerous. Thaddeus said you were to stay with me until he came for you, and *that* is what you are going to do."

"Back to Beth— Where am I?"

"Capernaum, of course. He brought you on an ancient donkey."

"*Capernaum!* But—"

"No buts. Now come on, get up and put your cloak on and let's go to the baths."

"But what will the people I'm staying with think if I don't come home?"

"Probably the same thing they thought last night. Thaddeus will tell them something. Now, come. A hot soak will do you wonders. I know the steward at the doors and he'll let us into the women's quarters even if we are after hours." The huge woman waddled as she walked, and because she had no idea where she was, Magdalene followed. She had to hold the hem of the borrowed tunic off the ground to keep it from dragging on the dusty road.

It was dark, the stars a dry twinkle in the heavens. It would have been a pleasant walk if the earth hadn't been playing tricks with her. Most of the time it stayed where it belonged, but sometimes it heaved up and danced under her feet, sending her sprawling into the broad back in front of her. The woman seemed imperturbable however, and each time Magdalene regained her balance, they started out again. She looked for landmarks to prove she was no longer in Bethsaida Julius, and everything was indeed strange and foreign. Suddenly, the Roman baths were in front of her and she was inside. It was dark and she gripped the tunic worn by Thaddeus' friend. *Oh. That's right. Thaddeus has no friends.*

She was unceremoniously stripped and led into the hot room, one towel draped around her head and shoulders and one to sit on. There were others sitting and lounging on the benches in the steamy room, the uncertain light making them all strangers. Her keeper seemed to know them though.

"Hey, Angel, who's your friend? She's too skinny to make

you any money." There were guffaws.

"Good evening to you too, Rebecca," the voice boomed.

Magdalene jumped at the name. Rebecca. The name of her old friend in Magdala. *She was dead.* Suddenly Magdalene wanted to cry, and buried her face in the towel to hide her tears.

"What happened to that pretty little thing you had with you last time I saw you?"

"The pig learned everything I could teach her and then slipped out with my best customer and set up housekeeping with him. Before I ever got a coin out of all my training."

There were snickers around the room. "We tried to tell you."

"Yes, I remember how you tried to tell me," Angel answered dryly.

Magdalene leaned farther back against the walls and kept her head covered, creating a steamy atmosphere around her face. She breathed the aromatic mist, flavored with mint and hyssop, and actually *felt* her pores open. Sweat started a slow trickle down her body, draining the effects of the wine out with it. The talk around her continued. Languidly, she listened.

"That new rabbi brought us luck. My business has increased twofold in the last month."

"Yeah. The Rebbe and that wedding. I had to buy two new girls to handle it all. Don't know what I'll do with them when business slows down again. I'll have to sell them or marry them off. Some stinking farm boy will come to town and think he's rescuing a poor helpless virgin again. He won't think twice about where she got all that money when they make their 'getaway'."

"Poor little farm boy . . ." a voice drawled amid general laughter.

"Angel, you got any plans for handling this business?"

Magdalene was suddenly aware that the women who shared the late baths with her were *business women.* She almost choked with laughter. Angel of all names . . .

"Nope. Can't say I have. But I'm enjoying it right well enough."

"That a new girl you got there?"

"No. Just a friend of a friend."

"For training?"

"No."

For a moment there was silence except for the drip of water from the low ceiling, and Magdalene released her breath. She had been afraid that Angel would give her away. After a time, the talk started up again, but on a different subject. Magdalene relaxed under the towel. She owed the large woman thanks. This was . . . fun.

Later, after enjoying a long sweat, the woman lifted Magdalene up, and half-supported, half-dragged her into the cool-room. She soaked a while in the tepid pool and when the room was empty, scrubbed the oily scum from her body with a coarse brush and a pot of soap held out by her keeper. After a quick dip in the cold pool, fed by mountain streams, they dressed in silence and departed by a back way.

"Roman's ain't much, but at least they brought the baths."

Magdalene shivered in the night air at the mention of Romans.

Thaddeus

The next morning Thaddeus found her engaged in animated conversation with Angel. He was surprised see her so at ease with the corpulent prostitute. And so happy. Another woman would have withdrawn from a sinner with distaste, even to the act of sweeping aside her garments to avoid being contaminated. But the Magdalene sat at the table, eating with her, laughing at a bawdy joke, one hand on Angel's arm to support herself as she laughed.

He stood in the doorway unobserved for some moments and watched the easy rapport between the two women. The Magdalene continued to surprise him. Against his better judgment, he found himself admiring her. After all, women were supposed to maintain their chaste dignity at all times, and so far, this remarkable woman had kicked him in the groin, threatened him with a broom, gotten drunk—very drunk—and become friends with a prostitute. Also, there were rumors that she was engaged in commerce. There was nothing here to admire. But he did. For some obscure reason, she reminded him of Jesus. He too, seemed

to take the common man, even sinners, at face value, not shun-
ning them, but seeking them out. He ate with the dregs of society
and laughed with them. Even *touched* them.

He remembered once as a child he had, unaware, made
friends with the son of the tax collector at the city gate. They had
played together for weeks, two loners with everything in common,
until his parents heard of it and explained the facts to him. The
next day, though it hurt, he had not gone to meet his friend, and
had turned his face away when they chanced to meet later. It was
the proper thing to do, the holy thing to do. But it had been
wrong. Inexplicably, Thaddeus was ashamed of his parents, and of
himself. Seeing the women together, he knew that, had Magdalene
been in the same situation, she would have disobeyed and
remained friends with a sinner. And he knew that she would
remain friends with Angel, speaking with her on the street and
seeking her out as women do to talk and drink tea and eat small
cakes.

Magdalene saw him at the door and gestured him in. There
were dark circles under her eyes and her face appeared even more
gaunt than usual. But only a fool would have failed to see she was
happy. She patted the mat she sat on. "Thaddeus. Sit down. Angel
and I were talking about you. She said you know where her sister
lives in Jerusalem and asked me to take her a message, when we
go there, that is if you would show me the way. She insisted that I
not go alone into that part of town, though if her sister is as kind
as she is, I don't see why not. I might even stay with her if I'm
asked."

Thaddeus' mouth hung open, suspended on his greeting, as
he stared at the guileless face before him. Surely Angel had told
her that her sister lived in a brothel. The best house in the capitol,
and the best known. If the Magdalene went there she would be
classified as a . . . a . . .

His emotions must have shown clearly on his face because
both women burst out laughing again. "I win," said Angel triumphantly. "Pay up."

"Oh my. Oh, Thaddeus," she laughed. Magdalene passed her
a copper fished from the secret pocket of her tunic. "You should
see your face." And suddenly both women were peeling with

giggles again, Angel's bulk shaking with mirth, Magdalene rolling on the mat.

He sank to the floor beside them, his eyes going from one to the other. They had a bet as to what his reaction would be when asked to take a woman to a brothel! He thanked God it was a joke. And the Magdalene moved a step further away from his traditional views of womanhood. He shook his head wryly. Leaving her in a prostitute's home for two nights had backfired. He had sought to teach her a lesson, but was being taught one himself. He would have to remember in the future not to expect her to react like *normal* women. Magdalene would never be predictable.

The donkey ride to Simon's rented house with the Magdalene left him even more shaken than finding that the two women had become friends. She kept herself properly covered, shielding her shorn hair from the view of passersby, but once in the town gates of Bethsaida Julius, she insisted on going barefoot in the warm air, kicking up small puffs of street dust until her feet were dusty brown. And he had been forced to carry her boots. Several men cast amused grins his way and he swallowed curses all the way back to the Fisherman's. All in all, it had proved to be a most trying and informative day. He thought the day was finished, that it could hold no more surprises than it had. He was wrong.

The tumult reached them down the street before they even turned the corner. Angry voices rose, ringing cries of scripture and warning. Glancing at each other, they hurried their pace, passing enraged men. Thaddeus recognized them as the Master's followers; they carried their belongings in packs, satchels, or baskets. They were leaving. He and Magdalene broke into a run.

In the garden, surrounded by the house, three red-faced men gestured wildly, quoting scripture at the top of their lungs, shouting about unclean men and sinners and remaining pure and showing mercy and other things having no relation to the rest. Around the men a crowd had gathered, vocal but not very brave, staying out of arms' reach of the three main combatants. A man, a new disciple to the group, picked up his bag and pushed through the crowd, an expression of righteous indignation on his face. As he reached the small opening that served as a gate, someone stuck out a leg and sent the man sprawling.

Thaddeus heard Magdalene stifle an ill-thought giggle, trying to smother another. Following her gaze, he saw Jesus sitting in the sun looking rested, fit, and calm. Instead of being concerned over the tumult, he looked placid, as if he were about to fall asleep. Even as Thaddeus had the thought, Jesus' eyes closed and his head nodded to his chest. Magdalene, shaking with laughter, begged pardon of those nearest her, separating them with a small hand and vanished through the crowd and into the house. Seeing her go, Thaddeus sank to the ground, out of the way of stomping feet and listened to the discussion, if it could be called that.

Jesus, though unconcerned with the argument, was the cause of the uproar. Today he had gone beyond his usual rebellion, eating with a publican named Levi, but had also asked the man to join his disciples. And the man had accepted. Many of the men refused to associate with a traitor who had taxed his own people and given the money to the Roman government. For the first time, the group was thinning. Watching Jesus nod, Thaddeus realized that the Rebbe had done it deliberately, knowing what the outcome would be. It had not been an ill-planned gesture, but a purposeful act executed with flourish. He wished he had been there to see it.

Jesus opened his eyes, met Thaddeus' gaze across the plot of ground, almost as if he knew what Thaddeus had just deduced. He smiled and slowly stood. He didn't shout, yet his voice boomed over the heads of the arguing men, "Any who are no longer my disciples may leave now and return to your homes. In two weeks Levi, Thaddeus, and Simon the Zealot will travel with me to Nain, and throughout Galilee." His feet were wide, rooted in the earth. "Simon, come. With all these *good* men leaving it should be simple to make a place for Levi in our group."

A dozen men took up their bags and left. One lifted the bottoms of his feet to the master, shaking the sand from his shoes in insult. Jesus made no indication that he saw the slur.

Thaddeus moved to the house to meet the publican, curious what qualities about the one man made him worth the loss of many *good* men. The word *good* rang inside his head as it had around the courtyard when Jesus said it.

Chapter Ten

Aemoa

The pain had begun as a dull ache in her lower back and radiated to her legs so that walking was an ungainly affair, as if she had heavy stones tied to her hips. It was a sure sign that her womanly flow was to start before the day was over, but until it did there was work to do.

Though several of the men had left, it had not taken long for others to take their places. Already she had prepared bread for baking, milked the goats and been to the well for enough water to last through breakfast. She heaved a sigh and glanced up at the gray sky; the sun should be up soon. Aemoa moved silently through the house on calloused feet, pausing once to massage her back.

She had hoped to never be inconvenienced by womanly flows again, but after a several month hiatus they were back with a vengeance. The only good thing was that her work would be curtailed by prohibition of law while her discomfort was upon her. And she would be billeted alone, out back in a small hut set aside for that purpose. She could use the rest. The other women were still asleep but would be glad to know that their morning work was all but done.

Stooping, she coaxed the flames alight in the small brazier she had brought from Nazareth. From a shallow crock filled with small cloth bags, she took out dried painkilling herbs for brewing. The medicine would make her sleep, but would also ease the cramps. She could tell this was going to be a bad one. While the tea was steeping, she gathered the mending into a basket and placed it near her loom, with a lamp, thread, and a basket of cloth scraps. There was an amazing amount of ruined and damaged clothing. The enforced inactivity during her menstrual would be put to good use and boredom could be held at bay with mending.

Padding back to the brazier, she bumped a stool in the darkness and roused one of the sleeping women who mumbled as she passed. She could almost make out the traditional words of greeting the day. The Magdalene joined her at the glowing clay pot, resting her head against the wall and stifling a yawn. "It's too early to be up running around the house," she mumbled. "Come back to bed."

"Humph. I've been up for hours while you snored." She nodded to a cloth-covered bowl. "The bread is ready to be baked and the water is drawn. I milked the goats, and got a bruised shin from your favorite for my troubles."

"Not *my* favorite. She hates me almost as much as she does the Iscariot, although she hasn't tried to gore me with her horns. Why are you up so early?"

"Couldn't sleep. My flows will start today. I hadn't had them in so long I thought they were stopped for good." She sighed. "At least I brought my blood rags with me. And speaking of which, you haven't had a flow since we found you. With your health improved, you may."

Magdalene's shoulders stiffened, and her voice was terse. "I think not."

"Why?" Only silence answered her. She looked at the woman in the uncertain light as complex emotions sparred on her face.

"I don't know. But I won't. Don't stare at me," she snapped. "I'll wash and then start the bread baking. Drink your tea."

Alone again, Mary rocked back on her haunches and considered the Magdalene's response. There had been revulsion on her face and, fear. Any mention of the past always brought fear. But it was different this time. Perhaps the poor child was starting to remember. Rising, she gathered up her pallet and began carrying things to her hut behind the house, against the wall that enclosed the back of the property. As she worked, she sipped the bitter brew.

The tea was strong and she slept through the morning, waking late in the afternoon to a muggy heat and a feeling of tension in the air. It was so intense she could almost *hear* it through the lingering effects of the drug. She turned her head on her pillow and stared through the palm fronds of her hut to see five men standing in the small yard. The sight held her still. Even had there been no heat to drive people to the coolness of the roof, these men would have surprised her. They were not the usual sort of followers her son attracted.

One, who had a quill tucked behind his ear, secured into his hair, was a scribe, two others were Pharisees, and the rest were Jesus' new students. They clearly thought themselves to be alone, though they still murmured.

". . . get back to Jerusalem with this, something will be done. No man who continually breaks the Sabbath can expect to be allowed access to synagogue or Temple. Jesus and his entire group of 'disciples' . . . *Disciples*," one Pharisee repeated scornfully. "As if the man had his own school in Jerusalem, instead of a group of bumbling illiterates." He controlled his scorn, his stubby fingers rubbing together viciously, mouth pressed tight.

"This time he went too far," one of the students said.

"What do you mean *this* time? He went too far when he *forgave sins* in the Temple. He went too far when he *healed* on the Sabbath. He went too far when he *harvested* on the Sabbath outside of Jerusalem. We would have taken him there and then but the people think he is a great prophet. The reincarnation of Elijah." He snorted, sounding just like a Gentile's pig. Sweat had stained the rich fabric of his robe in long streaks. "I've sent word to my friends about this incident. All we have to do is keep him here for a few days more and then we can take him and escape this place of pestilence for Jerusalem. We know his activities, and now we know the layout of his sleeping quarters, such as they are. We will take him here in the night."

"Pestilence," he muttered, glancing around the small yard. Mary froze, scarcely daring to breathe in the sweltering air. The man was one of the Jerusalem powerful, dressed in an ornate robe. And he was talking about taking her son in the night. "It takes Pharisaical training to deal with the Law."

The other Pharisee, a small, balding man, barked with

laughter. "I had thought the man intelligent, but he fell into our hands with no prompting. It was the error of a child, not—"

"He *is* a child," growled the sweating man. "A child playing at men's games, making mockery with intrigue and plots. The man is an imbecile to think he can break Sabbath without consequences. The incident with the wheat was damning enough, but this . . . this is how we stop him. All it took was a strategically placed, low-born cripple with a withered hand as bait."

The sweating man was angry, his tone tinged with a barely subdued violence as if he had been insulted and— Oh. She had warned Jesus of his quick tongue. Had said a thousand times, *Beware of the leaders. Don't let their questions make you hasty of speech. Don't taunt them with your knowledge and understanding of the scriptures. Someday, someone will trap you into a corner with words and then you will be in trouble with the powerful.* But it hadn't taken words. Only his own compassion.

"You say we have him, but could he have us? Could he be planning some—"

"Don't be a fool. This man isn't intelligent enough to set a trap for a hare, let alone set one for *me*. And as for his power, it is that of the Evil One, sent to lead the people from the truth of the Law. He has no true power."

"No," the scribe said, his tone sly. "He only healed a withered hand before our eyes. A withered hand we had all inspected. The withered hand of a trap set by you. Nor is he wise. Yet, he backed you out on a point of Law so far you became silent. You, Ishmeil, hand picked by the Sanhedrin for your knowledge of scripture and debate to keep an eye on this upstart. And the upstart defeated you with one quote. One."

In an instant, the Pharisee had the scribe by the throat, holding his slight frame, feet kicking, a hand's breadth from the ground. "You ever say that again and I'll cut out your tongue, you spawn of pigs offal." The little man's face mottled blue, eyes bulging from their sockets. "You squeak one syllable of it and I'll see to it that your 'proclivities' reach the ears of the head of your house. You wouldn't remain heir for long if your father heard of your preference for Greek boys. *Do you understand?*" He shook the little man.

The other Pharisee said, "Fight another time. We have work to do, and stopping here to talk isn't wise. This place gives me a bad feeling." He scanned the enclosed space and Mary shrank again into the shadows. "We have plans to make and men to hire, tougher men than our two colleagues," he said, nodding to the disciples.

"Anything for a fair price," grinned one of her son's followers. The men slipped out through the gate into the narrow alley, leaving the small area silent and smoldering with their words.

It was late that evening before Jesus and his disciples returned. They had been at sea and smelled of fish and salt and sweat. They washed in the back courtyard, and she turned her head away from the sight, giving them privacy. She couldn't help with food preparation, nor sleep in the house, nor join in the meal, but, sitting in the shadows with the baskets of mending, she heard everything they said while bathing, and afterward, through the open windows. The men spoke of nothing out of the ordinary, seeming to be intent on discussing aspects of the day's teachings and scripture. She writhed at the delay in getting to Jesus. She didn't think the Pharisees would come tonight, their plans were too uncertain, but they *would* come back, of that she was sure. And if Jesus was still here . . .

The night dragged on as she waited for her son to come near the small hut, but he seemed determined to thwart her. Never glancing her way, he didn't even go to the wall the men used to relieve themselves. Long after moonrise, he rose and walked to the door, carrying a small jar of oil for her lamp. He leaned against the courtyard wall and clasped his hands. "I know, Aemoa."

"What do you know?"

"I know about the Pharisees' plan."

"But how? I only just—"

"The Zealot was on the roof and heard them. He's been watching our newest disciples, and knew they were planning something. And because you were in the menstrual hut, you were here when the Pharisees came. It's time we moved on." She could see his teeth gleaming in the dark, grinning like a mischievous boy.

He finished with, "Are you able to travel? Would you like to go to Nain after the Sabbath?"

She sighed, feeling the tension of the long day drain away. "You don't think I would be left behind, do you?"

"I thought we would leave the first day of the week," he said softly.

"I can be purified by then."

Magdalene

Exhausted, she fell into her bedroll that first night of travel, expecting to be asleep before she hit. It was a surprise to find herself wide awake, with a mind too filled with images and scenes and snatches of conversation to rest. It had been abrupt, the order to travel, giving the women only four days to prepare, and one of those was the Sabbath with its enforced inactivity. Now, without enough time to assimilate it all, she was on the road, traveling with more than fifty people, eating and sleeping this first night in the open. She pulled her mantle over her ears to protect her skin from buzzing insects and snuggled deeper in the bedroll.

They had left Bethsaida Julius, singing and laughing. She had been surprised to see two Pharisees in the crowd that followed them to the city gate, one gesticulating and shouting into the ear of the hearty fisherman who laughed and slapped the smaller man on the back with such force that he quickly escaped and went back to his companion. There were vendors and beggars and dyers and she even thought she saw Angel before the crowd carried her past the colorful knot of women gossiping near the well. A group of men sang as they passed through the gates, and her fingers had ached for her well-packed lyre to play.

She kept her shorn head covered until they were well out of town, dropping her mantle only when her breath, hot under the wool, steamed her face with sweat. No one among the travelers noticed her shame any longer. She had begun to fade into the background like another willow along the shore they followed.

It was glorious to be strong again, her muscles firm and supple from all the weeks of walking about the countryside, her skin burnished from the sun to a golden bronze. Carefree, she sang and joked and scavenged for food with the other women. It was everything she had thought it would be when the Rebbe first proposed traveling to her, though there were many more in their retinue than she had expected. And she had never anticipated that the crowds would follow them around the Sea of Galilee, south toward the Roman road, but they had, for hours. The best part of the day were the last hours, when the women bustled to cook and feed the men who argued in small groups around the campfires about the exploits of David and Saul. She listened to their arguments as she served, stepping between sprawled legs, only a woman, a shadow with ears. After the meal, while the women washed the bowls and serving platters in the sea, the men gathered around the Rebbe with their conclusions and thoughts, and he taught them with simple words the meaning of the stories, his voice carrying to the silent workers sloshing in the shallow water. Magdalene had discerned the truth of the stories, and hid secret smiles in the darkness.

The men's conversation continued into the night, though many of them fell asleep where they lay, until only the most faithful twelve still plied the Rebbe with questions. She fell asleep to the gentle drone of the Rebbe's voice.

The second day dawned a brilliant red over the eastern hills—she knew because she was kicked awake long before the sun even thought to rise. Aemoa, purified after her stay in the menstrual hut, was already hard at work kneading dough in a shallow bowl when she emerged from her private ablutions. Rolling up her sleeves, Magdalene joined in at the task. Her shoulders ached with the roll and scrape, the two women dusty with flour in the faint light. Feeding fifty people was a major undertaking, and she was secretly delighted they would be in a village most nights, hopefully the guests of the town, each household sheltering and feeding a few men. This would mean less time together as a group, but it would also be less work.

By dawn's light, the bread was baked, oats had been cooked into porridge, and the women began the unpleasant job of waking the snorers. There were grumbles and bleary eyes from most, but surprisingly, from the Twelve who stayed up the latest, there were only smiles and yawns. Jesus was nowhere to be seen.

Thaddeus tugged at her skirt as she served him porridge for breaking the fast and was the only one who remembered a sheepish thank you, his voice gravely with sleep. She was warming to the womanizer, the sort of man she would have once avoided. Of course, all males were the sort she would have avoided in her previous life.

The next three weeks showed her a new and different world. A world where she had a place of purpose, where she was allowed to listen and even to speak when the men talked about the Law and God's intent. And she discovered that she loved to travel.

Chapter Eleven

Magdalene

It was the end of their fourth week on the road and the group was going home. Trailing behind them, looking for wild onions to season the night's stew, she had just caught up. Magdalene was tired, and glad that they would be in a town, not camping in the open this last night on the road. She could see Jesus ahead in the center of a milling cluster at the crossroads of the main street leading into a small village, the arched gate ahead. Dust motes swirled in the dry air, churning the scene before her into a hazy out-of-focus vision, like a dream on waking.

There were hundreds of people laughing, gesturing, jostling, crying out to him as they tried to get closer. Closer to Jesus. He was the center of attention for the whole town, sure and graceful even among the press of swaying bodies. He was holding a babe, one hand supporting the infant's head, the other its body, a familiar sight. He offered a blessing on the child, his voice indistinct in the rabble.

At the edges of the crowd, a disturbance ensued—a man on a horse. Magdalene faltered to a stop, pushed back loose strands of hair, tugging her mantle lower over her face. *Oh Yahweh, don't let it be real. Please.* But it was real. The man was real. The Roman soldier of nightmares.

Out of the bloody clutching hands of darkness he rode, pushing through the crowd, arrogant in his supremacy, his power. He swung down from his horse. A servant who had been running alongside him took the reins. Magdalene's throat closed in a spasm of terror. The Centurion touched Jesus. *Touched him!* And Jesus, placing the infant back in its wide-eyed mother's arms turned and smiled at the beast. Her breath came hot and fast.

She raced to the protection of the city wall, reaching out to Jesus, as if he might feel her warning over the distance. But she couldn't stop what was about to happen. The crowd thinned rapidly, the cowed populace retreating into the alleys and doorways. The Twelve, led by the Fisherman, his massive arms out to his side, gathered silently at Jesus' back, a semi-circle of power. The Fisherman reached beneath his cloak and gripped something. Metal caught the light, steel, a sharpened blade. A Maintz Gladius. A Roman short-sword. Where had he gotten such a thing? It was treasonous to own one. The Roman spoke, his words lost beneath the buzzing in her ears.

The sun glinted darkly off the fine hair on Jesus' arms. The dust settled in his beard. The Twelve edged closer, forming a tighter knot. The Fisherman half-drew the sword. It shimmered on his tunic. Her knees went weak and a dull pain grew heavy in her chest. She knew that sword. She remembered it. Memories slid over her, oily and pungent as rotted meat. *Romans* . . . She had stumbled over the sword when she found her family, dead and hanging from a tree, and dead in the brush, cast aside as if worthless. It was the Roman sword the murderers had left behind.

The Centurion standing beside Jesus was dressed in breast-plate and robe, a sword belted at his side. His servant, a youth with no armor or weapon, tied his sweating horse to a scrub nearby. Magdalene darted a look around; the Roman had brought none of his soldiers. Would the Twelve be enough? Her body shook as the soft rumbles of their speech drifted on the air.

The Centurion *bowed* to Jesus. Magdalene's eyes widened, her vision spiraling down to a narrow tunnel. He *knelt* and kissed the hem of Jesus' robe. Then, moving slowly as though his bones pained him, he gathered up the reins and led his lathered horse away. A soft clopping echoed on the dried, mud-brick walls. The servant followed.

She didn't hear the hoarse sob that tore from her throat. Nor did she feel the rough brick scrape against her fingers as she steadied herself. It was over. Jesus was safe. The Rebbe moved on into the town, the crowds following. Quickly, they were gone, leaving her outside the gates.

A boy, not yet ten, raced past her shouting the news to the

town. "Jesus of Nazareth healed the Centurion's servant. He healed him. And Jesus wasn't even there. The servant of the Centurion lay miles away in Capernaum! Jesus healed him. I heard it all. He healed him. Jesus healed a *Roman!*"

Magdalene's world quivered violently. No. *It was a lie. He wouldn't. No. NO!*

The people raced into the town, searching for Jesus, straining to get closer to the Rebbe. Jesus the Rebbe. Jesus the Wonderful. Jesus *the Traitor. The traitor.* Bile rose in her throat and she swallowed it back, sinking slowly against the brick wall.

When her body was again her own, she crept along the road, away from the gate, into the countryside. She took shelter in a copse of palm trees outside of town, sitting on a stone in the foliage, her knees drawn up to her chin, her arms holding her legs. Rocking, she stared into the distance, tears coursing down her face. Remembering. Remembering Romans. Remembering *everything.*

Dusk fell. The moon rose full and glowing, filtering between the leaves and patterning the ground with its brilliance. Her thirst grew. Her tears ceased to fall. The night was cool, and insects swarmed her. She covered her face with her mantle. Grieving over Jesus. *The Traitor.*

The Zealot

The long breath blew out of him in a tight line, almost whistling with its pressure. The Roman had gone, but his heart would take days to return to normal. The power old Reuven called *warrior's energy* pounded in his temples and a cold sweat beaded his brow as he fought for control, the control to remain calm and yet tend to his duties. He slipped away from the group of disciples and returning townspeople, located a new follower and sent him to see that the Roman did indeed return to his house in Capernaum, and did have a servant. If this was a trap they would know quickly. His heart constricted.

The Zealot had more peace in his life, more delight in living now than at any other time in his past. Jesus had swept aside the barriers, had opened his heart and soul, had learned his deepest secrets, fears, hates, and loved him regardless. He remembered the time on the mountain, the air filled with the damp scent of flowers, their bellies full and thirst sated as they sprawled on the sun-heated earth and talked. The Rebbe told them then how the meek would inherit the earth. How there was room for peace, joy, all the gentler emotions in life. Such promises.

It had given him a reason to live. He wasn't about to lose all that now. He would know ahead of time if the Centurion had set a trap, and warn Jesus away. But if it was a trap, how? How could a healing be used against the Rebbe?

One boy went to follow the Centurion, another, he sent to scout the periphery of the town for more Romans, still others went to the synagogue to see if Jerusalem Pharisees were here, and others he sent to the baths. He had done all he could except remain watchful and close to Jesus. Uneasy, he slipped back to Jesus' side, his eyes alert. He felt the Rebbe's eyes on him but refused to acknowledge him. He might see reproach there, or amusement. He could only do so much, but he would not be deterred from at least that. As he scanned the crowd, he saw the Magdalene pull herself unsteadily to her feet and lurch away. She looked drunk. And then he realized. *The Roman.*

He remembered her fear and wanted desperately to go to her and offer what comfort he could, but at that moment, the Rebbe turned with a throng of people down the street. Casting back his head, he noted the direction of her progress, that she seemed safe enough and turned his concentration back to Jesus. It was good that he did, for Jesus thrust a squalling infant into his hands and told him to find its mother. He almost dropped the child who screamed even louder at being held by his shoulders. For the rest of the afternoon he was plied with children, errands, chores, miscellaneous trifles and once he heard the Rebbe's murmur, "Simon the warrior? Or Simon the nanny?" It was ludicrous. But he was happy, and the work kept his mind off the fears of Romans and traps.

Much later, as the last of the followers struggled in and the group settled down to eat in the public area provided for travelers, he relaxed. But no sooner had he done so than the boy he had sent to follow the Centurion raced to the group, his lungs raspy, his body flinging sweat. *I was right. It was a trap. The Rebbe is in danger.* Scenes of cold steel and blood whipped through him. Pushing through the disciples, he knelt at the boy's side and gave him a cup of cool water.

"It's true," the young man gasped. The disciples and the women went silent. "The servant was healed. We were on the road on the far side of town, and the Centurion was met by, it must have been a dozen soldiers on foot. They came to tell him that the servant was well. He hadn't needed to go to find Jesus after all."

Jesus smiled, watching the events play out.

"But then the Centurion asked them when the healing took place and it was the same hour as they spoke—Jesus and the Centurion." The boy's voice went breathy and he drank the water, handing the cup to a passing woman. "You healed him, Rabboni," he said to Jesus. "You really healed him. Without even touching him. They say he left his pallet and walked on his own." The boy drank a second cup and was taken by a fit of shivering. "Without even touching him."

Simon was pushed away from the center of the group by the Rebbe's mother, who wrapped the sweating, overheated boy in a cloth. He stared into the master's eyes.

"Are you relieved, Simon? I am safe and all your planning has been for naught. Did you think I did not know the nature of the Centurion's heart? That he asked with need and humility? I am not a babe, Simon, like the children I have given you today." The Rebbe's warm eyes held Simon's. "But thank you, my Zealot." He smiled wide, teeth white against his beard.

Simon began to shake, a cold sweat drying slowly on his skin. It had been so close. Or seemed to be. Perhaps he was a fool to be so protective of the healer. The people loved him, followed after him, composed new songs to his honor, placed his name in the old songs of praise, and those who didn't love him slunk away, muttering. But that was the fear. Men who were discontent and frightened always seemed to find one another and he had seen them in small groups on the street corners and fringes of the crowd whispering.

The Pharisees and the Sadducees were watching, listening, jealous of the Rebbe's popularity, and the Sanhedrin also. They were jealous of the Baptist as well, and because of that they had done nothing to see him set free from his prison cell, though they had the power. There were too many political factors at work. He blew out a breath into the night and sat against the nearby wall, pulling his blanket over his head to think. Surprisingly, sleep took him immediately.

A soft step near his ear roused him, his warrior's training bringing him instantly awake. The moon had moved to its height, shining clear and pure in the empty sky, blocked by Thaddeus' head as he stooped over him. "Simon, are you awake?" He swiveled to a sitting position, stretching. "Have you seen the Magdalene?" Alert, his mind uncluttered by dreams, he remembered the crossroads and her unsteady departure. "She's not here, Simon. Aemoa hasn't seen her all day and she didn't claim her pallet tonight. Do you know if she was to stay as a guest somewhere?"

"No. She isn't a guest. When was the last time anyone saw her?" His mind worked furiously covering all the possibilities, yet kept returning to only one.

"Before the noon meal, or just after. The Fisherman saw her then, but that was before we entered the town. No one has seen her since. The Rebbe was asking about her. I'm worried."

Thaddeus moved, allowing a shaft of moonlight to curve past him. From where he sat, Simon could see the city gate, locked against thieves. "She ran away." It sounded foolish even to his own ears. But Thaddeus said nothing. "I saw her in the crossroads, after the Centurion."

Light dawned in the other's eyes. "The Roman." He captured Simon's shoulder in a viselike grip, fingers digging into the soft flesh at the jointure of the socket. "You've got to find her, Simon. She's all alone. She's been gone for hours."

He nodded and left, hearing the wooden beam fall across the door behind him, his bare feet padding softly on the packed ground. Close to the city gate, he leaped to the flat of a wall and raced up, climbing to the roof. Carefully, so he didn't fall through into the house below, he crossed to the far side and lowered himself off and out of the city. At a fast trot, he headed to the spot he last saw her and from there away from town. He didn't bother to look for prints this close to town.

Three miles later, after checking half a dozen likely places, he saw a familiar footprint in the softer earth beside a fork in the path. She had the strange heel on her sandals used by the cobblers in Magdala. She had still been moving drunkenly, and there was evidence of a fall. Her state of mind must have been terrible. But why? She had seen Romans before. The most she had ever done was slip into a side street, tighten her mantle over her face and continue on by another way. Her sandals left the faint path and moved unsteadily toward a copse of trees. He angled to follow.

He knew he had found her by the soft, almost animal-like keening and he paused to allow his eyes to adjust to the deeper darkness under the palms. Slowly, she appeared, first her pale skin, and then her robe. She sat on a stone, her arms wrapped around her curled legs, hugging herself as she rocked, back and forward. Though he stood a distance away, he could see the tears on her face and occasionally, along with the strange keening, he heard a sob.

Now that he had found her he was uncertain what to do. He watched for some moments the childlike rocking, uneasiness growing in his breast. He had seen mourners rock like that, but there was something wrong with that analogy. She rocked more slowly than a mourner. It reminded him more of a woman he had seen on the outskirts of a village as a boy. He had come upon her one day quite by surprise, and paused to watch. He had recognized her after a time as the wife of a local laborer. She had been sent out of the town and into the hills, outcast by the village. She had been possessed. Like the Magdalene, she had hugged herself and rocked, her voice a low moan.

He found himself running back to the city with tiring speed, the wind burning in his lungs, his legs pounding. He reached the city with an aching side, his breath heavy, knowing he had run in fear. He could handle almost anything except the possessed.

Getting into a gated city at night was not nearly so easy as getting out. He was standing in the shadows, winded, his breath hot, when he saw the Rebbe drop from a rooftop, wearing sandals and carrying his staff. The Rebbe walked toward him.

"Take me to her."

Wordlessly, Simon turned and led the way back out of town, back to the copse of trees. The Rebbe asked no questions and Simon was glad. He knew what it meant to see the young woman rocking in the shadows. She would have to be sent away from the group, into the hills, or she would contaminate them all, every man, woman, and child. He had heard the tale of Jesus healing her and casting out her demons. But she had been re-inhabited by the unclean spirits. There was no cure.

He shivered in the night air, remembering the rest of his childhood scene. The crazy woman had turned her gaze to him, and he had seen the emptiness of her soul mirrored there. Through the pinpoints of her constricted pupils, he had seen such torment, such pain. And then she had changed. One moment her eyes had been dead and the next they were alive with intense emotion. Her demon had launched her at him, furious, grappling with him on the grass. Astonished, he tasted dirt as he rolled with her momentum, her hands reaching for his throat. Had she not slipped, he would have died there. He was sure of it. As it was, he had returned home that night with aching muscles and strained limbs. And now the Magdalene was rocking.

They entered the trees together. He was surprised at how silent the Rebbe walked. Almost like a warrior.

Magdalene

Settling about her shoulders, tangled like a ripped bridal veil, loneliness lay against her skin. The air was heavy with the scent of isolation and grief, damp and cloying. Her grief seemed to rustle with the movement of her ribs as she sobbed. Her chest rose and fell in painful attempts to draw in more air than her lungs could hold and then to expel, in a tearing ragged breath more than they had contained. The pain pierced her sluggishly beating heart, draining down into her like water into a chasm. She was drowning in the solitude and the emptiness and there was no room for more.

She had tried to resist the truth. Tried to believe that he had lied to the Roman, only pretending to heal the servant in Capernaum. It would have been an easy lie. But she knew he hadn't lied. He had healed the Roman's servant. He had healed the enemy.

She rocked, searching for comfort.

"Mary."

She stiffened, tears gleaming in the moon's radiance, filtering through the trees. *He always walks so softly. Just appearing, like a spirit.* And she shivered though it was warm.

"Mary." Softly. So softly. It was a command, a plea, a tender calling all at once.

She turned. Tears still flowed from her eyes, her throat was raw and the metallic taste of blood coated her tongue. She trembled, as haltingly, she whispered, "Why? Why a Roman?"

The night breeze ruffled his beard and hair. He had bathed, for the scent was clean in the moonlight, but his eyes were pools of blackness. Silence was taut between them. Her tears dried stiff on her skin as his eyes studied her. It seemed as if the entire night passed while she waited, but perhaps it was only moments. Time seemed immaterial in the darkness, fleeting and insubstantial. Eternal.

"Mary. If I was bleeding," he took a breath and his tone deepened, anguish filling it, "in a dangerous place, what would you do?"

Danger. She knew instinctively that this question was vital to him, and that it had many more meanings than appeared on the surface of the words. *Danger.* It could only mean Romans. Dangerous to her? And her mind saw a misty place, swimming in blood. Men with swords and shields, pikes and helmets. Romans. She shivered. Yes. *That is danger.* Slowly she focused again on the serene eyes before her, and moistened her lips with her tongue. This was a friend who asked this of her. *Romans.* Did he even begin to know their threat, their vile sickness?

He had helped one of them. *Traitor,* her mind whispered. But perhaps there was a reason. Perhaps he had healed for a purpose.

"Mary?"

A scene flooded into her. A bloody tree with her husband hanging from it, a Roman battle sword at his feet. Birds of carrion calling. She had forgotten the birds that had already come by the time she found him. And the flash of red in the brush. Her son. He had been there, in the brush. Hidden. Abused and beaten and . . . she took a shuddering breath . . . raped by the soldiers. She remembered. She had forgotten, and now she remembered. *Why did I have to remember, oh God? Why?*

"*Mary?*" His voice so gentle.

His questions. About Romans. She could run from the Romans. But if Jesus were hurt. . . She moistened her lips again. "I would . . . gather fresh linens, herbs. The ones the Egyptians use. I would go into the bloody place and dress your wounds . . ." Falteringly, she added, "I would not run."

His eyes were sad, melancholy, and his face in the half light was fearful. "And if they would not let you help me, if they made you watch as I . . . as I . . ."

"I would love you with my eyes," she whispered. "I would sustain you with my strength. And I would not leave you. I would not leave you with them. Ever."

He exhaled, relaxing, and his warm breath touched her cheek. With his fingertips, he brushed the side of her face, wincing at the rough traces of her tears. "What would the Fisherman have said to that question?"

All unexpected, she chuckled, and the salt cracked at the corners of her mouth and eyes. Her tension drained away, leaving her almost relaxed. Dear, impetuous Simon the Fisherman. "He would have attacked them with a weapon, or sworn to gather an army and rescue you, destroying all those who would harm you."

Her eyes locked with his and her laughter vanished at the look that possessed his features. "I have need of you, Mary. You belong here, in this time, with me. You are the best part of why I am here. Please don't go. Please trust me. Please."

Taken back by his intensity, she faltered. Hesitantly, she reached out and took his hand, warm and calloused, scented by the soap he had washed with, and held it to her face. "I will never leave you," she said, her voice cracking. She swallowed, her throat dry and painful. "Not even when you are in the place of danger."

Strange. She had meant to say *if you are in a place of danger.*

His eyes held hers a moment longer, before he pulled her to her feet. Silently, her hand enveloped his larger, calloused one, she let him lead her back along the trail into the small village. For reasons she never questioned, the gates opened to them, closing silently behind them.

The Zealot

In silence, the Zealot watched the tender exchange, and something cold inside broke away. He felt weightless, as though he floated in still water. As he watched, the two moved back toward the tiny village, leaving him in the shadows.

Chapter Twelve

Magdalene

The Days of Awe—the High Holy Days—were over. Past was the Day of Affliction with its five abstentions—no eating, no drinking, no physical relations between man and woman, no bathing or anointing one's body with oils, and no wearing leather shoes. Past also was the Day of Atonement. The High Priest had entered into the Holy of Holies, the Place of the Presence, the dread silent *Place*, to seek forgiveness for himself, for the priesthood, for the whole of Israel. There had been no mishap during the ceremony, and word had spread through Jerusalem and into the countryside that the Lord had forgiven the Israelites their transgressions of Law. They were clean again. The ten days of repentance were over. All angers, all afflictions, all feuds were put aside. All injuries, personal and business, were forgotten.

Now, in the seventh month, on the fifteenth of Tishri, in the light of the full moon of the vernal equinox, it was time for the Festival of Sukos. The time of thanksgiving and the time of remembrance. On the roof or out back of every home in the nation was a suko. A hut symbolic of forty years of desert wanderings. The Law of Moses required that for seven days and seven nights all Jews must live in huts partially roofed by green boughs, palm branches, or reeds, through which moon and stars might glint.

Within some sukos there was room for tables, chairs, sleeping mats, and the entire hut was decorated with harvest produce. Food was tied to the bough walls in bright bunches: herbs, vegetables, and even late fruits. Whole huts seemed edible. Here, families would feast, sing, visit, and sleep. The Festival was a time of frolicking and joy.

They had been in Capernaum for two months. And it was glorious to have a place to call home. Magdalene had used some of her profits to rent a small, furnished house. Its two rooms were plastered with limestone; in one was a built-up bed platform, her cedar trunk, and a chair; in the other room was a lovely low table and several three-legged stools, two rich rugs woven in the Persian manner, and all the cooking utensils she would need. Already the walls were hung with the first shipment of things sent from Nazareth and she expected more soon. Jesus had fabricated some of the ingenious window and door casements for her home similar to the ones in Nazareth and was to install them before they traveled again. And it was all hers. It was the only thing she ever had that was her own. Hers alone.

Standing in the center of the larger room she turned slowly, her arms outstretched. "Jason. Look at me. Would you ever think your foolish wife would do so well for herself? I have my own home, Jason. I wish you could see it."

She didn't notice that she invited him to *see* it, not live in it. It never occurred to her that she enjoyed living alone more than she had ever liked living with Jason. Such thoughts were treacherous. But it was so. She woke each day with joy and expectation, an overflowing excitement. She cooked for the disciples that slept on her upper floor, washed for them, cleaned her small home, listened to the Rebbe speak, talked with her neighbors, walked about Capernaum, handled her investments through her scribe-manager, and slept the sleep of the exhausted. It was wonderful. She was alive with living. All those that traveled with the Rebbe felt the same. She could see it in their faces, hear it in their voices. It was inescapable.

And now it was the festival. The Festival of Sukos!

The suko on Magdalene's upper floor was large, to accom-modate the twenty or so young men who slept there. Being a widow, and wealthy, she was considered above reproach and viewed as a matronly mother to the younger men. The older followers were stationed at the family home of the Fisherman, a shouting distance away. Lazarus and his sisters, Mary and Martha, had rented a house as well, and they were all close enough to visit and celebrate together.

She surveyed her home again, hopeful that she had everything she needed for feeding her guests. Yet, no matter how prepared she felt, she always ran out of something. At least there were fast runners in the group of young men who could be sent to the house of friends or to market for necessities. Excitement tingled through her and she couldn't help the wide smile that creased her face. *Sukos.*

Running to the back of the house where her own, small, private suko was constructed, she stopped and retied a sheaf of wheat at its door, then entered, stooping low beneath the short entrance. It was the best suko she ever had, the walls expertly made of palm wood tied tight with twine. She need not fear the wind tearing it down for even the foundation was well secured.

Jesus was an excellent carpenter. He had constructed a set of movable shelves to go into the suko, to hold the diverse tools and utensils she would need to cook for so many men. She crossed over to it and once again scanned it to see if anything was missing, but the small space was crammed full and if she had forgotten anything, it wouldn't have fit anyway.

She checked the wine in its casks; there was more than enough, provided no young man decided to prove his manhood by seeing if he could drink it all. She touched a cask. It was good wine and it was from her own vineyard. Her partner had decided to take a great load to Jerusalem to sell before the High Holy days and for Sukos. When he returned he had promised her a substantial profit. He had better be right because her purse of ready-to-hand coin was getting low, and she would need money when the group traveled again.

She sat, curling her legs onto a stool. No one had ever demanded that she provide for the group while on the road. No one if she discounted the Judean, the one called Iscariot, and she always discounted him. But she had taken it upon herself and found she enjoyed buying for the group's meals and clothing while they traveled. Someone stepped through the doorway, his shadow falling over her.

"My, my, my. Don't we look domestic?"

"One of us does," she said grinning. "The other one looks like a handsome womanizer."

"Oh, praise be. She noticed I was handsome. Does that mean I have a chance with the lovely maid? My heart leaps with joy."

She cocked her head at Thaddeus. He made a pretty picture standing there with his hands clasped in an attitude of silly delight. She wondered . . .

"I am no maid," she said, her voice deliberately wistful, managing not to grin, "but what would you do if I said yes?"

"I would bring you the sweetest flowers, the best, finest gold jewelry in the land, the most expensive perfumed oils, the—"

"Yes."

"Wh— What?"

"Yes.

His eyes and mouth gaped. He took a breath, like a fish thrown upon the shore gasping; he looked more fearful than delighted. Laughter burst from her and after a moment he nodded wryly. Their relationship had been established in a hurry, set and sealed and unchanging, filled with practical jokes, humor, and the friendly passes which she always avoided. But sometimes she still took him unawares for a moment. She was a friend, the rare female he didn't try to seduce, and Magdalene knew that he had come to depend on her for that friendship. "I brought you fresh autumn flowers for the Festival." He held out his hand, presenting the blossoms, only partially wilted, as though recently picked.

"Hmmm. Didn't Angel have some of this growing in her yard?" she said, touching one of the blooms. "And this. And—"

"All right. All right. So they're from Angel," he said. "But *I* brought them to you."

"Well, thank Angel for me and thank you also. I only wish I could thank her for myself, but since she won't allow me to visit."

"She's only guarding your reputation."

They had been over this ground before. She knew it was useless to convince either one of them, yet she still felt the unreasoning anger at being denied a friend so unusual and informative. But it wasn't worth the effort to argue today, not with the Festival so close.

"Do you want to visit her?"

"Who?"

"Who are we talking about? Angel. If you want to see her,

Festival is the best time to go. We could wrap you up in a heavy robe and—"

"Oh yes, yes, yes. Thaddeus, thank you," she said. "I love living here and it's wonderful having all the boys to care for, but sometimes I wish so much for variety. And Angel is so . . . so frank and charming and, oh thank you, so much."

"I would have done it sooner if I had thought it would bring you such happiness," he said. "But what will you do if the others learn you have been to see a *professional* woman?"

"Nothing at all. You would have a hard time convincing me you don't respect Angel. You would give her your last piece of silver if she needed it."

"Yes. I suppose I would. But I would also make certain that she paid me back. In full." He waggled his brows at her.

"You are incorrigible."

"Incorrigible, yes, but you have to admit. I *am* charming."

"Hmmm. Yes, but I believe there will come a time when you change."

"What kind of change?" he asked.

"I believe that one day you will become the model husband and father and no longer have the slightest interest in chasing women," she said playfully. "*That* kind of change."

"Never." He pulled a face, then grinned.

But she had seen a change already. Perhaps he had finally found a teacher who was controversial and intelligent enough to hold his interest. He had explained to her once that in the past, when he would find a new teacher with a new *angle* on the teachings, as he put it, he would soon discover holes in the fabric of their thinking. Finding one fault, it was easy to find others and leave disappointed.

But with Jesus it was different. The Rebbe opened up the ancient writings to his followers in new and revolutionary ways, and they never were able to pick holes in his reasoning. Jesus spoke with such authority and knowledge that Thaddeus was becoming totally involved, leaving no room for his other pastimes. She had come to the realization that he had little real interest in chasing women, but was, rather, bored with his life. Jesus relieved that boredom. He was . . . fascinating was too weak a word. She could not describe the challenge and attraction and hold on the imaginations of his disciples. It was beyond her experience. Beyond the understanding of any of the followers. But it was real.

"When do you want to go? She said something about after dark, night after next." He lifted a fine dark brow. "She is taking that night off from work and letting her girls go home to rest up a bit to prepare for the three days before the Sabbath. She, ah, expects a busy week."

Pulling herself back to the conversation, Magdalene smiled. "That will be fine. I'll prepare the boys supper and leave it hot. I'm sure they can find their way around a suko well enough to eat alone. I cringe to think what the dirty dishes will look like though. Do you think I could leave them until the next morning. No, I guess not," she said without pausing. "The food would be cemented to the bowls by then. I'll have to—"

"You go right ahead and be domestic, dear. I have to get back to the Fisherman's." He made a hasty exit.

Watching him go, she wondered if Jason ever strayed. But no. He often said he had no interest in other women. She made a wry face. He seldom even had an interest in her. She had often heard other women talk of the virility and incessant demands of their husbands in the bedchambers. But Jason had always been considerate. Almost always. Her thoughts had strayed to dangerous ground and she felt a flush of warning. She shook it away.

On the appointed night, Magdalene dressed with special care in the privacy of her home. Though she kept to the letter of the Law by eating and sleeping in the suko, she had found the need for greater privacy while she dressed and attended to her toiletries. She was not bothered so much for herself, but some of the boys were at the stage where it was not wise to tempt them overmuch.

She dressed in her finest linen tunic, oiled leather boots, her best jewelry and lace veil. She looked a vision and knew it by the appreciative gleam in Thaddeus' eyes when he came for her. "It's almost a shame to cover you up," he bantered. "You look so lovely that Angel might try to recruit you. If she succeeds, I volunteer to be your first customer."

"Aren't you the gallant. All that trouble for little old me."

"Sacrifices for a friend," he sighed theatrically. "I wouldn't want Angel to get a bad bargain."

"Bad bargain," she cried, laughing.

"Yes. Only the best for Angel." Smiling, he pulled the hot wool mantle low over her face.

"This is ridiculous," she said. "It's so dark out now no one could possibly recognize me. Can't I wait and pull this over my face after we pass the baths?"

"No. Put it on now. But as soon as we're out of this section of town, you may drop it."

"Oh. Thank you," she said sarcastically, wiping a hand across her moist brow.

"Well we could always go another day."

"No. I finally got an invitation and I'm going. Tonight. Let's hurry so I can get out of this wool."

"Fine. But you have to put it back on after we pass the baths. I hadn't thought about it until you brought it up." He accepted the fist she dug into his side with a grin and led the way out of her house. Wisely he said nothing about her having a big mouth.

The walk through the city was uneventful, accompanied by songs escaping through the walls of every suko they passed. The night was filled with laughter, and they found themselves talking of their families. Talking of the past. He asked her at one point, teasingly, how Jason would have taken to her being friends with Angel.

"Jason is dead. It doesn't matter what he might have thought. Does it?"

"No. Not really," he said seriously. "But I wondered." He changed the subject to a more lighthearted topic and quickly had her laughing. They laughed often on the way to Angel's, so engrossed in conversation they did not notice the shadowy movements of a boy, keeping pace with them, flitting into dark alleys and doorways.

Their words carried on the night air far enough to reach the ears of the watching lad as he followed them.

● ● ●

The Boy

The name *Jason* always had the power to arouse intense fear in him. Hearing it from the woman's lips, carried on the night breeze made his knees weak, his mouth dry. There had been a night when he had heard the woman's voice crying that name in pain and grief, blood on her hands. And he had been under the spell of that name ever since.

He slipped along the roads of Capernaum, not knowing why he bothered. He had checked on her a dozen times in the last months. She had forgotten her past, forgotten the demonic possession at the touch of the teacher's hands. But he followed, drawn by the name and the woman's voice. That name tonight had brought all his darker memories close to the surface.

The two people stopped finally at the edge of a street he knew well. He did some business here, off the leavings of the women's customers. It was how he made his pocket money. He watched carefully the house they entered and, going around back, located a window that opened into the room where they stood.

Amid much laughter, hugging, kissing of cheeks and lips, the two he had followed pulled off their heavy robes and sat. The man was tall and handsome with dark rich looks, Jewish and Greek, the mixture of bloodlines enough to make him totally arresting. The boy studied him, liking the sight of somewhat thinner nostrils than most Jewish men possessed. He fingered his own nose in the darkness. Was it similar? The man's eyes, however, were his best aspect. Deep, dark, enigmatic, they flashed in the lamplight when he laughed. The boy settled his feet deeper in the dust of the alley and watched.

Angel he knew. The corpulent prostitute was well known and well liked by all the denizens of this section of Capernaum. The man was handsom and laughed often, but it was the woman he strained to see. Her mantle dropped, revealing her short hair, her willowy neck, her graceful posture. It was at first only silly women's talk. The kind he had heard a thousand times. And then, after an hour of words, his heart lodged in his throat.

"How did you meet your Jason? Was it an arranged marriage?"

Mary, twirling a strand of short hair in her hand, answered, "Yes. My father chose for me when I came of age." He could almost hear her smile. "I was terribly spoiled and refused to choose between several possible suitors, so my father imported one. A very special one. In that no nonsense fashion fathers have, he informed me I was to be married. And I promptly threw a tantrum. I'm afraid I was horrid to him for days, but he refused to relent, even when I cried. He had already given his consent to an old friend. It was his son I was to marry. I saw Jason the day they signed the marriage contract." She laughed and a shiver ran down the boy's spine. Remembering. "I fell instantly in love. He had the finest face, the most deep, full, rich voice, as if it dripped with honey. He was a trader, my Jason was. And a good one too."

"What did he trade?" Angel asked.

"Oh, you know."

"No. I don't," Angel laughed. "What did he specialize in? Did he deal with caravans, wines, imported spices, jewels?"

"Y . . . Yes."

"Yes, what?"

"Yes. All those." The woman's voice sounded uncertain.

"Of course. But I suppose it doesn't matter. Most men feel that a woman would be too stupid to understand any aspect of business. Stupid men," Angel said. "How do they think . . . Well never mind. Come into the back room, Magdalene. I purchased a bolt of fabric last week. I'm to have a robe made of it . . ."

That was the last the boy heard for some time. It wasn't necessary to hear more. The Magdalene was remembering. He thought his heart would stop. Magdalene. Not even her real name. Disguised with cut hair, traveling in this part of town. She must be searching for something. Or someone. Perhaps she *knew*. Perhaps she *remembered*.

His legs trembled and he shivered in the cooling breeze. He wanted to leave. To run back to tell. He even made a half step away from the window. But in his mind he could hear a smooth sardonic voice asking, *Is she unguarded? Does she live alone?* And so he waited, feeling the strength seep slowly back into his limbs.

It was late when the man returned for her. The two women were laughing about how Thaddeus wanted her back home early and then did not come for her at the appointed hour. They spoke about the new teacher, Jesus. He was glad he had waited. He learned much. And when Thaddeus strode through the door and swept the Magdalene out into the night, he followed them as close as he dared. He still did not know if she lived unguarded. But he knew how to find out.

Odynius

"She's remembering, I tell you. They've cut her hair and made her sane, Jason's wife."

The one who spoke was just a boy, perhaps sixteen, with rough hands, soiled loincloth and bare, spindly legs finely dusted with pale hair. But it was his face that singled him out. A too-long nose began higher than his eyes. At the junction of his straight brows was a slight knot, below were flaring nostrils. Even without the strong jaw and full lips he would have been recognized as Greek. No Jew of pure blood was born who could boast his wide-set eyes. Even by Greek standards they were set far apart. When he was a child he was beautiful, and perhaps he would make a handsome man. But now, caught in the grip of adolescence, he was less than plain.

The one he spoke with was strange as well. Though pure Jew to the tonsures of his head, he was dressed in the Roman fashion in toga and Roman sandals and little else. He felt no shame in being thus attired, but rather, as he stretched and yawned on his couch, seemed to glory in the soft texture of the clothes. He eyed the boy a moment and thought it was a pity he hadn't spotted him younger. He would have brought a fine price in Rome as small child. He had tried to remedy this change in the boy's body by taking him to the very best castratos, the most expensive physician of the neutering arts in the land. But it was too late. Even with his testicles removed the boy had begun to change. Shrugging, he lifted his slender arm from the couch and popped a berry into his overripe mouth.

"So," he said languidly. "What of it? She was mad, possessed. Even if she remembers, no one would believe her, not even if she makes claims. It's been too many years. Besides, she thinks Romans were responsible." He smiled, his sensual mouth curling slightly. "And she is afraid of Romans. You saw to that quite admirably. I always wondered how you got her into the camp. Did you use your charm and sweet, little boy smile? Or did you slip to other means and use your sweet, little boy body?"

The boy turned away.

"Too bad you were too old for the trade, Shalmer. You fell to it with the same desire as a starving child to food, but with much more grace." As he spoke, he felt a hint of desire that his memories had stirred, memories of the young man before him as a child of ten.

Too old by almost five years to bring a profit in either Greece or Rome, he had nevertheless been trained to be a companion and lover to a man. He had been an apt pupil. Nubile and slim, graceful as a willow, he had danced with a gentle sway of hips, a quick thrust of thigh and pelvis that had ignited the desire of his teacher. Odynius usually preferred younger children, but the older man, then twenty-two, had taken the boy as lover. He had been most satisfied with him for several years, until the boy's body and voice began changing, and he lost his supple grace to adolescent growth. Sadly, he had sent the boy to the stables, losing a teacher of other young boys, true, but not able to stand the sight of his own lost pleasure. And when he could no longer bare the sight of the boy, he had sent Shalmer away, to keep watch on the widow of Jason Ben Shahar.

The Greek boy stood before him now, even in his disgrace, wanting to protect his master. Perhaps he should use the boy. Loyalty was a hard commodity to purchase, but, through love . . . Yes, he would reconsider. But not now. Now his desire was a flushed heat and he wanted one of the new Greek boys . . . Demitrius . . . Not his real name, of course, but more musical than the original. And young. Only four, but already he showed much promise. Not like Shalmer, but then no one would ever be Shalmer.

"Won't you even think of the danger to us? To you?"

The boy was still speaking. What was it he had said? Oh yes, the woman. Mary, Jason's wife. Widow. He had followed her today. She was sane again it seemed, and had been for some time, traveling with the great Rebbe's band. It was a good place for her, quite public. He could keep an eye on her and if she ever should decide to take action against his business or his pleasure, he could deal with her then.

"Yes. I'll put someone to watch her. Don't worry. I'll take care of everything. Now . . . send me Demitrius." He pretended not to see the pain in Shalmer's eyes as a servant went to fetch his latest replacement in his master's affection.

Odynius rolled over on his couch and felt the covers slither to the floor. The boy, Demitrius, had learned much since he had last sent for him. He would bring a good price, a fine profit in Rome when he finally went there later in the year. Odynius knew just the man who would buy the lad, too. He had a penchant for small, dark boys. And the fact that the boy was of Jewish blood would not bother him at all. Of course, if the boy had been of Greek or even mixed blood, he would have been priceless.

A soft knock fell at the door. Odynius covered himself and called a welcome. Shalmer entered, sullen and silent, his eyes downcast at the evident satisfaction on his master's face, jealous. Amused, Odynius gestured the youth closer.

Shalmer's adoration gave him pleasure. When his boys cried when they were sold, he knew he had done well training them. But with Shalmer it was more. He liked the thought of the youth's torment, punishment, because he had not remained a boy despite the expense of the surgery, not remained soft and supple, with liquid eyes, and oh-so-talented hands. Punishment, because he had grown into an ungainly youth with knobby hands and knees, and a body more clumsy than he had ever been graceful. It still hurt. And so, with casual cruelty, he asked, "What do you want, boy?"

Shalmer

Shalmer winced at the term. Once he had been *my love*, or *my pet*, or *my darling*. Now it was only *boy*. And he couldn't stand it any longer. He wanted to be held again. He wanted to be whispered to again, the way Odynius whispered to the boys he trained. But Shalmer knew it wouldn't happen. Odynius wouldn't welcome him back, not until he proved he was valuable. That was why he had come today. He had formed a plan last night in the darkness of his pallet in the stables, the pain still cutting from the sight of the child in Odynius' bed. He knew now, how he could win his master's love back. Last night it had seemed so simple. Today it was hard to speak. "I have a plan." His voice broke.

"A plan." Odynius' voice, by comparison, was smooth as buttermilk, cultured and soft and lilting with sarcasm. "A plan about what, *boy*?"

He swallowed, struggling against the lump that gathered in his throat and teased his eyelids with tears. "A plan about Jason's widow," he whispered. "She is in Capernaum now. I think someone should keep an eye on her at all times, and it should be someone you trust. Me."

"You." His voice was incredulous, and Shalmer chanced a glance at Odynius' face. There was amazement, but as he watched, the finely chiseled features changed, grew thoughtful. He felt the full attention of his lover's gaze for the first time in years, and almost shivered with the pleasure of it.

Odynius

Odynius considered the proposal put to him, for it had been given in undoubted sincerity. He knew the youth too well for there to be an ulterior motive. But he had one himself. If he sent Shalmer away, gave the lad time to grow up, to lose the awkwardness of adolescence, he might, possibly, grow beautiful again. Might make a fine teacher of young children. And it could be useful to have the widow better watched. She couldn't hurt him or his business, but it might be unpleasant if word about him got about. He liked it here and though a move to Rome or even Greece wouldn't be impossible, it would slow him down. Here he had contacts in the slave trade.

"My dear, boy," he purred. "I must admit you have a more

astute mind than I gave you credit for. And far more loyalty. You
are loyal? You aren't thinking of running away?"

He knew how loyal Shalmer was, but it gratified him to see
the shock and tears gather in his past favorite's eyes. "No, you
would never think of running away, would you? You still love me,
don't you, Shalmer?" The boy nodded, his movement's jerky and
without grace. "If you are right and this *woman*," his voice slithered
over the word, "is a danger to us, it might be useful to have you
there, to listen, and learn." At the boy's tense shrug, he continued,
"Well then, if she starts to think too often of the past and of us,
you will get word to me, and we will take care of her. Together.
We would not risk hiring an intermediary to do our work for us."

The use of the plural did not escape the boy's notice and he
swallowed, biting his lips to control their quiver, his eyes never
leaving the figure before him. "And, Shalmer," Odynius continued, "I would be grateful for this favor. *Very* grateful."

The boy's huge eyes were swimming with tears, and Odynius
considered bringing him into the bed now, to seal the bargain. But
the boy smelled of horses. "You will find a bag of coins in the
cabinet. I'm sure you remember the place? Get them and bring
them to me."

Slowly Shalmer dropped his face, disappointment glazing his
eyes, pulling down his mouth. Just as slowly, he moved to the
cabinet, withdrew the heavy bag, and carried it to the bed.

"Shalmer. When you return, things will be different between
us. Do you understand?" The boy's eyes focused on his. A smile
quivered, vanished, and settled on his mouth. He nodded once.
Satisfied, Odynius counted out a handful of coins and pressed
them into the boy's hand. "Go by the storeroom to choose a new
loincloth and robe. Get yourself a money belt for the coins, and
sandals. I want you to eat well while you are gone. You follow the
woman for a few weeks and then report back. Then we will decide
on our next move. Together." He deliberately made his voice
sensual and full of promise. Promise he had no intention of
keeping. Perhaps he could keep Shalmer on this mission for a year
or so. That would give him plenty of time to grow up and become
useful to his business again.

In Shalmer's eyes, he saw only trust and love. "Be careful, my dear," he whispered. "I don't want anything to happen to you while you are away." He let his fingers travel lightly over the boy's arm, making him shiver, "Don't forget me."

Shalmer shook his head, a look of disbelief on his features. Then he turned and fled the room. Odynius chuckled. And called for Demitrius.

Chapter Thirteen

Shalmer

Early the following morning, a vastly different Shalmer followed the teacher and a hundred or more of his followers to the seashore. Bathed and dressed in a fresh, but coarse linen tunic and loincloth, a new woven robe slung over his arm, he looked nothing like the scraggly waif who had clung to the shadows in the night. Spindly limbs hidden from view, there was more than a hint of the beauty to come in his bearing and features. Covert glances were cast from a group of young women and his lack of awareness of the sensation he caused only added to their appreciation.

Already informed of the price the Magdalene charged for rooftop lodging and meals, he had slipped the coins from his belt when he arrived. But there was no one in the house. It was dark and empty of even the least of the furnishings he had hoped to expect. His belly rumbled plaintively.

"Barbarians," he muttered. Following his words, he heard a burst of laughter from the rear of the house, and remembered that it was one of their religious festivals. Their god asked them to do strange things, and this festival where the whole population slept outside, even in the rain, was one of the strangest. He wondered if they made exception in the case of sickness or age, but supposed not. He walked around the house.

The hut in back was miniscule but the laughter came from the rooftop. He followed the sound up steep stairs to discover a huge suko; it could sleep a dozen men comfortably. And the smell that wafted through the cracks set his mouth watering. Lamb, thyme, coriander, and the sweet scent of apricot. He pushed away the hanging cloth door and stepped into the room. The talking, which had been loud as he entered, stopped, and several of the young men chuckled nervously. Prepared for this, he smiled. "My father's house was only recently converted to the religion of his wife's family. There hasn't been enough time for the color to wear off yet."

This was greeted by guffaws and back slapping, only slightly tainted with relief. And then his hand was grasped by long slim fingers and he found himself staring into the dark eyes of his past. He tensed, waiting, knowing that this was the moment that would decide his future here, but there was no recognition in their black depths. Mary of Magdala was smiling.

He was surprised by the beauty of her smile, but then, he had never seen it before. The last and only time he had been this close, she had been rocking on her haunches, holding her tattered robe close with bloody hands. Now, she was truly beautiful. All that in only a heartbeat, and she spoke. "Don't let them tease you. You're Greek, aren't you?"

"Ye—Yes. But my step-mother raised me in the way of the Law. Are you the one they call the Magdalene?"

"That is my name."

"They say you cook the best food in all Capernaum." It was not a lie but he doubted if anyone could create delights like Dava. The cook had served delicacies to Odynius even a king would have drooled over. Just thinking of them made his stomach cry with hunger.

She laughed. "I think that was a famished belly talking. Are you hungry?" His stomach spoke again. "Well, I suppose that's one way of answering. Come. Get a plate. There is enough to feed another tonight."

"Is there enough to feed another for several nights?"

She frowned. "Well, I don—"

"I can pay," he said, thrusting the coins into her hand. "And I can work also. I can help with the cleaning and I'm very good with goats and horses."

She smiled. "Well, I suppose I can find room for one more. There aren't any more of you, are there?"

"No. Just me."

"Alright. You may sleep here on the roof. I'm afraid the Festival has brought so many people in that it will be a little crowded. But you can squeeze in somewhere I'm sure. How long will you be staying?"

"I won't be leaving."

When he saw her quizzical glance, he quickly feigned devout intensity, "I will follow the Rebbe for the rest of my life. So I'll stay as long as you will let me." He had heard more than one man speak with such fervor, and although it was extreme, these people were fanatics. She smiled again, accepting his explanation.

"Come, eat. And thank you for the coins. But if you work well, we can negotiate on your time here. I can use a helper. Where are you from?"

"Jerusalem."

"You've come a long way." She dished up a bowl of stew and tore off a hunk of bread. "You traveled alone?"

"No. With my father. He's a pottery merchant. He agreed to let me stay so that I might study under the Rebbe. Uh, where can I wash?"

"Outside the suko there is a jar and bowl. Use those." She smiled up at him again. "But hurry. More will be along soon and after that it is every man for himself."

He stepped outside with relief, glad that he had remembered to wash. Years before, Odynius had coached him in the finer points of Jewish behavior, and he remembered a great deal from living so close to his lover. But Odynius had never kept to the Law in any respect, and he feared he would stumble on some obscure point. To have neglected to wash would have been worse than any other mistake. It would have ruined his story about conversion right away. Only a Greek would eat with dirty hands or out of a dirty dish, and he had to be even more careful than most. His Greek features set him apart from the first moment, and the others would be watching for failure to observe the Law. No Hebrew would have dealings with a member of another race or religion. Many did not even consider conversion to be binding. He wished he could have claimed half blood, but his coloring wouldn't allow it. There wasn't a Jewish eyelash on his face and it was always wise to stick to more plausible lies. And he had to keep his castrato status hidden. The Hebrews would throw him to the street if they knew that he had been castrated.

The stew was good, well seasoned and probably cooked all day to achieve the tenderness of the meat. The vegetables had been properly added at the last of the cooking and were still crisp. He was surprised at the woman's culinary abilities. She wasn't a rival of Dava, but his time here would not be spent longing for better meals. After eating the stew and fresh bread, he shared in a cobbler made of simmering apricots and cinnamon spice. It was delicious.

However, later that night, he was sorry he had taken Dava's advice before he left that morning. Dava had stated emphatically that to have a bedroll would make him stand out among the poor followers he had thought were the sum of the rebel teacher's disciples. But here every man had a blanket, or roll. Some even had cots. He had nothing. There were several young men lounging around in the cooling shadows, belching and discussing the day's highlights. Unable to sleep for the noise, nor able to join in the theological reasoning about the Rebbe Jesus and the prophet called the Baptist, he slipped down the stairs and into the street. There were no Gentiles on this side of Capernaum, and the sounds of Festival surrounded him. From every house came laughter and singing and conversation of the foolish fanatics. And he felt very alone.

He wandered for hours, stopping only to purchase a wool blanket, soap, a vial of oil for anointing his body, and a satchel to carry it in. He ignored the quick depletion of his store of coins. The purchases made him feel better and were worth the price. Eventually, as the sounds of celebrating settled for the night, he made his way back to the Magdalene's house and crept to the roof to sleep.

The rest of Festival passed without event. So also did the Shmini Atzeres, the eighth day, The Celebration of the Law, Simchat Torah. The Jew's religion was not simple, yet not as complex as he had feared. He wasn't bored, nor was he unable to follow the conversations around the low table at evening meal. To his surprise, he found himself joining in the evening discussions, delighted that his comments weren't dismissed out of hand but were listened to and considered. When he was told by the oldest of the boarders that he had an astute mind, he flushed with pleasure and later found that he listened more closely to the Rebbe's lectures.

It was a change to be in a group of men who hadn't the slightest interest in his body, but only in his mind and perceptions. Yet, he had fantasies about Odynius' pleasure at seeing him and how his teacher and once-lover would take him in his arms and pull him to the silken couch. The couch of his dreams. The couch where last he had seen Odynius and the child, Demitrius.

But he had nothing to report, and no reason to report in early. He followed the Magdalene whenever he could escape from the other young men and slip back to the house. She was living quietly and properly as a widow making her living by taking in boarders, and sometimes by selling embroidered tunics in the market. She did the marketing, took long walks, but never again to the street where Angel lived. She was proper. But she still was the Magdalene, Mary, Jason's wife. And he knew what that meant to him and to Odynius. For she was no longer possessed.

On the day he was supposed to report in to Odynius, he spent hours washing and anointing himself with scented oils, and dressed with care in his clean tunic and sandals. He combed his hair, which he kept short and swept back from his face. The other men teased him about the lovely lady he must be going to see and he hid a secret smile at their inquiries, one that did nothing to dispel the others' interest. Leaving early, he traveled by a circuitous route, losing the last of the ones who had followed him through the marketplace. Heart pounding, he arrived at the door and knocked, touching the lintel out of habit.

Odynius met him at the door himself, smiling an amused, slightly cynical smile. "You're becoming the very proper little Hebrew, aren't you, boy? Well, wipe your feet and come in. I'm busy and haven't much time."

It wasn't quite as he had imagined it, neither the greeting nor the interview that followed. Odynius was preoccupied, distant, even irritated. After his short speech, explaining the Magdalene's habits and lifestyle, he waited for some comment, but Odynius stared out the window, his face in a shaft of harsh light, the fine lines at mouth and eyes magnified. Shalmer knew there wasn't much to report, but he had hoped for more. "Odynius?"

"What?"

"Are you all right?" He had meant to make his voice soft, concerned. Instead it cracked on the last syllable and Odynius glared at him.

"Why don't you grow out of that? You used to have such a lovely voice." He looked over Shalmer, taking in the hem of the tunic that was an inch too short to be beautiful, and woven of coarse cloth. "You used to be lovely all over and quite useful. But now you bring silly tales of widow's weeds to bore me, and you sit like a gawky colt on the stool I made for you when—"

Abashed, tears started at the corners of Shalmer's eyes. He remembered when the stool had been made. It was one of the sacred memories, the precious ones of his time with Odynius. It had been some winter party when he had danced for Odynius' guests and sat at the head of the long table, the pampered pet. Later, after he had pleased the guests by his dance, Odynius had presented him with the gift—the beautifully carved stool with the low back. Now he sat on the stool with bony knees high in the air, his arms wrapped around them to keep from sliding to the floor. Even from his own viewpoint, he was ugly, no longer the graceful boy who had been so charming. He felt lost in his too-large body with too-long arms and legs. *A gawky colt.* It fit.

"You're not to come here again wasting my time with drivel. I sent you to act as my eyes and ears. If she is a threat, she won't act quickly. It will be a slow process. The next time you come, it had better be with some new development. Listen. Watch her. Talk to her about Jason. Perhaps she will let something slip about her plans. Then and only then come to me. Do you understand?"

Tears slid unnoticed down Shalmer's cheeks, opposed only by the slight fuzz that glistened there. He studied his hands, the knuckles white. He should leave. Pride demanded it. He should stand and curse the man he had loved and storm out. But he had no pride where Odynius was concerned. He had nothing. Suddenly the arms he had dreamed of were sliding around him, cradling his too-big body, rocking him. He sobbed and fell against Odynius crying.

"Why do I always hurt you, little one?"

Shalmer wasn't sure Odynius had spoken. Perhaps it was his

imagination. But the gentleness in the voice whether real or imagined had its effect and he calmed.

Odynius wiped the tears still clinging on Shalmer's parched face. "I want you to stay with Jason's widow for a while longer. We have to know how much she knows about the business. About Jason's part in it all. About . . . the rest. Do you understand? What you are doing is very important to me. To us. It might take a year. Even longer. But there will come a time when you can leave this job and come *home*." He combed his fingers through Shamler's fine hair, pausing for a moment at Shalmer's mouth. It was a tender gesture. Shalmer closed his eyes.

Odynius

Gently, he shoved the boy out into the street, whispering admonition, setting another date for more information to be exchanged. Perhaps more than information, but he promised nothing except with his lying eyes. Shalmer believed that he would take him back, him a man nearly grown. Shalmer was a fool, and no longer a boy.

The Zealot

It was late in the year, just after the autumn "former" rains, when the plowing was complete and the fields were ripe for planting. The first snowfall had speckled the ground white before melting in the warmth of day. The sky was bright and blue in contrast to the bare waiting earth heaped in furrows. He sighed and rolled over, plucking a dry twig from the brown grass near his face and tucking it between his teeth. He reveled in the peace. It had been months since he had come here to spy on the Rebbe and ended up staying, a convert to the new teacher. He had not once longed for the excitement of the hunt. The kill.

Now he woke each morning with joy, barely concealed. The excitement and expectation of each morning was always completely satisfied, and at the end of the day, he fell into bed, his soul full until he could hold no more.

It was Jesus. They all felt it, the Twelve. They spoke of it in low whispers, amazed at the similarities of their feelings, amazed at the changes that each had undergone. They shared their life histories, even the painful parts, and had grown closer than brothers in the months of travel and quiet stay in Capernaum. But now there was something new in the air, something which all could feel but none could name. There was a look on Jesus' face when he thought he was unobserved, and the teacher had spoken in low-voiced conferences with his mother for hours at a time but not shared the subject of the talks. Something was about to happen.

The Zealot squinted his eyes at the sun. Perhaps they were to make the long awaited journey out of Galilee. Perhaps they were to travel again, carrying Jesus' message to the people. Most Rebbe's who shared the acclaim and renown of Jesus would have retired to Jerusalem and opened a school, living the rest of their lives in peace and financial security. But not Jesus. Not once had he suggested that. To Jesus, the only way to spread the teaching was to be among the people, talking and preaching the word of God.

This new approach had started whispers about who Jesus really was. Even in his own heart he thought the rumors might be possible. If the Messiah had truly come to raise up the people and throw off the yoke of Roman tyranny, he would first have to reach those people. He would travel among them talking, preaching, healing if he had the gift. But Jesus couldn't be the Messiah. He didn't teach revolution. The Romans who listened on the fringes of the crowd, the outcasts in the conquered land, couldn't fault with Jesus' preaching of peace.

Rolling over on his stomach, Simon buried his face in his arms, smelling the damp, rich earth. It reminded him of his childhood. He had always been surrounded by the smells of earth and fresh growing things, the acrid odors of lamb and shepherd dogs. It had been an uneventful childhood, marked by only the sense of peace and the single great trip to Jerusalem when he became a man at the age of twelve. That had been a turning point for him, the end of the peace of childhood and the beginning of the hate that had sustained him for most of the intervening years.

Destitute, his mother and younger brothers and sisters had not been able to make the pilgrimage to Jerusalem for his Bar mitzvah. Coming home he had been so excited and so eager to share all the wonderful sights and experiences of the Holy City with them that he had run ahead of his father and their companions to reach the house first. When his father had finally caught up with him, he found his son curled up on the ground holding himself, crying unmanly tears into the soil of the graves outside their empty house. Five graves in all, heaped with rock to keep out the night scavengers. Five victims of his mother's typical generosity.

The neighbor woman staying at the house to tell them of the deaths and help them begin the mourning had been cold and distant when she relayed the news of the sickness that had entered the house with a traveler. The Roman merchant had lived and gone on his way, leaving the woman who had been his hostess and nurse carrying the contagion. They had all died. All. That day, he had begun to hate. Even now, had never shared the story of his Bar mitzvah. He had kept it locked within, twined with hate. The only respite for all the years until now had been with Nirit, and she had been murdered.

Lying on warm earth, he became aware of a tickling on his nose, and realized he was crying. A tear dripped from his nose to the ground. It had been years since he thought of his mother. She had been the most gentle soul, tall and quiet, with a grace that reminded him of the Magdalene. Strange, the Magdalene reminded him of the two most important people of his life, Nirit and his mother. This very morning, he had taken her a trinket picked up at the market. He had walked in and surprised her by cupping his hands over her eyes as she kneaded dough.

"You'll never guess who."

"Of course I'll guess. Let's see, it must be the Zealot, because only he and Jesus walk so quietly and it isn't Jesus."

Dropping his hands, he had commanded, "Put out your hands."

"Simon, I've dough all over me."

"It doesn't matter. Put them out anyway."

Sighing, she stood and held her floured hands out.

"Now. Close your eyes." When she had obediently lowered her lashes, he placed into her hands a small glass bead through which a silken thread was strung. It was a necklace, delicate and beautiful, with gold filigree worked into the etched glass surface. When she opened her eyes, her smile spread slowly, as if she released it by measure, lighting first her lips, then her cheeks, and finally resting in her eyes, a faint glow of pleasure.

"Oh . . ." she breathed. "It's beautiful. It really is beautiful, Simon. Is it for me?"

He took the necklace from her hands and slid it around her neck, careful not to touch her skin as he tied the thread in a knot. There had been tears in her eyes when she turned to face him again, but she had been smiling.

Rolling on the ground, he again faced the sun, its feeble rays warming him. Yawning, he slept. And dreamed of Romans. They had surrounded him and were creeping slowly toward him. He could hear the vibrations of their sandals striking the earth as they walked. He waked, disoriented, in an empty, sunny field, a boy running toward him at top speed. "Simon. Simon. come quick. The Rebbe wants you."

His legs had stiffened as he slept and it took a moment to rise and slip into his traveling trot. Even so, he quickly outpaced the younger man. The city boy fell behind, his steps uneven on the hard road.

Simon rounded a curve into the city. Taking a shortcut through an alley, he arrived at the Fisherman's house unwinded, having run off the last of the dream's effects. The rest of the Twelve had gathered and were waiting on him.

"We're to travel to the south of the sea, Simon," a voice called out.

Recognizing the voice, he turned to Andrew. "So? We've done that before."

"Ah. But not by boat," the young man grinned triumphantly.

"By . . . by boat." Simon's voice was curiously empty. The boy eyed him strangely and then turned to his elder brother. No one knew how boats affected him. Especially in rough water. Simon held in a groan. Perhaps the Rebbe would allow him to stay in Capernaum.

• • •

Magdalene

The city felt empty without the Rebbe and the Twelve. Leaving behind the women followers and sending the lesser disciples home to visit families and to help with the autumn planting, they had begun a special teaching and training trip. Word trickled back into Capernaum about the teaching and the usual healings—more than could be believed. And there was some rumor about a storm on the sea so severe that their boat nearly capsized until the Rebbe called out to the heavy sea and told it to quiet.

Two months after their departure, the ground had been soaked soft by several early snowfalls, making the planting easier, and Magdalene walked out of the city often, keeping watch on the progress of her fields. Sometimes she was accompanied by the young man, Shalmer, one boarder who had stayed on after the Rebbe left. He claimed he lived too far away to make the visit and be back when the Rebbe returned. The boy could be morose at times, sunk into his thoughts, while at other times he was light-hearted, amusing, even droll, asking questions about her and her past. In other young men who boarded with her, she would have taken his attention to mean he was infatuated, but none of the usual calf-looks and long sighs escaped him.

She had commented on Shalmer's accent during one of their walks. It was Galilean and not a clipped accent like the Judean, Judas. Shalmer had blanched at her question and mumbled that he was often teased about his accent back in the capitol. His father and mother had been raised near here and he spoke as they did.

He was a strange boy, and Magdalene was glad to be free of his company today, as she went to the market, his absence making her feel curiously free. She slung her long-handled basket as she walked between the vendors. The noise was almost deafening, calls of the fish market blending with the shrill screech of the first vegetable vendor at the junction of two territories. She looked over the pitiful offerings of vegetables and decided to use her own dried things in the fish soup she was planning for tonight. It was a blessing to feed fewer men for a while. Before, when she went shopping, she had been forced to take her old donkey to carry enough food for only two days. Now, two days' purchases fit into one basket: eggs, fresh fowl, wheat flour, barley and a box of dried fruit. When the fruit had been soaked and cooked with honey, it would make a lovely sweet treat.

Her necessary shopping done, she slipped to the cloth section of market. Here, she fingered brocaded fabrics in every color of the rainbow. There was silken purple on bolts, crimson heavy wool robes in the regional fashion and in the newer Greek style. She even found a stall where Roman togas were sold, the wife of some Roman official haggling over the only yellow toga offered.

Magdalene walked on before the bargaining was concluded, her attention drawn by gold jewelry dangling at the next corner. She had a little time and always saved this favorite area of the market for last, lingering over the assortment of gold and silver, precious and semi-precious stones, chains, bangles, necklaces and rings. The merchants knew she would purchase nothing. Already she was pegged as a looker, but because she never asked to see anything that was pushed back, and because she smiled so beautifully, she wasn't snubbed by the dealers. Some even stopped her to talk. Today though, there was a break in her ritual.

Almost finished, she decided to look in on one last booth before she went home. This particular vendor sometimes sold her a cup of wine or tea while they chatted over the selections. Today, as she sat cross-legged, sipping a hot herb drink, she could tell her friend was in a state of excitement. "Tell me, Peleg?" she said, "before you inhale flies in your excitement."

The old woman beamed, her wide face crinkling into a thousand wrinkles. "I have made a sale, my child. The sale that will make a rich woman out of me. A man, a *foreign devil,*" she said licking her lips, "has offered me a king's price for a ruby set. He saw it and did not even offer to haggle. He has gone to get his purse. Hee hee. I am to be a rich woman now. *Rich.*" She slapped her thighs with child's delight.

Magdalene smiled. "Let me see this marvelous ruby set, Peleg. I would share in your good fortune and in the fool's folly."

Looking both ways to make sure no one would see and possibly steal her wealth, Peleg pulled a heavy bag from the folds of her robe, holding it in her cupped hands. "See the future of this old woman before you." Carefully, reverently, she pulled open the draw string of the bag and poured its contents into Magdalene's hand.

For a moment, everything stopped. She was holding a gold band worked with ruby chips and black onyx. A costly ring. A familiar ring. Jason's ring. The world seemed to tilt and shift, the light darkening into a tunnel, centered on the ring. Magdalene took a breath that felt thin and insufficient. "How much did the foreign devil offer you for this set, Aemoa?" she heard her voice ask calmly.

"One gold stater, child. *One stater*," the woman hissed with glee.

"I will give you one stater and five shekels." Silence followed. It drew out so long Magdalene was forced to look from the ring into the old eyes before her.

"You would ask me to break a bargain. A bargain is sacred."

"One stater and ten shekels. And you may follow me to my house and take payment now."

Peleg's face creased once more into a smile. "A bargain made with a fool from Jerusalem is no bargain at all. Sold! And not for a fool, but for a wise woman who knows her gold and jewels. Do you live far, Magdalene?"

"It's only a little way. But what will you tell him, this foreign devil?"

"Nothing at all. Amos," she shouted. "Amos, come here. I will be gone a little while with my dear friend. While I am gone, pack all the wares and take apart the booth. Quickly! Oh. And if the man comes back—you know the one—tell him I was suddenly taken ill and had to be carried away. Hurry, Magdalene," she groaned, as she creaked slowly to her feet. "Hurry."

Magdalene pulled the jar which held her store of coins toward her, surprised at how heavy it seemed, how weak her arms were. She had found the ring Jason always wore. Impossible, but true. She had tilted the ring into the light as she sat at the booth and saw the mark of the master who had made it. The Shahar signet ring had been in the family for generations.

Slowly she counted out the promised coins, not caring that she counted out a greater sum than most men earned in a lifetime. She went back into the main room where the Peleg waited and placed the coins in her hand. They clinked heavily into the vendor's palm and dully as Peleg counted them. Satisfied, Peleg held out the purse holding the ruby ring. It was light in comparison to the fortune in coins, yet Magdalene scarcely noticed the difference as she emptied the ring into her palm again. The window light caught the ruby as she slipped it onto her middle finger. It was already warm, as though still carrying the life-heat from Jason's hand. She curled her fingers into a fist to hold the loose ring in place.

The old woman was backing out the door, smiling and nodding her head. It was a strangely odd gesture, her hand tight around her waist to hold the bulge of coins in place.

"Wait. Don't go."

She saw the look of fear and avarice on Peleg's face. "No. I'm not reneging on our bargain. I only want to know where you got this. And when."

Peleg paused. "I don't know who I bought it from. I don't ask them names when I'm offered a bargain. I paid his price and he left."

"What did he look like? Was he tall, short?"

"It was years ago I bought this. Five years. And he was a Greek boy. Lovely and delicate. A man's toy. The boys who pleasure Romans and Greeks in the baths and temples. He said it was his. I gave a fair price." But her tone suggested otherwise.

"A Greek? Did you recognize him? Had you seen him before?"

Peleg resumed her backing. "No. Never. I have to go now. My family is waiting for me."

"Please. Think, Peleg. It wasn't perhaps someone you might have seen since. Someone you might know if you saw him again?"

The woman's eyes widened. Though she quickly shook her head, Magdalene saw the recognition there. The woman knew who had sold her the ring. Or she had seen him since. She *knew.* Magdalene took a step toward her, but the old woman slipped through the door. In the second it took Magdalene to run into the street, the old woman had vanished. The street was silent and still but for a dog digging in a ditch across the street. She was gone, not a dust mote wavered in the air to mark her passing.

The gold was warm against her skin, and Magdalene opened her hand to look at the ring. Jason's ring. He had been wearing it the morning she left for Rebecca's. The morning she passed Romans moving out of the town. The morning he had died. It, along with his fingernails, had been missing when she returned. How had a Greek child come to sell the ring?

Chapter Fourteen

Magdalene

It was the worst part of the year, the skies always a hazy gray, the world dark and dank, the earth damp, the paths thick and slick with half melted snow and mud that never dried or froze completely, but broke through at the weight of a foot. The weather had deteriorated, growing colder the morning after Magdalene's visit to the marketplace and the purchase of Jason's ring, and she spent a great deal of time alone in her house, stitching tunics and embroidering fine designs on the hems in the lamp-lit, flickering darkness. It was a time of forced introspection when her dreary thoughts paralleled the cold weather.

She had not been aware that her earlier activity with the young followers and with her business concerns had masked a deep emptiness, a deep aloneness. She missed the presence of the followers and disciples, the tense discussions about Jesus' message versus the message of the Baptist, the desert prophet. Missed the angry shouting matches and convoluted theology, yet she refused to attend synagogue and turned down the offer of company from other women.

Other than to market, the only time she left her house during the months of self enforced isolation was when one or another of the Twelve made the trip from wherever Jesus had led the group, back to Capernaum with messages or requests for money for supplies. And the only time she refused to respond to the requests was when the Iscariot came. Because he had damaged her dowry girdle, the Iscariot never got money from her.

From the visits of the Twelve, the women learned about the cure of Jarius' daughter, and heard again about the calming of a great storm on the sea—this told by the Zealot with shudders and a slightly green face. They heard of a mob scene in Nazareth, when Jesus had nearly lost his life, and they heard a strong re-capping of the new teachings Jesus gave the people. These were almost enough to bring the Magdalene out of her lethargy, being told in story form, like a riddle with several meanings. Yet, nothing seemed to help for very long.

Only when Jesus came to Capernaum, sending the Twelve out alone to teach and preach, did Magdalene feel an opening within her and begin joining the small, intimate group at the Fisherman's house for the evening meal and conversation. As always, the presence of Jesus was healing. With the Rebbe and the few disciples wintering nearby, she began to grow, slowly at first, then with a sureness that surprised her. She began to take part in the more intricate discussions, displaying a sharp mind and quick memory, especially in quoting the Baptist. Though not on a level with the Twelve, she could still follow the disciples' discussion, its train of underlying thought, and was once the first to pick out a flaw and reach an obscure conclusion. Jesus was proud of her, she knew. She could see it in his eyes when he nodded slowly at her, a smile on his face, and she warmed, opening even more to life and what it might offer her.

It was at one such discussion, the women sitting in the shadows around the walls, that a disciple asked about a story Jesus had told. "Rabboni, tell us about the parable of whole cloth, and what it means."

Jesus grinned and drained his wine. "Magdalene, you are a worker in cloth. Tell us what happens when an old cloth is torn and ragged, and a foolish seamstress repairs it with new cloth."

Magdalene caught her breath. He had never called upon her like this. She moistened her lips. Blinked. And seemed to see, in the dark of her mind, a cloth, ragged and frayed, blowing in an unseen, unfelt wind. It was the vision of herself, as she had been, the day Jesus healed her. She said, "The repair will not hold. The old cloth will fray even more quickly at the seams. And the cloth will fall apart." Her brows came down, as she thought. Jesus had, in a way, healed the tapestry of her soul, not by repairing the damage to her, but by—

"Yes," Jesus said, holding her eyes in the flickering light. "Old cloth cannot be repaired with new cloth. The whole cloth must be remade anew. In such a way must *we* be remade anew, by the Father, to his glory and for His purpose."

That was what he had done when he healed her. He had made her a new being. She had been reborn. The old Mary was dead and gone. Magdalene was born, a new being, in Jesus' eyes. He nodded at her, before turning away to answer another question. But Magdalene's hand reached into her robe, to the small pocket sewn there, and the ring she had bought for a king's ransom. The gold was warm against her flesh, as if alive.

For weeks the habits of the small group continued while the Twelve preached in the countryside and the earth warmed in the steady rains that would provide a bountiful first harvest. Magdalene learned and grew and she found peace, though from time to time, she would catch a pained look on Jesus' face. He would stare out at the sea, pausing in the cut of a fish he was cleaning, or pause while smoothing a newly-carved cup, his gaze on the grain of wood he had shaped. Someone would speak his name. Sometimes he would look up. Sometimes he wouldn't hear at all. He was pensive. As if waiting.

She was away from the house shopping for three boarders who had joined her household, when the word came that shattered the quiet, peaceful weeks. Thaddeus met her on the street, the first time she had seen him since his return from the mission of the Twelve. Her face froze in the act of a smile at his expression. His usually handsome face was drawn, pale, his hands clenched, knuckles white. There were traces of tears on his cheeks. "The Baptist is dead."

Magdalene's grip on her market basket weakened, and she scarcely noticed when Thaddeus took it from her. She had heard the Baptist speak once, and had boarded several of his disciples when they came to speak with Jesus. His arrest had startled them all, but like the rest of Jesus' disciples, she had thought it only a matter of time before he was set free from Herod's prison. "How?" she asked. "What happened?"

"They put his head on a great silver platter. It is said the feast continued around his head, amid obscene jokes." He choked.

"And for *lust*, Magdalene. For a *child* who *danced* for Herod while he drank. *His own niece.*" His voice was tortured, tears at the corners of his eyes.

Taking Thaddeus by the hand, she slowly led him back to her small house. She had thrown back the shutters to receive the day's unexpected light and warmth, but it felt cold now, despite the sunlight streaming through. The house was empty, the brazier still glowing hot from the last meal. She pushed the door shut on its stiff wooden hinges, the creaking loud in the silent room. The sob from beside her made her whirl and she caught him to her, scarcely able to hold him for his shaking.

"They cut off his head," he cried. "His *head*. That man could talk into the teeth of a sandstorm, Magdalene. He could be heard over the blare of the trumpets in the Temple. Why did that *bastard king* do this? Oh, *Magdalene*. The Baptist is dead. *Why?*" His words were lost in tears and stopped, choking, in his throat.

Her own eyes were dry as she held him in strong arms, her hands smoothing his hair like a child. "*Why* is the wrong question, Thaddeus. *Why* is always the wrong question. There's no answer to the question *why*. There is only an answer to the question, 'How do I go on?'" But her thoughts were on Jesus. He loved the desert prophet. The Baptist was his kinsman—in spirit as well as blood. She wondered who was comforting Jesus now? The sound of wailing began in the house next to hers. She shivered where they sat in the corner.

Evening shadows lengthened and they were joined by the young followers as night fell, those that had boarded with her, and others who had rushed in from neighboring villages. There were older followers as well, among them the Zealot, Thomas, Matthew, and James the son of Alphaeus. Their grief eventually quieted and, exhausted, they talked with muted whispers.

Someone had lit a lamp and its feeble light tossed irregular shadows through the room. *Its wick needs trimming*, she thought. Her furniture had all been turned upside down, and all their shoes were piled by the door. *The signs of mourning.*

Joints stiff, Magdalene rose in the shadows to prepare food for her guests. There was not nearly enough, but she passed around a few pennies worth of tough, day old bread and a few bites of pickled fish. No one seemed hungry.

From outside, she could hear the sounds of mourning as the whole city was swept up in the news of the death of the Baptist. He had been a prophet, the first prophet to come to the world in centuries. He had prophesied that things were changing. He had prophesied that the Messiah was to come. He had told some that he knew who the great one was. And Herod had killed him, and placed his head on a charger. An arm went protectively about her shoulders; she felt its weight, its warmth. Turning, she looked into the dark eyes of the Zealot.

Of the large group seated on her floors, they were perhaps the only two who had not known the Baptist. With him, she felt less isolated in the sea of sorrow. Suddenly the door burst in, the small light revealing Phillip looking harried and disheveled. "Is he here?" Startled faces looked up at him. Magdalene thought, *No. He's dead.* "The Rebbe. Is he here? I've looked everywhere for him and no one has seen him. Not since— Not since he heard."

The Zealot, always the first to react, was on his feet, his legs bent in a slight crouch, like an animal about to pounce. "Who saw him last?" he breathed.

"Aemoa. She said he looked ashen, but he never spoke, just turned to leave. I thought he might have come here. We can't . . . can't find him anywhere." There were tears in his eyes, his fair skin streaked with traces of dirt and tears. Phillip's black hair, which he wore long and swept back with a gold clasp, had worked loose and hung in tattered threads around his face.

It's longer than mine, she thought.

The Zealot joined Phillip at the door, his steps silent and graceful even in the dark and crowded room. There was a whispered conference between the two and the others of the Twelve who had gathered in her house. She couldn't hear, and waiting, isolated, her mind was caught up in a frightening scene. "He's going to the wilderness." Her words were strong and clear in the near silent room. She was surprised she had spoken, but she knew she was right. He had told her once he went into the mountain wasteland to the east when he was troubled. He had once been tested there, when he was most troubled about his life and the direction it would take.

The Zealot nodded. "Yes. He would go into the desert. To be alone."

"But is he safe there?" Phillip cried. "He was distraught. His mother fears for him. We should follow. Just to make sure he isn't hurt. What if he fell and broke his leg in the dark? You know how he likes to walk at night. We have to go *now*. He's in *danger!*" The small man's tone rose to a frightened pitch. "What if Herod takes him as well?"

"There is nothing we can do tonight," Magdalene said, hating the words that fell from her mouth, but knowing they were true.

"What do you mean *nothing?*" the small man almost choked on his words. He pointed to Simon. "You tracked the Magdalene in the dark by only the light of the full moon. I saw you. I watched. We could get torches, lamps. We could—"

"No," Simon roared. His anguished voice, so used to command, brought Phillip's tirade to an abrupt close. His eyes threw black fire at the trembling man before him. "Jesus wears only ordinary shoes. I can't track him at all in the darkness. Perhaps not even in the daytime. Do you know how many pairs of shoes there are in this city just like his? Thousands! How can I— How could anyone?"

There was an eerie silence in the room. Then from the rear, in the shadows where her eyes could not pierce, there came a young voice. It cracked with intensity when he spoke. "I, uh . . . I saw him. The Master. At the seashore when I was coming here. He was boarding a boat. You won't be able to track him. At all." The thin voice stopped, then spoke again, stronger this time. "But you're right, ma'am. He did go into the wilderness. I sat and watched until his boat was out of sight on the horizon and it headed to the southeast."

"If he did go southeast by boat, then there is only one place he could have been set down," said Thomas, his speech a soft contrast to the others in the room, practical and emotionless. "I've been there. We can reach it by foot in two, three days. Or we could take one of the Fisherman's boats and be there sooner."

Again she heard her voice speaking as if it had a will of its own. "We will take the boat at dawn. There's a great deal to do before morning. Phillip, go tell Aemoa that we have located Jesus, and where. She will know what to gather. Thomas, you have friends in the marketplace. We will need supplies. I'll tell you what to buy. Matthew, go find the Iscariot and bring him here for we will need money from the treasury to buy the supplies and he has most of it. James, you are the fastest. Go quickly to the shore and find the Fisherman. It's time for him to be casting off for the night's fishing. If he is gone, make a deal for the cost of a large boat to take us to the southeast shore. I'll pay for the boat. Thaddeus, go find Jesus' closest disciples."

No one moved. Everyone stood, dumb, looking at her. She put her hands on her hips. "*Well?* What are you standing here for? We've work to do. Simon, I'll need your help." Still no one in the room moved, but stood or sat with mouths ajar. "I said, *Go!*" she shouted. "And you younger men go back to your families. I can't be bothered with you now. *Get!*"

The room exploded with movement, bodies, arms and legs all standing at once, throwing shoes as each man hunted for his own. One of them knocked over the lamp, leaving the room in even more confusion, and the noise of their leaving was deafening in the darkness. As her small house emptied, she heard the strained sound of the Zealot's deep voice. He seemed to be crying and, with an effort, holding in his sobs.

"Simon?" He didn't answer and she hurried to light the lamp from the brazier of glowing coals. When the room was bathed in soft, even light, she turned and saw the Zealot, crouched in a corner holding himself, rocking on his heels, muffling his mouth with the stuffed hem of his robe. She slipped her arms around him and tried to comfort him, but he pushed her away, seeming to be even more convulsed than before. Finally he opened his eyes and through his tears, she saw laughter. *Laughter?*

"Oh, Mary. Magdalene. You were magnificent. You, you should have seen yourself. Most of those men have not been spoken to like that by a woman in years. You should have been a . . . a Zealot." His laughter came forth fresh and he quickly stuffed the hem of his robe back in to stem the sound of levity in the mourning city.

Exasperated, she put her fists to her waist as the Zealot turned and started righting chairs. "Simon, you act like you haven't ever seen me before. I am not a weak, foolish woman. I do things like this all the time." *But not really,* she thought. *I've never taken charge of a roomful of* men *and sent them scurrying like so many rabbits.* Despite her worry over Jesus, the humor of the situation struck her as she remembered the expressions on the faces of some of the men. It had been amusing to see the crowd digging in the pile of shoes, backsides high in the air.

Holding in a smile, she helped the Zealot up-right the furniture. Later, she brought out her money bag and directed Simon to strap it around his waist. The leather bag held enough coins to rent a ship and a little extra for emergencies. The Iscariot would have to do the rest. He likely had enough money to feed the whole nation in his money belt.

By dawn, Simon the Fisherman's boat was loaded with the Twelve and the women, and was far out to sea, moving slowly into the sunrise. No one slept for the first several hours of the voyage, the events of the day still too painful and fresh to allow for relaxation. But later, their bodies in uncomfortable positions, draped over fishing supplies or their own belongings, they fell into exhausted slumber. Her eyes wandered tiredly over them, as she remembered the last several hours in Capernaum.

It had been almost midnight before all the Twelve had gathered in her house, with their respective chores done. The prices the market vendors charged for late purchases, especially after some had retired for the night, had been exorbitant, and the Iscariot had resisted spending so much money. But Thomas had been unyielding. She wondered if he had found it necessary to take the money by force from the diminutive secretary, as there was now a certain enmity between the two that had not been there before. She and the Zealot had helped to carry all the provisions to the seashore and onto the boat. It was an odd assortment, piled haphazardly on the deck. It reminded her of the pile of shoes in her house.

The faint breeze, cold with the season, touched her face. How far ahead was Jesus? What were his thoughts? Did he know that those who loved him were following? Would he even be there when they arrived? There were so many different trails one could take from the shore to the wilderness. How could the Zealot find the one Jesus had taken?

She could see the Rebbe in her mind, his face etched with fatigue and sorrow, lines, usually faint, darkened with tears, his beard dusty like the first time she saw him, in the market in Magdala, the moment he touched her and brought back her memories and her mind, clearing away the screams of the darkness and the demons. That memory was as crystalline now as the day it happened. All she had to do was call it to mind and she could once again feel that purity and warmth and security. She wondered, if he touched her again, would she still be as broken and frayed as a torn tapestry, or would she have fulfilled his vision and become new cloth.

A light touch on her arm pulled her from her thoughts and she turned to see Aemoa, her gray eyes tired, yet still filled with that compassionate determination that was hers alone. "Do you think Simon can find him? The desert is so vast." She rubbed her arms with her hands under the long sleeves of her wool robe, trying to warm the chilled skin. "I made sure that Joseph taught our son the places of all the stars and that he knew the position of the moon in every season. It helped Joseph more than once to know such things." She looked up at the graying sky and they could hear the soft calling of sea gulls, diving and whirling in the air above the boat. "Jesus has been here before," she said. "He knows this area. He couldn't get lost here. Or hurt."

"No. Of course not," Magdalene agreed. "Your son is careful. He walks with steady, sure steps. He is graceful, but without the predatory stance of the Zealot. He wouldn't fall into a hole, no matter what Phillip thinks." She smiled into the worried eyes of Aemoa. "Jesus will think we are silly for our concern. We should have more faith in the Rebbe." Her words again surprised her.

She rubbed her eyes with the tips of her fingers, felt the scratching of a rough nail on her lid. Dropping her hands, she encircled Aemoa's arm with hers and squeezed comfortingly. "Get some sleep. We'll be there soon and we'll need our strength to find Jesus. Come. I'll find you a place."

The older woman smiled. "And what about you? Won't you

need sleep too? Or are you the indefatigable one?"

"No, Aemoa. I'm tired. I'll sleep near you." She yawned widely. "Let's kick the Iscariot out of wherever he is and take his sleeping place." She was gratified to hear a gentle snort and led the way to the back of the boat.

It was more difficult than she had thought to find the Rebbe. What Thomas had called one docking place on the shore was actuality a length of beaches lined with rough dwellings, small fishing villages. They stopped at each, a man splashing through the water to the shore to ask for news of a boat docking from Capernaum. Each stop cost them an hour or more, and it was late in the day before they found where Jesus had been let off, in a filthy Gentile village of mud and wattle.

Magdalene sagged with relief. She had begun to worry if Jesus had left on a boat in the first place, or was back in Capernaum waiting for them. By nightfall, they had unloaded all the supplies and found lodging in the flea-infested shacks. It was a second miserable night, and Magdalene tossed and turned in the cold that descended on them from the desert. Could Jesus freeze in the night without shelter? Her only warmth was the back of Aemoa pressed close, and Jesus hadn't even that for warmth. He was alone. And she was afraid.

Dawn came slowly, but at the first hint of light, Magdalene was up and securing the packs the men would carry, nudging tired forms into action before they could even greet the day with prayers. She had no need for prayers when Rebbe could be in trouble. There was only need for movement and speed. But then, she didn't pray.

They were ready to leave by the first real light, fasts broken and the group assembled. Then because Aemoa was exhausted, Magdalene spent some coppers on the purchase of an old donkey to carry her, knowing that Judas had enough money to take care of the emergencies. The donkey was a steady beast who would carry Aemoa well, she was assured. Magdalene had her doubts, but as he was the only creature to be had, she paid the price and led the bedraggled donkey back to the hut and his burden. She settled

Aemoa, with a minimum of argument, on the bony back. Turning to Simon, she nodded once, firmly. "Still think I would make a good Zealot?"

"The best." His eyes were tired, his slender muscled shoulders stooped.

Her eyes narrowed and she said, "You spent the night following his trail, didn't you?"

He sighed. "Yes. The boy who saw him leave and watched for a while, took me by torchlight down the path, or up rather, and I found a few traces of his walking staff in the dirt."

"Oh, Simon. You need your sleep more than the rest of us. How are you ever going to keep going as tired as you are?"

"I've gone far longer without sleep. I had to mark the trail." He shaded his eyes and stared up the path. "It rains in the desert this time of year."

She hadn't known. She was untraveled.

They moved from the Gentile village, pairs of suspicious eyes following them from the doorways. She was glad to be free of the dirty town. Two days later, nearly out of supplies, fatigued, irritable and damp from a cold rain, Simon smelled smoke, and they found Jesus. He was sitting in a natural depression, not large enough to be called a cave, a small fire blowing in the wind, his walking staff leaning against the stone wall at his back. The Rebbe watched them as they straggled, exhausted up the hill to him, no trace of surprise showing on his face.

Judas, the Iscariot, was angry, and reached Jesus first. "We've been looking for you. What do you think you're doing all the way out here in this devil-filled place? Do you know how much it cost us to get here?"

A trace of a smile twitched Jesus' mouth, which only made the Iscariot more angry. While he stomped and muttered, throwing angry glances at Jesus, the Fisherman knelt at Jesus' side and felt the master for broken bones, his great, reddened hands tender on Jesus' skin. Half smiling as the others came up the hill, Jesus said, "I'm not broken, Simon."

No one spoke after that, only went about setting up camp in a tight circle around where Jesus sat. Magdalene, busy with a stiff, knotted rope, watched as Aemoa sat heavily beside Jesus and ran her long fingers over his face. He looked tired, dehydrated, with dark circles under his eyes, but he was clean, a sharp contrast to the members of the group. They had found no water as they tracked Jesus and had gone on slender rations. No bathing, little drinking.

Aemoa's soft voice was lost in the relentless sounds of setting camp. Jesus' reply was crisp and clear, his voice echoing off the far walls of hills. "There is a fresh pool lower down, a spring with a small stream. You can wash there, Aemoa. You look tired." Again she spoke, unheard, and he answered, "No. I brought no food. I've been praying."

Magdalene smiled, turning her head so Jesus couldn't see her face while he endured the fury of his mother's rage. Several others of the group were doing the same, while the Fisherman laughed aloud at Jesus' plight. Her tirade put a new light on the situation, lifting the sense of heavy sorrow and anger from the backs of the apostles. A tenor voice started singing the Vintage Song, an old favorite, and Magdalene looked up with surprise to see Andrew singing. The Fisherman's baritone followed his younger brother's notes and they all joined in, an oddly merry sound bouncing off the walls of the hills.

Soon, so quickly she could hardly believe it, the camp was set up and a tasty stew was bubbling in a goatskin bag slung over a fire, the tops of the flames well below the level of the liquid in the bag. The camp was neat and orderly, sleeping rolls pulled under the low overhang which had sheltered Jesus. The men had bathed while the women prepared the stew, those who had fresh clothing, changed, and those who did not, wrapped themselves in loincloths while their tunics and robes aired. Jesus sat throughout the process, watching them as they worked and ate. But he didn't speak again, sadness pulling at his mouth.

The women left him with the Twelve sitting around him singing, trying to make him smile, and went to their own bath. The men seemed to think Jesus was fine now that they had found him, but the women speculated to themselves that he was different somehow. More subdued. Aemoa felt it the most, this change in him, and her face was worried, though he was safe and unharmed, apparently waiting for them.

Simon caught a hare, and set more traps, and there was wild winter wheat growing near the pond for bread. After adding the fresh meat and grain to their supplies, they determined that they had enough to last two more days in the wilderness. The decided to stay. They talked and sang and enjoyed the respite from the latter rains for the two days. Jesus relaxed in their company and once joined in a song. Some of the sadness leached out of his face, but grief for the death of his kinsman had left deep traces.

Magdalene enjoyed sleeping under the stars, curled around Aemoa and wedged against Joanna's back. They needed this time alone as a group, it strengthened their bonds, and even the enmity between the Iscariot and two others eased, though Magdalene felt no lessening of her own distrust. She had tried to forgive, but he was . . . shifty.

No one thought about how they would get home. Perhaps it was foolish to feel so carefree when they didn't have enough food to make the walk back to Capernaum. The Fisherman had sent his boat back with his workers and another wasn't planned to pick them up. But after the fears and horrors of the Baptist's death, it was good to relax.

In those days in the wilderness, Magdalene developed friend-ships with other women who traveled with Jesus. There were Susanna and Joanna, the wife of Chuza, Herod's steward; Joanna had brought word of the Baptist's death. There were the three Mary's: Mary, the wife of Cleophas, and Mary Salome, the wife of Zebedee, both half sisters of Mary, Jesus' mother. There were other women, all of different backgrounds, yet all concerned with the welfare of the men who followed Jesus. They were the providers, the ones who did the cooking, sewing, marketing, planning. The ones who found where they were all to sleep when they entered a village or town for the night. And they all, without exception, sat and listened when Jesus spoke, their faces turned to his with rapture. They too were captivated by the authority of Jesus of Nazareth.

He had treated them as no other man had. Indeed, he regarded them with the dignity of disciple peers. They had never heard him utter the traditional prayer of the morning thanking God that he had not been born a Gentile or a woman. They sensed in him an uplifting spirit, like a fountainhead of equality.

At the end of the second day, they packed up what little supplies they had left and made preparations to leave for the coast in the morning. Their plan was to signal a boat from shore and hire it back to Capernaum, promising payment on arrival. But that night, with ominous clouds hanging over them in their sheltered valley, they heard, carried on the wind, the sounds of people. Many people. By morning, they were surrounded on every side by . . . thousands.

The hills around them, which curved in a natural amphitheater, were covered with masses of humanity. There was no place that wasn't crowded with groups, entire families, seemingly entire towns. They washed and drank from the once-clear stream, thirsty after walking along the well-marked path of Jesus and his followers. And they waited.

Magdalene couldn't believe that so many people could be so quiet. So still. They had started from Capernaum, a large group of several hundred led by the followers left behind, mourning the loss of the Baptist, sensing of change on the air, scenting the fear. They had walked for four days through the countryside and along the shore, gathering others in their wake, spreading the news about the death of the Baptist and the location of the one he had named as his successor, this Jesus of Nazareth, the teacher who mourned in the hills of the desert. And they had come, even after they ran out of supplies, hungry, and thirsty. Not one had spoken of turning back. Now, lining the hills, they waited, utterly silent, respectful, for Jesus.

He'd said not a word, his face heavy again with sorrow, his hair appearing lined with silver in the dull light of the strange morning. The people didn't call for him. Didn't shout. But still he didn't speak. The disciples and women who had spent the last days with him were fearful that he wouldn't speak at all, casting wide-eyed glances at one another, fidgeting. But Magdalene watched him as he gathered himself, as he filled inside with something new and powerful.

Slowly, Jesus stood, unfolding his frame with grace. As he stood in the shallow cave and surveyed the great, silent multitude, Magdalene saw the change continue over him. His sorrow vanished, replaced with the strange, enigmatic expression of . . . compassion. He felt for them. The rebbe that mourned, felt their sorrow, their fear.

And he spoke.

Afterward, Magdalene couldn't have said what his words were, nor even the content of them. But a sigh went through the crowd at his first word, long and drawn out, as though they released their held breaths together and inhaled for the first time in hours. Her scalp tingled with the power in the air, in his tone, and tears spilled unnoticed down her cheeks. All day, no one moved as he spoke, his voice strong, echoing in the hills, his form outlined against the rock at his back, the cloudy sky above.

At evening, Aemoa brought him bread saved for their trip back to shore, the last crusts of it and bade him eat, but he refused, saying that no one in the hills had eaten nor was likely to. He ordered the Iscariot to send the fastest runners to the nearest town and bring back food for all the people. He would eat then. But Judas claimed he had no money, that the Magdalene had spent it all on supplies. And even so, he said that not even two hundred pennies worth of bread would feed the crowd. There were five thousand men out there, plus the women and children. It was impossible.

Magdalene searched through the packs of supplies again, hoping to discover at least something, and missed the rest of the conversation. Thaddeus told it to her later, how a small boy, in the elem or naar stages had brought Jesus his lunch, forgotten all day in the excitement of hearing Jesus speak for the first time, and offered to share it with anyone who was hungry. Several of the followers had laughed, and almost pushed him away, but Jesus had called to him, bade him sit down and then called for the crowd to sit as well.

In the sudden silence, Magdalene turned then, to hear him bless the meager meal. And the hair-prickling sensation returned, even greater, stronger, as if power rushed over the ground and up into the sky.

Jesus passed small loaves and fishes out to the Twelve and told them to feed the thousands of people. Two fish and loaves. They began to break it, and toss it in baskets. Few knew where the food came from, the feast that was passed out that day. Only later when they had gathered up the scraps and counted the bushels left over did the story get out. The miracle. The feeding of the five thousand in the hills of the desert.

The heavy rains, which had held off for so long, coming only as showers, broke that evening as they walked back toward the Gentile village by the edge of the sea. The wind that blew off the water was cold, and the lowering clouds promised more poor weather for the disciples, the followers, and the thousands in the desert. With the storm, the crowd broke up, many heading north along the shore, back the way they had come, to towns and villages left empty by their leaving. Others followed Jesus all the way to the shore, to be with the great man for a day longer, hoping to hear one last message, one last word or promise.

Magdalene worried now, with the cold seeping into her bones leaving a dull ache, how they would get back to Capernaum. Thaddeus, trudging beside her, reading her mind, said it was a long swim. At his words, she stumbled, the hem of her robe fraying against the path. The desert soil grew full of moisture, becoming pitted and runneled by the excess, and her boots, soaked, stretched and flapped at her ankles. The wet leather ground into her skin, leaving blisters, and finally only raw flesh. The straps of her pack cut into her tired shoulders and she shrugged them against the weight but it did little good. And still Jesus pushed on, not allowing a rest. He acted as if he had a specific time he was supposed to reach the beaches.

Magdalene slogged along in the mud, her mind was as tired as her body, straying away from deep thought, back to the pain in her heels and bones and shoulders. Glancing at Aemoa sitting on the old donkey, she saw again the gray lady of her memory, but now with rain in her eyes and plastering her clothes. The Zealot pulled his robe high as the donkey on which she sat splashed water at his feet.

A shadow fell on the ground, scarcely indistinguishable in the dim light and pouring rain. It was Jesus. Looking up, she absorbed the tired lines of his face, the unhealthy pallor of his skin, lips slightly blue with cold. He looked . . . old. His eyes were as dull as the leaden sky, sunken into purpled folds of lids. His flesh was so thin she could see blue veins and red lines of capillaries beneath.

She felt a flash of anger. It was his fault she was so cold and wet. If he hadn't gone off into the desert— She could see, suddenly, that he knew her thoughts, and she dropped her eyes, ashamed. Tears blinded her and she stumbled again, almost falling. He caught her elbow for an instant to steady her, then, still without speaking, passed his staff into her hands. The wood was smooth and warm from his touch and from years of use, and she felt tears start again.

She wiped her eyes and leaned into the staff, the wood strong and supportive as he slipped into the crowd. Later, she told herself it was only the kindness in his eyes that gave her new strength, but she made the rest of the trip to the shore with a lighter step, the wood lending her warmth.

They reached the poor village along the shore at dusk. There was a boat waiting in the night shadows to take them to Capernaum, the very boat that had brought Jesus here.

Capernaum was much as they had left it, yet quieter, subdued. With the death of the Baptist, many of the followers had departed for home, feeling it was now dangerous to be the disciple of a rebel rebbe. Yet, new followers poured in to fill the ranks of the departed, many angry, wanting to destroy the king who had beheaded the Baptist. Others simply had nowhere else to turn. All had listened to the Baptist, heard his message, accepted his calling. Many came and pledged allegiance to the new teacher, Jesus of Nazareth, named by the Baptist as the chosen one.

The Rebbe never asked for his staff back. A new one appeared in his hands within a few days, one of fine-grained rosewood, carved with scripture. Perhaps presented by a new follower. Magdalene kept his gift, taking it with her everywhere.

Chapter Fifteen

Thaddeus

The number of cities and towns they visited astounded him. Thaddeus had traveled through this part of the country many times, but hadn't seen—really seen—the people. Always in a hurry, often in a wheeled cart, behind a donkey or mule, he had bypassed the poorer, rougher places, staying in the larger towns which boasted an inn. Now though, he was seeing how the people lived, the poverty, the fear, the constant search for food that was never enough. He was living it with them. It was spring and they stayed in many of these towns, camped in cramped dusty places while Jesus talked, healed, and spoke of promise, of how God had not forgotten the poor, the downtrodden. It was a strange message for a prophet, a *new* message. A message for the people instead of messages for kings and rulers, as the prophets of old had told.

The women worked hardest of all while they made their slow way to Jerusalem for the Pesakh, the festival of Passover. They foraged by day, shopped in the meager markets, and at night cooked enough food for the followers and all of the hungry that cared to join them. They even made the Sabbath meals good and properly filled with ritual. Their ability to feed so large a group at the leanest time of year amazed him.

He had never expected to see Magdalene stalking a strange market alone, shopping for food and supplies, ignoring any Romans present. She even uncovered her face to share a word with a local woman or child, teasing and laughing, unconcerned that her hair would cause comment. She was changing, his Magdalene. She had become quite . . . capable.

Capable. It was the word he used to describe her to the

stranger who sought him out several days ago to ask of her. He had been sitting on the ground near a well, half asleep, his head bobbing in the heat, a day's journey from the capitol, when first approached, waiting for Simon the Fisherman. He had been embarrassed to be caught sleeping, especially by such a well-dressed man. He had felt at a disadvantage from the start.

"You are Judas Thaddeus of James, one of the followers of the Rebbe Jesus of Nazareth."

It was a statement, not a question, and showed the man had done much research into his family and lineage. Thaddeus climbed to his feet, pulling his robe and his dignity around him as best he could.

"Yes, I am Jude Thaddeus. And you are?"

"You are an educated man," the stranger said, "far more so than most of his followers. I recall seeing you in several synagogues in Jerusalem." The stranger smiled and threw back his mantle. "I am Joseph of Arimathea. Perhaps you might remember a session of the Sanhedrin where we discussed the question: 'How many devils can inhabit a man at one time?' Ah . . . I see you do recall. Will you to tell me about this man you follow. I assure you I am not here to carry back tales to Herod. I leave that for lesser men." His black eyes glistened with eagerness, like the excitement on the face of Jesus' youngest followers. "From an educated man's viewpoint, *tell me about Jesu*s." The last was spoken overloud, and Joseph looked around, quickly replacing his mantle as though suddenly aware how exposed he was.

So, Thaddeus thought, *he is here without Sanhedrin sanction.* Thaddeus relaxed. There were many of these men, wanting to learn, to sit at the feet of a celebrated teacher and discuss the scripture, yet fearful of the condemnation of their fellows, fearful of association with a man already branded a rebel and plotted against by leading factions.

Thaddeus motioned the man away from the well and into the shade of newly green trees. Here they sat and talked, and he shared the Rebbe's words, the message of a new way of seeing the Lord, a new way of interpreting God's word and what He wanted for the Hebrews. Joseph leaned forward to catch each teaching, his body all but quivering with the need to learn more.

By the end of the day, Thaddeus agreed to arrange a meeting between the two men when Jesus went to the Holy City, and he would make sure that he was present when they talked, though no others. He promised. And then, when he had thought his conversation with Joseph of Arimathea was over and stood, the man asked a strange thing.

"The woman who travels with you. She is called the Magdalene. She has shorn hair. Tell me about her."

Thaddeus' swelled with anger. He had thought this man above such remarks, such base needs. "She is no prostitute. Put that far from your mind. She would have none of you. She is a good and simple woman, a widow whose husband died at the hands of Romans. She markets and cooks for the men, listens as they moan about their wives and sweethearts. She works hard and gives much. And her hair is short because the Rebbe healed her and his mother could not save her hair. Think no more of her. She is not for you."

The man smiled, frankly amused. "Your Magdalene *is* safe from me, my friend. *I* have no designs on her." His inference was plain. He did not have designs on her, but he wondered at the force of Thaddeus' words.

Thaddeus smiled ruefully. "We all feel protective of her. She is . . . special."

"And that is what interests me. I feel I have seen her before, and Magdalene is no real name. Tell me about this paragon of virtue, her real name and of what she was healed."

Thaddeus rose and walked toward the town walls, aware the Arimathean followed. When Joseph was again abreast, Thaddeus said, "Her name is Mary. She was sitting in the marketplace in Magdala. I only heard this. I wasn't with Jesus then. She was rocking and singing about Roman soldiers and dying. Telling passersby the things they most wanted kept secret. She was clearly possessed." He glanced at the man and accepted his nod of understanding. "When Jesus appeared, she pointed at him and screamed that he should kill the Romans for her, to avenge the deaths of her family. Jesus healed her instead. Simon the Fisherman told this to me. He saw it. He says she had seven devils." Joseph nodded again, intent. "Later she joined the group and stayed at the Rebbe's house in Nazareth for a time as her body grew strong again. She is quite capable now. Why do you want to know? Is that the woman you thought you knew from somewhere?"

"I don't know." He shook his head and his long tonsures fell forward, well oiled with the expensive scent of myrrh. "No, no. It cannot be. I thank you. You have been most helpful. Seven devils you say. In Magdala.

"When will you set up a meeting between Jesus and myself?"

It took Thaddeus a moment to follow the abrupt change in subject and they settled on a time and place for the rendezvous. All in all, a strange talk.

Magdalene

The din was incredible. Even from a distance as she climbed the incline to the Temple, she was enveloped in it, the frightened lowing of animals, the shouting of the sellers, the cries of the penitents and bellowing of the priests, the sounds carried to her on the fresh wind. Today there were few women making their way to the Temple. The women were in their homes involved in the final preparations for the evening meal, the removal of Hametz— the leavened substances. They also had to build a great bonfire into which Hametz would be thrown at Erev Pessah, the start of the seven days of Matzah, the days of unleavened bread. Today, they sweated over hot fires and ovens, hurrying to finish the final details in time to wash and purify themselves before the men returned and the advent of evening was announced from the temple walls.

Instead, she was joined by thousands of men, some carrying one lamb, others leading small flocks of them to sell in the Temple to those whose lambs would be judged unclean by the priests. Every adult male of Jewish descent who could afford it had undergone ritual purification in the baths near the Temple, and then had entered the Golden Gate bringing the sacrifice of the lamb, the perfect yearling lamb, the paschal lamb of the Passover. It would be butchered by a succession of priests in assembly lines, each priest responsible for a different aspect of the slaughter, each priest certifying as to the lamb's cleanliness and purity of form and internal organ, until at last it was returned to its original owner gutted, blooded, and ready for roasting, its blood thrown on the High Altar. She had heard it said that over a hundred thousand lambs would be sacrificed in the one afternoon allotted to it by the Law. Incredible. And for the first time in her life, she was here for Passover.

She came before dawn to pay her coins, to enter into the darkness of the grotto baths, strip, and lower herself into the icy water, pouring more over herself with the ewers until she was clean enough to enter the inner Golden Gate. Twenty priests had bent their backs into the weight of the great door, pushing it open, and she had shivered with cold and awe as she entered the Women's Court with hundreds of others to offer sacrifices and confessions, still wet with the ritual purification, to go before the One God.

She was virtually alone in the crowd of men, pushed and hurried toward the women's baths, and then again to the great door that marked the first opening of the Temple walls. The shadow of the immense wall fell across her, dropping the temperature sharply. The walls, higher again than the height of fifty men held the cool of winter still. The front wall of the Temple grounds was deep, the sounds of footsteps, voices, and the raucous calling of frightened animals rebounding off the stone passageway. The wall housed rooms and porticoes, living quarters of the people who ran the Temple. Its cold seeped into her bones until her teeth chattered. She pulled her wool robe and mantle closer, covering her face in the darkness. Flickering torches lighted her way, though she could have found it regardless. Her father had told her abut the Temple from the time she was old enough to speak and she knew it better perhaps than her own home.

The daylight ahead beckoned her into the Outer Court and she waited expectantly for the chill to pass her shoulders as it had on the day before when she stepped out again into the sunshine, into its brilliance and the vast space that was the Court, dominated on the far side by the Inner Temple. The Holy Sanctum.

Again, as she had expected, she was caught up by the majesty, by the feel of the polished stones beneath her feet, of the walls that surrounded her, the sounds, the smells of incense, and the flush that mounted her face as she walked the space of the Outer Court. Gold ornaments glittered in the sunlight. The priests moved with strength and vitality, their white vestments sparkling in the sunlight as they hurried through their duties to be ready for noon and the beginning of the sacrifice.

Over the clamor of vendors, animals, and hundreds of voices, she could hear the uneven beating of her heart and had to resist the impulse to press her hands to her face.

It was the Temple.

Near her, a simple country man looked around and almost dropped the lamb he was carrying, his mouth held open in awe at the wonder of the Temple. She felt a momentary jealousy against him, for he would carry his lamb up to the priest, would see the first cut, would experience the holy rapture of the ceremony and know himself cleansed of every evil and sin, while she, a woman, would be banished to the Women's Court, peering through the latticework. And then that thought was carried away, for she saw Jesus ahead in the crowd, striding toward the Inner Court, and she hastened to follow, to keep from losing sight of him so that she could find a place to the east, in the Women's Court, where she could watch him and hear his words.

Her heart skipped with irregular beats. She saw where he entered and ran as quickly as she dared to the Women's Court. The court was empty, hollow, the sound of her footsteps echoing on the stone walls, the sounds of the rest of the Temple muted here.

She paused, searching through the latticework, moved, and searched again until she found him, surrounded by the others, the Twelve, all with their lambs. And John, Jesus' kinsman, held two, carrying the burden of the Rebbe. She leaned forward, her hands curled tightly into the rough stone. Her face scratched against it and she pulled back slightly. He was going to speak. She knew it. Her heart beat painfully, and she breathed deeply to ease its pain. Aemoa had told her to remember his words carefully and to report them to the other women.

A man brought his son to Jesus, cradling the youth in his

arms. The boy was shivering following his purification, yet fevered, his limbs twisting with pain. Jesus put his hands on the boy, murmuring. And instantly the boy's body went still. A moment later, he raised his head and looked around, confused. "Abba?" he asked. His father burst into tears, burying his face against his son. Around him, the silence spread through the inner court, like the ripples in a pond.

From the shadows a voice spoke. "By what authority doest thou these things? And who gave thee this authority?"

Magdalene looked for the speaker, but he was out of sight. From his accent, he was a Jerusalemite, well educated, wealthy.

Jesus answered and said, "I also will ask you one thing, which if you tell me, I, likewise, will tell you by what authority I do these things. The baptism of John, whence was it? from heaven, or of men?"

Magdalene sucked in a breath. It was a political challenge as well as a scriptural one. If the challenger said John was only a man, ordained only by men, speaking only as a man, then the people might grow angry, for John the Baptist was universally accepted as a prophet. But if the challenger said John was a prophet of Yahweh, and yet he had not followed the prophet's requirement for repentance, then he was undeserving of his rank.

The man answered Jesus, and said, "We . . . cannot tell."

And Jesus said, "Neither tell I you by what authority *I* do these things."

Magdalene fell against the latticed wall, letting it hold her up as the challenger came into view, his rich robes and his prayer shawl heavily tasseled. He was surrounded by other Pharisees. A low wind began, a rustling sense of power that raised the hairs on the back of her neck.

Even in the raucous outer court all sound died, the assembled there ceased speaking, clothing stopped rasping, the animals quieted, all sound, through the entire Temple died; even the priests stopped their preparations for the sacrifice. Jesus' voice, pitched to carry through the crowd, filled the Inner Court, bounced off the far walls and echoed back. Those nearest him sank down on benches and to the floor, arching their necks to see, straining to hear as he threw back his heavy mantle, his chin clean-shaven in honor of the day. And he taught. Using simple words, phrases that any unlearned man could understand, he taught the scripture.

Magdalene's hands wrapped around the lattice, fearful, for he challenged the Pharisee faction on their own ground, speaking of those who wore their robes and prayer shawls long in false humility and pride. And the Pharisees were insulted, angered that a country teacher should call them hypocrites.

Jesus spoke almost uninterrupted the whole morning, growing hoarse in the building heat, He healed three blind men with a touch of his hand and that angered the Pharisees too. Everything he did angered the men of power. Yet, as the hours passed, they did nothing, and she knew that, for whatever reason, the danger she sensed had passed.

Then, at the sun's zenith, the shofar sounded, the ram's horn, signaling the beginning of the sacrifice, the tones echoing through the Holy City. It was noon.

There was a mad rush toward the opening where the first priest stood, his knife, used only for this ceremony, gleaming at his belt. Magdalene moved from her place and found another where she could watch more closely the process of the slaughter. Prayers filled the air, the chanting of the priests, the bleating of the first animal as it was inspected by the first priest, counted, approved and passed on. The first cut was clean, across the arteries and windpipe in one crisp motion. The lamb's blood poured into the waiting container and the lamb and the blood were passed on to a waiting acolyte.

Her fingers curled more deeply into the cold stone, her lips parted, as she breathed the scent of heavy incense laced with the salty, metallic scent of blood. The noise of the men and the animals was intense, high pitched and echoing again and again off the stone walls. She moved along the latticework that separated her from the scene, seeing two rows of priests, each going through the same motions of slaughter and passing on the dead.

After the first cut and ritual gathering of the blood, each animal was passed on as it was gutted, the entrails and organs inspected by slippery red hands for blemishes or irregularity of form. Then it was skinned, the valuable pelt thrown into a growing white and red-splashed pile, the digestive, unclean organs going into another, more gruesome pile, the clean organs to be burned at the altar handed into the keeping of an acolyte. The procedure was fast, systematic, and within minutes a hundred lambs had been sacrificed.

The priestly robes were splattered with blood from the first moment, the robes that would be worn only once, never cleaned, a memorial taken home as a prize after the year of service was over, crusty with blood, to be hung in a chest and brought out often to tell of the experience. And when they died, the priests would be wrapped in the robes of office for burial.

The floor was running in blood, and, as Magdalene watched, a priest slipped and was injured on his own knife. He was replaced quickly, efficiently, by a clean-robed priest, eager for his hour of service. The blood was taken in and dashed on the Sacred Altar, the Rock Moriah of Father Abraham. The blood would drain through holes in the rock, into the hill beneath. And this one day of the year there would be so much blood that it would drain out of the rock into the valley below.

After thousands of lambs had been slaughtered, the floor was deep in blood. It pelted the lattice work of the wall separating the Women's Court from the rest of the Temple. Blood splattered her face through the openings in the stone wall. She was sprinkled with it.

A strange cleanliness began at the touch of the blood and drained into her soul through her pores. Her breath came quickly in small gasps. A silver bracelet cut into her flesh where she leaned into the wall, but she ignored the pain. It was a part of the moment. It was a part of the sacrifice.

She would have no paschal lamb, but would share with Aemoa, the Twelve, and Jesus, the one he was to bring back to the rented house. She watched the lamb Jesus had chosen as it was entered into the ritual. The priests seemed to take special care in its inspection, searching for some, any, blemish. It had none. It was perfect. The priest made the first ritual cut and passed the lamb on to the next priest.

At the end, Jesus took possession of the lamb, its legs tied together, the salt used in the blooding still caked on its sides. He was smiling as he turned away, she glimpsed into his face for a moment, and saw that he too was caught up in the thrill of the ceremony, his clothes splattered with the lamb's blood. He moved away, out of her sight. But Magdalene stayed, pressed against the lattice.

Hours passed as exhausted priests, their robes dragging in the pools of blood, were replaced in the line by others, still clean. The sight of slaughter, far from being horrific, brought her peace, calm, as if taking away the remembered pain: Jason's pain. The pain of his blood. The scene of the destroyed house in Magdala. The scene of bloody death. The memory of her son, lying in the bushes in his tiny red robe, which she had forgotten for so long. All the horror was slowly replaced with this, the scene of the Temple slaughter.

Poor Jason. Poor Jason. Holding her place at the women's wall, watching, she gave him up to Yahweh. It was the last, final part of her healing. Strength grew within her; she could *feel* the changes, and wondered if others would see them.

The Zealot claimed to see such changes already, but she knew the truth. She had lived with herself too long, knew the sickness, the hate, the fear that claimed her soul. But she was strong now. Jesus would see the changes in her. He would know. He would share this with her.

She gave herself totally to the slaughter, staying until the last lambs had been given to the last supplicants, the poor who couldn't afford to purchase a sacrifice, supplied out of Temple riches. The light was failing when she turned and stretched stiffened limbs. A priest, rounding up the last people of the day prior to closing the great doors, steadied her as he led her through into the Outer Court. His robe was splattered with blood. Exhaustion and elation in equal measure were etched into his face.

She walked through the cold walls and the great escarpment. She passed down the hill.

Somewhere in her mind, in the thoughts generated by the sight of all the blood, was a determination. She would seek out the truth about Jason soon. Not just yet. But soon. First, though, she would see if she could still worship like a Hebrew. Like the Mary she had been, but with the strength of the Magdalene.

The walk home was warm after the cold of Temple stone, and she felt light, carried on the breeze that swept up the city streets like a seed on the wind. People ran past her, hurrying to get home before the blowing of the shofarot, the dozens of shofar, signaling the end of one day and the beginning of the Passover. But Magdalene refused to hurry, glorying in the sunset, so bright on the horizon, the evening smells that permeated the air. There was the dry scent of bitter herbs, unleavened bread, and above it all was the smell of roasting lamb, rich in its own drippings. And wine. Some of it was hers. She had seen to it that her own wine was sold in the streets and bazaars for the festival. Her partner had agreed. He was a greedy man and she had made them a lot of money in this holy season.

She arrived home, preceding the blast of the shofarot by only minutes. She washed and changed out of her dress, knowing she would never wear it again while she was alive. She had already determined that she would be buried in the dress. Clean, Magdalene stood back, watching the bustle in the rented house, a half smile on her face. In the house she had rented for the festival week were fifteen men, all the women and children, and their supplies, all in only one room. The other room was locked, containing the furniture and furnishings and utensils still possibly contaminated by Hametz. There had simply not been enough days to ritually clean the entire rented house, hence the clutter in the one scrubbed, inspected, and rescrubbed room.

The woman from whom they had rented the house had declared the house kosher according to the Kashrut—the dietary laws of food preparation—and ready for Passover. But one did not trust strangers for things as important as kashering for the Passover meal.

The women had kashered all their own utensils while she stood at the latticework wall. Items used for broiling had been cleaned and brought to red heat, glasses had been soaked in water for three days—this done while on the road. Metal utensils—only those made in one piece could be used this week—were immersed in boiling water. Pots used for cooking had been filled with water, brought to a boil, and then red-hot coals had been thrown in, making the water spill over without cooling off, thus kashering the rim. Everything within the house, including walls and ceiling, had been kashered. All Hametz—leavened substances—had been discarded. They were ready for the ceremony of ceremonies, the one that made them a *People*.

The Zealot

There was a secret smile playing across her face when she entered. She was glowing, as though she had a lighted candle behind her eyes. Her fingers were interlaced loosely at hip level. Disheveled, obviously tired, she carried herself with such poise, such grace, that his throat constricted. Once again, she reminded him of Nirit. There was dried blood in her hairline. The folds of her mantle were thrown carelessly across her shoulders, her head uncovered, which was so unlike her, with her fear of being seen, shorn.

Concerned, he moved closer, peering down at her. The silver-streaked, black hair was shining, curled around her face. "Are you all right?" he asked. "We've been here for hours, waiting for you. Worried." His kept his voice soft, making sure it carried no farther in the crowded room.

"I am fine, Simon." She touched her face where the blood had splattered, remembering the feel of the blood there. "I went back to the Temple." Her smiled blossomed suddenly, and it was as if the sun rose again, out of time. "Oh, Simon," she whispered tautly. "I spent all day at the Temple."

His eyes went wide. "The whole day!" He knew what she had seen—the slaughter of sacrifice. She shouldn't have seen that, not in her state of mind. He still remembered the sight of her rocking in the moonlight, mad, possessed by grief. She grasped his wrist gently, curling her fingers around it. Inexplicably, her touch comforted him, and he looked deeply into her face, into eyes that were calm, like the dark silence of a deep well.

"I stayed from the first cut until they closed the Golden Gate. I saw it all, Simon. Everything that they will allow a woman to see. The blood of sacrifice and redemption splashed onto me. I heard the Rabboni, the Master, speak and silence the Pharisees. It was . . ." She shook her head as if words failed her, her voice intense.

"It was wonderful."

He understood what she meant. The Temple experience often did strange things to people. He had felt it himself more than once. He shook her hand free of his wrist. "I'll go with you to wash your face again. Pay attention to your forehead."

He led the way around back and waited on one side of the screen as she tilted the large jar that held their communal fresh water. He heard the splatter and her soft humming, recognizing the tune of the prayer the priests chanted as they returned the purified lamb to its owner. He wondered if there was some reason, some law that prevented Magdalene—a woman—from its use, but let that thought drift away.

When she returned, they walked back into the room and he left her to take his place at the low table. It was too low for couches, in the Roman tradition, but as they had to recline around the table by Law tonight, they rested on their sleeping mats, pillowed on one end to raise them. Magdalene's clean bare feet passed him as she joined the other women.

Aemoa in her white mantle, her face soft in the dying light, spoke the blessing for the candles, beginning the Passover ritual. "Blessed are You, Lord our God, King of the universe, who has sanctified us with His commandments, and commanded us to kindle the Yom Tov light." She lit the first candle, her features flaring with the taper.

The youngest child asked the first ritual question. It was the Fisherman's son, long-haired, his black eyes wide at his honor. "Why is this night different from all other nights?"

Jesus, the leader of the Seder, the ceremony of the Passover, answered. "On all other nights we eat Hametz and Matzah, on this night Matzah only; on all other nights we need not dip our foods into condiments, on this night we do so twice; on all other nights we may take our meal sitting up straight or in a reclining position, on this night we all recline."

The Zealot closed his eyes and pictured the scene, thousands of years ago when the Israelites left the land of captivity so suddenly that they could not bake the bread they had ready. Instead, they had rolled it into balls and set it on their heads, where the sun eventually baked it hard and unleavened.

The ceremony went on, each child taking part. Above it all, around it all, woven in so he would never forget this Pessah, this Seder, was the sound of Jesus' voice, still hoarse from the morning teaching in the Temple.

"Our Fathers were slaves to Pharaoh in Egypt . . ."

They each drank from the four cups of wine, the symbols of all that is good in life, ate the bitter herbs dipped in salt water, the reminder of the evil that is slavery and the tears shed by their ancestors, the Matzah. The ancient words spoken in the Rabboni's solemn voice echoed in the Zealot's mind, never to be forgotten.

"Who has commanded us the eating of the Matzah?" the child said.

"He who has commanded us to eat Maror," Jesus said.

The cup of Elijah, the ceremonial cup which would allow the old prophet to visit this house, was of the finest green glass, massive, with two handles, one on either side. The Zealot saw the Magdalene staring at the cup, a tender expression of pride on her face, and he wondered fleetingly if the cup was hers. They sang the old songs, the Magdalene's clear, slightly off key voice crisp in the crowd. Everything about the ceremony was beautiful. Tears started, and the greatest warrior of the Zealots allowed them to fall unchecked as Jesus passed the sops.

As the ceremony meal passed, the Magdalene's face reflected rapture. On Jesus' face was exhaustion and sadness. The Rabboni was always so sad now. So driven. He had changed when the Baptist was murdered. And then that thought too, slipped away.

That night, after the ceremony, they slept lined across the floor, wrapped in their respective blankets, all but Jesus. Simon, with his Zealot training, heard the Rabboni stir in the night, though it was odd for any Hebrew to sleep poorly on the night of the Guardian of Israel. At sunrise, Jesus was gone. *Into the mountains to pray again?* the Zealot wondered. Or perhaps into the Temple? Jesus would return. When he again found peace.

The crowds of people started home after daybreak, and by evening, the city had lost half of its pilgrims and appeared, by comparison, nearly deserted. The Twelve and their traveling companions would stay until Jesus returned, then perhaps they would leave. He would tell them where they would go next. The

ꓔy for another day, and when he returned,
ᴄd, and thirsty. His face was calm. Resigned. Not
ᴏn noticed. Not peaceful at all.

Magdalene

Their travel in the next months was driven, harried, as if Jesus was concerned he might miss some small section of the country, some small group of Hebrews living in the predominantly Greek and heathen cities to the north. They traveled through Phoenicia and the Decapolis, Caesarea Philippi. They spent days in the smaller towns and weeks in the larger cities, Jesus teaching in the synagogues, on street corners, and in homes.

The group grew and shrank, those on the outer edges constantly changing as new men would hear of the teacher, prophet, and healer traveling through the countryside and join them, replacing those leaving in disgust and anger because Jesus espoused an idea or thought that was strange, or refused to side with the Hebrew against the Romans, or simply because Jesus sat at meat with, and even touched, the unclean ones he chanced to meet. He was the Rabonni—radically revolutionary, but not in the way other people expected. His message was of peace and forgiveness, of love and harmony.

Magdalene felt herself flowering beneath his words. She would sit at the fringes of the groups listening to him, her body heavily swathed and sweating in the summer heat, not moving for hours and she could actually feel herself glowing. Growing. With the words of forgiveness ringing in her ears, she could, almost, look at a Roman soldier without fear, and she seldom ran when small groups of the killers would pass her on patrol.

Though lately she had had strange dreams about Romans. Dreams about hands, pain, screams, and fire. For once, the dreams were not connected to Jason. Strange dreams that should be left for sleep and not examined too closely by day.

Best, Magdalene had learned to pray again—simple and joyous prayers, thanking God, the Father, for bringing Rabboni and his followers into her life. *Jesus.* His face shone with such love and passion when he spoke. His voice filled with tenderness, compassion for the injured, the sick, for widows and orphans, for the least powerful of the people. He spoke to women as easily as to men, treating them as equals, as if they could think and reason. And sometimes he looked at her, his eyes liquid and fringed with those long lashes, and shared a smile with her alone.

Magdalene didn't have to worry about anyone thinking she was in love with him. She was not, and perhaps never would be, an eligible widow. Her monthly flows had not restarted when her spirit was cleansed of demons and her mind was healed. The death of her woman's body left her among the females of society not suitable for marriage—too young to be included among the gray and bent women who were of no use to a man, and too old to join the eligible widows.

She was able to move back and forth at the outskirts of both groups, coming and going as she pleased. The greatest benefit to being barren was that she missed none of Jesus' sermons and none of his quiet nights while banished to a menstrual hut. While all of the other women spent a week or more out of each month living in isolation, she was constantly available for service to Jesus and his followers.

When his voice gave out from hours of shouting to crowds, she was there to fix a soothing herbal tea. When he needed to laugh, which was more and more often these days, she was there with some silly comment garnered from the crowd, some amusing observation to share with him. She kept his meals warm, his tunics mended, took his sandals to be cleaned and oiled. And Magdalene, as a woman who was not a woman, followed him everywhere, always with a bit of pickled fish and loaf of bread to share with him, for he so often forgot about the simple things in life, like food.

With the disciples, they traveled all through that long hot summer, kicking up huge clouds of dust wherever they went. She heard one person say that he could always tell when the Rabboni moved, because half the earth went with him. And it was true.

In late August, with the sun more scorching than she had ever remembered, the group of travelers stopped in Capernaum to rest for a few weeks. But it was long enough to have the fuller clean her clothes and to bathe and wash her hair. She shopped in the market, buying new tunics for the disciples and one for Jesus, purchased a new outer dress for herself, to replace the one stained by temple blood.

Magdalene enjoyed the chance for solitude she found on this stop, and found peace in the privacy of her own home, though she still shared her rooftop suko with many of the younger followers. She missed the time with Jesus, of course, but it wasn't difficult to find him at any time in the day and bring him his lunch or a cup of water.

Magdalene also found time to visit Angel, spending afternoons in the cool of her home, chatting and drinking spiced wine. Over time, their conversations evolved from bawdy humor to discussion of Jesus. Angel had developed a great interest in Jesus and asked questions about the man who talked with women as if they were equals, and who actually touched the unclean people of Jewish society. Magdalene hid these visits from Thaddeus. He was still her self-proclaimed protector and he could be difficult about Angel.

At the end of September, Jesus pulled them out of Capernaum with only two days notice. With the rains threatening to come early, Jesus wanted to be in Judea for the Feast of Sukos. They had one month to cross the countryside, a journey that would normally have taken them six weeks. Jesus would have to hurry, stopping at fewer towns. *Impossible.* He would never do that. Magdalene sighed. *Men.*

Somehow they did reach the Holy City in time for Sukos. Not bothering to rent a house, Jesus and the Fisherman threw up a suko on a rented roof in less than a day. It had three rooms and four removable walls, little more than screens, for privacy. They wouldn't be here long, but the sense of a home that was theirs alone and not their hosts' was delightful. It lent a feeling of gaiety to the feast.

The week of Sukos flew by and Magdalene spent almost every day in the Temple. She had expected it to be restful. Uneventful. It wasn't. And she began to be afraid. The Pharisees and Sadducees followed Jesus, asking questions of him, topics of Law, quagmires into which he could slip and fall, questions which could cause him to be denounced. With each baited question, Magdalene became more afraid and followed Jesus more closely than ever. Yet when the worst trap was laid, there was nothing she could do to help.

Magdalene had come early to the Temple to pray and, finding Jesus teaching, had sat in the Women's Court and listened. He spoke about simple things, because the crowd was of the poorer citizens, the less educated, and he addressed them in a carrying voice, for there were many of the heathen blasphemers and Samaritans in the outer Gentile court, sitting in small groups, listening. Magdalene liked the clean, pure words, unsophisticated and sensible. As at the Passover, she leaned her face into the cool stone of the women's wall and listened.

He spoke for an hour into the hush of attentiveness. So engrossed was she, she scarcely heard the commotion in the Outer Court until it reached Jesus. A small crowd of scribes, Pharisees, and a few Sadducees, their anger like a dark cloak about them, moved into the Inner Court where Jesus taught. Though they were louder as they approached him, Jesus' voice never broke, nor wavered, nor did he look their way. He told his story through to the end, and then sat, ignoring the important men, until one, younger than the rest and reckless with youth, called out to Jesus.

"Rabbi. Rabbi!"

Jesus was sitting on his heels, and he rocked back, eyes closed, as though unaware, as though praying. Magdalene's breath went ragged. Her heart hammered unevenly. She curled her fingers, as if to sink her nails into the stone. *Something was about to happen here, something dangerous.* It was apparent in the stance of the influential men, in the way the spectators scuttled away from Jesus.

A young woman, her clothing ripped, exposing red welts across her flesh, was shoved into the midst of the men remaining around Jesus. She staggered and fell, clutching at her torn clothes, not quite managing to cover her breasts. The crowd, seeing a woman obviously caught in the act of adultery, surged forward and closed around Jesus, only to pull back slightly at the angry gestures of the men who held her.

The reckless young man who had spoken first, reached to the

woman and, laughing, pinched her through a rent in her tunic. When she flinched away, his face flushed an angry red, and he slapped her, a stinging blow. The young woman moaned and trembled, crossing her arms over her breasts. Several men moved closer to better stare at the beaten woman, lust and violence on their faces. Magdalene's mouth was dry as the dust on the floor.

Swaggering, the young man stepped to where Jesus sat. "Rabboni," he said loudly, "this woman was taken in adultery, in the very act. Moses, in the Law, commanded that such should be stoned." He tossed a small stone, smooth as if from a creek bed, into the air and caught it. "But what say you?"

Jesus, as though he hadn't heard, began to write with his finger in the dust of the Temple floor. The silence was potent and Magdalene could the smell the sweat of confrontation on the air. Slowly, the court settled, though uneasily. Waiting.

The young man, emboldened at Jesus' silence asked him again as he poked a finger at the shivering woman. "What say you, Jesus of Nazareth?" He tossed the stone again, catching it deftly. "Can you not respond to so simple a question? Are you deaf, man? Perhaps *you* need to be healed." There was no laughter at his remark, and for the first time, the young man seemed to notice the silent crowd edging in close. He looked from face to face and lost some of his swagger; he touched the long tassels on his prayer shawl as if for reassurance and regained his brazen smile.

Slowly, Jesus stood and looked into the young man's face. The youth's lips twitched, his brazen expression fled. He looked away, growing pale. Jesus' gaze traveled slowly from one to the other of the Pharisees, the Sadducees, the scribes. As one, they seemed to shrink and pull away. Finally Jesus smiled, though sadly. He nodded to the small stone in the young man's hand. "He that is without sin among you, let him, first, cast a stone at her."

No one moved. No one said a word. Jesus stooped down again, and wrote on the ground. From her place in the Women's Court, Magdalene couldn't make out the character he drew, but perhaps it was from some part of the Law which reminded the important men of their own duplicity in the scheme. One which made *them* equally guilty before the Law.

There was no sound for a moment, not even the whisper of a

breeze. An older statesman, who held a stone ready in his hand, turned and walked away from the center of the crowd. His hand, trembling, dropped the rock with a ringing clatter. He broke into a run at the sound, as though the rock had been aimed at him. Slowly, still without words, others left, from the eldest first, to the youngest last, their footsteps echoing in the silent chamber. Through the spaces in the latticework, Magdalene could see the woman, the young, brazen man, now pale and shaking, and Jesus. The man moved as if to speak, but his voice wouldn't come. Silent, he turned away and walked after the others. The woman bent and gathered up her rags, covering herself, still trembling, her eyes never leaving Jesus.

His face solemn, Jesus, stood and looked around the Temple as though surprised and seeing it for the first time. His gaze fell on the young woman staring at him, her face tear streaked.

"Woman," he said gently. "Where are your accusers? Has no man condemned you?"

"No man, Lord," she whispered. The silence that fell between them seemed to build. Her trembling slowed and stopped.

"Neither do I condemn you," Jesus said. "Go. And sin no more."

Later, the tears dry on her face, Magdalene pulled herself away from the latticework wall and went home, her footsteps silent in the empty Temple.

Chapter Sixteen

Thaddeus

"You what?" Thaddeus exploded. "You told Angel *what?* I thought that was a joke! I can't believe you would tell her something like that. All right, *promise* her something like that," he said, as she started to interrupt. "Well, you're not going. I won't have it. And don't you raise those brows at me, Magdalene. You are not going to that side of town. Not today, not ever. Don't ask again," he shouted.

"Fine, Thaddeus." She smiled sweetly, but there was something in her eyes that gave him pause. "I'll ask one of the others to take me to see her. I promised Angel I would make this visit while I am in the capital, and I'm going to keep my promise. I'm going to see her sister, with or without you."

"Magdalene, you don't know that side of town. It's—"

"No, I don't." She grinned. "That's why I'll need a guide. Angel gave me directions, but I'm afraid I won't be able to follow them. I *would* hate to get lost in the Holy City." She tapped her cheek. "Perhaps Shalmer would act as a guide. We haven't seen much of him since we got here, but he should know this town well enough to show me the way. Would you find the boy for me please? Surely someone must know where his father lives."

Thaddeus shut his eyes and blew out a breath. He had known the argument was lost before he even started it. She had *changed*. She was more stubborn since they got back to Jerusalem and he didn't know why. There was no reasoning with her now. She had promised Angel she would take a message to her sister and visit for a while and she would go no matter what. But perhaps . . . "All right. I'll take you. But not today. Day after tomorrow. I promise."

"Today, Thaddeus. We're leaving in the morning," she said

triumphantly. "I overheard Jesus tell you while we served bread to break the fast. You, dear friend, are trying to deceive me. I will go today, now. Will you take me, or not?"

He rubbed his forehead. She reminded him more and more of his wife. She had started out sweet and gentle too. *Women.* Of course, any woman who would attack a man with a broom at their first meeting was not sweet and gentle. He snorted at his own blindness. "I'll take you."

"Now?"

"Yes. Now. Are you ready? Do you want me to carry anything?"

"My, my, my. So helpful," she teased.

"Don't push me, Magdalene," he growled. "You don't know what you are getting yourself in to. Do you have any idea who her customers are? Do you think a whore could operate a thriving business on Jewish money in the Holy City? It's probably *Roman* coin she takes as payment. Yes, *Roman.* Are you going to *swoon* if we run into a rowdy bunch of soldiers out on leave, visiting a famous house of pleasure? Didn't think about that did you?"

Her face fell, her levity draining away. "Yes. I thought of it," she said softly. "But this is something I have to do. For me as much as for Angel." She took his arm and led him out the door, covering her face with her veil and her heavy mantle. "But I thought that with the sukos and all the visitors in the city, the soldiers would still be on emergency duty schedules."

"*Probably,*" he grumbled. They walked in silence for a while as children ran, screaming past them, playing catch-me on the narrow, winding, residential road. "What is Angel's sister called?"

"Atarah."

"Atarah." He felt a slight chill. He knew that name. He said, "They chose a venerable and respected name; obviously it's not her own."

"Don't be catty, Thaddeus. Can you find her place?"

"Yes. I can find it," he muttered.

"I'm sure you can," she said demurely, ignoring the frustrated look he cast her.

The noise of the crowd was raucous, making conversation difficult, and so he didn't reply. Which was was perhaps wise.

Magdalene was being difficult, and a public argument was to be avoided.

The procession of pilgrims leaving Jerusalem slowed and grew congested, forcing the pace into a crawl, which made the noise only louder. There were whole families with most of their belongings piled on their heads, too poor to own a donkey, and there were others mounted on camels or donkeys, or riding in carts, too wealthy to walk. It was a strange mixture even to Thaddeus, who was accustomed to the sight. For the Magdalene, he was glad she had covered her face, for he was certain she walked with her mouth open.

Behind them, he caught sight of the boy Shalmer, doggedly following them from a distance, shadowing them, making himself noticeable only by his haste. His desire for the Magdalene was getting out of hand. The boy never let her out of his sight. Thaddeus debated bringing the subject up with her, because she seemed blind to the soft sighs and longing eyes of the boys who traveled with them. Instead, he merely pointed out Shalmer's progress to her at an opportune moment, just as the boy tumbled over a large basket of goods packed on the verge of the street. Magdalene laughed softly. She had a beautiful laugh, but the point was made without his saying a word.

"I would guess that my journey into this particular part of the city would bounce me from the pedestal he put me on. No young man wants to see the object of his dreams visit a prostitute. I will appear somewhat less than a temple virgin now."

Thaddeus disagreed, but kept his council. This young boy's admiration had already lasted longer than he had thought it would. He had a feeling that nothing Magdalene could do would make him less infatuated.

He led Magdalene to Atarah's home, which was also the back door of her business. It had changed greatly since he first visited here so many years ago. Then, Atarah was one of only three girls, now, he could tell by the additions to the upper stories of the house, that it sheltered a much larger business, and a much more profitable one. He tried to leave Magdalene in the lee of a high wall and go to the door alone, but she would have none of it.

"I see no reason why I shouldn't come with you. As soon as I tell her who sent me she will let me in."

Thaddeus gave up trying to get her to stay out of the way while he reintroduced himself to his once mistress. He could only hope she would appear not to recognize him in front of Magdalene.

They were told by a house servant to wait in the patio; the wait was short. Magdalene's memorized message from Angel got the prostitute to the door faster than Thaddeus thought possible. One moment the doorway to the patio was empty, the next, there she stood. Always a tall woman, slender as her sister was portly, Atarah favored colorful, loose flowing clothing that clung to her willowy curves, accentuating her foreign stature and rich, dark skin of her Egyptian father. High cheek bones and sloe tilted eyes smiled at him from across the years and he felt his knees go weak. But Atarah never even glanced at him. Her smile and out-held arms were for Magdalene.

The exotic woman laughed at Magdalene's expression. "Oh! My dear, elder sister plays a small joke on you. She didn't tell you we were but half-sisters." The familiar laugh, low and hoarse, filled the courtyard. "My father was one of several tribal chieftains my mother entertained later in her career. Angel, however, was the child of her true love. Tell me. Is my sister still, ah, taken with much eating?"

To his surprise, Magdalene laughed. "She told me you always called her fat. She said to tell you that she loves anything that is forbidden to her. And yes. She is happily portly." Thaddeus sighed in disgust. The two women were instant friends.

Atarah used Greek boys as personal servants, pretty things who seemed more feminine than their mistress. As they brought deep cushions to Atarah's private parlor and served drinks, Thaddeus wondered which of the silent, feline boys were still slaves. He knew that Atarah sold them their freedom after a few years of service, keeping the boys on afterwards as servants if they wished. He knew that some of them earned their freedom sooner than others by acting the woman's part for certain high ranking Roman soldiers.

One of the boys was assigned to his needs with a flick of Atarah's hennaed and buffed nails. Still she hadn't looked at

Thaddeus. He sipped at his chilled red wine as the women talked and nibbled at grape leaves seasoned with flavored vinegar, the taste of balsam wood light on the leaves. The boy's eyes never left Thaddeus' face, and he was uncomfortable with the attention of the beautiful youth.

Thaddeus followed the conversation with part of his mind, the rest bent on the difficult problem posed by Jesus that morning. It dealt with guilt on a point of Law and the right to judge another who was just as guilty but perhaps in another area. It was a sticky problem and his concentration slipped away for a while to be brought back abruptly by a sudden strained silence in the room. He blinked rapidly to clear his mind and took in the shocked face of the Magdalene, the embarrassed face of their host.

"What . . . What did you say?" Magdalene's voice was breathless.

"I . . . I . . . It was nothing important. I must have the wrong Jason in mind. After all, there are a great many men named Jason, and—"

"Not many men named Jason who lived in Magdala. And fewer of those can call themselves traders. Even fewer who can afford to make their way to the Holy City more than once a year. I want to speak to this man you claim came from my husband so long ago. I know how they are used. Angel explained *that* side of your business to me before I left." Her voice was harsh.

"But, my dear. The man met this trader so long ago he would not remember who— And even so, he was trained elsewhere. I'm sure I must have been mistaken in thinking I might have known your husband. One meets so many."

"I will speak with him. Now." Magdalene's voice was unyielding. Hard. Her face was strained with tension and pale with shock. Thaddeus groped blindly in their words for a sense of what he had missed, what Atarah had to do with Jason. If the man had been one of her customers, it was only natural Magdalene would be upset, but he didn't think that was it. Atarah would never have mentioned a past *business arrangement* to a wife. It simply wasn't *done*. And Jason had been dead for many years. Too long for the emotion on Magdalene's face.

No. This was more than that. This was something Atarah had

let drop in their search for mutual acquaintances or family, something ordinary, something *known*, and thinking Magdalene already knew it. Something about one of Atarah's servants, and about Jason, who was a trader. What did Jason trade in? Magdalene had never . . .

A cold fear began roiling at the base of Thaddeus' spine. Why would one of Atarah's *special boys* be called in at this point in the conversation? The look of pity on Atarah's face was explanation enough. Pity and something deeper. A look that said she too had once faced the impossible, the painful, and wouldn't deny the other woman's right to do so.

Atarah clapped her hands once and spoke in flawless Greek to the boys sitting wide-eyed at the raw emotion in the room. Quickly they rose and left, not completely successful in hiding their relief. As the curtain fell on the room, blocking the slight breeze from the hall, Atarah turned on her cushion and faced the Magdalene squarely.

"You are a guest in my home." The song of a bird started outside the open window, its call melodious, seeming to accentuate the husky quality of the woman's voice. "Under ordinary circumstances, I wouldn't continue with this conversation, but there is strength in your face. I think you are not like the usual woman with her whining and carping and weakness." She brushed the side of her face with one tapered finger. "I am a believer in the right of the strong to know the truth even when it is painful. Tell me what your Jason looked like."

"He was beautiful," Magdalene whispered. "Dark, like me. His eyes flashed with laughter too often, or grew hard with his thoughts. Jason could speak with his eyes better than most men can with their voices."

"Did he have a scar, a mark, a mole, something unique? Perhaps a trait that would set him apart. What you describe is handsome but like a thousand other men." Thaddeus was surprised at Atarah's tone. A silky purr—sarcastic. Insulting. Then he realized she was giving the Magdalene something to fight against, something to hold back the tears, to make her angry. And it worked. Magdalene threw back her head, the short hairs coming lose from the braids that held them.

"Yes, he had a scar. There are thousands of men with scars. That isn't unique."

"Then perhaps you will tell me what makes this Jason unique," she said, smiling with the corners of her eyes.

The smile had its desired effect and the tension drained out of Magdalene's shoulders. She almost smiled herself. "He had a scar on the inside of his arm, here," she pointed, lifting her arm, "And here," she pointed to her face at a spot near her upper lip. She looked away, swallowing past a dry throat. Atarah clapped again, this time calling out in Aramaic for juice and wine to be brought in again. Magdalene continued, "He used to say he got them rolling with a boy with a knife as a child, over the results of a reprimand from a teacher at synagogue."

"But he really got them from a young woman he tried to tumble. Yes?"

The effect of her words was unexpected. Magdalene's face went flat for a long moment, then found a soft expression, like a child who has just fallen asleep. Peaceful, almost. Her lids fluttered down, covering her eyes and a smile touched the corners of her lips. "Yes." When she opened her eyes, she was relaxed. Calm. "Forgive my anger. I prayed that I would learn the truth about Jason's death and I knew it would be hard. It's a surprise that the Lord would teach me so much about his life as well, and that I would find that harder still. So. Tell me about Jason the Trader from Magdala. All traders specialize. What *trade goods* did my husband specialize in?"

The curtain was drawn aside preventing response, and a slender young man entered the room carrying a tray on his arm. He could have been anywhere from eighteen to thirty, his face unlined and smooth, without a hint of beard, his hair long and oiled, gathered with a gold clasp at the base of his neck. He was painted at eyes and lips, and he served with a grace so practiced and smooth, so fluid, it was as if his body was encased in water. As if he danced. When he presented Thaddeus with a glass of wine, their eyes met briefly and Thaddeus was certain of the man's sexual preference. Strangely, for once, he didn't feel threatened by it.

"Would you please join us, Martine?" Atarah asked. "I would

like you to hear this conversation and to add to it if you wish." It was most definitely a request, not an order, and issued in her most gracious voice. The man was a friend, not a slave, and if he had worn a Roman slave collar, it had not been for long, as there were no scars on his collarbones.

"I would be delighted." Martine placed cushions where he could view each of the other three unhindered, and settled himself slowly, relaxing effortlessly into the pillows. He appeared tranquil, so peaceful of face and form, that he instantly put them at ease. Yet, there was a simmering tension below the man's calm, an energy that seemed at odds with his exterior.

"Martine," Atarah used the diminutive form of the name as though to a favored child, "this young woman was sent by my sister to meet with me, I think with a purpose. She is the wife of an old business acquaintance." She stared at the man intently, and Thaddeus felt Martine's tension grow, a hum as yet low key, filling his eyes. "Her husband was killed several years ago in Magdala. His name was Jason. A trader by profession."

Martine, his training impeccable, did none of those things that might show reaction in an ordinary man. Only a slight tensing of the taut skin around his eyes and a practiced question on his brows. If anything, he was more relaxed than before Atarah spoke. Yet, there was something different, less peaceful about the man. "Yes?"

Atarah smiled with her lips, her eyes equally cool, boring into Martine's, giving and sharing in a silent conversation something more than her words implied. "She is called Magdalene. She is here to help feed and clothe the followers of the Rabboni Jesus."

Martine inclined his head. "A worthy and learned man. A generous woman." Was there sarcasm laced into his words? No. He spoke the truth.

"She knew nothing of her husband's business activities. A typical woman of the times," Atarah said. There was a slight emphasis on the word typical, and Martine nodded again. "She still knows nothing, but she seeks to learn. And from what I gather, she has educated herself well. She has become one of those rare women who grows. A *strong* woman."

Martine's face was still, his eyes now freely studying the

Magdalene.

"Martine?" Atarah said.

"Yes."

"Would you tell her about yourself? About your past. I think she deserves to hear. And perhaps you might gain something for yourself as well." When seconds trickled by, she said, gently, "Martine?" Silence filled the room as a variety of emotions passed under Martine's skin, paused a moment in his eyes and then were replaced by others even more enigmatic. Magdalene never moved nor broke contact with his eyes. Martine looked again at Atarah. She was smiling sadly.

"You presume too freely upon my reverence for my past. For the scarred ghost of the child I was."

"There comes a time when it is right to speak. When it is weak to remain silent. Angel sent her to me, I think in part so she could learn the truth if she wished it. You know my sister. She would do you no harm. She would send no trouble to us."

The song bird resumed singing outside the window. Thaddeus hadn't heard it fall silent.

"If you wish," Martine said softly. "I'll tell this woman Angel sent to you, about Jason the trader. And perhaps we shall see if she is the woman you think. *So strong.*" His last words were slightly insulting.

Thaddeus' leg had gone to sleep, and yet he couldn't move. He was nailed to the floor with confusion and an overwhelming curiosity. He wished he had listened to the conversation between the two women. He wished for an instant of privacy and a large bush. He wished for—

"Jason was a slave trader who specialized in small boys."

The effect on the room was astounding to a shocked Thaddeus. Nothing happened.

"He bought young boys from their families. Jews, Greeks, Nubians, any nationality as long as they were attractive and quite young." His voice was carefully expressionless, as though he spoke by rote. "He then turned them over for their training to a man in Capernaum. When they were sufficiently . . . capable, they were again sold, to the highest bidder at special auction, here in the capitol or in Rome if they were unusually competent and beautiful. He looked at Magdalene. "Have you ever been to a slave auction, Magdalene?" It was the first time he had spoken to her, and his voice, so neutral until now, was suddenly hard, almost rough, hiding a deep anger.

"Yes," she whispered.

"Do you know what your husband was responsible for? Do you have any idea what happens to children when a drunken buyer— When they *try out* their purchases for the first time? Do you know what they are allowed by Roman law to do to any slave who shrinks away, who shows fear or tears or who *displeases* them? Your husband was a murderer. A mangler of tiny boys. Your *husband*." He spat, the spittle landing at Magdalene's feet.

Magdalene's eyes were fastened on his face, her hands clasped in her lap. There were tears on her cheeks. Martine went on, his eyes boring into her. "My twin brother and I were sold to your husband by our *dear* uncle when both our parents were killed by plague. Their bodies were still warm from the fever when he herded us into the room where Jason was and took the silver he offered. 'Twin boys,' I remember him saying. 'Odynius will be pleased.' *Odynius.* That was his partner. He was responsible for our training. He taught us how to stand, how to serve from a tray, how to dance, how to please our owners in every way. *Every* way.

"Do I offend you, lady?" He smiled, showing he didn't care if he offended or not. His voice was pure, silken venom. "Atarah, you should take her to one of those *special auctions*. She would be thrilled seeing little boys walk across a stage swinging their hips and smiling, all painted eyes and fear, wondering which man will buy them and what he will do to them."

Magdalene stared into Martine's face, her eyes swimming, tears running down her face to drip off her jaw.

"It is said that fear has a smell. It is true. Afterward, a special auction, after the first boys are sold and sitting on their masters' laps in the crowd, then the real fun begins. Wine is served and food, and when everyone is slightly drunk, they bring out the *very* special boys. My brother and I were very special. Odynius had *enjoyed* us and so our training was longer than most, and my brother was fond of him. He loved the man, wanted to please him. He would have done anything to be allowed to stay with him."

The silence in the room was deep and no one moved. Thaddeus was numb and tingling from the waist down. He knew the others in the room had forgotten him. He was unnecessary here. He shouldn't be here.

Martine was watching Magdalene. What was he looking for in her face, Thaddeus wondered. What did he expect to see? There was pain, sadness, even a touch of horror mingled there. And she seemed older. Why did Atarah allow this? Why had Angel sent Magdalene here? Thaddeus remained silent.

"We were purchased by a Jew. Does that shock you, Magdalene? He was a very wealthy man in the capitol and his use of boys was little known. I think he was looked upon as a lonely but pious man because he never married, a kind man as well, giving a home to homeless boys.

"He was a goat," Martine hissed, his face contorting. "The things he did to us—" He looked away. "After a year we had enough. We were going to run away, back to Odynius. At least there we were not left bleeding and bruised and kept locked at night in a hole in the wall. My brother said Odynius would protect us."

The song bird chirped once as though startled.

"The night we planned to leave we were called upon to perform a certain service. A game we played while our owner, drunk on wine, watched. My brother, secure in the knowledge that we were leaving, taunted him. Angered him. I was afraid, but my brother couldn't seem to stop. He went on and on, until—" Martine swallowed. He seemed to have difficulty drawing a breath.

"He beat my brother to death while I watched. He did it slowly. And then when he was finished, he cut out his tongue and sat it on a plate in front of me and told me to eat it."

The Magdalene sat still. Silent. Pale.

"I killed him. I didn't know I could do it or I would have done it sooner, before he killed my brother. It was my fault. If I had killed that . . . that monster sooner, my dear brother would still be alive, with me, today.

"Do you know what it is like to live with only half of yourself, Magdalene?" Martine's voice was tortured. "That is how it is with me. Half of me is dead, killed because the other half wasn't willing to act, wasn't strong enough. And all because of Jason. Your *husband*.

"I smiled when I heard of his death. I sent inquiries about it and decided it was a fitting way for him to die. It was simply five years too late."

Magdalene

The walk back to the rented house was silent, the only diversion the sound of crickets and the low rumble of the masses, boarded up for the night. Even the spring air that brushed against her, wood and dung smoke scented by family meals, seemed a part of a dream. Magdalene's feet dragged on the path between buildings. Twice she would have fallen if not for the warm pressure of Thaddeus' hand on her elbow. She was so . . . tired.

Her brain whirled, new knowledge colliding with old love, new questions seeking answers. She had felt strong since the day of the temple sacrifice, capable of looking the truth squarely and shouldering the past no matter what it held. But she wasn't strong. She was weak in the face of reality's heavy burden.

Jason. A slave trader, specializing in small boys. How had he kept the truth from her, from the town? How had he lived a double life for all the years of her marriage? How could she have been so stupid? A fool.

There were many things she had refused to remember, things that were too painful to think about. Now, they beat at the confines of her mind, clamoring to be recognized, to be heard. Jason turning away from her in the night. Jason with the presents, the costly gifts and gentle words begging to be forgiven. How could she have forgotten the pain of those times. The bruised whelps, the aching wrists, the difficulty of breathing with broken ribs. She had *forgiven*. How could she do otherwise? She was only a woman, chattel, a possession. He could murder her without fear of repercussion. And he loved her. She knew it. It was there in his eyes each time afterwards. The love and the shame. And then he would be so good to her, so gentle. For months he wouldn't raise a fist against her, going and coming on his trade routes. *Slave trade routes.*

And she had loved him. Loved a trader in human flesh, small boys, and pain.

Suddenly they were standing before an open door, the light of many lamps bathing them in a soft glow. She blinked, turned away and back again. They were home. Home to a suko, the lamplight shining through the cracks. She tried to smile, but the room seemed to waver. There were people talking. She could feel the pressure of Thaddeus' hand on her arm and she leaned into him, resting in his solid warmth.

Jesus was talking to her, and then Simon. What were they saying? Something about Jason. They must know, they must all know about the boys and what he did. But they were smiling, laughing, gesturing. Then they slid away, back to the fringes of the crowd that moved like seaweed in an angry sea. A face moved toward her, smiling. *Jason. My God, it's Jason. Jason.* And the world mercifully slid into blackness.

Thaddeus

Thaddeus caught her before any of the others realized she had fainted and swung her up in his arms, striding past them, issuing orders for her bed to be laid out, calling for water and Aemoa. He ignored the look on the stranger's face. He knew this man. He had met the man in private, and the stranger did not indicate that he knew the Magdalene. Not then.

Gently, he set his burden on her rolled out mat, lifting her mantle from her head and using it to cover her body. She was cold and he chafed her hands between his own, her cold, blue nails scratching his palms. Aemoa removed her boots, brought out blankets and pushed him away so she could tend to the still form.

His anger, held in check by concern, rushed up and through him, a blazing path of fury. Freed from the burden of his friend, Thaddeus lashed out. He rushed into the front room, caught the stranger by the robes and beard. Crashed with him into the wall. His body and hands were weapons. He pounded the man's head into the limestone and clay. "You bastard. You miserable . . . miserable . . ."

"*Thaddeus!*" The voice thundered, commanding. A steel grip twisted his wrists. When he didn't let go, a blinding pain ran up his left arm and it dropped, useless.

The shocked silence in the room penetrated slowly and he released the stranger. The Zealot's hands were fisted, ready to hurt him again. Andrew's eyes met his, pleading; the Fisherman's were wild and confused. Anger drained out of him and Thaddeus fell into the Zealot, cradling his numb arm. He was pushed out of the lamplight, into the night, and slammed into the courtyard wall. Facing him was the Zealot, Jesus, John, and the man who had caused Magdalene to faint. Thaddeus stepped back, remembering to breathe, trying to find a center of calm. Prickles of pain ran up his arm; the Zealot had twisted it at an odd angle, ready to cause more pain if he didn't calm.

The Zealot said, "You will tell us what that attack was about." It wasn't a question. "You took the Magdalene and went off into the city all day, then you came back, *after dark*," he said, "both of you looking as if you saw death. We try to introduce her brother-in-law, Magdalene faints, and suddenly you are beating our guest's head against the wall. What happened?"

"Who is he?" Thaddeus' voice sounded whispery.

"I am Mary's brother-in-law. Joseph."

"You're not a Judean. Mary is," Thaddeus said. The stranger looked to Jesus for help, but the Rabboni said nothing, watching them all. Thaddeus glared at the stranger through the dark of night and said, "You asked many questions and pled for secrecy last we met. Now you are here, claiming the Magdalene as family. Tell us what changed. Speak."

"Yes, I am from Arimathea." Joseph's voice was wry and strained. He rubbed his throat, hidden behind his shaped and oiled beard. "But I am Jason's brother. We had been parted for many years. And," he glanced at Jesus, "secrecy is relative."

"Did you know what your brother traded in?" Though he tried, there was no way for Thaddeus to keep the revulsion from his voice. It shook with the effort of speech.

The man firmed his mouth. "For coin? Yes. I knew."

He lunged at the man, brought up short by the searing pain in his injured arm. The Zealot smiled, teeth gleaming in the moonlight. "You never learned to fight. I'll *break* the arm next time. Understand?"

"Yes. I understand. Now you understand. That spawn of a goat she was married to was a slave trader, specializing in the purchase and *education* of little boys for the use of Romans. He was an abominator. His wife didn't know, and he abused her with whips and fists. I want to know if it was a family way of life. Maybe this *Arimathean* has a penchant for raping little boys and beating women too."

The Zealot said to Jesus, "Since his arrival today, he asked me questions about our Magdalene. Lots of questions."

"When *we* spoke, he arranged a meeting, but he failed to appear. Perhaps he thinks he can hurt the Magdalene. He needs to know he would have a hard time getting away with that."

The pressure on his arm had slowly stopped, and the Zealot backed away. Now the fighter faced the stranger with a feral smile, his teeth bared, his body deceptively loose, far too casual. "Explain."

"I'll go back inside and tell everyone it's all right out here," John said, sounding amused. He walked back into the house. His lighthearted response to the tension eased the situation and the men looked from one to another.

"I appreciate the *delicacy* of this situation," the stranger said. "I wanted to explain all this to Mary but I'm afraid my family resemblance changed that. I assure you the resemblance is only superficial. My brother and I were far different in temperament and personality. That is one reason we hadn't spoken for years. In fact, I met Mary only once before the rift between Jason and myself." He pointed to a wine shop down the street. "Can we not sit like good men and talk?" He ended on a quick breathless note, his hands slightly extended palms upwards. A gesture of peace. Jesus nodded and The Zealot raised from his slight crouch. Jesus turned to the shop and the others followed.

The story that came out over the next few hours, delivered around a table in the wine shop, was one of brothers tainted by a lifelong rivalry, one brother's sexual preferences for children, and, a rift that could not be healed. Each man contributed a part of the story, Jesus, the discovery of a possessed woman and her healing. Thaddeus told of the previous meeting with the Arimathean, months before. The Zealot spoke of meeting of the stranger and his subsequent introduction to Jesus. And the most difficult part was told by Thaddeus—the story of Jason's life and what it had become.

The sharing ended with Joseph. "I have been remiss in my duties to Mary, the one called Magdalene. I want only to make amends, to give her a home in the city if she desires it. To care for her as befits her station in life as a widow."

"So. What now?" Jesus' voice was pitched low, into the silence around the table.

What were they *supposed* to do, Thaddeus wondered.

"Mary has had a shock. She may not be able to travel, even if she chooses to go with you," The Zealot said, jutting his chin at Joseph. "Do you intend to claim her fortune? Who killed Jason? Was it Romans? There are too many questions to turn her over to you."

"Nothing has changed for me," Joseph said. "I will give her a home, with me, if she desires. I left her alone, at the mercy of others for too many years. I could have helped her had I tried, had I cared." He looked at Jesus and quickly away. "I never tried to see if she needed my help. I never tried to find Jason's killers. It's time I took up my lawful responsibilities."

"And her fortune?" Jesus asked, his eyes piercing in the dim light of the shop's lamps.

"It is hers. I have no use for blood money."

Jesus and the strangers' eyes held, a rueful smile on the face of the Arimathean.

"When she wakes, we will ask her preference. *She* can decide." Jesus said as he pushed himself away from the table.

Ordinarily such a comment would have caused surprise. A woman did not make decisions regarding her welfare; she did as the men in her life dictated. But Jesus was different. And so was the Magdalene. For once, a woman would make up her own mind, if a woman had such a thing, Thaddeus thought. Wisely, he kept his mouth shut on that thought.

• • •

Aemoa

"I don't like it. It isn't right to leave her alone like this."

"Aemoa," Jesus sounded slightly exasperated. "She isn't alone. She has no less than three personal servants, chambers larger than our house in Nazareth, a doting brother-in-law, and soon all her personal belongings will be here. We are not leaving her in dire straits. What do you want me to do? We can't delay our travel, and you can't stay. I need you with me, especially now."

"But couldn't I stay at least until she wakes?"

"She's had a shock and a very tiring time here. It may be days before she wakes for more than a cup of soup at a time. Joseph has promised to send a runner to catch up with us as soon as she wakes or if anything goes wrong or— Aemoa, please. Don't worry. This way is best. I would have asked her if she had been awake, but one thing I've learned about the woman, she can sleep deeper than anyone I've ever met. We have to leave her with Joseph."

"Fine," she blew the word out, filled with irritation. "All right. She stays with Joseph. But I want a few minutes alone with him first. No interference from you. Understood?"

Jesus nodded, murmuring. It was only later she deciphered that he said, "Poor man."

Aemoa almost missed the appointment with the Arimathean. There were so many supplies to buy, even more to pack, and this time, without the Magdalene, she worked alone. Joanna and Susanna had elected to remain in the Holy City visiting relatives, shopping, and relaxing. Before they left, the two women had given enough money to the Iscariot to pay for a month's supplies, but it was no recompense for the loss of able bodies. The women would catch up in a month, traveling with one of Joseph's messengers. The Arimathean had promised to send runners to keep them informed about the Magdalene.

Aemoa washed with extra care before the meeting, putting on

a new veil beneath her mantle and all her Sabbath jewelry. She knew how to dress when meeting the wealthy. No matter what one wore, one always covered it with a slightly superior smile.

She wanted to meet with him on her own territory, keeping the emotional advantage, but she had given in to the temptation to see his home. The Zealot had already visited there and come away with approval on his face—approval and not a little awe. She, however, would not be so easily cowed. This stranger would find her a stern judge.

She was a little winded when she arrived at his house. She had meant to be early, throwing him off balance, but had gotten lost in the part of town where wealthy homes all looked alike. Perhaps she should have accepted his offer of an escort. But no. She had things to set straight with him and did not want to be in his debt.

An obsequious servant bowing and grinning and pulling at his hair showed her through the massive stone gateposts and closed the heavy wood door behind them. Within was a garden of strange greenery, not native to the dusty Holy City, but brought down from the mountains and planted to give shade, obviously at great expense and with a great waste of water in the dry seasons. Shameful. There was, however, a patch of herbs growing in the back of the garden in the native soil and sun. She gave grudging approval to that at least.

She touched the lintel on the door and whispered the proper words as she entered, noticing the servant do the same. Taking her to a sumptuous chamber, he offered her water in a large ewer for cleaning the dust from her feet, and a small servant girl to assist her. He backed from the room, and left her in privacy. The small Gentile girl's hands were clean and she was properly respectful as she assisted with the removal of her sandals and the washing of her feet and hands, the application of scented oil, one so light it vanished into her skin. Aemoa approved.

Later, after an acceptable interval for her toilet, she was led by the servant who had first greeted her, though the large house to a library. She had never seen a library. She had never seen more than one book at any time before in her life, and that had been the single scroll in the synagogue in Nazareth. This library held more than a hundred books—scrolls, wax imprints, engravings, parchments and vellums. She was awed and having trouble fighting the reaction, which did not bode well for the rest of the interview. She had to remember to keep him in his place. In awe of *her*. Yet now, that seemed impossible.

The room was high-ceilinged, with small arched windows in the Persian fashion, high overhead, their shutters thrown open. Heavy tapestries were pushed to the sides, tapestries clearly meant to cover the windows to keep out cold and damp. Aemoa had never heard of such. Rich carpets covered tiled floors. Tapestries covered the walls. A fire burned in the small bronze brazier beside a massive desk of strange design with intricate carvings on the legs. His hands were steady as he pressed the sharp edge of a stylus into the soft heated wax before him. His focus on the detail was complete. Impressed in spite of herself, she moved to watch, holding her breath for fear of disturbing his concentration. She didn't know Joseph was so learned, a scribe as well as a member of the Sanhedrin and a leader in one of the finest schools in Jerusalem.

"Please sit. I'll be right with you."

She jumped at the sound of his voice and almost fell onto the cushioned stool, barely noting the fine detail of the embroidery work on the fabric.

This will never do, she thought to herself. *I am supposed to be a little haughty. A little condescending. Not falling over my own feet.* Her over-awed mind refused to listen. She tried to breathe smoothly steadily, in the manner of meditation, but she jumped at the sound of her own lungs. This wasn't going well at all.

Joseph put down the stylus and dusted his hands together, smiling. "Forgive me for keeping you waiting. But when one is repairing a wax imprint, one can't stop the work at will. The wax determines the time of labor."

She nodded sagely, as if she were familiar with wax imprints, trying to regain the upper hand in her own mind. "Would you like refreshment?" he asked. Without waiting for her reply, he called for fresh juice and cakes. *A good host.* She wasn't supposed to think that.

"You're wearing a new veil," he said smiling charmingly. "It's lovely. Attractive to your coloring. I complement you on your choice."

Why . . . th . . . thank you. It was a gift," she said, and flushed.

He raised his eyes and directed the servant to lay the refreshment on a small table so she could serve, deferring to her with his eyes. Everything very proper. More than proper. Exquisite. Suddenly she blew out an irritated breath and relaxed. It was stupid to maintain an anger that had no cause. "I hope you don't think me rude for wanting to see where Magdalene will be staying."

"Rude? Never," he interrupted. "You are a good and kind woman who saved my sister-in-law's life. Your charity puts me in shame. If not for you . . ." He let his words trail off as she poured juice, as if he admired her grace with the fragile glass cups. "You are a woman of women. I have been told by everyone about your care of her. I thank you from the depths of my heart." He smiled again and a warm flush swept through her. He was easy to speak with. A gentleman. She passed a cup to him. The juice was delightful and as they sampled the small cakes, he told her of an amusing moment in his local synagogue.

When she finished her cake and drained her juice, he continued, "I'm sure you want to inspect Mary's quarters and each of the servants I've chosen to care for her in your absence, question them as to their experience. They have been waiting since your arrival. Would you like to speak with them now?"

"Thank you. Yes," she said, and didn't tell him she hadn't thought about *servants*.

"Afterward, we can proceed to the rooms I have set aside for her. I don't know how I've managed all these years since my wife died, and I would appreciate any suggestions you might have for Mary's comfort. I have never cared for an invalid in my home, not that I expect her to be bedridden for long, but I believe I have considered most of her needs."

"Oh, I'm sorry about your wife."

"No. Really." He waved away the concern. "It was years ago. I have managed to muddle along without her. It wasn't easy, but . . ." He shrugged slightly. "Enough. I didn't invite you here for sympathy."

She nodded smilingly, not bothering to correct him with the

information that she had invited herself. Most stridently. "I'm sure any servant you have chosen will be most adequate. Does she have a lady's maid? She will need someone mature and skilled with hair and skin. I had to cut her hair, you know." She waited for an unkind remark to this, but none was forthcoming.

"I think Samantha will meet with your approval. They are all bondservants, not slaves, their services purchased subsequent to your sanction. If any are lacking in any way, they will be replaced." He stood and lifted a metal bell on the desk top, gave it a ring, the tone startling in the high-walled room. Aemoa had never known anyone wealthy enough to own a bell.

The door opened instantly and Aemoa stood as three servants filed in. Two were female, small delicate creatures, and one was male, huge and hairy. Dressed plainly in similar smocks, their hair was pulled back from their faces exposing clean skin. There was no lice or dirt.

Stepping up to them, Joseph began to list their abilities. "The man may look rough, but until this morning, he worked for one of the leading physicians in the city. He is knowledgeable about herbs and has inspected my medicinal garden, pronouncing it useless, and making extensive suggestions. He seems competent and, by size alone, will make a good bodyguard. The smaller girl is untrained, but may act as an escort for Mary—Magdalene—" he flashed a smile at Aemoa, "—when she is up and about. She knows the city well. She also claims to sew, though I hired her primarily as a companion. Samantha, however, is my prize," he said, standing before one of the most willowy creatures Aemoa had ever seen. The girl was fair, with a Greek nose and jaw, and ash blond streaks in her hair. Her eyes were her most arresting feature, however. They were blue!

"I stole her from the wife of the Roman prelate. There, she acted as hairdresser, seamstress, and housekeeper. She is Hebrew through her mother, and wanted to return to the service of her own people as soon as her time of bonding was over. Instead, I bought her papers, at an exorbitant price, might I add, for the remaining two years of service. Her duties have been explained to her and she is willing to work with Ma—agdalene for as long as she is needed. What do you think?"

Feeling foolish for her previous distrust of the Arimathean, Aemoa looked up at Joseph. "You have chosen better than I would have dreamed. Tell me," she said with a grin. "What do you do when you are not at the desk working on books. Are you looking for a wife?"

He laughed at the open coquetry on her face, dismissed the servants, and led her back to the table. "Madame, your son told me you were a wonder, and I admit to striving to impress you. I had no idea my plan was working so well."

"I an indeed impressed. And forgive my teasing, sir. Magdalene could not have a better home. But don't forget. If you mistreat her, you will have me to deal with."

"Yes," he sighed. "You, the Zealot, and that Thaddeus creature. I've been receiving threats all morning. I'd be a fool to do anything to displease the girl."

"You mean—"

"My home has been full of visitors all day, all issuing the same ultimatum. 'Care for the Magdalene or else.' She must be quite a woman to instill such protective feelings in her friends."

"Oh, my . . ." Aemoa covered her mouth.

"No need to be embarrassed. Would you care for another cake? My cook has replenished the serving tray. He will have a tantrum if you don't eat them all. He's the height of temperamental about his saffron delicacies. Takes it as an insult if they're not all eaten."

"A man in the kitchen!" She had not intended to sound so shocked. It was just that—

But her host was laughing. "Yes. I know. It is strange. He is one of only four or five I know of. He was sold into slavery as a child and served in Egypt. He knew nothing there but the art of the kitchen. In fact, I was the only one who even thought of employing him when he finally escaped and returned to Jerusalem. But now? Would you believe Herod himself tried to steal him away from me? What that man can do with lamb would not be believed."

"I'd like to ask him a few questions about these pastries. How did he get them so flaky . . ."

Chapter Seventeen

Shalmer

The pain in his chest had lessened slightly with rest, but he couldn't sit for much longer. The urgency that had driven him out of the city at a run was still with him, pounding in his temples, pressing at his lungs. He had beat the Magdalene back to the rented house, had concocted a story for the remaining boys out of partial lies, a story about a death in the west, his need to go there and rejoin the group at a later time. And had taken off at a hard run.

She knew. *She knew.* She would do *something* to them now. There were many possibilities. She might call in Roman officials, she might involve the local authorities. He had to reach Odynius. If he could get there in time, they could avoid disaster. They could run. Odynius had connections in Rome. They could hire a ship, taking what boys he had in training, and they would be safe. But he had to reach his master first, bringing with him the traveling schedule of Jesus of Nazareth so that Odynius could find the woman if he wished to act against her.

Odynius might hold him to blame. Would he call him a fool for allowing her to reach Atarah's house? But what choice did he have? He had not known where she was going, and she had not been alone. Thaddeus was with her. Beautiful Thaddeus. Did he know too? Did they know enough to tie it all together? No. Perhaps not. Just a name. Odynius. Jason's partner.

It was all his fault again. Odynius would know that as well as he. Better perhaps, for, after the last time, after Jason, Odynius had been left with the loose ends, the questions unanswered, the soft palms to be greased with money.

Gods, what was he to do? He had never prayed before, feeling foolish lying prostrate before a carved or molded idol

begging it for help, plying it with sacrifices. But now, now everything was different. Fear beat a painful rhythm in his chest. What
if Odynius didn't believe him? What if he let him take the blame?
What if Odynius ran, but ran alone? Exhaustion was making him
think strangely, but he couldn't stop.

Please. Please. You loved me once. You have to love me again.

It was almost dawn before he had recovered sufficiently to
press on, the stones bruising his tender soles through his boots.
He was running again, blood pounding through his veins faster
than the tattoo of his feet. Running under the pinkening sky,
waves of purple clouds in the sluggish dawn. Pleading with
Odynius with each ragged breath. He knew he had to stop, had to
take off his boots and line the soles with fabric, with wads of moss
to protect them. Otherwise he would never make it to
Capernaum. His feet would give out. Where had he learned that?
Oh yes, The one they called the Zealot. And then, soon, he had to
buy a mount. A horse, one with sturdy legs, big barreled and
stocky. One that could take the pace he needed to reach
Capernaum in time, Capernaum and Odynius. For the first time
he regretted the loss of the few coins he had spent for clothes.
Even that slight loss of change could make a difference in buying
a good mount.

And then, ahead, was the answer he had needed all along. Just
around the curve was a Roman patrol traveling north, ten men in
uniform, the gleam of polished metal bright beneath the dust.
They had fresh horses which meant this was a recent posting. He
knew what to do. He had been trained by the best. Without being
seen, he left the road, found a clearing and washed the sweat from
his body. It was a waste of precious water, but it was a wager; in
all wagers something was chanced. If he was wrong about the
soldiers, he chanced a long thirsty day and a solitary night. But if
he was right . . .

Once he was clean, he slipped on the special tunic he had
purchased. It was intended for Odynius, for a night together. But
Odynius would understand. Silken, it had the hue of apricots
which made his skin appear more roseate and delicate. It was also
slit, calculated to show more of his legs than was considered
modest. His legs had displayed a dramatic change in the last

months. Where before there had been only stringy sinew, he was now lean and muscled, slightly furred with shimmering blonde hair. He combed his hair, stuffed the soiled garments into his bag, and moved back to the road. If the soldiers had been moving before dawn, they would soon take a break. That would be the time to overtake them. He would know almost instantly which soldiers to approach. Some would turn away in disgust, others would leer, amused at a ploy so obvious. And if he was lucky, there would be one, at least one, who looked at him with hunger. He would know him the moment their eyes met. And for that he would travel the rest of the day with the soldiers, perhaps on horseback. And the next day if he could, if they were going in the same direction. Then, at night, he would scatter the horses, taking the best. He kept behind them, matching their pace. Waiting.

It came sooner than he expected, the sight of shade close on the roadside determining a rest spot. The soldiers and their mounts stepped off the road, onto and across three graves showing signs of various ages, the whitewash still bright beneath the dust. Whitewash! It was foolish. The Jews thought a man could be tarnished and damned by touching a grave during a holy season. At least that was how he understood it. He just avoided the graves, didn't bother to ask why he should. Romans were more to his way of thinking. A body was just a body. Once dead it didn't matter what one did to it. Alive, it mattered only a little more.

The dust settled around the soldiers as they slid off their mounts, or dropped their weapons to the earth, the dull clink of steel and bronze ringing in the still air. They had wine. His stomach grumbled appallingly. It wouldn't do to have his stomach give away his desperation. He had brought no food. *Stupid*. There were some things he would not tell Odynius about this trip. When his stomach quieted, he approached the group of men, hips swaying, smiling.

Magdalene

She woke slowly, aware of movement close by, a blur that wouldn't quite come into focus. Her eyes seemed out of sync, giving the world a doubled look, too many of everything and nothing familiar. All around her was white and lapis lazuli. Her head ached. She closed her eyes again and slept.

It was dark when she woke next, the incessant buzzing of an insect near. She raised her hand, swatted it away, and when she laid her hand back on the bed it was soft. A *real* bed. Not a traveling bedroll. Her hand followed the wrinkled sheets and discovered that she was a foot off the floor, the thick mattress resting on a wooden frame. How delightful. Jason had told her about these beds once. He had said that she, ". . . should try one. It is like sleeping on a cloud."

Poetry from Jason had been strange. Usually he was only poetic about the intimate relations they shared . . .

Intimate relations. Is that what Jason had on the mattress that was like a cloud? He had been so insistent about the delights one might have while pillowed in a deep mattress. She pushed the thought away. Again she slept.

The call of a bird finally woke her, a mourning dove, so close by its call echoed slightly. She opened her eyes to the white and lapis lazuli room, its white walls tinted pink with sunrise. How she could say it was rising instead of setting she didn't know. Perhaps it was the sounds that surrounded her. Slumber. Peaceful, Accustomed by now to waking in strange places, she felt no anxiety. Eventually someone would wake and tell her where she was and where to meet Jesus for the day's travel. She wouldn't be rude and wake her hostess. Instead she would spend the moments doing what she had done for the last several months. She would worship.

It was strange how easy it had been, even the first time. It was like a song half remembered that returned in full as soon as she opened her mouth to sing. Peace had come with the worship. Such peace. And strength. It wasn't hers, but it may as well be. It was just as Jesus said. It was so easy to worship once one let go and reached for God. The adoration came from within.

"Our Father who art in Heaven . . ." she prayed, following the example given by the Rabboni. But today's experience in personal worship was cut short by a rustle near the foot of the bed. A stifled yawn, a short sneeze, and a face creased by covers peered over the bed's foot, balanced between her opposing big toes. It was an astonishingly beautiful face, even wrinkled down one cheek from sleeping too long on one side. And the woman's eyes were *blue*!

"You're awake. You *are* awake, aren't you?" the lovely creature asked.

What was so amazing about being awake? It was morning after all. "Yes. I think I'm awake. Who are you?" That sounded terribly ungracious. "And good morning."

"Good morning. I'm Samantha. Your maid. Wait right here. I'll get Joseph. Don't move." The girl leaped up and ran from the room. There was a hall at the foot of the bed. What a strange house. She hoped her new maid could say more than short, disjointed sentences.

When did I get a maid? And who is Joseph?

Without waiting as ordered, she threw back the covers and swung her legs to the floor, which was made of wood. The smooth grain felt strange under her feet. She was still testing it when she was joined by another young girl, not so attractive, but with gentle features.

"She's gone after the master, you know." Her voice was soft, Judean.

"Good morning. I'm Magdalene."

"Yes. I know. Shall I help you with your dress? That is an improper way to meet him, with the hem wrapped around your thighs."

"The floor is wood."

"Yes. I know. It feels strange to sleep on wood. You can feel the vibrations from people walking, even talking sometimes. Your dress?"

"Oh. Yes. Of course. Is there a wash basin? Did she tell you she's my maid?"

"Samantha? Yes. I'm your maid too."

"I was afraid you might say that. What is your name?"

"Immea, ma'am."

"Immea, I need a proper tunic; this thing I'm wearing is almost sheer. This Joseph will be able to see right through me. To me. Where are my clothes?"

The girl giggled.

"You shouldn't be out of bed!" a male voice roared. She couldn't see who because at the moment it started she had the sheer tunic up over her head. If this was the elusive Joseph she was going to have a word with him about entering a lady's room unannounced. Especially when the lady in question had gotten tangled up in her tunic leaving the main parts of her naked. She jerked the tunic back down and grabbed a coverlet off the bed.

"The medications haven't worn off yet. You shouldn't even be able to stand." His voice was unpleasant, low and growly.

"Who are you?" she demanded, holding the thick cloth in front of her.

The man stood over her, arms akimbo, scowling, "You should be in bed."

Magdalene drew her shoulders back. "I have *been* in bed. I am out of bed now. Who. Are. You?"

"He is your servant" a man said from the doorway. Magdalene turned and saw him there. And her world tumbled in a slow arc. "*Jason . . .*" Slowly she sat upon the low bed.

"No. I am not your husband. I am your brother-in-law, Joseph." He snapped his fingers. "You two, come with me. Immea seems to be the only one who knows what to do for our guest. When Mary is presentable, she may join us for a light repast. Would that be acceptable, Mary Magdalene?"

"Brother-in-law? Where is Jesus? Thaddeus? Aemoa and the women?"

"Yes," the man said. "Jason's brother. Your traveling companions have gone on, leaving you in my care. If you are willing, that is, to be my guest. I have given my word to the Rabboni that if you are displeased with your place of honor in my household, I will send you to them with an armed guard. But I hope you will give me a chance." His familiar brow creased, just as Jason's had. He gestured with his right hand, just as Jason had done. Magdalene's heart clenched. "I hope you will stay for a while, Mary of Magdala. We have much to discuss. Much to share."

• • •

Shalmer

The soldiers were rough, demanding, and it was harder than he had thought to please the three who were eager to share his services, each desiring to sample the techniques of a well trained whore. The whores one could afford on soldiers pay were not of the quality nor expertise offered by their young traveling companion. As long as he showed a desire to please and some small variety of style, they agreed to subsidize his trip north to Capernaum.

Shalmer sought to please, able to find respite only when they were on the road. But at least they were satisfied, giving him gifts of an occasional coin, a small trinket. They promised him many eager and willing customers in Capernaum, assuming he was headed north to set up a business for himself. But they left him exhausted. He had planned to travel with them for a few days and then steal a horse and all their purses, making good time into Capernaum. Instead, they kept him so busy far into the night that he was too tired to even think of running away, and he was never alone to make an escape. At least one of them slept with him at all times.

A trip he had hoped to make in less than a week was taking over two. The soldiers were slowed by the many new streams birthed by the last stormy rains, and stopped every night in some small town. There were crevices etched into the earth, some too deep and treacherous for the horses. These they traveled around, seeking different routes, making note of where extensive road repairs were needed, the reports made out by a clerk who traveled with them, detailing the locations and extent of damage.

The edge of Shalmer's fear was dulled by time and activity. He had time to think about what he had heard while crouched at Atarah's window, listening to the conversation within. Their knowledge was very sketchy. All they had was the name Odynius, a general description and a location he had long ago vacated. The only one who might have recognized Odynius after all the intervening years was Martine, and he was not traveling north. Atarah had only met Odynius once and that was when she smoothed the way for Martine's freedom after the death of his owner. It was all years ago when Jason was still half of the partnership. Odynius had changed in the intervening years. He had become Jewish again. No, on the whole, things didn't look so bad. If only the soldiers who offered him their protection at the moment weren't so . . . robust. If only he could sleep for a few hours.

They finally reached Capernaum near dusk on the eighteenth day, the city wall towering in the distance. Shalmer slipped away in the bustle of the crowds entering and leaving the city, ducked down behind a camel and turned into a side street. This was *his* city and he knew its back streets and alleys well. He had several destinations in mind and a great deal to do before evening and the moment he knocked on Odynius' door. He couldn't be troubled with long, sweet goodbyes from the soldiers.

After a bath and massage, his skin softened by steam and palm oil, he purchased a new silken tunic to replace the soiled one the soldiers had worn thin. He visited the wine merchants and bought a small cask of the Greek wine his master preferred, and lastly, at dusk, a twisted loaf of bread and soft, tart cheese. His heart beat wildly in his chest, keeping pace with the steady rhythm of his feet as he moved toward Odynius' house.

It was all as he remembered it, and his breath came pained as he stood in the outer court and looked at the whitewashed house, its lintel unadorned and stark in the falling light. Within were the couches of pleasure, the rooms of the dance, the large kitchen, the dormitory and training rooms. And Odynius.

He breathed slowly, pushing the tension out, inhaling calm and the scent of brazier fires, cooking meat, spices and herbs, wine and urine where passersby had used a wall in an alley. He went to the door, knocked and waited. He heard no noise from within, but the door opened slowly, revealing the Dava, the houseman and cook; a strange expression on his face. Without asking, Shalmer was shown into the house and left alone.

Odynius swept in, resplendent as always in a dark purple tunic, a smile of welcome on his face. It was obvious he had not been told who awaited him as, first confusion, then recognition crossed his face. Dava stood aside, enjoying the scene, then dropped the curtain and was gone.

"Shalmer."

"Odynius. I came as fast as I could. I—"

"You've changed. You're all grown up. Yes . . ." he breathed, circling around, staring. "You've *changed*," The expression on his face could have suggested pleasure and Shalmer felt an answering glow. "You will make a wonderful teacher for the boys," Odynius said.

It was not what Shalmer had hoped to hear.

Magdalene

Though the food on the table was superior, she pushed small morsels around on her plate with the flat loaf, taking an occasional bite whenever Joseph looked at her. The silence between them was overlong and would have been uncomfortable except for the easy camaraderie that had sprung up between them in the last week. Joseph had begun to allow her time to accept the things he said, the explanations he made about her own past. Some of the facts he had shared corroborated the things she had learned from Atarah, others threw a new light on her relationship with Jason. She had scarcely known her husband, and what she remembered about him had been colored over the years by her own mind, perhaps a protective measure because of the way he died.

"Try the lamb. It's delightful" Joseph said. "Aemoa told me you would eat me out of house and home, but from the evidence of tonight, she must have been addled." His voice was bland, lacking the advisory tone another man might have used, and he punctuated his remarks by taking a mouthful of dripping lamb stew on soaked bread. After he swallowed, he said, "It isn't un-lawful, what my brother did for coin. Nor so unusual. Many of the boys who are indoctrinated into that way of life find a strong preference for it and don't change even when they can." He took another mouthful of lamb, chewed and swallowed. "You must have been made aware of the fact by—what was his name?—at Atarah's. You said he seemed calm, peaceful."

"Martine. No. He was not a joyous man. My husband lied to me," she said tightly. "Jason posed as a good and pious Hebrew, he shared my bed, he fathered our child. And then, when he was gone from me, he took small boys to his bed, doing things I can't even imagine. He then sold them into slavery. One such boy was murdered. Martine lives with the memory of that incident branded into his mind. Do not talk to me about it not being *so bad*. It was horrible. There are no words to show how horrible Jason was."

"He posed as a 'good and pious Hebrew.' And his beatings were a part of that."

She shrugged, surprised at her own resignation. "Most women experience such things. It isn't unusual."

"Is that the argument you used to rationalize it, to protect yourself at the time?"

"It isn't a rationalization," she said with more heat. "It's the truth."

This time he shrugged and sipped his wine, allowing another silence. Angry, she stuffed a large bite of lamb into her mouth and chewed with great deliberation never taking her eyes from his face. He was imperturbable. He seemed emotionally indifferent when discussing Jason's way of life. To her, that was unacceptable. *Jason* was unacceptable.

"Don't you ever react to anything? Have you no emotion at all?"

Patting the corners of his mouth with a napkin, Joseph raised his brows in mild amusement. "I think we have enough emotion at this table. *One* of us should remain calm and as you seem apt to fly into rages or tears at the slightest provocation that leaves only me."

"Slightest provocation! I don't think—I"

Joseph gestured with a languid wave, a *See what I mean?* motion. "I have lived with the fact of my younger brother's way of life for many years. Nothing he did would surprise me. You, however, have just learned about him. You have a right to emotions. I went through my share of them."

Magdalena put down her sop of bread. "When? How did you find out about him?"

"I went to one of the auctions."

"You what!"

"Unlike most slave auctions, some, the ones advertising the

castrato and young boys, are held in secret. As a member of the
ruling Sanhedrin I found out about one, and was sent to investigate. I saw Jason in the background, herding boys, straightening
tunics, drying tears. I cried more than a few myself that night."
His eyes looked bleak in the half light. It was the first emotional
reaction she had seen on his face.

"Why didn't you stop it?" she whispered.

"I went with that authority. However, there were several,
highly placed Romans present, regular patrons. My guards and I
knew better than to raise a hand. When I reported to my
superiors, I discovered that they were willing to look the other
way on *minor atrocities* as long as the sales were not widely known,
were attended by Romans, and as long as they didn't interfere with
their own purses." His voice was disgusted, tinted with an ancient
anger. "The most I was able to accomplish was to see that the
auctions were made even more secretive, harder to locate, and
therefore less profitable. And of course, I saw to it that Jason
never got another penny from me or my father again."

"You told your father . . ." she breathed.

"Yes. It was, in part, what killed him. He disinherited Jason,
fully and with great pomp. There was no way he could inherit."

"But I thought . . ." Jason's ring could not have been the
family ring. Another one of Jason's lies. One in many. Her hand
automatically sought it where it hung suspended on a chain
around her neck.

"Ten years? That was just after our wedding."

"Yes. Though I did nothing against him until after the cele-
brations. I knew our father was unwell and I wanted to see him
happy for a time. Also I had hoped that marriage to you might
change him."

"And it didn't."

"Oh, for a time. He wasn't at the next auction, but it wasn't
long before he was back again. It was nearly a year before my
agents received word that a new castrato physician had been set
up near Capernaum, financed by Jason's coin. I went to my father
that very night. He was dead before the year was out. But I could
not allow Jason to sully our name. And Father would have heard
about it sooner or later. I knew he would have preferred hearing it

from me."

"You loved the old man, didn't you?"

"Yes. Very much."

She swirled wine in her stoneware cup, watching the play of dark red against the glaze. A servant moved to take the dishes and bring another course. It was strange to see a table cleared and know she would not be washing after. It was even stranger to be eating with her host. Women seldom ate with men, a woman's place being to serve and then eat what was left, with the children. Joseph seemed to enjoy her company. Another most unusual man, much like Jesus.

"One more thing. I've been saving it for last, hoping you would be well enough to hear. I've sent out inquiries to find who killed Jason."

The words passed through her as meaningless vibrations. Strange. *Ridiculous.* She knew who killed Jason. Surely he . . . Magdalene stared at her brother-in-law, feeling a flush rise on her cheeks. "I know who killed him. Romans killed him. All you had to do was ask. It was Romans. I passed them as I entered the town. I found him afterward. I *know.* It was Romans."

"Why would Romans kill someone who provided them with a bit of Roman life in a distant colony? Why would they open themselves to trouble from an illegal death? If they had wanted Jason dead, all they had to do was concoct a fake sentence of treason," Joseph said gently.

A piece of lamb caught in her throat. Slowly, she forced it down, her throat working with the pressure until it was gone.

"It wasn't Romans, Mary. I don't know who it was, but it wasn't Romans."

Her breath stilled. *Not Romans?* Of course it was Romans. It *had* to be Romans. She had found the sword. *But it could have been placed there. Or dropped by the murderers.* It was not impossible to acquire Roman weapons. The Zealot had told her that there was a thriving black market in Roman weapons. *Not Romans? Then who?* A Greek boy sold the ring.

"Not Romans. Not thievery," she whispered. Her mind made the intuitive leap. "His business partner?"

"Perhaps. We'll have a better idea when I hear back from the men I hired. They should return from Magdala in a month."

"It's been a long time, Joseph. A very long time. They might learn nothing."

"In that case," Joseph said, sopping the lamb drippings, "we'll make enough noise to draw out a tale-teller or two. We'll offer up coin until we learn something, like where this elusive Odynius is."

"Odynius . . . It's a Greek name, isn't it?" she fingered the ring again.

Odynius

Odynius stood over Shalmer's couch and studied the boy. It had been only months since he last saw Shalmer, and the boy had been agitated, his body all angles and bones, lovesick and silly, moaning over his abandoned teacher. Now, his lashes were long, curling delicately against his cheeks. He had gone from a gawky, graceless youth to a beautiful man with a firm, virile body and a wicked smile. If Odynius enjoyed men full grown, he would take Shalmer to his couch, but, though the youth didn't know it yet, and wouldn't know it until his usefulness was over, there was no chance of that, ever.

Shalmer puffed out a breath and turned on his pillow, waking. Soon he would open his eyes and ask the same question of the morning before; he would have to consider the things the boy had told him. Would have to make a decision about the woman. She was a threat. She knew too much, and yet he still hesitated. After all, he was in no personal danger from her. He was not guilty of Jason's death, except perhaps by association, and his friends and customers would be adequate protection from the accusations of a not entirely sane woman. But he had to consider his export business and the children in his care. He had planned to go to Rome in two years' time, as soon as he had made enough friends in high places and had enough coin to cover the expense, or he could find a new partner to back him.

The Magdalene's accusations, founded as they were in partial truths, might make it difficult for him to stay in this house. But he could move. And with Shalmer to assist in teaching the boys, he could increase his product and his profits. Shalmer had great promise as a teacher. Yes, he would search out the woman and deal with her.

Shalmer

The days flowed easily into weeks as Shalmer worked with the new boys, always waiting for Odynius to come to him. Believing his master's soft words and the promise he saw in his eyes, trusting in the little gifts he was brought: embroidered shifts, a fine silver statue of the goddess Diana, a new pair of shoes of the softest pigskin. Shalmer was especially fond of the boots, liking the way the soft leather swallowed his ankles. He thought again how foolish the Hebrew people were in regard to their abhorrence of swine. No animal hide in the world could be cured to the softness and suppleness of pigskin.

Odynius and Shalmer made plans together, inquiring through agents about houses in nearby towns and in Jerusalem. Inquiring about the cost of moving to Rome. And they sent spies to follow the group traveling with Jesus. They sent others to make inquiries about ships leaving for Rome, to ask, discreetly of course, about the town for men willing to do violence for a price. Together, they would take care of the Magdalene and the threat she posed permanently. She had a strong mind for a woman and had recovered from her possession, which few ever did. This time there could be no mistake. No return. This would be the last time the specter of Jason's death would interfere in his life. He would finish what he had begun so long ago. This time would be the last, that was a promise to himself and to Odynius.

It was a simple plan and it would be easy to take her, once he got her away from the group. He would call her to a hut, claiming that inside was a sick child. Instead there would be men with rope, sharp knives and orders for no noise. After making sure that she was securely trussed, they would take horses and head for the coast and a ship. Simple, that is, if he could get her away from the protection of the Zealot. The only ones he feared in Jesus' close little group were the Zealot and the hot-headed Fisherman, the one they called Peter. Together they could wipe out an army, the Fisherman by bellowing, and picking up and swinging anything within reach, and the Zealot . . . the Zealot could kill silently, with his bare hands.

Yes, it would have to be gently done, and that meant doing most of it himself. After all, the Magdalene trusted him.

In his fourth week in Capernaum, however, their plans suffered a setback when Odynius was accosted on the street. Not injured, precisely, but certainly questioned, and by members of a gang of cutthroat thieves with a strange sense of morality. They felt it simply a way of life to steal and rob, rape and pillage, but felt anyone who would touch a child was immoral. To this end they questioned Odynius about being a lover of boys. Odynius got away, but not before he was thoroughly humiliated, and he arrived home bruised and in pain. The next attack culminated with a blackened eye, a bloodied nose. The assault ended there only because the Roman guard arrived. It was on this attack that the men whispered the name.

"For Jason," they said.

Though it left his face masked with bruises and unable to appear before his clients, it served to cement their concerns about the Magdalene, for who else would have set the men on him? Only the woman—who had vanished from Jesus' traveling group. The kidnap and eventual death of Jason's widow would be the finale of their plan. It had started with the bungled killing of Jason which had left the woman alive, and would end with her death.

Chapter Eighteen

Magdalene

Magdalene looked over the bag of trinkets she had purchased in the jewelry market. Once this would have delighted her, to spend all day in the midst of pretty things, buying with no thought as to price, and coming home to a beautiful house with servants who cooked, cleaned and prepared her baths. She had no duties, no responsibilities except to grace Joseph's table on the evenings when he wasn't entertaining, and to amuse herself. But after the months on the road with Jesus, in which each day had been filled with work and study, inactivity was wearing. She missed Jesus and Aemoa with a fierceness that was suffocating.

It had been close to two months since she had first waked in the strange bed on a wooden floor to the realization that she had been given the chance to understand her past. The first things she learned about her husband had been heartrending, but since, she had been intrigued with the ways Joseph went about gathering his bits and pieces of information. She had been impressed with the way he could draw conclusions and reconstruct events from years ago.

But lately Joseph had withdrawn from her, sharing less and less, dining alone rather than with her, and even restricting her actions. Where before she and Immea had had the run of the city and all its markets, now she was forced into the company of a man who could only be described as a bodyguard. At first, she had found it amusing to be followed about the women's market by the abashed man, but after today, it would have to stop. He had refused to allow her to enter a tapestry shop which she frequented often. He bundled her away with no regard to her dignity, to the amused titter of the vendor.

Her suffocating loneliness and her anger had come to a boil within her as he the man carried her off. She wanted to be with Jesus. She *needed* to be with Jesus! Come dawn, she would pack her things and seek out the traveling band, and nothing Joseph might say would dissuade her.

Tonight she dressed with special care and waited for Joseph to join her for the evening meal so that she could tell him her demand, but he didn't join her, staying in his library with men, talking *business*. Business which excluded her. Her anger grew as she reclined at the table in the main room, drinking wine and eating fruit, pushing away the meat delicacies Dava had prepared for her.

Finally the men left, and fortifying herself with an extra glass of wine, Magdalene firmed her jaw and stepped briskly to the doorway of Joseph's study. The door was open and the light from several lamps streamed into the hallway. She marched into the room, heedless of the fact that she had not been invited, and took a padded stool. He didn't look up. She cleared her throat. His lips twitched, but he made no other move.

"Joseph."

He looked up with feigned surprise. "Mary, my dear. Did you enjoy your meal? Cook tells me you approve of his cooking by clearing your bowl every night."

"I did not come in here to discuss cook and his ego."

His eyebrows shot up. He grinned and put down his stylus. "I wondered when you would loose your temper with me."

"I've not lost my temper with you, Joseph. Yet."

"Ah," he said, drawing out the syllable as though she had said something of great significance. He pushed out his chair and leaned against the wall at his back, templing his fingers at his waist and studying her intently. "I heard about the scene at the market today."

"From that man you hired," she said righteously.

"No. From Immea. She has a great regard for you, and seems to feel you are capable of caring for yourself. She gave me quite a setting down for assigning 'that great beast,' I believe she put it, to guard you."

"Immea?" She could not quite keep the amazement out of

her voice.

"Yes. In fact it is the first time I've been spoken to in that tone of voice by a servant since I was a toddler. It was quite reminiscent of my maid, scolding me." He looked up at her ruefully. "How is it you are able to win such trust and affection from so many different *types* of people? From servants and slaves and vendors and prostitutes. And speaking of which, you had a caller while you were out today. Atarah, I believe she was called, planted herself in the center of my hallway and roundly denounced my houseman for keeping her waiting. The poor man has a fair understanding of languages, prides himself on it, and he said he had never been insulted in so many languages at one time. I would not like to loose such a valuable servant. I believe he would take it well if you would apologize for your, ummm, *friend*."

"Joseph, stop being sanctimonious and tell me what Atarah said. I owe her a visit."

"What?" Joseph's deadened tone alerted her, and she felt her hackles rise in spite of herself.

"I. Owe. Her. A visit. Wipe that look from your face. I choose my friends and I go where and when I like. And you will call off that bodyguard. I won't have him interfering in my life."

"But—"

"No buts. He goes or I go. Back to Jesus."

"You are hardheaded and stubborn. Totally unreasonable. And you are a woman and will do as the head of your family requires."

Magdalene sat up slowly. "As the head of my family requires?" she quoted softly. "You are not the head of my family. Jesus is." Joseph's eyes went wide. "And if you insulted my friend today," she said, "I'll never forgive you."

"You may not call that woman a friend. Do you know what she does for coin?"

"Yes, I know. But how would you know unless you have visited her establishment? You have the grace to blush. So it's acceptable to use the services of a prostitute, but not acceptable to be the friend of one."

"You cannot know what you are talking about. You're only a woman. The scripture clearly states it is better to empty your seed—"

"Do *not* hide in the scriptures to protect yourself. If you need the use of a prostitute, say so. Hypocrite."

"Fine. I have occasionally visited in her place of business," he said, his teeth grinding at the insult, "when I was young. What business is it of yours?"

"Visited in her place of business," she mocked.

"Woman, mind your place," he said softly.

"My place? My place is with Jesus," she said, just as softly. "My place is serving food to thirty or a hundred men a day. My place is scrubbing clothing in streams, and comforting the dying. My place is in a position of respect at the side of a man who doesn't regard the type or quantity of a sin in a person, who sees all sin as equal and all of us as equal, man and woman, Gentile and Jew, freeman and slave, prostitute or one who uses them." She stopped suddenly and took a breath. Her heart was racing, her face felt hot when she put her palms to her cheeks. "I'll be leaving to join Jesus in the morning."

"Why wait till then?" he said, his face cold with fury. "You can leave now!"

"Thank you. I will," she said calmly. Magdalene stood and walked out of the room up the stairs to the room she had used. It was with great satisfaction she heard the sound of something shattering in the library.

When she entered her apartments, she was surprised to see Immea calmly laying out her clothes, packing them into several bags. The girl looked up when she entered.

"Our master has a temper."

"Yes," Magdalene said.

"We can be ready to leave in a few moments. Would your friend Atarah put us up for the night?"

Suddenly Magdalene laughed, the sound ragged and torn. She had never stood up for herself before. Not ever, in her entire life. And the anger had been . . . freeing. She touched her burning face and huffed out a breath. "I think that is a wonderful idea. She did, after all, invite me for a visit. But are you sure you want to go there with me? You know what she is."

Immea lifted one brow, pride showing in her small strong

face. "A slave is often little better than a prostitute and I have never been better than another woman. I will not allow you to go alone, in any case."

"You are a bond slave. I cannot afford the coin to buy your last two years of service."

Immea smiled, her odd blue eyes twinkling, and lifted her head, the gesture almost regal. "I can. I might have purchased my freedom any time in the last weeks, but I stayed for you. And now, we will travel together. If you will have me."

Three days later, Magdalene had discovered where Jesus was, and had placed inquiries as to joining a band of travelers heading that way, but had found no one to travel with. An apologetic Joseph visited her at Atarah's and requested, politely, that she return to his home to wait for Jesus rather than chase after him. He had discovered that Jesus was supposed to return to the Holy City for the celebration of the Dedication of the Temple, and he agreed that she might leave with the band when they departed.

Magdalene returned to Joseph's house to find things were vastly different. She still had to contend with the bodyguard she called a barbarian, but he no longer interfered with her activities. Atarah was a regular visitor, taking Immea and Magdalene, in the cool of the afternoons, into the dark underbelly of the city, to learn about Jason and his death. The lovely prostitute took them, heavily veiled, to places that Magdalene had never imagined existed. She met the proprietors of bordellos, the entrepreneurs of the city who could provide any pleasure a customer might desire.

She was taken to small black markets where Roman and Hebrew men could purchase ambergris for a fraction of the market-price, and to the flesh markets of the slave trade which she left in tearful silence, in agony for the children sold by drunken parents and hard-voiced hawkers. She learned much about the *Holy City* that most of its residents never would. She saw many of the city's leading citizens, the Sadducees and Pharisees, faces covered, entering the houses that catered to exotic sexual tastes, and leaving later with secret smiles. She learned things she never would have thought possible, things beyond her imagination, things that left her in a cold rage, seething with anger and frustration. But with Atarah's help, she learned to view Jason with more patience and understanding. The woman was gentle with the frailties of men, amused at their double natures: what was righteous and politic, versus what they secretly desired.

Things were better with Joseph too. He had a deal of luck in locating Jason's partner. The elusive Odynius was in Capernaum. He had the man watched and harassed for several weeks and decided from the reports of his agents, that the man knew more than he was telling. Joseph also had a nameless fear that Magdalene was in danger from the man, though he couldn't say precisely why—hence the barbarian bodyguard. But overall, it was an improvement.

As the time for Celebration and Jesus' return grew near, Magdalene began to frequent the Temple and the families of those who had sons traveling with the Rabboni, asking each day if they had heard when Jesus would arrive.

Thaddeus

Thaddeus leaned against the wall of the Temple, the entire city visible below him. He felt listless, frustrated, and though he knew why, was powerless to do anything about it. Jesus had stood him there, in the shade against the wet, cold stone wall, his feet in puddled rainwater and told him to watch, but hadn't told him what exactly to watch for. His directions were so oblique as to be senseless, only that he was to stand here, and watch, and when *it* happened, handle it as he saw best. Things were happening at the center of the group around Jesus, exciting things, and to be shunted off with a useless job was unbearable. If the nameless *something* didn't happen soon, he would go mad.

Before noon, in the distance, he heard a crier announcing the arrival of a caravan. Could this be the thing Jesus had told him to watch for?

The city struggled alert at the news of something stimulating after the weeks of rain, and people moved with varying degrees of speed to the market where he could hear braying and shouting and the rumble of many feet. He watched up the road. It was a huge caravan, with many of the usual followers that attached themselves to caravans and its hired mercenaries for safety—travelers, vendors, pilgrims, farmers. Already these followers were dispersing to the various corners of the city, the muted sounds of farewells echoing from the walls down the now deserted streets.

A figure, vaguely familiar, passed through the crowd and walked with two others down the street toward him. He strained to recognize them but the man was hulking and the tall woman was a servant. The figure between them was heavily veiled, and though her walk was familiar, the sun was in his eyes. She was almost upon him before he recognized Magdalene and with a whoop, he ran to her and tossed her into the sky.

"Magdalene! I can't believe it, we've missed you. Aemoa is always complaining how much she needs you. Where did you—"

Magdalene was torn from his arms. A huge arm slammed into him. He hit the stone wall. And was held off the ground in a vise-like grip that threatened to tear one shoulder from its socket.

"Nobody touches the lady."

He found himself looking into the most fearsome face he had ever encountered, and swallowed the scream coming from his throat.

"Mistress Magdalene, you want I should break his arms or put him down?"

"Please put him down, Barbarian. The gentleman is an old friend." Magdalene's voice was grave, but Thaddeus could hear strangled laughter coming from the back of the other woman's throat.

"Oh," replied the raspy voice.

Thaddeus felt the ground beneath his feet again and stepped quickly away, straightening his clothes. The man who had accosted him was a head and shoulders taller than the Fisherman. Thaddeus took another step back; he didn't want to be too close in case the man decided to break his arms. Something like this always happened whenever he touched Magdalene. He should have learned by now.

"Please, you and Immea go on to the Temple. I'll be along directly." She looked at the hulking man and said with some asperity, "I am perfectly safe here, in the shadow of the temple walls." The dour brute grunted, and the girl giggled as they left, but not before Thaddeus got a warning look from the guard that caused him to take another step away from Magdalene.

"Where did you get *that*?"

Magdalene sighed. "He was a present from Joseph, I think to punish me. You can't imagine how hard it is to shop with that man standing behind me. Are they gone?"

"Yes," he said leaning out into the street.

"Good!" Her voice was almost singing and suddenly his arms were full of woman and he was being hugged till the breath was squeezed out of him. "I missed you so much. You don't know how much. I have been going crazy for weeks wondering how I was ever going to reach all of you and here you are, the first person I see today. Thaddeus, I'm so glad to see you."

No more the skinny fragile thing of his memory, she was now full-fleshed and rounded and he disentangled himself with regret, looking over his shoulder after the guard. Holding her away from him, he studied her. Her brows were plucked like wings, her skin glowing with the finest oil, and her eyes were more alive than he had ever seen them, sparkling with unshed tears. There were no loose tendrils of short hair flying from beneath the mantle she wore, and her mane was piled on her head, braided and glistening in the Greek fashion. She was beautiful and he touched her face with the back of his hand in a fleeting manner.

What he was feeling must have shone in his eyes for she smiled a soft smile and didn't reach for him again. Instead she turned and started walking away from the Temple, back in the direction of the market, all the while telling him about the last weeks and the things she had seen and done. Her conversation gave him the moments he needed to compose himself and he was grateful for the wisdom in her that gave him the respite. This was why Jesus had put him there, in the lee of the wall, to wait.

Later, sitting in a wine shop with bread and cheese, she told him about Joseph and Atarah and the slave markets and about Jason and the things she had learned. It took most of the afternoon and her servants came looking for her. Eventually he sat silently in Joseph's home drinking watered wine and watching the play of emotion on her face as the shadows lengthened.

He was glad to see her, and his gladness was mixed with awe that he should care at all about protecting a relationship, a friendship, with a *woman*. Until Jesus, it had never occurred to him that a woman could be a friend. It was only recently that women had been considered, by some in positions of leadership, to actually be people. Though second class people to be sure. But not to Jesus. To him they were equal creatures with men—a novel, almost revolutionary, thought.

As the Magdalene questioned him about Jesus and the others and listened with parted lips and delight to the things he said, he felt another feeling growing within. His desire to protect her. This was another thing that Jesus had intended him to learn from the encounter, he was certain. Thaddeus' lifelong knowledge about women and their place in society, their intelligence, their abilities, was undergoing a drastic change in the presence of Magdalene. She was the best of womanhood. She left him in awe of her. And she did it unknowingly.

Chapter Nineteen

Magdalene

Magdalene was back on the road with Jesus, this time traveling faster and lighter, protected by Thaddeus and Joseph's barbarian bodyguard on one side and by Immea and Simon the Zealot on the other. The change in the Zealot was remarkable. From the moment Immea first greeted him, the wiry warrior could scarcely take his eyes from her, and afterwards left her side only when summoned by Jesus. Magdalene felt like a cautious mother supervising her virgin daughter. She was careful not to let the girl out of her sight. Her barbarian guard, either in love with the girl himself or under orders from Joseph, glared, his eyes on the back of Simon's head, yet the Zealot seemed blithely unobservant of another's scrutiny. Magdalene gave the bodyguard the care of the donkeys and hoped they would keep him busy, but strangely, they were meek as lambs, and Magdalene could only pray Barbarian would hold his temper.

Slowly, they traveled to Peraea, the Land of Gilead, east of the Jordan River, once even slogging through a sudden snow storm that left them and wet and chilled. Magdalene leaned often on the staff Jesus had given her, but her bones, never strong after the years of malnutrition, ached, often forcing her to ride one of her donkeys. Before they stopped in Medeba, Magdalene took sick with a congested head, her illness temporarily defusing the situation between her traveling companions as Immea had to spend hours nursing Magdalene. The servant girl also took over her mistress' duties in the group of disciples. Immea was too busy to torment her admirers.

Magdalene, so ill herself, was among the last to hear of Lazarus' illness. It surprised her that Jesus had not left to go to

Lazarus immediately, and felt guilty that Jesus might have stayed because of her. Thaddeus set her to rights on that, telling her about the Pharisee who sought to advise Jesus and the Publicans who flocked to hear him speak. According to Thaddeus, the Rabboni was too busy to leave and it was the opinion of those closest to him that he would heal his friend from here.

When she was better, well enough to sit with her embroidery, Thaddeus and Magdalene talked about the relationship between Lazarus and Jesus. It was strange that a man like Lazarus, so simple and unassuming, would hold such esteem in Jesus' heart and mind. Though everyone appreciated the quiet man, Jesus' regard for him seemed too great for the man's qualities. Magdalene wanted to talk with Jesus herself but was isolated in her rented room to regain her strength, and Jesus stayed on the winter roads teaching and preaching. It was a long, cold, lonely, and miserable winter.

Whether Jesus had really been waiting for her recovery before he left for Lazarus in the south, she never knew, but on the day the icy rain stopped, the group moved out of Peraea at a leisurely pace. Only once in the next few days did she see Jesus. Then he simply appeared at her side and touched her shoulder. Strength began to flow into her from his fingers. He whispered her name and vanished again into the crowd. The sound of his voice carried her all the way to Bethany. *"Mary."*

Magdalene's strength had returned in full by the time they neared the large town. Warmed by fresh spring breezes and heartened by the signs of budding trees, she left the donkey and walked part of the distance they traveled each day, always leaning on her staff, smiling and humming little songs. On the day they were to reach Bethany, she trailed behind Jesus, swinging her arms, thumping the ground with the staff, as she tried to match his stride.

Though the disciples asked him questions, Jesus didn't reply, deep in thought, his head cloth pulled low. The one time Magdalene glimpsed his face it appeared drawn down as if with grief, a strange emotion for a man going to visit his dearest friends. Like the others, she shrugged off the thought and

concentrated on the skyline looking for the first sign of Bethany—
a large ancient tree that legend claimed had sheltered the lovers
Solomon and the African Queen as they rested after a day's hunt.

As the tree came into sight, Magdalene caught up with Jesus
and took his hand, chattering. His hand was cold, clammy, as if
winter were still emptying the skies over them, and it slipped from
her grasp as if dead. Magdalene pulled at his mantle, and it fell to
his shoulders. His eyes were glazed and dull, his lips stretched
away from his teeth in agony.

"Rabboni, are you . . . ill? Would you have me call Aemoa?"
Lifeless, he walked on toward the town, past the tree. Magdalene
stared after him a moment and finally followed, her heart
pounding in her chest, a familiar tightness.

They passed small groups of people, most of whom paused in
conversation and watched with expressionless faces the procession led by Jesus. As the group moved into the town, silence
rippled ahead of them, ominous, and Magdalene found it hard to
breathe in the stifling atmosphere. Finally, mutters came from one
group, perhaps a little drunk.

"Look there. It's the one they thought was the Messiah.
Claimed he healed diseases."

"Too bad he didn't come when Martha summoned him. He
might have had Lazarus up and about by now, instead of rotting
for days."

"Oh, don't tell me you believe all that nonsense about
healings. It's a hoax. He can't do anything."

"Martha believed he could."

"Yes," the first speaker shouted. "Martha is a *woman* too.
Easily fooled. And her brother is *dead*. I wonder what she'll say
now about the *great man* she tried to summon."

Jesus walked on, and Magdalene understood. *Lazarus* was
dead. Tears started, but whether they were for Lazarus or Jesus or
herself she couldn't have said.

Ahead of them in the street appeared a small group moving
toward them. At its head was Martha, and when she stopped, so
did the others. Her face was haggard and dirty with the ashes of
grief, streaked with tears and heavy lidded, the prohibitions against
washing strictly enforced. Stepping forward when Jesus paused,

Magdalene touched the woman's hand and whispered the correct words, "May the Lord of Consolation comfort you."

Martha ignored the courtesy and stood silent staring at the Rabboni. When she spoke, her voice, while always harsh, was hoarse from days of loud grieving. "Lord. If you had been here, my brother would not have . . . *died.*" Her voice broke. Exhausted, she fell at his feet, one hand touching his sandal. "But I know, that even now, whatever you ask of God, God will give it to you."

Magdalene was stunned. What was this woman asking of Jesus? Her mind must have slipped in her grief. Did she think he could—

"Your brother shall arise again."

Magdalene breathed a sigh of relief as Martha's eyes focused clearly on Jesus' face. Slowly she rose to her feet and brushed the street dust from her dirty robe. As if nobly born, she nodded her head at Jesus' response and said, "He shall rise again in the resurrection at the last day." It was correct according to the Law, and now there was reason in her eyes, though her face was even more haggard.

Then Jesus said, in a voice that would have carried from wall to wall of the great Temple, "*I* am the resurrection and the life! He that believes in *me*, though he were dead, yet shall he *live*. And whosoever lives and believes in me shall *never die*." He surveyed the silent crowd, meeting stunned eyes that lowered or turned away. He turned to Martha. Softly he said, "Believe you this?"

Magdalene stared back and forth between the two. There was a heated feeling in the air, an expectancy, a feeling of power, like the air before a lightning storm. The hairs on her arms lifted, shivers prickled down her spine.

Looking up into the face of her friend, Martha's eyes widened. Uncertain, she whispered, "Lord, I believe that you are the Christ, the Son of God, which should come into the world. That I believe." With regal bearing, Martha swept her robe aside and went up the small rise into town.

The feeling that had caught Magdalene in its grip lessened slightly with her going and she stepped to the side, rubbing her arms, trying to shake the lightning-like effect from her. Trying to place it. To remember why it felt so familiar.

Moments later, another group descended upon them, this time at a run. A small frame fell at Jesus' feet, exactly as Martha had fallen. Magdalene recognized the slender form of Lazarus' and Martha's sister, Mary. She was a delicate girl with a thin face and passionate black eyes. All her spirit was in those eyes, all her feelings clearly expressed. This young Mary had never been able to hide the slightest thought or emotion from the world. Everyone knew her secrets, her hopes and fears, her loves. Whenever she was near Jesus, the girl scarcely took her eyes from his face. Though only thirteen, she was madly in love with the Rabboni. Now, her eyes were brimming over with tears, her face tight with tears only recently dried. She raised her face to Jesus' white one. "Lord, if you had been here. . ." she whispered. With this, she dissolved in tears, clutching at Jesus' feet.

Jesus, his mouth slack with grief, slowly raised his eyes from her to the people that had followed. The mourners were crying loudly, sharing in the proper distress of grief. There were no paid mourners here, but true friends. Magdalene wiped tears from her own face, recognizing several of the mourners. They had journeyed with Jesus or stayed nearby in Jerusalem. When word reached them of Lazarus' death, they had traveled fifteen miles to mourn.

A breeze blew up from the town, carrying a hint of the lightning power, now weaker, erratic, like eddies in a stream as it twists around a bend. And she heard the groan. Low and rumbling, it was tortured, filled with anguish. The power rose, and her skin pebbled hard. She looked at Jesus. The sound he made was pure, distilled pain, low and fading, and few seemed to have noticed but her. "Where have you laid him," Jesus whispered.

"Come and see," several voices said at once and suddenly they were all moving the same direction. Toward the town's graves. The feeling of power grew and Magdalene felt dizzy, as though she might fall. The air was cold and dry, yet burned as she breathed.

And then she remembered. The marketplace in Magdala and again in the clearing at her home. And to a lesser extent, when Jesus had touched her shoulder on the journey. She had felt it then, the lightning power, overwhelming and exhilarating. She had been lifted on waves of lightning and emotion just like this. Power. *Jesus'* power. *Something is about to happen.*

They stepped down rough stairs into a narrow cleft in the rock, its walls bordered with caves. Grave caves. The mourners raced to one at the lowest level, some pointing. Magdalene was still on the steps at an angle from the grave, separated from Jesus, facing him. Tears streaked his face, though she couldn't remember seeing him weep before. He was sobbing silently, or so quietly the mourners' distress covered the sounds. Tears glistened on his cheeks and rolled into his beard.

The breeze lifted her robe, tingling with power. The sensation was growing, burning along her skin. Magdalene fought for breath, watching the crowd. Everyone seemed caught up in this feeling, this power and Jesus' tears. If there were words spoken then, Magdalene didn't hear them. She saw only Jesus as he walked, stiffly, as if in pain, to the stone covering the grave. It was as though he himself was rigid with death as he touched the stone with one hand.

Martha brushed by her on the narrow stair, and stopped at Jesus' side gesturing, and Jesus' mouth formed words, but Magdalene's ears were roaring now with the force that seemed to be building in the cleft of the rock. And she couldn't hear.

Jesus gestured away from the grave and back to the stone, almost angrily.

Three men came from the crowd and put their shoulders to the stone. Magdalene forgot to breathe. When Simon the Fisherman joined the men, the stone began to roll away. As it moved, Magdalene fell against the stairway wall at her side, unable to stand alone. She was battered by the feeling. The power. The stone was rolled to the side and Jesus raised his arms, fingers curled into claws and shouted into the sky. Magdalene closed her eyes and slid along the wall to the steps. *No. No. It isn't possible. No.*

Slowly, the roar cleared from her ears and she rested her head on the rock. The sounds of the crowd were loud, the voices still senseless. She breathed deeply and shuddered at the rush of air into her parched lungs. There was shouting and screaming and the smell of rotting flesh. At last she opened her eyes and saw them. Saw *him.* Wrapped in stinking grave cloth, the coarsely woven cloth stained with death fluids and decaying herbs.

Jesus has raised Lazarus from the dead. She closed her eyes again and let the blackness take her.

The Zealot

Simon, his fingers wrapped tightly about a walking stick watched as Magdalene stumbled, paused, looked around uncertainly as though she had just waked, and then moved on. Her movements were slow, like the creaky tread of the aged, and her eyes, when she bothered to focus, were frightened. She had been like this since he had found her at the tombs, asleep in a crumpled heap in the dust. A length of burial cloth, still stained and smelling of rot, had found its way to her and lay twined around her ankle. When she had waked and realized where she lay, she had grabbed at his tunic and said strange things. Now, the words played over in his mind, tight with her desperation.

"Simon, you must stop him. They'll kill him. They'll ambush him in the streets. Stop him, please."

"Stop who, Magdalene?"

"Didn't you feel it? Didn't *someone* feel it? I can't have been the only one. It was so familiar." Here she had shuddered and wrapped her arms about herself. "There was something else here this time. They're going to kill him, I know it. Stop him, Simon. *Please stop him.*"

"Jesus? You're talking about the Rabboni?" In his exuberance he had at first missed the depth of her distress. "You haven't been into Bethany tonight. He isn't in danger; they *love him.* Everywhere they're talking about him. About making him *king,* about uniting the people behind him to overthrow the Romans. He *brought Lazarus back from the dead,* Magdalene. Didn't you see it? No one could oppose him now. The Sadducees will have to accept the resurrection of the dead as fact. Even the Pharisees will have to accept him. No one can deny he's the *Christ.* He's said all along he's the Son of God, and he proved it. Right here! We're planning a triumphal march all the miles to the Holy City. All of Bethany is going. Don't you realize what this means?"

"Pharisees? Sadducees?" She had gripped at his robe, twisting the wool in bone-like fingers. "Do they know about this?"

"By next week, the whole nation will know of it. A month after that, the whole world."

She pulled at his clothing, surprising him with her strength. "You idiot," she hissed. "Listen to me. How do the Pharisees know? Tell me."

Her face, pale in the moonlight, carried fear and some of it passed into him. He quieted and said, "Two were here, and they left before dark to take the news back to the city. They—"

"You should have stopped them," she whispered. "They'll *kill* him now. We have to keep him away from the city. We have to."

"They've tried to stop him before. They even tried to stone him, but they can't touch him. Not once have they been able to lay a finger on him. And after today, they'll have to back him against the Romans. They'll *have* to," he insisted.

"No. They'll never give up what they have. They have power. They're in charge—"

"In charge," Simon snorted and jerked away. "The *Romans* are in charge. They are the only ones with power."

"No. That's not so. The priests and the Habberin have more power than you think. They are the ones who keep our young men from being conscripted into the Roman army. They are the ones who stopped Pilot from erecting a statue of Caesar. They rule the Temple and the people, and they grow fat and rich under the Romans. They aren't going to give *any* of that away. The rich and powerful will kill Jesus first, no matter how much Jesus means to the common and the poor. You have to stop him from going to the capitol. He's too great a danger to them."

"All right, all right. You're afraid of an attack, an assassin of some kind. I admit that could happen. So to relieve your mind, I'll make sure he's never left alone. He'll be surrounded by us at all times. I promise. Will that satisfy you?"

"No. Yes. Oh, I don't know. I lived with Joseph just long enough to see what being that wealthy and powerful could accomplish. And Jesus said the *meek* would inherit the earth. The *meek*! Not the Pharisees who own it now. For the meek to inherit, the Pharisees have to die."

Simon stroked his beard as he pondered her words. Could the Sanhedrin contemplate the death of Jesus? Would they resist the loss of power and prestige that a king would represent? Habberin—a pupil of the Law. The Law said it was death to murder, yet they had already tried to kill Jesus. *Habberin.* He had respected the men that comprised that group for so long and then seen them do such unholy, unlawful things. All for the good of the people . . .

He would be extra careful to guard Jesus during the days before Peskah, telling only the Twelve where the Rabboni would be at night and in the vulnerable hours of the day. Perhaps only the Twelve could be trusted. Magdalene just might be right.

Thaddeus

Their entry into Jerusalem was spectacular, better than any could have dreamed. Word ran ahead of them in the streets that, "Jesus of Nazareth has raised a man from the dead. The Messiah is come. The *King* is come." The people, already drunk on Festival excitement and wine were caught up in it, tearing the boughs from nearby palm trees, laying them in the way for him. Many, mostly those who had been in Bethany, pulled off their robes and spread them in the street, gathering the clothing back again after he passed and holding it to their chests in religious fervor. *The King was come.*

He rode on a donkey, a young foal, the symbols not lost on anyone. Kings always rode a donkey on their way to be crowned. And he had requested it himself. He was ready to be crowned. King. Messiah. Deliverer, Prince of Peace—once the Romans were defeated.

Thaddeus could scarcely contain himself. It was beyond anything he had ever hoped to see. The people parted in front of Jesus and closed in again once he had passed. They sang the songs of praise and victory—the old songs of David, sung anew for the Son of David. There was a feeling of gaiety and joy, hilarity and a tremendous noise in the air as people rushed from all quarters of the city to join the excitement. Many had heard Jesus speak in the past or seen him do some miracle, others, many, many others heard for the first time about the King, the Miracle Worker, the One with the power over death. *The Christ. The Messiah.* Tears ran down Thaddeus' face as he joined in the singing. The Twelve formed a cadre around Jesus, protecting him from the touching hands, lifting those that cast themselves down in the street before the small hooves could crush or injure them.

All in Jesus' following were caught up in the excitement; the Fisherman, Peter, was singing in his booming voice; Andrew was quiet, with a look of utter adoration on his face. The Zealot was half-heartedly on the lookout for assassins, Magdalene at his side looked tense and solemn. Phillip was laughing; Thomas was thoughtful; Aemoa was crying; all were brought out of their usual selves in the light of the strange, the unique, the never before. *The King.*

Only some instances caused Thaddeus the slightest pause. The first was a group of Pharisees whose loud praying was interrupted by Jesus' entrance. They stood close together gesturing angrily at the spectacle. *The Habberin, jealous over the loss of audience, might spell danger.* The second was the sight of Shalmer, a new, well-dressed, prosperous looking Shalmer standing with a wealthy merchant, watching the scene with tense eyes. Why would Shalmer, once so ardent a follower, be standing on a street corner, his arm held—was it possible—by a Roman? Why was he scanning the crowd so closely? Where had he been all the past weeks? But small concerns vanished before the crowd's exuberance.

Magdalene

The days of Peskah were almost upon them, and Magdalene should have been happy, lighthearted, filled with delight at the sight of spring in full bloom. She should have been looking forward to the festival in the Holy City. Instead she was frightened, bewildered, and lost in the changes. It was the power.

Ever since she had been swept up in the power at Lazarus' tomb, she had been pushed along by its final eddying currents. Her skin burned. Her hair raised up as if lightning struck. She saw danger everywhere—in the eyes of the soft-bodied Pharisees who tried to keep up with the fast-traveling group and failed. It was in Shalmer's face glimpsed at the edge of a crowd. It was in Joseph's voice as he recited the information about the Romans who had come to Magdala after Jason's murder, searching for his wife. It was in the movements of the Zealot who worked to be at Jesus' side each moment of the day. Even greater though, it was in Magdalene's heart, in the painful pounding and inconsistent beat. In the difficulty she had catching her breath. Fear. The fear of the dreams that had returned. The fear of Jason's blood-soaked hands.

Jesus hadn't helped. When she went to him one night, searching him out in the moonlight, pouring her pain and fear out at his feet, he had simply smiled and spoken enigmatic words. "Do you remember the marketplace at Magdala? The answer starts there. Remember the vision of yourself."

All she could recall of the marketplace was a vision of a torn tapestry, the ends fluttering in the breeze, much as Lazarus' death shroud had fluttered in the breeze. That and the feeling of power. There had been nothing else except the calm of Jesus' eyes. That memory she clung to, for it was seen less and less now.

Her fear grew and Magdalene found herself darting at shadows. Her only consolation was in taking over the work that the Zealot normally did. Now when a child was brought to the Rabboni for blessing or healing, she carried it to and from its mother's arms. The children kept her busy.

The Zealot

It happened so suddenly, so quickly he found himself rooted to the earth, stationary for the scant moment it took for the violence to start and escalate into bloodshed. He was getting slow. His reflexes, once so sharp that he could stop an opponent before he moved, were rusty, his mind even slower than his body. It took the sight of dark red blood to activate him. And then he was almost too late.

He had been following Magdalene for most of the day, worried by an oblique comment Jesus made as they had their morning meal. Something about the unanswered questions in her life and the proper timing for the solutions. Final solutions. It had started him thinking, and watching. And by noon he had picked out the forms following her.

There were two of them, both dressed in rags, filth, and grease, both Gentiles, quick, with the fine movements of practiced thieves. Both carrying the stink of the unwashed, ritually unclean, and pork. His nostrils twitched in disgust.

They flitted after her, keeping her always in their sight, one or the other of them leaving her each hour for a short time and then returning. He followed one when next they parted, hoping it was the right move. It had been too long since he had worked at stealth, where surprise was the rule rather than the exception. He no longer trusted his rusty instinct.

The largest of the two left her trail and slipped into the crowd. Quickly, the Zealot glided after, his feet silent on the roadway. The thief was a fool. He didn't even watch to see if he was followed. He went straight to a small house and entered the courtyard. Three horses stood in the yard, two bridled and saddled, the third strapped with a pack. A man stood with the horses, and he seemed familiar by his stance though his face was in shadow. The larger man joined him and the two men conferred before the larger of the thieves vanished again, back the way he had come. Simon waited, knowing that the identity of the third man was the most important thing.

Instinct. Reuven's leathery old voice had done its job well. Breathing evenly, his body still, Simon stood in the foliage of sprouting palms as the thief melted away. The slender man followed, his face catching the sunlight briefly before he covered it with a rich head-scarf. *Shalmer.* But a different Shalmer. Harder and more bitter than he remembered, his smile curved into a twist at the corner. Cynical. Angry. Coldly beautiful.

There was no time to wonder at the change in the boy—the man—as he moved after the thief, leaving the horses. *Instinct.* Simon followed the two men on a route straight back. Shalmer paused once, to stand over a loose bundle of clothing in the shadow of a building. He moved on.

The Zealot paused too. The bundle was Magdalene's

Barbarian, bleeding from a head wound but breathing. When he looked up, Shalmer was gone. Vanished into the crowd. At the sight of the guard's blood, dark in the shadows, the old sensations returned. Suddenly. In full. The skin on the back of his neck prickled. Tiny hairs raised. His breathing deepened, and his heart pounded again to the old rhythm of *war*.

The Zealot in him came alive fully as though he had never put it to rest. For a moment the nightmare he had carried in his heart for so many years returned. The sight of Nirit, her legs spread and her face bloated. And then that too was gone. He turned into the crowd, sure of his direction, sure of Shalmer's prey. *Magdalene*.

Just ahead, at a corner in front of an alleyway she stood, talking to Shalmer, the old Shalmer, the mask of boyhood once more on his face. He was frantic, begging, his acting faultless. Had Simon not seen him before, he wouldn't have known it an act. He took Magdalene's arm, urging her into the crowd, back to the house with the horses. There could be little doubt; there was no other place. The Zealot had only moments to find the two supposed thieves and stop them. Immobilize them.

He didn't have to look far. They were in the most obvious place, the larger of the thieves standing taller than the others of the crowd, the smaller man beside him.

It was more quickly done than the Zealot had hoped. He left them both unconscious, bruised and beaten, the larger man's throat compressed until he was comatose. The smaller man he put out with quick jabs to the kidneys and then to the jaw. *Different tactics for different body types*. Reuven' words. *Instinct*. That left only Shalmer.

He raced to the house where the horses waited, tails twitching in the noon sun. The house was empty, no furniture, a dank smell of mold coming from the walls. The horses moved restively in the yard as the fighter found a place in the second room, deep in shadow, with a view of the street. He stooped to his heels in the gloom and waited.

The minutes slid by. Sweat began to pour down his back with the strain of waiting. He used to be so good at waiting. Where were they? Had he placed her in greater danger with his actions?

No. This was where Shalmer would lead her. *Instinct. Calm.* He breathed slowly, deeply, forcing the fear away. Finally, they appeared, walking toward the house. He watched from within, hidden by shadow.

Shalmer should have traveled with the Greek players one heard of so often. He was skilled. He was, at the moment, a terror-stricken boy. "You have to hurry. Please. His fever is so high. He's burning up."

"I *had* to stop in the market for medication. I could do nothing for a fever without supplies, Shalmer." She was tired. The dazed look in her eyes more pronounced than this morning. She had carried that look around with her for days. And her voice was a monotone. "When did the fever start?"

"This morning."

"Had he eaten? Drank? Have his bowels moved?"

"No. Nothing. Nothing at all. Hurry."

The Zealot tensed. Waiting. They walked into the house, Magdalene still questioning, but Shalmer no longer answering. They stood just inside the doorway, their eyes adjusting to the dim light. Shalmer dropped the boyish mask, a cynical smile touching the corners of his lips. Simon recognized the signs of victory on the boy's face. But what had he won?

"Sit down, Mary."

"Wha . . . What?"

"I said sit down." He pushed her, none too gently, to the floor.

Simon almost made his move then, but the soft whispery voice of his teacher touched his ear. *Never attack too quickly. If there is no danger, wait. Your enemy may give something away, some vital piece of information, some question or answer you have been seeking. Wait. Listen.*

"But I thought you said your father . . ."

"I did say. But as you see, no one has been here for quite some time, either sick or in health. And I don't remember my father."

"Then what . . ." Confusion filled her eyes. Good, the Zealot thought. There was no fear. Yet.

"We may have a little wait. You should rest. It will be the last rest you have until we reach the sea."

"The sea?" Her voice was a whisper. But her hand tightened on her staff.

"Yes, Mary. The sea. We are going on a little cruise, you, myself, and Odynius." She started. "Ah, I see you recognize the name. Yes, Odynius. Jason's partner. You have him to thank for your life. I would just as soon have finished you off, but he thinks you might bring a good price from the soldiers in Rome. You remember the soldiers, don't you? You once had quite a time with soldiers. A night of lust and passion. Their lust and passion, of course. It left you rather the worse for wear."

"Soldiers? What are you talking about? Soldiers . . ." She tried to rise and he shoved her back to the ground.

"You kept screaming about their hands and about a baby." He smoothed his hair, which was oiled and curled in the Greek fashion. He smiled again, and his words were deliberately cruel. "As I recall, you were pregnant."

Magdalene was staring at the damp walls, her eyes unfocused. "Hands."

"Yes. Something about hands and death and pain and . . ." He tapped his chin. "I do believe you were crying." He laughed and walked around the perimeter of the room, eyes going from Magdalene to the windows, the light outside ruining his vision. "I watched what they did to you. It was most satisfactory. An appropriate punishment for the threat you posed. You talked too much, Mary. A common habit among women, I understand. You complained far and wide about the massacre. Soldiers came to town to investigate. But, you know soldiers. They aren't the most dependable of men. They are easily sidetracked, led off the scent."

"What are you talking about?" She was shaking now. And she dropped the staff. It toppled slowly, and landed on the dusty floor with a crack. Simon almost leapt at Shalmer, but heard again Reuven's voice counseling patience. He clenched his fists and waited.

"You don't remember, do you? I often wondered, after the fiasco at Jason's house. They weren't supposed to harm your son. He would have brought a good price in the market." He smiled that strange, hard smile and looked at his nails. They were buffed, gleaming in the semi-darkness. "You placed a complaint to the wrong man, one of Odynius's friends. He *had* to send a troop to investigate, but fortunately we heard about it first, and our men showed up. Doesn't any of this jog your memory?" At her slow shake, he continued. "Pity.

"You were not quite in your right mind even then. You were easy to approach. All I had to do was whisper Jason's name and you followed. Trusting little soul. A drug in the wine I passed to you and you were ready for your night of passion."

Magdalene was shaking, her face white in the dim light.

"It isn't uncommon for brothers or sons to sell their sisters or mothers. I brought you to them, bartered a good price and watched them use you. It was not the first time I had seen a man and a woman together, of course, but it was the first time with so many men and only one woman. And it was the first time where the woman was not willing. You left a few scratches and bruises, but they got their money's worth. And I got extra from their commander for my own services. Still not bringing back any memories?

"Why, Mary, you look pale. Not as pale as that night, of course, but really most unwell. The soldiers never found you again. Even when they got into Magdala the next morning and started asking after you, you never came forward. And most strange, no one could find you. After you aborted your baby, you crawled back to Magdala and went to some old woman's house." He laughed.

Magdalene doubled up on the ground, retching.

Still Simon waited. He was boiling inside. But *instinct* . . .

"I thought I had taken care of the threat of Jason forever when you were possessed by demons, but somehow you recovered."

"The ring," she whispered, wiping her mouth with the back of her hand. "You were the Greek boy who sold Jason's ring."

"Ring? Ah. The ruby ring he wore. Yes. I took it, sold it. Odynius gave him that ring. I Never understood what use Odynius had for Jason. Do you know the strangest thing about all this? They weren't supposed to kill him. They were only supposed to geld him, as I was gelded." He sighed again. "A great deal went wrong that day. But, of course, you know that."

His gait gently flowing, Shalmer walked to the doorway and looked about. With his back to the room, he continued. "Odynius almost lost his business because of Jason and his foolish talk to the wrong people. I won't allow that to happen. Not ever." There was a short pause. "Where is Odynius? He should have been here by now." Shalmer turned, blinking into the poorly lighted room. "Magdalene?"

The Zealot, concentrating so on Shalmer, at first missed the slow movement of the woman on the floor. She rolled silently to her feet and, crouching, slipped up behind Shalmer. As he turned, she attacked, still mute. It was the awful deathlike silence of her lunge that caught them both by surprise.

Startled, Simon stood gape-mouthed and watched as she ripped at the tender flesh of Shalmer's eyes. Blood, black in the tomb-like dark of the room, gushed from Shalmer's face and his mouth opened in a high-pitched scream. And the Zealot in Simon moved. He charged, reaching for the downward arching arm. Heard the sickening crunch of bone and soft flesh. Heard the breath go out of Magdalene in a half-cry, half-moan as the blow landed. Heard the voice of the murderer and rapist as it cursed and his own voice in the guttural cry of the warrior. There was a moment of impact. His body felt the jar, and then another. And it was over.

Too soon. Too soon, some part of him cried. He was filled with fury. An impotent rage. And his only outlet was already un-conscious, bleeding on the floor.

He tied up Shalmer, tightly enough to stop the flow of cir-culation to his hands, hoping Shalmer got gangrene. He strapped Shalmer's inert frame to one of the horses. Magdalene he carried in front of himself on another beast. He remembered riding, but it wasn't until he found himself at the Arimathean's door that he knew where he was going. *Training.* As soon as he saw Joseph's shocked face, he started shuddering.

Later that night, his mind restored by sleep and wine, his body purified at the temple baths, Simon related all he had heard to Joseph: Shalmer's original plan of revenge had been carried out far more effectively than anticipated, by men hired with stolen money. A stolen Roman sword the only clue. A broken woman sold to soldiers and repeatedly raped, the complaint effectively silenced.

Odynius was in a Roman jail, awaiting trial, the highly placed bureaucrat he had paid for silence had been sent back to Rome in disgrace. He had a private cell bought with private funds. Shalmer was in the communal cell next to him. Some of the men there had been imprisoned for years. Most were desperate. Most didn't care who or what the new man was or if he was willing or not. He was a vessel, more useful if he was beautiful, but if he was a scarred castrato, injured and bleeding like Shalmer, they didn't complain.

Magdalene was asleep in Joseph's house upstairs, her nightmares quieted by a sleeping draught, Immea at her side. It appeared to be over.

Magdalene

There was a dusty taste in her mouth that no amount of water or wine would wash away. It was bitter, sour, like the after-taste of vomit. And perhaps that was the answer. It was the sickness of Shalmer. Her stomach ached with the memories of his words. The bump on her forehead ached, and Immea told her she had an ugly bruise. But Immea couldn't see inside where the real bruise lay.

She had been sold to Roman soldiers. Used.

There had been dreams of Jason's hands. Had it been Roman hands she really saw? Roman hands that accused. Roman hands that reached for her in the old nightmares?

Oh Yahweh, Adonai. Abba. Help me. Help me.

And Jesus. He must have known. That day in Magdala when he looked into her eyes, healing her tattered soul, forcing out the demons of the past. He must have seen it then—that shame, that horror. *Why don't I remember?*

And where was Jesus now? Several of the others had come to visit, to offer pity. Or bearing false smiles of comfort. Comfort that masked curiosity, asking what was it like . . . After the first few, she had refused more visitors. Oh, God, would she ever be able to walk the streets again?

"Magdalene? May I come in?" It was the hesitant voice of the Zealot, the soft shuffling of his feet on the strange wooden floor. She kept her face to the wall, her breathing steady, hoping he would go away. *Please go away.*

"I have a message from the Rabboni, Magdalene. He said I was to stay until you agreed to hear me. Even if I had to wake you, though I know you aren't sleeping."

There was no escaping it. Slowly she turned and faced the doorway. Dark circles ringed his eyes and a heavy stubble marred his cheeks. His lips were cracked. He looked harried. As though he hadn't slept in days.

"Simon?"

"Magdalene. Let me come in. Please." It was only now that she heard the exhaustion in his voice. Was this for her? Fear eased its painful grip on her heart. Dear, dear, Simon.

She nodded her assent and he pulled aside the cloth door, his eyes darting about the room. She smiled. "My fearless Zealot. There are no armed men here to fight. Do *I* make you hesitate?"

"It is no easy thing the Rabboni sent me to say."

"Sit. Take the stool."

He stepped back rather than forward, clutching the door, standing in shadows. "After what you went through I didn't expect you would see me. See any man."

"Jesus knew to send you, Simon. Of all men, you are the most gentle one I know. And you saved me from a life worse than any death I would ever have imagined." She held out her hand and the Zealot entered the room, pulling the padded stool to her bedside, and sat. Taking her fingertips in his, he perched, like a bird poised for flight. "It must be weighty words for you to feel such distress," she said softly.

"If I understood them, it would cause me less concern."

"I only speak one language, Simon. If it is Greek, you need have no fear of my reaction."

The wiry man relaxed slightly, a tentative smile pulling at the corners of his mouth. "No. It is in a language you understand. It's only the words that make no sense."

"Perhaps we can unravel a truth from them together."

"First." He stopped and took a deep breath. "First he said I was to tell you my story. It isn't easy. I've told no one all this before. No one but Jesus." Slowly he began, his words halting and pained. It was the story of a young girl and a shy man. One given to playing the flute more than to speech. A girl far too gentle and above the station of such an unassuming man. It was the story of their love and courtship, a story of laughter. And as he told it, he seemed to remember some things as if for the first time. Others were fond memories, told with soft voice and gentle tone. Magdalene laughed with him. And cried with him when he spoke of finding her lying in her own blood, cold, with the buzz of flies in his ears as they lapped at her blood.

He told her of his flight, of finding the Zealots, of the training and the hatred. The sleepless nights and sounds of death. Of the first rotting piece of flesh he had tacked to the wall of the cave in the hills to the north.

When he finished, she was silent. Sharing in the rebirth he had found with the Rabboni. The peace he knew for the first time in years. The love he held for Immea. They smiled into one another's eyes at this confidence, for they both knew it was no secret. A blind stranger could have seen how he felt about her. Hands clasped, they were silent for a time. Simon stood, breaking the touch that had bound them. There was misery in his eyes. "I don't like to say words that have no meaning for me. I don't say them to add to your pain."

"Simon. Jesus never made anything *easy* on me." At the surprised look on his face, she said, "He could have healed me from the wasting sickness that first kept me in Nazareth. He could have healed me of the congestion of my head this past winter. He could have taken away my pain at the loss of Jason and my son. He never did; he forced me to grow. Tell me what he has to say."

He took another deep breath and exhaled, the sigh like the sound of surrender. His shoulders rounded forward in weariness. "He said to tell you that it's time to stop hating Romans. That part I understood. He was speaking to me as much as to you. Then he said you were to think back to Magdala, to the day he first touched you, to the power that gripped you when he pulled you to your feet. He saw you then as you were and as you could be. He said, 'It's time to become complete. A tapestry of many colors, made of new thread, not repaired and easily torn.'" He spread his hands helplessly. "It makes no sense to me."

"No, it wouldn't. But I understand. Thank you, Simon." Her voice sounded calm but empty. Hollow, like the empty place that opened inside her at the words. "I would like to be alone for now. But would you tell Immea to come to my room later." He nodded, and relieved, rose from the low stool to go. "Simon? Thank you. Thank you for everything." Simon flashed her a smile and was gone, the cloth door moving in the breeze of his passage.

Magdalene turned her head to the wall, closed her eyes, and looked at the empty place inside her. It had been filled with demons. Then with illness. Then with fear and hatred. Living with Jesus, traveling with him, had left it empty and dark. A place prepared for . . . something.

"Abba. I accept." In an instant, Magdalene was swept up in the power of Jesus, just as on that day in Magdala. There were no eddies of weaker power, no small currents to fear. Just pure crystalline power. An awareness of the emptiness inside her and the vastness of the nameless God. The darkness gave way to His Light. Heat and His power fell onto her. Magdalene gasped.

She saw herself as Jesus saw her. She understood. She was nothing without Adonai to fill the emptiness, to light up the darkness of her soul. She was complete. Whole. The tapestry that was her innermost spirit was vibrant and beautiful, depicting a vision—herself, standing straight and tall beside the Rabboni, whole, beneath his gaze.

Slowly the vision faded, but it left her with a strength she had never had before.

When Immea came for her mistress, Magdalene was already washed, dressed, and packed, humming a little tune. "It's time to rejoin the Rabboni, Immea. We have a Passover meal to prepare for a king. For the King of the Jews."

Chapter Twenty

Magdalene

The wind, scented with the smell of wild flowers and with cinnamon incense blown down from the Temple, brushed her face and billowed through her clothes, as she rushed down the street. The Holy City was silent, sleeping, the recitation of the Hagada over, the Passover meal finished, the children sleeping, the Temple quiet, even the nesting birds were mute in the peaceful darkness. She had seldom walked alone in the night. Fear was too often a companion. But not now. Never again. She had faced all there was to face in the world of fear and had survived. She was no longer afraid. Even the night was a friend.

She had left her house, moving into the night shadows. This was not a time for sleeping. It was a night for singing, for praying, for laughter and movement. Today of all days there would be silence at the temple walls. Priestly exhaustion. The scent of rotting blood and incense. Places for the pious to pray, even in the night. Jesus had spoken here last year and several times since. She recalled his words and their enigmatic meanings. For days she had been considering them in relation to her vision, and to her understanding of scriptures.

Jesus was the Son of God. Change was coming.

Somewhere in the city there was an uproar, the sounds of shouting carried to her on the wind. She ignored it all and lengthened her stride. The scent of cinnamon and spice grew stronger. It reminded her of the previous Passover when she had stood in the Temple all day watching the slaughter, blood splattering her face. She lifted her head into the spiced breeze, smiling into the darkness. It had been a good day.

The noise level grew. Still, she ignored it. Until it burst

around the corner. A man, naked, his face blurred by motion, ran past her shocking her out of her thoughts. The noise exploded— men shouting, the sound of steel against steel. Gentiles roaming the streets, using the festival as an excuse to drink and carouse, celebrating their own festival of spring?

She increased her pace, following the dark street to the Temple, seeking a return to the silence she had enjoyed, her mind on Jesus. Two more men ran toward her. Magdalene jerked toward a doorway in the narrow street, but they collided with her, sending them all sprawling into the hard-packed dirt.

Without a word of apology, the men leapt to their feet and ran on. Stunned, Magdalene sat, her legs splayed in the dirt. *That was Phillip.* She was certain of it. He looked as if he was . . . running for his life. He was afraid. She knew it by the smell of his sweat against her clothes. From his direction, he seemed to be running from the noise. Was there a riot?

The sound of footsteps echoed down a side alley, loud and lose, as though their shoes were improperly secured. Two new forms appeared, one small and silent as the night had been. The other larger and breathing like the bellows in an iron forger's shop. It was Simon-Peter and Andrew.

"Simon," she called. "Stop. Wait! What is it? Peter!"

They were gone.

The noise level grew, and now she could tell it was anger, harsh and coarse, ululating in the breeze. Growing. Others were running away from the sound. A cold fear started at the base of her stomach. She who had called the night a friend, was now not so certain. Friends could become enemies in a heartbeat.

Another runner ran on a parallel street, and Magdalene darted down an alleyway hoping to intersect him. But he was gone, leaving only the sound of his feet as he sped away. Off to the right she heard yet another and ran, planning better this time. She came out of the alley between houses just before him. Her fear, only a nebulous question until then, froze. It was James.

Without thought for her safety, she threw herself into his path, ducking her head to avoid the worst of the impact, and together they fell, rolling, tangling in her skirts and his robe. He gagged, his fear multiplied at the collision, with no outlet but his mouth and fists. He struggled, tearing her tunic, the ripping sound only magnifying his frenzy.

Magdalene, without thinking, drew back her arm and slapped him resoundingly across the face. His struggle and gagging stopped at the loud crack of her hand. "By the hair of the high priest's bald pate, you are going to tell me what is going on. Do you understand?"

"Magdalene. We have to get out of here," he gasped, gulping in great draughts of air. "Come. Hurry." He grabbed her hand as he struggled to find his feet. Baring her teeth, she gripped for a handful of his hair and twisted it cruelly. "James, I'll pull out every strand if you don't tell me what has happened." She ignored his yelp. "You're the fourth of the Twelve I've seen in the last few moments running like kicked dogs. Now tell me *what is going on.*" With each of the last four words, she yanked at the tuft of hair for emphasis. "Tell me."

"We have to hide. They've taken him." He swallowed hard, as if his throat was dry. "In the garden. Judas led them there, temple guards, or maybe mercenaries hired by the Sanhedrin were with him. I don't know who exactly. They had weapons, swords, knives, torches. Judas *kissed* him and the soldiers *took* him! They'll be after all of us!" He pulled Magdalene, moving away from the still-growing noise. "Come! We have to get away!"

Fear exploded through her, filling her center as fully as the light of Yahweh had done. She pulled back against his steps, halting him. "*Jesus?* They took *Jesus?*"

"Priests and Pharisees and a mob of men and . . ." He stopped, gasping for air. "There were too many of them for us, Magdalene. You understand? Just too many. Peter pulled that sword he carries and cut off someone's ear, I think, but it did no good. There were too many of them. We have to run. Come!"

Yanking on the tuft of hair, ignoring the pained grunt when her hand came away with most of it, she said, "Find the others. Then go back to my house. You are to take what money you need. It's stored in a jar, Aemoa will know which, and divide it among you. Then you separate and go into the section of town that houses the prostitutes. Go separately, you understand?" The words came from part of her that was still rational, still thinking.

She listened to her own voice in surprise as it issued orders, barked commands. And James paused, some of his fear evaporating at the sound of authority. "Find the house of Atarah. Thaddeus can tell you how to find it. Give her the money and she'll hide you. You can trust her. Tell her I sent you. But go *separately*! We can meet for messages at the house of James and John's mother at dawn and again at noon. You tell the others. I'll try to have some information by then. Get the money from Aemoa, understand?"

"Yes, but what can you do?"

"I have Joseph as a source of information. And as a woman I can travel into places you could not. One of the rare good things about wearing a mantle at all times of the year is a certain anonymity." The wry tone of her voice and the rational thought behind it did more than the tearing of his hair. Reason replaced the fear in his eyes.

"Be careful, Magdalene. See . . . See if Joseph can get him away."

She smiled grimly. "I will. But he can get away anytime he wants. *If* he wants."

She left the temple area quickly, using the darkness as a cloak, her head wrapped in the wool mantle. As if from a distance, she watched the sure, purposeful steps of the woman she had become, the woman called Magdalene as they took her on a circuitous route to Joseph's house. Time seemed to slow, dragging out like glue from a renderer, almost painful in its viscosity.

She banged on the door and forced her way inside, then waited, patiently, as a new and disapproving houseboy roused his master and dressed him in a robe for an interview with a demanding woman.

Still amazed at the change in herself, Magdalene listened to herself as she told Joseph what she had heard and done, calmly taking in the distressed expression that filled his face when she told him of the presence and composition of the attacking men in the garden where Jesus was taken.

From his reactions, she knew Jesus' situation was serious. As James had feared. Yet, the insulating calm continued even when Joseph dressed and left the house, shouting orders for his servants as he ran. His last words rang in her ears. "Stay here, out of sight. I'll be back as quickly as I can. Don't worry, but don't leave the house." Within an hour she had made a stop at her rented, dark house, checked to see that the crock with her money was gone, retrieved what she needed, and arrived at James' mother's house. Inside, she could hear the women crying and moaning softly among themselves. She let herself in by the only door and latched it after her. They looked up in fear at her entry, gathered around the low table in the light of one candle.

"It is no wonder men leave women out of war and government," she said brusquely, setting her bag by the door. The insulting words caught their attention, and silence spread through the room. They looked to her. Waiting. As if she were their leader. But there was no time to consider that now.

Dropping to a vacant cushion, she accepted a cup of watered wine and explained what had happened and what she had done. She was terse and pedantic, even with Aemoa, surprisingly. It seemed to restore the balance in the room. "How many of them have come?" she finished.

Aemoa said, "Of the Twelve, seven have come, demanded money, and gone with no explanation. As they told me, I took it from your hidden place and brought it here."

"Good. But this house smells empty. This will be a busy day. The men will need sustenance and perhaps travel supplies." The women immediately set about baking the only kind of bread that was allowed for the next week—unleavened—easy to prepare, easy to travel with. She ignored her own thoughts about the death that had come with the first unleavened bread in the history of her people. When she left the house, the women were busy, their tears had dried, and their fear had abated, at least temporarily.

It was dawn when she made her last stop, shoulders stooped with exhaustion, at the darkened house of her friend. Atarah must have been watching at the window, for no sooner had Magdalene raised her hand to knock, than the door opened and she was enveloped in Atarah's bangled, scented arms. "Thaddeus came. He told me what happened. Come in. Martine, wine, quickly. Seven men came during the night. I did the best I could at such short notice. They are scattered throughout the city, in places where no one would think to look for them. Only the impetuous one, Peter, has gone to the Temple, to spy out the whereabouts of your Rabboni. Is there any news?"

"Peter." Magdalene shook her head. "No. Nothing. But thank you. It's good to find one person thinking rationally this dawn."

"Two," said Martine standing in the doorway with a tray and decanter.

"Two, then," Magdalene said, smiling slightly. "You have no idea of the confusion. It's mad. And from what I understand it could all have been avoided if they had kept their heads. Jesus could have gotten away."

"My dear, from what you have told me about your Jesus, had he wanted to get away, he would have," Atarah said. "It sounds as if he *wanted* to be captured. I've heard the story seven different times already and pieced together enough to know."

Magdalene nodded then shook her head in denial. It was true, but she didn't want to believe that he had wanted to be captured. How could he become king if he was in the hands of the temple leaders? She had listened to the Zealot enough to know that revolution comes only from the people. Never the leaders.

"Your Jesus is too smart to be caught by the dogs who run the Temple, unless he wants to be in their power. He allowed them to take him."

Unable to protest the obvious, Magdalene sighed softly, "He isn't *my* Jesus."

"Humph," Atarah said tartly.

"The strange thing is that just before the trouble started I was thinking about how peaceful it was in the city. Do you mind if I rest here for a while, before I go back to Joseph's?"

Three hours into the day, she was awakened by soft voices, one of them familiar and angry, Joseph; others placating. When a door closed soundly, Magdalene rose from the couch she had slept on and walked on trembling legs into the hallway. Atarah and Martine were still conferring in whispers, their backs to her, their words sharp and hissing.

"No need to whisper on my account," she said yawning. "I'm

awake. What's happened? Is he free yet?"

Atarah and Martine, their faces taut and pale, turned to her. "He told us to say nothing," Atarah said slowly. "But as you know, I've always believed the strong have a right to the truth."

Magdalene nodded, but put a hand to her chest. Her heart ached with that familiar, tired heaviness.

"Jesus has been charged with crimes against your Law. Foolish, stupid crimes, yet he refused to speak for himself. They say he's been mute all day, despite the beating they gave him, your *holy* men."

"Those in power are seldom holy," Magdalene whispered.

"They took him to Herod who took Jesus' silence as a taunt. He's been before Pilot at least once. It's very serious."

"I have to go to him."

"Magdalene, wait." Atarah's voice was gentle yet unyielding, her eyes full of pity. "They scourged him. Thirty lashes with the cat." Magdalene flinched. The cat had nine tails, each barbed with metal or sharp stone. Most punished with the cat did not survive it, yet it was not called a death sentence, and did not require a trial of any kind. "He can scarcely stand. He looks . . ." Atarah glanced at Martine and back to Magdalene. "They tortured him, beat his face with a reed, tore out part of his beard. When the soldiers had him, they played the Game of Kings. Crowned him with thorns. He's lost so much blood he's having difficulty breathing." She paused, glancing at Martine who looked away, shaking his head. "They want him crucified."

"Cruci— . . ." The world did a slow tumble and refused to right itself. Crucified? The image of Jason, tied to a tree, staring sightlessly down, hit her like a fist. "Ja— Jesus . . ." *Crucified?* She ran past them pushing at the outer door with such force that it shook the house when it hit the wall. And she was running through the streets.

Houses and markets, shops and bakeries passed by on either side, blurred by speed and tears she was ignorant of. There were flashes of faces, some startled, others fearful, fingers pointed in the sign to ward off demons. Still she ran, her body, hardened by months of travel over every type of terrain. Each step slammed into the ground with the rhythm of her fear. *Ja-son. Je-sus. Ja-son. Je-*

sus. Je-sus. Je-sus.

She ran until the cramp in her side forced her to walk, her mind lost to the passage of time, fighting the awareness of her loss. Admitting the loss of the Rabboni would be admitting defeat. Accepting death. He was the *Son of God.* He had power over *death.* But would he fight? Or would he die? How would he choose?

Somehow, she found herself at the door of James' mother's house, her breathing hoarse and labored, her body quivering with exhaustion and wet with sweat as though she had fallen in the sea. A salty sea. A sea of tears. *Jesus. Jesus. Jesus.* The door opened slowly and she looked into the face of Salome. A caricature of Salome. Fearful. Mourning. *They knew.*

She allowed herself to be drawn inside, her body stripped and washed and dressed again in fresh clothes. Her hair brushed free of tangles. All the while she stood, silent, staring away from Aemoa who moved about the room upturning furniture, each piece, one by one, overturned. The first sign of mourning. Aemoa removed her shoes and placed them by the door. The other women removed their shoes as well, the pile growing. The house was silent. It reminded her of the silence of the clearing at Magdala. Nothing there but the wind. The wind and death. *Jesus. Jesus.*

"He has been sentenced," Salome said.

"Joseph, your brother-in-law, came looking for you and left word," Joanna said. "They are taking him to Golgotha."

"Today?" she whispered. "Even with the Sabbath to start at sundown?"

"Yes. It seems the Habberin don't keep the Sabbath." Refusing to meet her eyes. Joanna and Salome moved away. Later, she could not remember which of the two had spoken.

Again the city passed before her eyes, but slowly this time and unmarred now by tears. Magdalene was leading the way, at the head of the women. Salome told her it was because of her words. She had stated calmly that, "This time, he won't die alone. Not this time." And then she had walked out the door, her staff, Jesus' old staff, in her steady grip. They had all followed. She didn't remember having spoken. It didn't matter. Each step, each tap of the staff murmured the word, *Je-sus. Je-sus. Je-sus.*

With each step it became harder to stand beneath the weight of grief, and she leaned into the wood he had carved, the wood he once leaned on. *Jesus. Jesus.* He had given her this staff to help her carry the weight of living. With the thought, her shoulders squared, her step grew more sure. Her head rose, eyes staring ahead. Her movements, once stiff, went willowy and graceful, full of pride, the pride in her Rabboni. Men—unaccustomed to the sight of a woman walking, her hair unbound and head un-covered—moved aside, allowing them to pass.

Golgotha rose steeply before her. Barren. Rocky. Lifeless. The hill of execution.

They arrived before Jesus, and for a time she hoped he would not come. But the sounds of a mob, drunken, mocking, and cheering, were carried to her on the wind. *Jesus. Jesus. Jesus.*

Yet, some small part of her mind still hoped. *Perhaps his power is only waiting. Perhaps he will chose to defeat death.*

Jesus. Jesus. Jesus, beat her heart, whispered the breath in her lungs.

She led the way to the side of the hill, out of the way of the soldiers who were there, laughing, shouting jokes. Digging the deep holes that would support the trees. They ignored the group of women standing in the sun's scant rays, all but the one whose head was uncovered. Her they shouted to. Called out asking her price. One of the men barked an order and the shouting ceased. Magdalene heard none of it. The crowd had arrived. Leading the way was one, no three men. Three carrying heavy crossbeams. One was a black man, a free man, dressed in rich robes, tears on his face. A fourth man stood a little apart, head bowed, swaying. He was bloodied. So beaten she almost couldn't find the face of her friend, her Master, in his swollen, blood-crusted features. Her eyes devoured him. *Jesus.*

His robe was stiff in the breeze, dark with blood. Thirty lashes with a cat of nine tails. She tried to count how many single lashes that would make, how many individual tears there would be in his flesh. She gave it up when he raised his battered head and looked at the crowd. At her.

Her heart seized painfully. Sudden tears fell in trails. *He has decided to die.* Magdalene could see it in his face. He would not call his power.

There was no recognition in his eyes and he dropped his gaze, swaying dangerously. Behind her, she could hear the tears and cries of the women. She stepped away, distancing herself from them. She was not ready to mourn. Not yet. Jesus needed her. And if he looked at her again, he would see courage in her eyes. Strength. And love. But he had always seen that. Love. She loved him. *Loved him.* Had from the very beginning, that strange day in Magdala when his eyes held her in the warmest embrace she had ever known. When he gave her back herself.

She loved him, with all her heart and all her soul. And he had known it, had *always* known it. For he was the only one who could see into her deepest, darkest heart. The only one who had truly loved her, just as she was, even broken by Romans and by her own countrymen. He had challenged her, encouraged her, laughed with her, letting her lean on him. And now, *he* needed *her.* Needed the strength he had shared with her. She would not mourn. Not yet. Leaning on the staff, she held him up with her eyes.

The black man carrying Jesus' crosspiece, stopped, and lowered the heavy beam to rest on the ground. He wiped his face, smearing tears, his eyes on Jesus. It should have been Peter carrying that cross. Or the Zealot. But they had all run, leaving only this stranger, this man who mourned, to help the Master.

"The Sabbath!" a soldier near her spat. He was a Roman from Macedonia. "Well, their weekly day of laziness means this one will suffer more, for a shorter time. I can accept that."

Magdalene's breath caught as she understood. There were several ways for a man to die on a tree. He could be supported with ropes and a block of wood between his legs, living for days if it rained and he was strong, dying finally from thirst and loss of blood to the chest. Or he could be stretched between ropes tied to crossed poles, his legs broken with great rods—the cripplers. Or he could be nailed to the tree, wrists and ankles pierced with great spikes, and no support for the body except for one tight rope. If the crippler was used in addition to this method, then a man would die in a matter of hours. It was the most cruel method. The fastest.

Let it be quick, she prayed. Because of the Sabbath, he would suffer only a little while longer. The screams of the two other men carried on the breeze, away from the hill. Jesus stood to the side, barely able to stand. The last to be hung. *Let it be quick.*

The soldiers took the crossbeam from the black man and pushed him roughly to the side. He joined the women, his tears clear on his face. His hands clenched and opened in pain and fury and fear, his eyes on Jesus.

Soldiers disrobed Jesus roughly. Aemoa shuddered a sob, and the man who had carried Jesus' cross, took her hand, holding her, supporting her. Aemoa leaned into him for comfort. One of the other women fainted. Magdalene didn't look back to see who. Didn't blink. Didn't look away.

His back was a crusted mass of meat and muscle, dripping in some spots with thin, very bright blood. There were deep purple bruises marring his chest, neck, and face, over which fresh blood dripped from the thatch of thorns that encircled his head. She had not seen them before, not consciously. They were proof of the final type of torture they had used on him, the soldiers' Game of Kings, played on the man the people had hoped to crown king.

His disciples had fled. The women who followed him stood a little way off, not able to support him, not able to help him. Now, others, strangers to the city, in town for the celebration, mocked him. She heard the taunts as if from a distance.

"King of the Jews! You are no king of ours!"

"Fool! You are nothing!"

"Heal yourself and kill the Romans!"

She closed her mind to them, focusing so tightly on Jesus that she saw nothing else. Magdalene tried to hold steady as they laid him out on the cross, his flayed back to the rough wood. But when he moaned, she began to shake. Tears coursed down her face like rain from storm clouds. She let them fall, wrapping her arms about herself, holding herself steady with the force of her will. The soldiers bound each of his arms to the crosspiece with rope.

A soldier with pale hair and blue eyes—from Germaina, or perhaps a Celt—raised a mallet, aimed at the spike held by another soldier, and let it fall. The clap of wood against iron was dull, the echo lost beneath the crowd. She had expected to be deafened by it. Had wanted to be deafened by it. But the sound was blunted, faint as it pierced the skin of his left wrist. The Master groaned, his eyes half shut. The second blow separated the two bones in the Rabboni's arm and entered the wood. After that it was a steady, hollow sound, the wood vibrating with each strike. Despite herself, Magdalene moved closer, her steps lost beneath the sound of the mallet. The soldiers didn't stop her, didn't seem to even see her.

They stretched out his right arm. The Rabboni's breath came in gasps with each mallet strike. Satisfied with the prisoner's arms, the foreign soldiers placed his right ankle on the vertical tree. One of the soldiers, a big man, sat on Jesus' knees, to hold his legs still. The one with the mallet drove a spike through the Rabboni's right ankle bones, then placed it over the left. The big man holding Jesus repositioned his knees to either side of Jesus' legs, and the mallet descended, hitting the spike again. Magdalene was so close she could hear the grind of bone and sinew. It took three more strikes with the mallet before the spike touched wood.

Tears made his form waver in the afternoon light. And it was with surprise that she saw tears fall from the eyes of the big soldier holding Jesus down on the cross. His tears fell across the Master's shins, mixing with his blood. Trailing around to the cross beneath him.

The awful rhythm stopped and the soldier lowered the mallet for the last time. Others moved up. Gripped the crosspiece. Heaving, they raised the tree and dropped it resoundingly into the hole in the ground of Golgotha.

Jesus' body flapped like a torn, loose garment in the breeze and she prayed he was unconscious. He was not. As soil was added to the hole and tamped down, he opened his eyes and stared at the crowd. The soldiers stepped back. Magdalene rushed forward. Reached him. Put out a hand and touched his shin. It was cold with the shock of his torture.

Magdalene slipped to the ground at his feet. Her knees in the packed-down dirt. Her arms went around his shins, cold, cold, cold flesh and the unyielding tree at his back. She held him a moment. Willing her warmth into him. If he was coming down from the cross it would be now. But he didn't stir except for the awful sound of his breath. Rasping. Gasping. As irregular as her heartbeat.

His blood was crusty against her hands. Damp from the Roman's tears. Her grip loosened and she slid to the ground, fingers on his ashy, purpled toes. Then her fingertips slid to the cross, its grain rough. She sobbed once, the sound broken.

She felt the drop hit her scalp, heavy and slow. *His blood.* It splattered down, through her hair. Another landed, with the finality of his death. *He will not save himself.* She knew it. *He could. But he will not.* She looked up. A third fell onto her forehead. It slid down her face.

The power started then. Like a slow-moving breeze. Not like before, not the almost violent strength of the resurrection of Lazarus. But it rose up. And it came from within her. It started at the core of her being as she willed him to look at her, blocking out all sound. All others. All but Jesus.

Look at me. I'll help you. I'll share your strength back with you. Just look at me. Her eyes never wavered. Were never blinded with her tears. Never weakened. Even as his blood fell onto her. Slow, steady drops, marking his choice, his choosing of death on the cross.

Jesus spoke several times in the next hours, his words passing through her unheard. His eyes, only his eyes, became her world. *Look at me. Let me help you. I'll be your strength. See what you made me become. I'll never leave you. Never!*

The light changed as the Earth went dark—early, far too early. Cocks crowed in the false night. Two of the soldiers who had hung him began to weep. The crowd of drunken revelers dissipated, their carousing ruined by the tears of the Romans and the unnatural darkness, leaving only the women and the black man and the Romans, and in the shadows of the buildings, hiding, a few of the Twelve.

Finally, as far-off lightning flickered and thunder roared, he looked at her. For a moment lost on the rest of the world, the Master stared into her eyes. He knew her, acknowledged her strength, and somehow, smiled at her.

Holding her with his eyes, his mouth moved. His words—his last words—filled the air. Others heard them. Others spoke of them later. She remembered only his eyes. Only his choice.

And he died.

Epilogue

Magdalene

She sat in the window, still and silent, staring at Joseph's shadowed garden below her. Not seeing—not really—the acacia tree below her. Its slow, sad swaying reminded her of another tree in another of Joseph's gardens. His burial garden. That tree, younger by many years than this, had also moved with melancholy slowness.

That strange morning, the day after the Sabbath, the third day after they had put Jesus, so hurriedly in the tomb, the women had gone to the garden to unwrap his body and wash it, to prepare it with spices and herbs. They had forgotten about the stone and the Roman soldiers left to guard it. They had been grieving and exhausted and not thinking, but needing to do *something* to honor the Rabboni.

The horn of morning had sounded from the temple walls, its eerie sound winding mournfully on the scant breeze, as they climbed down the rocky wall to the bottom of the old quarry, newly transformed into tombs. The tombs of the wealthy.

Joseph's tomb, the newest of them all, newly carved into the stone, not yet used and freshly landscaped, was easy to find. It was the one with the young acacia tree near the opening, its branches bent with twine to form the graceful shape of its destiny. The tree had seemed to weep.

The women with her had cried out at the latest horror, the final indignity. Had wailed at the sight of the open tomb. The Roman soldiers had run off, leaving their cold, dead fire and their meal, and their swords scattered. And the tomb. Empty.

The other Marys ran off as well, terrified. Weeping. To tell the others. But she stayed. Alone. Once again, empty inside and broken. Watching the sun rise over the horizon. Weeping. Since the cross, she hadn't cried. All the long Sabbath day with its secret hidings and intrigues, its silent movements from safe-house to safe-house carrying messages, making plans—remaking them— the fear like a shadow of bird wings falling across her, she had not cried. Not until she saw the tree in the garden of tombs, the empty tomb, its opening yawning and black as death.

Her tears started then, blending with the tendrils of fog that settled in the low places, obscuring her vision.

His tomb was empty. He was gone. Stolen. The final dese-cration.

She was alone, as always, always alone, beneath the slender tree, her clothing muddied by the dew-touched earth. *Gone. Gone. Jesus is gone.* She would not be able to touch him again, even in death. She would not be able to wash his skin and sweeten his cold flesh with herbs and spices. She would not be able to love him. Never. Ever. Gone.

"Mary." Soft.

"Mary . . ." Softer. A whisper.

The sound of her name. The sound of his voice a caress. And tired. So very tired. She had heard him speak like that so often.

"Mary . . ."

It had been Jesus. Risen. And her heart, filled with loneliness and pain, flared with the power he had left with her. It roared in her chest, in her ears. Jesus. Risen!

Days ago. Days. And he had not been to her since.

The tree in the dusky garden below quivered as if with a contrary wind, calling her back to the present. To the now. He had not sought her out since the garden of death. The garden of life. The garden where he had forbidden her to even touch the hem of his robe. Yet others had touched him since. *Others had!* Not her. Was it because she was a woman? Was that it? Was that why he had not come back to her?

Why had he not let her touch him? She didn't understand. She was his friend.

The tree below her moved again, impatient for the dark. For night. For its sleep. She closed her eyes. And days passed. And sleepless nights.

• • •

It was days now, weeks really, since the Peskah, since she had seen him in the misty gray dawn, haloed at his back by the pale sun on the horizon, wavering in her tears. She still had not seen him since. Not once.

The Twelve all told her she had been honored by being the first. That he had chosen her above them all to be the first to see him, to speak with him. *The first.* And they spoke with conviction and fire. But that fire hadn't touched her. Hadn't warmed her. Still she waited.

It was easy at first, that waiting. Wonderful things were happening among the followers of Jesus, their numbers were growing every day. The disciples were allowing anyone to join, man, woman, slave, and freeman. Even Angel and Atarah had joined the group, sharing their riches with abandon; the sisters and their friend Martine had given up their past way of life. The black man who had carried Jesus' cross had been welcomed, sharing that he had traveled for forty days to sit at the feet of the Rabboni and learn, and had ended carrying the Master's burden instead. Most odd of all, the Roman who had sat on Jesus' legs while the nails were driven through his flesh had been welcomed. All had been accepted into the group freely. And Jesus had appeared to many of them, talking and sharing and preparing them for the future.

But still, Jesus had not come to her.

Magdalene would fall asleep at night hearing the sound of her name on his lips, as in the garden of the tomb, when he spoke to her. *"Mary . . ."* She remembered his voice, soft, plaintive, loving.

And the soft overtones of her name would still be quivering on the air when she woke long before dawn. Dawn. She had grown to hate it. With its long gray shadows arching slowly across the strange, wooden floor. Dawn brought, each day, the memory of the events of that pale day in Joseph's other garden. The garden of death. Of life. When Jesus rose . . .

"Mary."

Tears started at the corners of her eyes. He had come. At last.

"Mary . . ." Breathed softly.

Slowly, she turned, her eyes brightened by the tears that spilled down her cheeks. His own eyes were no longer tired, his smile steady, strong. His face clear and glowing, as if a lamp threw its light onto him. "Rabboni," she whispered.

"I would not have left you without seeing you again. You need not have feared."

"You are going then," she whispered past the pain in her throat. "Back to your Father. Back to Adonai."

"For a time," he said. "Only for a time. It will not be so very long before you join me."

"I've traveled with you before. Will you not let me go with you now?"

"No. But I will come soon. Ask the others. I have told them."

There was much to ask. To say. So little time. "I . . . I was strong for you," she whispered. "I did not waver. Not even when they dropped the tree into the hole. Not even when your blood coursed through my hair like tears. I loved you with my eyes. I shared my strength with you."

"I know." He was still smiling, a light from somewhere near catching in his hair, glistening. "I am proud of you, Mary." He was going. She could feel it.

"I love you," she whispered. "I don't want you to go." Her tears slipped down her cheeks, obscuring his face. He wavered with her weeping. His eyes grew dim, the light going. Had he heard?

"I love you." *Please hear.*

"I know. Mary . . ." His hand moved in the growing dark. And then he was gone, the room fully dark with night. Slowly her hand rose to her face, her fingers touching hesitantly to the warm place on her cheek. Was it dry?

She was never certain—not completely—that he had touched her face in that last possible moment as he went. Taking her tear with him.

The End

And The Beginning

www.ingramcontent.com/pod-product-compliance
Lightning Source LLC
Chambersburg PA
CBHW030647260626
47157CB00007B/2526